The Witchery

To MCF

The Witchery

Prologue: Omnes Colores

Media vita in morte sumus.
In the midst of life we are in death.
—The Epistle of Saint Paul

I DIED BY FIRE IN THE FALL OF '46 . . . 1846, THAT IS.

The timbers and the colors came crashing down. The fire was a kalei-doscope cracking a thousand, a million colors: omnes colores. . . .
Yes, all the colors came. Reds rose from the timbers as they tumbled, and in shattering the windows burned blue. From the bricks there is-sued a violet hue, though how it was they'd been empurpled I cannot say. Sacks of milled corn burst not as golden bombs, but showed in-stead the greens of inland seas. Mirrors standing sentinel against the warehouse walls twinned the flames till their backing mercury burned, and it was then all the colors came. . . . Piled rugs of pied thread fast fell to ash. Tea sets, candelabra, cutlery all smelted down to silver. . . . And all of it—the fire, my pyre—seemed a . . . a mere and simple surprise, yes. Surprising, too, that I had no fear; for all the while I burned I knew I would not die.

. . . He had been right. . . . I would ascend to a nameless state. Such that now I wonder:

Am I a god? Am I a goddess? Am I a ghost?

As a teen I'd been told by my saviors, *You are a man, you are a woman, you are a witch*. And so, by the time I walked, nay, *ran* into those flames some two decades later—oh, what a fool I was!—the news of my true state was as naught; for I was what I was, simply so. Ask any dreamer who has had a dream come true and you will hear the same: What had once seemed impossible yet comes to pass, simply *is*. And so I simply *was* man, woman, witch: spawn of two persons leaving no other legacy, but more truly myth-born of Hermes and Aphrodite, and thus fated to bear that appellation I disdained all the long years of my life: hermaphrodite.

The heat of it blistered and blackened the splitting skin, which yet seemed mine. And oh, the pain of such a parting from life! Too, my witch's blood boiled like that of sisters staked and blazed in ages past, burned by those believing themselves allied to Heaven's higher cause, those who held that the only way to stop us witches was to kill us, burn our bodies and our blood—the former but a vessel for the badness borne on the latter—and thusly keep us from accessing an Afterlife. Oh, but as the colors came, as the Work was done, as my body burned and my blood boiled, there came a transubstantiation: from man, from woman, from witch, I ascended, yes.

To god? To goddess? To ghost?

I sit shipboard now, sailing, and would pay heed to neither calendar nor clock—so rarely must we dead contend with capital-*T* Time—were it not for she who hosts me; for though this body is freshly dead, still it begins to stiffen even as I . . .

———————————— ✳ ————————————

Stay. Understand, sister, and shy not from this moribund fact: In order to write, I must either speak—and the speech of the dead takes many forms—to an amanuensis, some sympathetic scribe; or, lacking such a one, I must insinuate myself into a corpse whose eyes I can open, whose muscles I can maneuver despite a heart grown still and blood that can no longer course. . . .Yes, yes, yes, it's a squishy and slimy and stinking business; but I have grown used to it. So, too, will you, *je t'assure.*

. . . the hiss and whisper of cloth catching flame . . . the sizzle of burning salt . . . the burst, the boom of barreled alcohol . . . the staves like arrows afire flying from off the concussed casks . . . Yes: all the wares of the house went up, and down, down the walls came by the bright light of day; for all, all was lost to the strange play of the elements: fire, yes, but wind and water as well. . . . And when later I was summoned home, was resurrected and rose, I could only wonder what I was:

    God? Goddess? Ghost?

I have determined to pass these sea hours purposefully; and the tale I purpose to tell is this: *How it was I died.*

To do so, to tell my tale, I have sought and found this hostess— she in whom I saw the seed of fever had been sown. . . . The newly dead are preferred for their pliability, of course; but here—on this swelling sea—I hadn't much choice, and were it not for Yellow Jack I'd still be silent, searching for a hand, a *literal* hand by which to initiate this volume, this return to the Shadows; for my companion keeps watch in the cabin adjoining, and cannot help. . . . This child—whom her father refers to as Missy, but whose name is Lucy—has fallen to the fever of late. I would guess that she is, *was* not a decade old, but I can say with certainty that she is newly dead, a fact as yet undiscovered; for I dissemble well. Whether or not my hostess carried fever onto this ship or found it here, it is too early to tell. Those who will mourn her are yet hale, or as hale as this heaving sea allows; and were I to dwell on a description of their complexions, to paint a portrait in words, I'd opt for pinks and the lightest of sun-born browns, with perhaps just a hint of the greenish hues of the seasick, but not yet that yellow that portends the onset of fever.

Oh, but jaundiced indeed is the tiny hand that holds this pen and that will soon harden to inutility; and it is that same hand, with the memory of so immature a script in its muscle, that renders these pages childlike. . . . Just now I have chanced to try her, or rather *its* left hand: no luck: our little Missy was right-handed in life, and must remain so in death. . . . Begging pardon of said penmanship, I write on with all due haste; for though I may give to this unconscious girl's casing *the semblance* of life—quite easily, in fact, with moans and groans and whatnot; though I worry that I cannot put her mourners off for more than a day or two, whereupon this body will begin to betray its true state—*enfin*, soon this Missy's family will come to this compartment, discover the girl dead and gone, and along with their shipmates grow eager, despite their sorrow, to quote St. Paul and commit her body, *this body*, unto the deep, sending down within it, unto the seafloor, that sickness that might yet make of this ship a floating morgue.

. . . Yes: already these thin limbs are stiffening, the fingers brittling, the vision blurring as the eyes unmoor from their muscle; and it is with effort that I bend this golden brow over the page before me seeking to educate, to edify whosoever finds this testament, this my last *Book of Shadows:* You, sister, I suppose. . . . Indeed, it is with Time that I must contend; and so, onward:

Rather: backward. Back to when the body that hosted my soul was my own. Back to when I was alive and once again on the run. . . . Stay:

I was not running. Better to say I'd set off in search of something: *a reason to live,* I suppose it was.

Ironic, that.

. . . The year? Let 1837 suffice as starting point; for by then I'd been Stateside nearly a decade, fugitive from my native France as well as the laws of both God and man. And in the course of those years I'd brought myself low, so low I'd nowhere to go but . . . elsewhere. And so indeed I set off, searching and wondering—as the sad traveler will—would I ever succeed in leaving my truer self behind?

Where was this "elsewhere"? *Alors,* though I know not where my tale will end, I know where it begins, yes; and so, hence:

To Havana.

Part One

Nigredo

 *Chapter One*

It is a melancholy of mine own, compounded by many simples, extracted from many objects, and indeed the sundry contemplation of my travels, in which my often rumination wraps me in a most humorous sadness.

    —SHAKESPEARE, *As You Like It*

WHAT A SIGHT: HAVANA HARBOR SEEN BY LATE DAYLIGHT.

I remember it well; for indeed we arrived at sunset, and sadly heard it told that we hadn't time to enter the harbor before dark. This the firing cannons of the Morro Castle made clear: the harbor, indeed the city itself, was closed till next the sun rose. It was slight consolation hearing our captain opine that it was just as well, that the harbor would be too crowded to navigate at night. And so we found a good offing within sight of the Morro's walls, near enough to hear the bells of the city count out the quarter hours; and there we lay off and on all night, tacking in accord with the winds and the water.

For hours I'd watched the silver-green isle of Cuba rising from the blue, ever more anxious yet knowing not that the *Athée*—aboard which we'd sailed from Savannah—was racing the setting sun. Had I known this, had I known that each evening the Morro's cannons announced that crepuscular closing of the harbor and city, I'd have been sick from nervous upset; for though I'd been sent to Havana, I had only the vaguest notion of what, *of who* I'd find there.

Would Sebastiana d'Azur—my discoverer, my Soror Mystica, who'd absented herself for so long, who'd cast away her courtly renown after the Revolution and retired to her crumbling chateau upon the Breton shore— . . . would Sebastiana herself be there? Who was the "we" of whom the aged witch had written so cryptically? *We have a surprise for you,* said the letter sent to me in St. Augustine. Would I have to face again Sebastiana's consort: the man, the menace, the faux demon Asmodei? He who'd hated me from first sight. He who'd sought to harm me. Oh, but Sebastiana's absence had surprised me once before, had it not? In New York. In years past. When I—so deeply needful, so lost—had gone thither, as again she'd directed, by post, only to find yet another epistle apologizing for her absence and consigning me to the care of a houseful of whoring witches. (Mistake me not, sister: I loved the Cyprians, and still mourn their loss and the dissolution of the Duchess's House of Delights.) More likely I, nay, *we*—yes: I had a companion aboard the *Athée*— . . . more likely we would walk alone among the Havanans with no clue but one: Somewhere in the city there lived a monk whom Sebastiana, in her directing letter, had identified by the single initial *Q.*

And so, though I knew not what, or who I would find in Havana, still I hoped to find such things fast. Thus, each wave separating the schooner *Athée* from its mooring in Havana Harbor was a hated thing. . . . But mark, for so it was the case: the waves had been few as we approached over the Straits, and our six-day sail from Savannah had been smooth, too smooth and slow: often we'd been becalmed, and had lain in want of wind.

※

Finally, *finally* all aboard knew the sight of the Pan de Matanzas—that Cuban mountain molded by a great hand in mimicry of a loaf of bread—and nearer, nearer there could be seen sown fields of cane and coffee bordered by tall, wind-waltzing palms. Nearer still, and the lighthouse could be discerned in detail, so, too, the forts of the Morro and Punta flanking the harbor's entrance: like fists of stone they were, wrapped round the harbor's narrow neck and seeming to strangle the inlet. And beyond, faint as my fate, the city itself climbed the hillsides: buildings in pastel shades, showing roofs of reddish tile.

The *Athée*'s sails had been unfurled to steal from those swaying palms what winds there were; and we beat toward the harbor as best we could, forsaking the changeable hues of the Gulf Stream for the sapphirine seas nearer the island. I imagine now that we truly hurried; for our captain must have known that the harbor would close come dark. By the light of a low, westering sun, flying fish rose beside us: silvery knives they seemed, hurled shoreward by the hand of Neptune. Seabirds were ten times more numerous, now we were nearer land. Gulls cried, and signed their chalky Xs on the slate of the sky. . . . So near, yes; but it was then, with the gulls wheeling overhead, that we aboard the *Athée* saw a schooner on the opposite tack make for the harbor even as the signals were dropped and the first cannon fired. Of course, I concluded the worst: here were pirates, espied by the Cuban guard and now taking shot. But no: my companion—even more anxious than I to debark, surely—passed to me the dire news had from the captain just as the lighthouse spun to cast its first beam upon the sea: the city was closing.

And so it was that, our suit for entry refused, the *Athée* bobbed another night at sea. Suddenly I found myself in possession of the thing I wanted least of all: long starlit hours to worry about what was to come, and to worry about what we'd done; for yes, a crime had been committed, such that we—the crew and cast of the *Athée*—were now

one fewer than we'd been when setting sail from Savannah. Of course, none but Calixto and I knew the why, the when, the how of the crime that had been committed: murder.

Indeed, we two wanted off the *Athée* come dawn; and all that starry, windless night I sat wondering how best to achieve this. How best to avoid the captain, and Cuban customs, and the inquisition sure to come?

I'd locked and left my house on St. George Street, in St. Augustine, not two weeks prior, my departure prompted by two facts:

Fact the first: As said, Sebastiana had written directing me toward Havana; and promising the disclosure of certain "secrets" in that city; and:

Fact the second: I knew I'd die a wasting death, or lead a lifeless life in anticipation of the Coming of the Blood, that sickening spill that comes—sometimes suddenly, burstingly; sometimes slowly, as a malaise that can have no other cause—to claim every witch on the last of her days, regardless of whether she loves life or has suffered a surfeit of it . . . yes, I'd do naught but long for my own Red End if I were to stay in that house all alone, hearing its walls echoing, echoing the stories of all I'd lost. Through said losses, and the survival of same, I'd grown stronger, much, but only as a witch. As a man, as a woman, *enfin* as me, *I was weak,* and hadn't the will to welcome or use said powers, powers that somehow I'd siphoned off the dead, as we few witches who are death-allied must perforce do whenever we encounter massed souls still clinging to life. . . . *Ego sum te peto et videre queto.* Which is to say, *The dead rise and come to me.* . . . What these powers were, specifically, I could not have said, and cannot say now: The Mystery of Mysteries.

And once I returned home from deep in the Florida scrub, I returned to the shelter, the safety of St. George Street: a ship returned

to port; but soon enough—in the accusatory quiet, in the stillness of an unhappy house—I came to understand that though ships may be sheltered and safe in port, they are built to sail. And so I set off upon receipt of Sebastiana's letter.

Set off for Havana, I supposed; though in truth, I might have ended up elsewhere. Indeed, I'd have gone as happily—that is to say, *un*happily—to Havana as to another place unknown; for I sought only motion, any sensation that yet proved I was alive. And all I knew as I rode inland from St. Augustine, seeking again the river St. John, was that I would ride its odd, northward flow to the sea, and let the sea decide my fate. This I did, hurrying not; for I no longer held to much hope—of salvation, of happiness—and only hope could have hurried me.

Hélas, I set out over rutted roads and long, long stretches of scratching scrub. Had I been in a hurry, I'd have hired a horse. Or taken directly to the sea at St. Augustine rather than heading slightly northward (as indeed I did) when my desired destination—Havana—lay to the south. Instead, caving to coincidence—I'd take whatever boat would come—as well as a nature too melancholic, and being ever mindful of the river's living metaphor, I sought the confused flow of the St. John's and told myself I'd reach the sea in time; whereupon I'd reset my sites toward Cuba. . . . *Motion*—be it northward, southward, or wayward—would suffice for now.

I'd sailed the St. John's a decade prior, when first I'd come to Florida; and so, when finally I achieved the river again and saw its oaks overhanging the slow flow, their Spanish moss dripping down as a living filigree, I may even have been—dare I say it?—*happy*; for a spell.

I secured passage aboard a passing sloop of slight burden already laden with lumber, named the *Espérance*. I had money enough to ensure that I'd not be expected to earn my keep, neither upon the St. John's nor in the sloop's home port of Savannah (not so northward sitting as to be *wholly* off course, thought I). Mind: I am not lazy, or rather was not lazy then—admittedly, we dead might sometimes be said to laze—but rather, I feared that work of any sort would result in my weaving myself into the ship's web of ropes, or worse: falling overboard into that river crowded with crocodilians. . . . No: I told the captain *in terms certain* that it was not a working passage I sought. I had not come to "hire on," but rather would pay handsomely—and *handsome* is aptly chosen, as I traveled, then, in manly guise—to be let aboard, whereupon I'd secrete myself all the way to Savannah so as not to be any bother at all.

As said, the *Espérance* sailed low in the river, its shallow belly full of pine planks. Too, more boards had been laid upon the deck and fastened with strapping. Though space had been left abaft the mainmast for the pumps, sitting close unto the bulkhead, the rest of the sloop was crowded, quite. Pine was profit, and no shipboard space was spared: so very redolent it all was of pitch and planed wood. Neither was there a bunk to spare belowdecks. These—hammocks, in fact, in which the sleeping crew swung—were claimed by those who, to judge from their limbs, tarry to the elbow and knee, had felled, hewn, and stacked the sawn pine. So it was I was told to bed down as best I could. Such an arrangement might have put off another gent—so I hoped to appear: a youngish gent of some means and strange ways; in other words: *a man best left alone*—but of course my relief was great at not having to share close quarters with six well-salted types. No: I'd have bared my breasts and strapped myself to the bowsprit, sailing as the *Espérance*'s figurehead, if it had meant securing that solitude that had long been requisite to the keeping of my doubly-sexed secrets.

The first day of the sloop's homeward passage ended without event; but not so night number one.

I'd been sitting amidships, well free of all stays and sails and such troublesome stuff, and had scribbled away the late hours of the afternoon. It's likely I dared not write in the *Book of Shadows* I then kept—too dangerous, this—but yet I recall having in hand a stub of pencil and some pages now lost, bound in a book of blackest kid (a hide nearly as dark as my disposition). All was well, with the salts too tired to trouble themselves with me. But then the sun set, and we—nay, *I alone*; for no man of the *Espérance* seemed equally troubled— . . . I was beset by so many millions of mosquitoes it seemed the swarm, with some coordination, could have lifted me bodily from off the deck and dropped me down in Savannah, sparing me the sail. But rather than carrying me thither, those pests determined to sup upon me, to stick deep their syringes and *draw, draw, draw.*

Others of the men seemed immune to the bother and bite, and took no action but to concede as little skin as possible to "the skeeters," rolling down their sleeves and slacks. A few lit smudge pots and carried them about like lanterns. The reflected lantern light threw ghostly swimmers in the drink. Later, the salts retired to their swinging hammocks to drink and sleep away what stings they suffered. Me? I had no refuge but the night, and the darkness, which—fortunately—hid what happened to those stinging things once they'd supped too much of my witch's blood.

Yes: soon the chore, the challenge, lay not in fending off the skeeters' bite but rather in concealing the myriad specks upon my skin; for the pests, witch-fed, fell dead with their stingers still sunken into my skin. No doubt by daylight I'd have seemed some species of dalmatian dog, bedotted by the dead creatures. Indeed, even by moonlight I could see my exposed skin darkening to black: looking down at my hands, I saw what seemed the black lace gloves of a lady of Spain.

The two men of the watch I heard snigger. One of them winked at me with an ivoried eye, evincing delight that this dandy come amongst the crew suffered so. I thought to refute the sniggering, to say that in fact I was not suffering the skeeters but rather was . . . *both-*

ered by them, merely. Instead, I said nothing. Which is not to say that I did not act in my own defense; for—and now it seems I may have willed this—he of the ivoried eye soon was struck by a thunderous fit of coughing, one which caused him to gulp greatly at the black, buzzing air and swallow down skeeters by the battalion. Had I brought his barking on? I did not know for certain; but yes, there came a *soupçon* of guilt, such that I rose and betook myself nearer the bow and further from the men of the watch. But when behind me it seemed I heard more sniggering, the guilt soon was gone and I fell to wondering, pointedly, what I could conjure to stifle the men. Were there catbirds in the shoreside trees who might be willed to dive, to dart about the men's heads? Or perhaps a snake might be induced to drop down from the branches overhead, branches that looked sulfurous now, well nigh infernal in that light coming from the braziers bolted onto the bow and crowded with tarry knots of pine? Such were my thoughts—I do confess it—when I turned to see not the sniggering men of the watch, but another of the crew: the cabin boy, name of Calixto.

Cal—as he was called—had brought me a bit of luncheon earlier on. Whether he'd done so of his own accord, or had been directed to action by the captain, I cannot say. Regardless, I'd been grateful for the fare, though it was but a bit of lobscouse—beef and bread, this is, cooked together without benefit of spice—along with a skin of switchel to wash it back. Now here came the boy again, burdened by a smudge pot and a mass of netting; which latter I supposed he'd cast over the river, for certain species of fish—like certain species of men—surface only after dark; the difference being: such fish one might sometimes seek, whilst such men are best left alone.

But no: on came Cal, toward where I sat. . . . And if earlier the sun had seemed to gild the boy—as indeed it had—now he was ensilvered by the moon sieving down through the trees.

———————————— ✳ ————————————

As before, he said not a word, this blond, sea-bred boy of some sixteen, seventeen years of age. Rather he set straight to work; and by the scant light of the moon, and the flickering flames of the smudge pot and braziers, I watched in wonder—wonder that soon ceded to delight; and delight that ceded to gratitude in its turn, gratitude deep as the surrounding dark.

He had not come to fish. It was no seine he had in hand. It was netting of a much, much tighter weave: muslin, I suppose. It was a square, one side of which was weighted by a piece of driftwood stitched into its hem. Strings depended from the remaining three sides; and these—in an athletic show, done so fast I knew not what I watched—Cal tied fast to the boom, and to the shrouds, and to a davit, till finally the net hung upon the deck as a tent, a triangulate refuge from the swarming skeeters.

Quickly as he'd come, Calixto disappeared. I stood in wonder. A moment more and he returned, this time burdened by bedding. Crude bedding, yes, true, but bedding nonetheless. This he proceeded to set upon the deck. And then, carefully, he tucked the edges of the net beneath the pallet, all save one side, which now he raised up. With the smile of a gallant, he motioned me into this odd construction. I knew not what to say, knew not what to do. Words of thanks stalled in my throat. But then the cabin boy nodded me on with a measure of urgency, and—as he scratched at his own welts, and I'd not be the one to cause him a moment's more suffering—I verily dove past him, ducking beneath his arm as if the boom were a sort of fallen maypole and he a suitor. Suffice to say: I may have let slip my masculine mask; but if so, I took it up forthwith. From within my shelter I thanked him. I sought some pocketed coin (thinking this was owed to—and sought by—all who did me a courtesy). All the while, the boy spoke not a word.

Having tucked me tightly in, he stood. I looked up at him. Stay: no doubt *I stared* as if I'd never see him again. He'd not have seen me staring, of course; for I'd long since had to sport, *at all times*, those blue-lensed spectacles that hid my eyes, eyes which—in time with my increasing strength—had grown fixed, and now, no matter my mood, showed constantly *l'oeil de crapaud*, the Eye of the Toad, or the true witch's mark, the sister-sign (so called because the circle of the pupil cedes to the shape of a toad's splayed-toed foot). . . . Yes, doubtless I stared. What? Did I think he'd swim from the *Athée?* That I'd wake to learn he'd ascended somehow, that indeed he'd been the angel he'd seemed? . . . Sadly, soon I saw naught but his back; for he turned on his heel and headed off, dissolving into the dark.

I may have sputtered a second thank-you. I may have bade him good-bye or good night. Regardless, my words broke not upon the boy. He was gone, and I might have spoken with equal effect to the trees or the stars and moon beyond; for now I lay upon my back, staring up. And it was in that same pose that I'd eventually fall asleep, knowing not that age-old superstition of sailors: To sleep topside, with one's face full to the moon, is to invite ill fortune.

. . . Indeed.

 *Chapter Two*

That blush, perhaps, was maiden shame—
As such it may well pass—
—EDGAR ALLAN POE, "Song"

ONCE OFF THE RIVER AND ONTO THE SEA, THE *ESPÉRANCE*
demanded more of her men; and boy. All but the latter
could be heard cursing her—always *her*, as is the custom
of the sea— . . . cursing her as though she were some
sea whore, at once desired and disdained. But their actions belied the saucy epithets they spewed: they tended
the ship with care. She, in turn, provided safe passage
seaward and toward Savannah.

I grew less and less at ease whilst sailing aboard the
Espérance; for I felt shamed, in a way, seeing the crew so
busied. True: I'd been aboard ships before; but I'd not
acquired any sailorly skills. Indeed, I was better suited
to the hold than the decks, being only slightly less burdensome than the tons of pine planking the ship had
taken on.

It was our second, perhaps our third day out that I

thought to offer my services (such as they were) to the captain. Surely there was *something* I could do; for I stood as tall as any of the men and, in accord with said stature, was strong. (In sisterly terms I was *very* strong, but of course that did not signify: Would I see to my assigned chores by the application of Craftwork? No indeed.) . . . Mightn't I stand watch? Surely I could scrub something? The shipboard scrubbing—against that corrosive salt borne on both the water and air—was incessant.

. . . It seemed I'd donned a man's pride along with the kerseymere pants and the piebald vest I now wore over my blouse (a *full* blouse, the better to hide my swaddling, which in turn hid my breasts: smallish, yes, but big enough to betray me). How I yearned then for a skirt or dress, and the solitude such apparel would have afforded me. As a woman, I'd have been seen as mere ballast aboard the ship, shunned, left to amuse myself and while away the sea hours as I saw fit, as long as I roused neither wrath nor desire, nor impeded the ship's progress in any way. . . . Oh, to be shunned, yes: it seemed a fate much preferable to that of a man with no purpose. *Hélas*, my dress had been decided: I'd boarded as a man, and a man I must remain until Savannah, at least.

Just as I stood, determined to seek the captain and offer said services, a wave broke upon the bow of the *Espérance*. Not much of a wave, mind; for, as said, the sea was then quite placid. Yet the boat bucked, and from deep in its bowels there came a moan not much louder than the one I made whilst falling back upon my buttocks, landing such that my own bones creaked in chorus with the ship's. . . . Best to stay put, I supposed. Best to stay out of the sailors' way. *That* was the service I'd offer; and to do so I need not apply to the captain at all. . . . And so, there I sat that sunny spring day. Land lay off to port. As I looked to it, I wondered: Was it Florida still?

Whilst staring at the shore and drifting into dreams, I'd taken up a spare length of rope. I refer to it as spare, though already I knew that nothing aboard a ship is spare: everything has it purpose and its place. More apt to deem the rope *stolen*, I suppose—by me. Still, there the rope lay in its knotted, rat-gnawed length. Perhaps I thought I'd appear useful, tasking myself with the untying of the rope's several knots. (Manly pride is not doffed as easily as manly attire.) . . . And thusly was I occupied when I heard the captain's voice, and a reply falling from on high:

It was Cal, in the rigging, calling down an echo of the captain's command.

. . . The Captain. Who now stood before me, staring down.

I bade him hello. And though I'd also learned not *to expect* kindness from a ship's captain—leastways not once the sails are set and one's coin is irrecoverable—still I was surprised at his silence, the more so as it gave way to an open show of scorn; for the captain laughed. *At me.* And quite coldly, too. The sound both shamed and chilled me.

With a harrumph the captain turned, leaving me to the Gordian task I'd set myself. No doubt I redoubled my efforts at untying the rope—I'd show him!—but I might as well have sat trying to peel the white from off a seashell. I'd naught to show for my efforts but blistering thumbs and split nails, one or two of which I'd bent back to the quick. That, and an increase of shame that took the shape of sweat, pooling at the small of my back.

So it was that when I heard a single word spoken—"Why?" —I supposed it came from the captain, returned to mortify me more. I lifted my head in hopes my tongue would prove itself a lash, that somehow I'd say something to . . . But of course it was not the captain. It was he: Cal, come down from the rigging to stand before me and wonder, aloud, "Why?"

"Why not?" I countered, defensively; for I'd spoken before I saw that it was he—Cal—and not the surly, shaming captain who'd come.

Indeed, at first I was unable to see who it was stood before me. Something—the ship or the sun—had shifted; and he was haloed: darkened by the sun behind him, and darkened the more by the glasses I wore. And when he moved, just so . . . well, then I was truly blinded: the sun came in a vicious shaft, and the sunshades were all but useless. Only when the sunspots cleared, only when sight returned, could I see Cal standing before me. Thusly, toe to top:

His broad feet were bare, and each took his weight in turn, in accord with the slight roll of the ship. His toes maintained a simian-like grip upon the smooth deck; a deck that he himself swabbed each day at dawn. Simian indeed; for I'd seen Cal climb that rigging wherein he was so sure of himself, swinging as a monkey might, vine to vine. Oh, but no monkey, this: Cal's skin was hairless, or rather the hair on his legs—exposed, south of his scarred knees—had been rendered golden by the sun, and barely showed against skin of a similar shade: bronze, let me say. The calves were as muscled as the feet seemed, and so, too, was this true of his forearms and hands: it is the gripping strength of the extremities that keeps one safe when sailing, and the muscles of survival develop fast. Points north of his knees were concealed by those duck trousers dirty with tar spots and whatnot, patched with canvas strips and held to his hips—barely—by a belt of rope. Truer to say the trousers *hung from* his hips, and hung low enough to show what I'd only ever seen on statuary: that V whose angles decline from hips to crotch, and which I've heard referred to—by sculptors, anatomists, and, well, the whoring Cyprians (connoisseurs of another kind)—as Apollo's Girdle. Above the knotted belt there rose a plane of belly, marble-hard and just as white; for Calixto was rarely without the shirt he then wore, its lower buttons undone. It was red fading unto pink, and if once it had been wool, now it was worn as smooth as chamois. Oddly, the shirt did not button all the way to the neck. It was donned over the head, I suppose, and from the shoulders it hung as an untailored square, seeming more pennant than shirt. Only its well-ventilated sides—strapping crossed from the back to front panels, each so crudely tailored I was certain the boy had sewn the shirt himself—let show the shape beneath; and through its open sides I saw that plane of stomach, its muscles segmented, strong from hard use. This shirt, or shift, was sleeveless—many a sailor has troubled with sleeves, as they beg to be snagged at by stays and wound up in winches; and so it was I fastened strapping round my own full sleeves, tying them tourniquet-tight—and showed arms well muscled, and rising to shoulders that squared off the boy's body, granting him a semblance of strength that, when first I'd seen him, I'd not remarked; for it was *the boy* I'd seen then, not the emergent man.

Indeed, Cal had at first appeared . . . dare I say it? Winsome. Yes. There was something quite appealing, quite . . . *light* about the boy. I'd not have deemed it strength, no. Rather, he was . . . radiant; a being into which both sun and sea had insinuated themselves. Blond he was, through and through; and blond only because the Maker—in a rare show of economy—long ago chose not to make men of gold. But something even more precious than gold shone forth from Cal when he smiled with lips drawn in lines too perfect, too precise, painted too pink, and parting to show teeth strongly white and a foretooth rather charmingly chipped. Indeed, when he smiled—infrequently, at first—one saw not the rest of his face. Rather, the sum of the smile was so great one saw not its component parts: the nose crinkling, the downy cheeks shifting on their prominent bones, the eyes shining to shame a sea that knew, or thought it knew, every extant shade of blue. And all this, all this was topped by a mop of sun-streaked curls that Cal would cut—with whatever blade was at hand—only when they fell to obscure his sight.

Here was a boy made to the Botticellian standard. And before him I sat wondering . . . Stay: to say *I wondered* implies a clarity of thought which then I lacked; for, simply, I was stunned. Had I been able to wonder, a question such as this might well have come: *Do I want this boy, or do I wish to be him?*

I'd asked such questions of myself previously; for such was my relation to beauty whenever I found it in human form. So it often goes with the homely. . . . Stay: to qualify: As a child I'd deemed myself homely, mistaking difference—oh, I was different, that much I knew—for ugliness, with self-loathing the result. This was a judgment no nun or fellow pupil disabused me of. Rather, the taunting and subsequent, much-sought solitude of my youth only reinforced it. Later, having learned beauty's broader terms, I saw that I . . . well, if I was not a beauty to beg the bristles of a Botticelli's brush, still I was . . . *Enfin*, I was me: tall for a girl or even a boy, lean, long of limb, and graced with a face others saw as . . . plain, I suppose. I was blond, pale of complexion, and therefore fast to flush (which trait I hated second only to my hands, which I thought too long-fingered and strong). And I'd eyes of a greenish-blue hue; though later, of course, the iris would nearly be overwhelmed by my misshapen pupils holding to the Toad's Eye. *Not* appealing; but so be it . . .

What I mean to say is this: Though I no longer saw myself as *monstrous*, hardly, still I quelled before such beauty as that borne by this boy nearly half my age. And so there I sat, sun-struck, beauty-blinded, and dumb; and suddenly so *very* serious about the rope I had in hand.

"Why?" he asked again, with a nod toward the knots.

I could not think of an answer both suitable and true; for I knew a man would never speak of the shame I'd sought to keep at bay with busyness. Neither could I continue to ogle my interlocutor. So: silence, and sideways glances; till the boy sat down beside me—standing, he was perhaps six inches shorter than I: *tall*, in other words—and said, whilst proffering his right hand, "Cal. Short of Calixto."

"Henry," said I; and though this was a lie, it had come to seem the truth; for I'd not used my given name—Herculine—in a long, long while.

"Henry," said I once more, careful to prune my pronunciation of the French that sometimes fogged it, and did, betimes, till the day I died. No, not *Henri;* but Henry. At times I wished I'd chosen a name with greater care, a name with greater flair; but I had not, and could not do so now without confusing myself further. I'd grown accustomed to Henry, and answered to it without hesitation. So Henry I'd have to remain, though always, *always* I'd be Herculine at heart.

. . . Herculine? *Qui était-elle?*

A being of Breton origin born into a doubly-sexed body, back about 1806 or so. Unlike the date of my death—*d. October 11, 1846*— the date of my birth was uncertain, as often it is with orphans. . . . An orphan, yes. I was six (or so) when the tale of my life turned trite, taking on those characteristics common to the heroines of the novels I pored over in my youth. I was sent to the Ursulines by my dying mother with naught but a note stuffed into the pocket of my Sunday shift; and if *maman* told the nuns my date of birth, well, they never told me. At the order's convent school I was raised by . . . Stay: my too clever pen wanted to write the word *wolves*. As in: *I was raised by wolves.* And well I could have been; for certain of those Ursuline sisters were downright lupine in both appearance and aspect. *Mais hélas, non:* I was raised not by wolves but by nuns, nuns to whose care I was consigned by my mother, dying of the Blood. (Was *maman* a working witch? Did she know her true nature, and sense that the Blood—that dreaded, rubicund flood—was coming? I cannot say. And if once I could recall my mother, I cannot now. Of course, *I could have.* I could have tried to divine a dream of the past, one wherein I might have seen her, maybe even found the father I'd known not at all; but this I never did, owing to an abiding fear of divination; for the divining of dreams is not mere sisterly sport, and sentimentality never seemed reason enough to risk a Sighting.)

That convent school under Ursuline command—which I deign not to name—clung to a cliff; or rather, I recollect it as a cliff though I suppose it was but a dune, down the friable slope of which sand and rock tumbled into the bay and from thence into the channel beyond. There, upon those far northern shores of France, the tides were, indeed *are* extreme, and seemed to me salted tongues coming in continuum to lap at that strand above which we lived our lives to the *tick, tock* of the Church's clock.

We were sixty-odd girls far from town and tribe. Within that cold, stony pile, the sorority committed itself to one of two worlds. The nuns and those whose fates had been decided by plainness or poverty, myself included, looked toward the Hereafter. We worked to assure our ascension. The balance of the girls, while yet made mindful of Christ, his sufferings, et cetera, were prepared for ascension of another sort. They would return to the world and rise within the Home and rule over such types as me: those who, if they chose not to affiance themselves to the Savior, were destined to slave in sculleries or schoolhouses, as maids and schoolmistresses.

Luckily, I was let to study; for I'd an aptitude that was recognized by the mother superior, Sister Marie-des-Anges, whose kindness would cause both her fall and mine. (The charge? *Satanic congress.*) From the shelves of Mother Marie's library I culled all I could. I read promiscuously: papal bulls were as one with the novels of Mrs. Radcliffe and the plays of Shakespeare, whom I'd adore all my days; such that:

> *I, thus neglecting worldy ends, all dedicated*
> *To closeness and the bettering of my mind.*

"Closeness"? At the convent school? Well, more about that anon
(as the Bard would have it). . . . For now let me say that if I opened a
book written in an unknown, or *as yet* unknown language, I did not
shut it but rather reached down the proper dictionary to set beside it.
Words were a refuge. What friends I had were fictional. And through
those books I lead a thousand lives, each better than the graceless one
I'd been given.

Thusly did the years pass; and still I lived all too literally within
the libraries of that convent school, preferring the ashes of life to its
fire. Secreted there—as opposed to the *dortoire* with its abhorred inti-
macies—I could keep myself apart, could keep the secret of my very
self. Of course, it would be years, many years before I'd learn that
Latinate term I so disdained, and which again I commit to these pages
for clarity's sake alone: *hermaphrodite*. And though I could list the
Ptolemies by the dates of their reigns, and could distinguish Pliny
from Pliny the Elder by a line or two from their respective pens, and
though I had adequate Greek by twelve or so, still I did not know that
a growing girl will one day bleed as a matter of course, or that a boy
will one day wake with the salt of salacious dreams spent onto his skin
or sheets. I had the ancients, yes, but I knew no man of my day; for
they—predators all—were kept at bay, beyond our walls. I had the
heroines of novels beyond number, but I had no mother, no sister, no
kindly cousin to tell me what a girl must needs know. In short, the
scales of my self sat imbalanced. And neither were they righted, or
brought into balance when finally I learned, or rather was told my true
nature. *Man, woman, witch.*

At nineteen or twenty, what was I to make of so strange a pronouncement? And one delivered by saviors—so I soon deemed
them—chief among whom was a witch, Sebastiana d'Azur, insisting
that I, too, was Witchkind. Worse still were those in league with this
witch: Father Louis and Madeleine, priest and paramour, incubus and

succubus, who came before Sebastiana to offer proofs of my perversion, of the too literal strangeness of my person. *Mon Dieu*, what a show that had been! . . . *Enfin*, when finally I knew what I was, the knowledge seemed of scant significance. Truly. For still I was lost within myself; and if earlier I'd had but one world to find my way in, here now was the Shadow World as well.

And now, more than a decade after my "discovery" and my initiation into that other world, *the* Otherworld, there I sat beside Calixto, quite literally at sea: as lost as ever I'd been.

Sitting beside me, Calixto set his hands on mine, as if together we might untie those stubborn knots. This, of course, caused my heart to hammer. Soon our hands were joined in a strange admixture of courtship and combat, and I grew confused: Who held to whom? Doubtless it was I who held too long to Calixto's hands, yes, past all purpose; but I remember being loath to let them go, so intrigued was I by their many textures: the smooth webs spreading from forefinger to thumb, the calluses marking the underside of every knuckle, and oh, the warmth, the wonderful warmth of his hands, *of him*.

Perhaps to reclaim at least one of his hands, Cal gave mine too great a shake: a greeting; such that the rope slipped from our mutual grip. . . . How I always *hated* that aspect of meeting men as a man: the too-hard handshake; but, in this case, the ensuing ritual served a secondary purpose: it recalled me to myself. And soon I'd summoned sense enough to say, "Calixto . . . Spanish, is it?"

Smiling, he offered no answer. Instead, taking up the rope, he asked—in an accented English that told me I'd guessed correctly—"Why worry about knots that is . . . that *are* no good?" His voice was deep, but deepening still; and in its tone I heard that his mistake had embarrassed him.

———————————— ✳ ————————————

I nodded; which was no answer at all. And I watched stupefied as Calixto, taking up some sort of steely tool that I'd seen pegged to the mainmast, undid the knots in a trice, as another man might undo the laces of his shoe. The tool was a marlinespike: a needle the length of my forearm, and fashioned for the splaying of rope and the tying of knots. As he worked I watched not his hands—which moved too quickly to teach me anything—but his face; and though we sat shoulder to shoulder, and the sun came angling down onto him, still I saw no stubble upon his chin or cheek, none at all. More envy now, more of that heady mix of covetousness and craving, as I was acutely aware of stubble; for though mine came in as lightly and as blond as Calixto's, still I took care to shave it close when putting forth my womanly self.

"Here," said he, handing me back the now-knotless length of rope.

I took it, careful not to show too much gratitude. (A woman would. A man must refrain.) "Just . . . just busying myself," said I with a shrug of my shoulders.

"Now you can busy you-self by tying. Is easier, no?" He'd split the single rope into its several strands, and these he sat tying into a quite complicated knot. "To tie is easier than to . . ."

"To untie, *sí*," said I, proffering the word he sought; but quickly I negated the Spanish affirmative by shaking my head; for I hadn't much Spanish, and did not want to intimate otherwise. True: long ago, at school, I'd made it through *Quixote*, but to do so I'd needed a quite precise dictionary and well nigh a hundred candles. Rarely had I had occasion to speak Spanish, even in St. Augustine, where I'd earned my keep translating a variety of tongues by aid of study, yes, but also the Craft and a certain tisane I'd concocted.

"Here," said Calixto, setting his hands atop mine once again and shimmying nearer. If earlier we'd been shoulder to shoulder, now we were hip to hip as well. "Like this." I tried to still the trembling of my large and once-hated hands by holding my breath: vainly; for within a minute I sat both trembling and gasping for air like a landed fish. I resorted to concentration: a specialty of us bookish types. I'd concentrate upon the task at hand, or rather *hands*, plural; for Cal's were upon my two, our twenty fingers tying I knew not what types of knot. Oh yes, concentrate I did, such that the trembling stopped and my breath came regularly; and so it is that I could—thenceforth—tie a Turk's-head knot. And often I did, in later days. Not for its utility, of course; but rather because it came to seem a sweet souvenir, despite its reminding me that I'd committed murder on behalf of the boy.

Chapter Three

Now would I give a thousand furlongs of sea

for an acre of barren land.

—SHAKESPEARE, The Tempest

. . . CALIXTO. CUBAN-BORN BUT BRED TO THE SEA: HIS mother died on the brink of his tenth year and, his father seeking to drown his grief in that rum for which the island is famed, Cal was left to shift for himself amongst his several siblings and sundry relations. Soon it seemed the wiser course to quit Havana aboard any boat going; and so he lied his way aboard a whaler based south of Boston. Shipboard, he learned English, yet still spoke it brokenly when first I met him on the St. John's.

All this (and not a word more) I pulled from the boy aboard the *Espérance*, as we sat tying that Turk's-head knot.

"Havana," said I with interest. "You live there, do you?"

"I live *here*," said he, knocking his hardened heel

against the ship's boards. With a nod downward, he referenced that area where his hammock swung: the belowdecks, stinking of sap, sweat, spilled rum, and spunk.

"For how long?" I asked. I'd meant to inquire how long the boy had lived aboard the *Espérance;* for I did not yet understand that he'd meant to say he lived at sea, and spoke of his present abode as but a further particular of same. But Calixto misunderstood my question, answering thusly:

"To Savannah." And so I took another tack; so:

"And where to then?"

Calixto said he'd hire onto another ship in Savannah, as the captain of the *Espérance*—to whom he was in no way indentured—would sit awhile in his home port. And so, already I held to a hope that would soon become reality: Cal would guide me southward to the Cuban city. Or perhaps it's truer to say that I'd accompany him. Regardless, soon we'd throw in together, owing to circumstances as yet unseen.

From Savannah we sailed about the *Athée,* each of us having secured our own passage: I by dissemblance and the ready dispensing of coin, and Calixto by swearing sobriety and a willingness to work for wages that suited his age and station (or so said the hard-driving, Bible-bearing steward who spoke for the *Athée's* captain). The boy would earn, I supposed, three, maybe five dollars. I'd paid several times that sum, and would have paid much more to ensure I'd leave the Georgian shore at the boy's side.

The *Athée* was a topsail schooner down from Mystic, Connecticut, and bound for Havana with a bellyful of corn and other commodities set to be swapped for coffee and barreled cane (molasses, I mean). She put in at Savannah to offload two of her troubled crew. Luckily, we arrived coincident with same, and luckier still—or so it seemed at the time—we learned she sought two crewmen as replacements. Now, lest it seem I'd come to deem myself worthy of said term—*crew*—let me say that I was not one of the two replacements found. Calixto, however, was.

Glad as I was to find passage to Havana, Calixto was equally glad to leave Savannah; for he was no lover of land. Still, it took some cajoling on my part to get the boy to sign onto the *Athée*—another vessel offered him a berth—as it had been long years since he'd been home and . . . stay: not *home*; for Cal's siblings had scattered like shot in the years since his mother's decease and he cared not a whit where his father was. That said, I suppose he'd come to favor my company somewhat; for finally he agreed we'd ship together aboard that schooner that would have us both, the *Athée*. True it is, too, that I made mention of money: *I could hire him as a guide;* but this idea Calixto waved away, albeit less than wholeheartedly. Indeed, the boy might then have said—if asked—that he was in my employ, though we'd discussed neither terms nor the type of service to be tendered. . . . Mark me well, witch: though I had no wish to bid the boy good-bye, and knew he'd be a boon in Cuba—the language, the lay of the land, et cetera—I did not, *not* secure his company by witch-tricks or other sisterly wiles. I persuaded him, yes, and was perhaps passionate in doing so, but I did *not* call upon the Craft. To do so would have been dishonest. More: It was a mistake I'd made before.

For a dollar I hired a harbor boy to row Cal and me out to the anchored *Athée*. We boarded the boat as the day of her departure broke; but—oddly—we were met by no one. It seemed we'd signed onto a ghost ship. The truth of it all was easily deduced, however: the crew would keep to the city and its many pleasures as long as allowed. And sure enough, with the sun risen to its noonday height, here they all came.

We heard them before we saw them: the splash of the jolly boat's oars, and an admonition akin to "Row, rummies, row!" He who spoke this last had a voice—a rusty timbre as well as an accent tinged his tough-speak—that, though it chilled me, caused poor Calixto to blanch; for he had no need of sight to know who it was approached the *Athée*.

I moved starboard, from whence the jolly boat approached. I'd meet and greet this crew as a man might: I flexed my fist and fingers, readying them for that succession of hated handshakes. Turning, I saw that Calixto was gone from my side. And over where we'd stowed our simple packs at the base of the mainmast—Cal had told me that to choose our berths before the crew had come was to invite trouble— there he knelt, frantically tidying and retying his haversack. I'd yet to see the boy so discomposed: his manner had been constant, and constantly light aboard the *Espérance* as well as in Savannah. And though our association was a short one, any lesser species of beast could have seen, or sensed what I saw: *the boy was upset*. Fearful, in fact; such that it seemed he'd determined to leap from the *Athée*'s port side in order to avoid he who approached so loudly from starboard.

It was not the captain who came; for, drawn out by the approach of his crew, said officer appeared unseen from somewhere belowdecks to offer a greeting which, evidently, neither Cal nor I had merited— surely the captain had heard us, as we'd made no attempt to hush our inspection of a ship we thought empty. No: not applicable to us were those unspoken rules of congress and cohabitation, such as all seamen know. We were the waste of the lot: a ship's boy and a *fancy-man* with naught but cash to recommend him.

The captain stood stolid and silent at my side, and Cal recessed himself into my shadow—I felt his quickening breath upon my neck—as the lesser boat approached and I saw . . .

Mon Dieu! Surely the captain of the *Athée*, or those landed stewards hiring on his behalf, had descended to Hell and raked its 'scape with a fine-toothed comb. How else to account for the provenance of such types as now approached?

Let this list of the crew's deficiencies serve, thus: they lacked limbs, foreteeth, assorted fingers and toes, suitable attire, wit, hair, yes, and sobriety most certainly. Neither did it seem they'd any familiarity with such requisites as soap, brushes, darning needles, or eau de cologne. Worse yet would be a list of their excesses: rum—in its vaporish state—rose from the infernal fraternity as a secondary breath, and mingled with the scents of sea and shore; each to a degree showed his seeming contempt for the skin he'd inherited, and so had colored patches of same with anchors, ladies' names, Christs upon crosses, and designs less readily discerned now that time, the sun, and Newton's laws had found effect upon skin now wrinkled, hale, and sagging; and though the languages known by the lot were several, none apparently contained that commonest of courtesies: *Hello.* Indeed it seemed we *had* boarded a ghost ship, but *we were the ghosts:* Calixto and me; for not a single salutatory word was forthcoming from captain or crew. Thusly was the tenor of the trip established.

Though Cal sought landward passage aboard that jolly boat, he could not secure it; for the boat was laden not only with crewmen, but also those supplies that then were brought aboard by means of a man-chain, after which the dinghy was secured to the schooner's side. What's more: seeing that Cal sought a way off the *Athée*—as a lamb might seek its way out of a shambles—he of the aforementioned voice caught sight of the boy, and again spoke, saying by way of pronouncement, for all to hear:

"*Eh bien*"—yes: the foundation of that fearsome speech was French—"I see the sea has brought back to me my Jimmy Ducks of old, my Duxworth *d'un autre jour.*" Though all the men heard this, none of them seemed to consider the words that so discomfited my new friend. As for me, well, two things were evident: firstly, this aged salt knew Calixto; and secondly, the boy was not the least bit anxious to renew the acquaintance. As who would have been?

Diblis (so he was called) had cursed the earth for a half century or more. Leastways he was old enough to boast that he'd been to sea with both Nelson and Napoléon. Tales of his exploits at sea were oft shared; for he was our cook, and *would be heard:* any who ignored him went without.

Staring at the man that first night aboard the *Athée,* watching as he served us, overspeaking any who tried to take the floor from him, I wondered was he fish or fowl, and had he fought for the English or French, or both in traitorous turn? Too, I wondered what it was about the man—*hideous,* he was—that seemed to me so very familiar. Over old horse—thusly did I hear our salt beef referred to by the ship's carpenter—I wondered if perhaps I'd seen Diblis in some portside sink? I'd been to such places in Marseilles, in Norfolk, in New York, and points between. Or had he shipped to St. Augustine and fouled its narrow streets, such that I might have seen him thereabouts and . . . ? No. I knew what it was I'd remarked:

Diblis had about him a bluish cast, as do the newly dead.

Mistake me not: the man was not yet dead. No ghost, this. But Diblis had about his starboard . . . *enfin,* his *right* side showed a strange and lifeless pallor, a paleness well nigh blue, yes. Strange, this; the more so when it appears upon the living, and upon one side of them only. On Diblis it extended up his right arm toward the shoulder, from whence it spread like tentacles over his chest, neck, face, and upper back. Upon his arm and chest—which showed breasts rivaling mine in size; though unfortunately Diblis's were not bound, nor even shirted, but swung in steady, pendulous display—the blue contended with the colors of his many tattoos. Upon his neck and face, however,

that death-shade vied for dominance with a texture, a deep, dark pit-
ting that readily told its cause: on a day long passed yet still undoubtedly damned, Diblis had stood too near a misfiring gun of great
bore. Yes: it was half shot, half powder burn that had disfigured him
so, that gave him his ghostly hue. Too, the shirt he'd worn that long-
ago day—whether it were of French, English, or mercenary issue—
had been black or navy blue; for its shredded threads were still
recognizable as such, there on that face into which they'd been blown
too deeply to be retrieved by any tweezering surgeon. Remarkably, the
man's features were intact, marked only by ugliness:

Above a fleshy and full yet pointed chin, ever slick with grease, he'd
a miser's purse for a mouth: lips of thin leather drawn tight by unseen
strings. It was a mouth otherwise unremarkable, save for the breath
and words that issued from it, both equally foul. And lest anyone
doubt the alcoholic proof of his breath, Diblis had a nose so swollen
and red it told that if ever he'd entered a church it had only been to
search out and steal a bottle of sanctified wine. His left eye was somehow . . . watery, and the white surrounding the iris was not white at
all, but bespoke both the yellowish beige of butter and the brown of
a light rum. And his right eye was worse: a blue marble bobbing in the
creamiest of chowders. But it had not been blinded; for it did sometimes draw off to this side or that, and to find oneself fixed in its gaze
was to suffer something cold, something slimy: like cold lard smeared
onto skin. There was no doubting that Diblis was fully sighted. Indeed, it came to seem that he, too, had some supernumerary sense; for
he saw, or knew all, *all* that happened aboard the *Athée*. Thusly did he
have the ear of our captain, who preferred his charts to his crew, poring over the former whilst leaving rule of the latter to Diblis. And
nothing, nothing renders a man more despotic than the command of
men living in close quarters.

Somehow, the crew had sealed tacit pacts of their own with Diblis, and as long as they did their work and paid proper homage—deferring to Diblis on all matters, laughing at what he deemed humor, and complimenting whatever slop he served—they were let to keep to themselves. Not so Calixto.

He and Diblis had met before, yes. I'd learn that they'd shared a long sail up the California coast not two years prior. They'd been many, many months at sea, rounding Cape Horn before coming northward; and though Cal declined to tell me of the voyage in any detail—lest Diblis hear; or so I thought—it was clear those months had passed as years; for my friend—who'd have been but fourteen, fifteen perhaps—had been apprenticed to Diblis in that schooner's galley. The pantryman, the preparer of all cold foods, and the keeper of what livestock had been brought aboard—goats, chickens, ducks, and such—and so it was that Calixto had earned that appellation common to such a one: Jimmy Duxworth, or Dux.

That Diblis would prove himself both strict and unpredictable, mean at night and meaner in the morning—owing to drink—did not surprise me. And though I was told in whispers that he'd treated Cal so badly the boy had sought to quit the ship and take to the California wilds, and would have done so had it not been for the intervention of an unnamed protector, well, neither that nor any other story could have prepared me for the license Diblis took with the boy, for the degradation, for the depravity I'd witness aboard the *Athée*. Which soon was such that something had to be done about it.

We were eight about the *Athée*: the captain, Diblis, a crew of four, Calixto, and myself. Our cook and his Duxworth slept in the small hold called steerage, and three berths angled into the bow were shared by we remaining five (as of course the captain had private quarters). This latter arrangement made me the object of envy and enmity both; for

I was let to keep to my berth whilst the four useful sailors swapped theirs in accord with the watch kept above: two turning out as the other two turned in. Like as not, one or both men coming off the watch would fall to snoring only after a brazen bout of self-abuse—done none too privately, and as fast as possible lest precious sleep be lost—thus adding a quite gamy scent to the stink of our surrounds. Down in that hold, spices off-loaded long ago still were redolent, as were soured cetaceous oils that had seeped from their casks back when the *Athée* had done duty as a whaler; and, of course, there was the constant smoke of Diblis's fire: Each day at dawn he smoked us from our sleep by means of said fire and a shut, smothering hatch, such that I'd wake choking and hating him more than I had the day before.

As I was still of little use—with Savannah not a half day behind us, I'd been told to graft the block straps, point the ropes, and set the handsome nets over the shrouds; and at said direction I'd nodded, eager but soon falling still: I knew not what to do— . . . as I was still of little use, nay *no use at all*, Calixto was doubly busy: His galley work seen to, Diblis would send the boy aloft to do all the light work, and then charge him with scrubbing the decks and sweeping the wash water down the scupper holes, et cetera. Meanwhile, I'd sit at a safe remove perfecting my Turk's-head.

Once out of Savannah, we found those light, baffling winds and pleasant weather that made for slow going; for which I at first gave thanks, as red weather would have shown me for the landlubber I was. But soon I came to long for a gust, a gale, anything at all to fatten our sails and speed us toward Cuba; for I saw that Calixto suffered from his close proximity to Diblis.

But no such luck: Soon we lost what winds we'd found, and lay all but becalmed. The captain ordered subtle changes to our course, all to no avail. We'd gain no speed till the *Athée* traded the green sea for the faster blues of the Gulf Stream.

Slowed so, the men grew indolent and begged Diblis—the keeper of the kegs—to "up their daily cups." This he did, to an end easily foreseen: Drunken, the men grew silly, sleepy, or mean, sometimes all at once. And it was Diblis himself who was rendered meanest of all by drink. I was offered grog—for which I alone was expected to pay, mind—but I declined; for I'd no taste for the water-cut rum. What's more: Somehow I knew I'd need my wits about me, and soon.

And sure enough it was that very night that the abuse, the *true and intolerable* abuse, began.

I resisted sleep that rum-sodden night, hoping I'd be able to sneak topside and bathe with water drawn from our reservoir of rain. (I had only the privacy afforded me by night and the sleep of the sailors.) But just as I clambered down from my bunk—dropping down beside a Connecticut man, name of Chance, who lay face in and flatulent upon the lower berth—I heard words seeping in a hiss from steerage. This was not converse; for that stream of shaming words flowed *at*, only at and never from, my friend. I crept nearer, near enough to hear. No great effort, this: Diblis was drunk, louder than he knew—surely that blue burst of ages past had dulled his hearing—and steerage was separated from the larger hold by naught but a panel door.

Standing with an ear cocked toward that cabin, well . . . I heard enough to soften the hardest of hearts. How was it Cal, gentle Cal, had called down such invective upon himself? What could he have done to spur Diblis so, such that now I heard hatred, pure hatred, issuing from the older man? Wondering thus, and deeming the matter one for the cook and his boy to settle themselves—or wanting to see it as such—I crept topside. What could I do to spare the boy such shame? *Rien*. And so I had better leave off listening. Further: I convinced myself—it was a lie, and I must have known as much—

that Calixto was strong, a match for whatever devils were resident in Diblis.

Topside, unremarked by the men of the watch, I pulled the plug of the funnel-shaped reservoir and washed as best a clothed man can. I would not risk being espied myself, not even at night; for there was star- and moonlight by which to be seen, and I'd no wish to become the scapegrace of the *Athée*, that being the sailors would delight in deriding; for already I'd learned that mankind en masse—be they sailors at sea or girls residing in a convent school—*need* such a being. No: I'd keep to the shadows, wherein my secrets had been stowed long ago.

Having washed, I stood now at the taffrail, letting what wind there was dry my loosed hair, which hung then to my shoulders: short enough to be tied into a queue (as a man might), yet long enough to pin into some upswept style and augment with false hair and ornaments (as is sometimes a woman's wont). All was silent save for the songs of the sea and the ship: that chorus of wave-work and creaking timbers that is, in essence, silence to a sailor's ear. Damnably, I still could hear Diblis; and soon saw the reason why: I stood near that same hatch, now covered only by that grate which sometimes he'd close to smother us from our sleep. A vent of sorts, meant to free the smoke of his fires, save now the only thing rising up was sound, sound like steam seeping from some infernal fissure.

Soon I heard mention made of another ship. Or so I thought; for Diblis's speech was slurred by excess of spirits, and spleen. Other words came, too—*California, captain, cravings*, et cetera—concatenating one to another, like links in a chain, and contributing to a story which came together; as so:

It seemed Diblis referenced, in insinuating tones, those sea months he and Calixto had shared, sailing up along the California coast under the aegis of a captain other than our present one. Truly: Here was a tale the sordid particulars of which I'd no wish to hear. And so I determined to tie my still-wet hair into its leathern strap and slip back belowdecks to my bunk, and sleep, all the while wishing—for Calixto's sake—that the sun would rise and hurry to its height, and that by its first light the boy would find a way out from under Diblis's shaming thumb.

But just then I heard further words added to that alliterative list that caused me to stop, to take to a knee and turn my ear toward the open grate; for with these words Diblis's tale had taken a turn; and what previously he'd only insinuated, he now spoke. "The corps," said he. "Cocks," said he. "Corn-holin'," said he, speaking so that the *C*s cracked hard and the *O*s opened as deep and as dark as wells. So it was I learned Cal had been abused before. So it was I witnessed his being abused again, *right then*.

Now that I knelt, I could—craning my neck this way and that—see down into steerage. I crouched so close to the deck that my nose grazed the grate when the schooner suffered a light swell and tipped toward starboard. But I braced myself, both bodily and otherwise, and bent again to see what I could see. . . . Diblis: there, not three feet beneath me, squatting on the edge of his rumpled bunk, bare-chested as ever, such that the blue of his powder burns set in relief his many crude tattoos. He sat leaning forward upon his bunk, like some collared carnivore straining toward its bait: something, or someone as yet out of sight. I looked down upon his balding head, upon his back quilted here with color, there with tufted hair; and then, as Diblis rolled with the schooner, as he tilted back I saw down the rounds of his breasts and belly to . . .

A devil indeed, this Diblis.

Down past a protuberant brow, past that roseate nose, past breasts like those of a Buddha, nay more like the pointy teats of a beast, down past his barrel of a belly I saw the . . . *mais oui*, a ruddy, crooked stub of cock protruded. Yes: Diblis was naked; and now that his hands were behind him seeking balance, he had only those shaming words with which to excite himself, to fire those desires dredged up by drink—shaming words and the sight of Cal sitting across from him and . . . *caged.*

Would that I used the word figuratively; but I do not.

There across the cabin sat a square of wicker standing perhaps as high as my thigh and three, four feet wide. Its top was secured by means of a peg; and therein, upon a voyage longer than ours would be, one might have kept fowl or a lesser, four-legged creature: a goat, perhaps, there to be milked prior to slaughter. But now the goatish one sat outside the cage, and within it, crouched upon a mat of fetid straw, there was Calixto, naked and trying not to cry.

How I burned at seeing him so debased! I think now that had I not been rendered dumb by the sight, I might well have worked some sister-trick upon Diblis then and there: caused his heart to seize like a sprung clock, or bled him dry via foul orifices both low and high. . . . *Hélas,* I did naught but watch that first night; and for such inaction I will not even essay an excuse.

. . . Poor Calixto, sitting caged, brimful of tears, and having heaped upon him such invective, such obloquy—and let it be said that amidst Diblis's words were some I'd yet to learn in English or even French—but the boy met it all with silence. Not silence of the stony, dignified sort. No: This was that species of silence that—along with the tears that fell and his posture: he sat cowering in the cage with his knees drawn up—bespeaks guilt and contrition and a coming punishment that was his due. Seeing this pained me the more. And then, *maybe then* I'd have acted if only a drunken Diblis had not begun to lay out his case (as it were) against Calixto. This I'd hear. I had to.

Apparently, aboard that other ship, Calixto had become the pet of a senior sailor—senior to Diblis, at least, in rank if not age—and had received the perquisites of said position, whatever they were. . . . At sea, where all sustenance must be allotted, and all needful things parceled out, lives have been lost in battling over the last of a Bologna sausage; and said perks may have been of a like nature. Then again, at sea, bodily favors are sometimes sought, swapped, or sold. So: best to let lay the subject of sea perks, I suppose. . . . Evidently, Diblis had grown jealous and was jealous still; but was it the Keeper or the Kept he envied? The Handsome Sailor (so I imagined him) or Calixto himself?

This and many other questions went unanswered; for, of course, Diblis and Cal knew the story's particulars and had no need to speak them—save, of course, for those details that Diblis deemed *particularly* shaming and therefore repeated till my own ears burned. That said, let me here tell what came to *seem* true, and what later I had confirmed by Calixto. It seemed Diblis spoke of relations that had been consensual; and such sympathies on the part of the Handsome Sailor were easily understood by me. *Enfin,* I myself was already smitten, was I not? Too, I understood—without sympathy, mind—the antipathy that such a coupling might cause one such as Diblis, whose heart had hardened with disuse, whose soul had soured, whose ugliness both within and without was such that his needs—and needs he had, *évidemment:* there it was, his ruddy nub of need—would only ever be bought from the lowest breed of beings; or otherwise extorted, as at present.

Some clue—I forget what—told me the Handsome Sailor had left their common ship at a California port. Had he been hounded from it by Diblis? Had there been a scandal? Courts-martial or the threat of justice cruder, more cursory than that? I cannot say. Never did I sue Calixto for all the details. Regardless, the Handsome Sailor disappeared; and Cal—betrayed, abandoned?— . . . *alors,* the fate of so beautiful a boy, thusly marked, is too easily imagined. Suffice to say: Rough usage became the boy's lot when again the corps set sail. And though I do not know how long Calixto suffered, I do know that the length of such a tenure matters not at all: Irreversible damage can be done in a day, in an hour, in mere minutes. This I'd learned.

Aboard the *Athée*, that night, further debasement followed, Diblis speaking words with which I will not stain these pages; and by such words he so roused himself that . . .

Hélas, there are things which must somehow be said. . . . Suddenly, leaping to his horn-hard feet as best his bulk allowed, Diblis crossed to the cage and loosed his seed onto its wicker slats. There it clung. Fatly, he fell back onto his bunk. Sated, he was. His breathing was so heavy, so labored, it loosed fumes foul with rum, the which rose to my nose. Had I a match, I could have set fire to his very breath. I saw his thick lids growing heavy, their blinking slowed by the onset of sleep; and had Diblis opened his eyes just then, he'd have seen me hovering overhead, staring down, *seething* down at him. I saw, too, that soon he'd descend to a dreamworld too dark, too diabolical to imagine. But before he'd do so, this:

He sat up to seal a contract with his charge. He'd keep Cal's story, keep his secrets from the crew and thus spare him *attentions* akin to those he'd suffered on that other ship—and it was true: Such salts as those aboard the *Athée* would have needed little provocation to pounce upon a boy such as Calixto—if, *if* Calixto agreed to . . .

Hélas encore, Calixto agreed to let Diblis indulge himself upon his skin with needles and ink.

Yes: he'd let himself be tattooed. And the design proposed by a laughing Diblis for his Duxworth was this: He'd mark his parts—" . . . rump, sirloin, and shank," said he—as a butcher does beef, in lines indelible and blue.

So perverse a proposal! . . . To see Calixto so sullied, to see Diblis delighting in same . . . I could not, *would not* let this come to pass.

But to this proposal I heard the boy accede.

True: Had he not agreed, he'd have been left to sleep the night in that cage; for I saw that Diblis had rigged the wicker top, had secured its peg with a lock. Indeed, Cal had not only to agree to the perverse pact, he had to coax his jailer to free him; which—blessedly—Diblis did, taking from off the table a tiny key that turned in the heart-shaped lock with a rusted *pop*. Had the devil not done this, I'd have descended to do it; or from where I was, perhaps I'd have tried some sister-trick, and caused to burst both the lock and Diblis's dark heart.

But no: Diblis opened the cage. This done, I was surprised to see Calixto spring up from within and secure with all the menace he could muster additional assurance that Diblis would not, *not* let slip his secrets to . . . *to me!*

Yes: Cal made Diblis swear he'd not whisper a word of his history to me.

And Diblis did swear it—an oath worth less than the rummy vapors accompanying it—before falling back across his bunk, an action amplified by the creak of wood and, soon, a rib-rattling snore. It was then I half hoped, half feared that Cal would avenge himself upon the sleeping Diblis. But no: The naked boy simply stepped from the cage and crawled abed, and there he lay curled and crying, his back turned toward his tormentor. I saw his unblemished skin so pure, unmarked but for those freckles constellating his heaving shoulders. The poor boy hadn't even strength enough to draw a blanket over himself against that shivering brought on not by cold, but by the shaming he'd suffered.

Before taking leave of that despicable scene, I had another long look at the boy and saw, *saw* what it was Diblis would do: the blue tattoo.

I'd not let that come to pass. *No.* I knew not what I'd do, but Diblis would not, *not* claim Calixto in that way. He'd not render indelible the boy's baseless shame.

I was determined, indeed; the more so as I sought sleep that night and heard again and again those words of Calixto's: his asking, his insisting that his secrets be kept from me. *Me*, who'd always been the keeper of secrets. Not the Shamer, but the Shamed. Why? Why me? Surely Cal knew I'd not harm him, no matter what I learned of his past. Surely he knew I'd never use him as the others might. Could he think I'd condemn him for once having given himself—heart, body, or both—to the Handsome Sailor?

To these and countless other questions no answer came but one: Calixto cared what I thought, *and so cared for me.* No one else had, not for a long, long while. So it was that not one but two who sailed aboard the *Athée* cried themselves to sleep that night.

 *Chapter Four*

. . . our natures do purpose,
Like rats that raven down their proper bane,
A thirsty evil; and when we drink, we die.
—SHAKESPEARE, *Measure for Measure*

THE NEXT DAY AT DAWN, CALIXTO CAME TOPSIDE FULLY
clothed; whereas previously he'd worn naught but those
duck trousers and the faded red shirt, now he'd pulled
on a worn sweater—despite the season's heat: already it
was warm, and by noon the sea would seem to steam—
knitted in wool dyed a powdery blue, or perhaps faded
to that shade from its original indigo. It was too big for
the boy: he'd had to cut its sleeves, such that the wrists
were frayed. Elsewhere there were holes, holes that
showed the skin it seemed Calixto sought to shield from
Diblis. But no shield, no sweater could assuage his
shame; neither could it put off what it was he'd agreed
to; and it had been agreed—or rather implied, I
suppose—that the tattooing would commence that
night, when next Diblis was sufficiently drunk, desirous,
and ready to indulge himself.

I heard it said that if the winds rose, and if the currents of the Stream were as strong as sometimes they were, we were two days, three at most, from the Cuban port. So it was I wondered: Could we, could Cal somehow stall Diblis, somehow put him off and flee into the city at first chance? It wouldn't be easy, no. More: Already I knew that the world of sailors was a small one, if improbably so, given the world's expanse of sea—hadn't Diblis and Cal encountered each other of late, having shared a Pacific ship not two years prior?—and so, even if Cal could escape the cook, doubtless there'd come another encounter. And if not, Diblis had only to loose rumors amongst the men of any seaport and watch his words spread like the red of chummed waters, drawing to Cal sharks of all sorts. No: Somehow Diblis's silence must be won. But how? What could I do if Cal did not confide in me? . . . I'd the long hours of daylight to think of something.

. . . Sharks. I'd been told that they abounded in the waters beneath and all about us. So it was I kept watch over those waters—smooth as slate, unworried by the winds—searching for a slicing fin. Was I hopeful of hurling Dibles overboard? No. Not yet . . . The sun on the sea was no deterrent; for of course I sported those blue spectacles I'd asked an oculist in St. Augustine to craft long ago, so as to hide my Toad-turned eyes. Yes, with nothing else to do but worry and wait, I watched for sharks: a strange game. None came. I saw schooling fish and pods of porpoises, and that lesser species of dolphin so unappealingly blunt-headed yet with a skin so iridescent it lights the very waters through which it swims. I'd see a similar iridescence hours hence, but it bore no beauty then: it was the scum coating the waters of the Havanan harbor, discharged from all the world's ships—oils spilled from both bilge and barrel, sailors' slops, et cetera. . . . *Enfin*, I saw no sharks; but still I kept watch, and of course did not bathe, could *never* have bathed as the men of the *Athée* did later that day, Cal included.

Typically, the sailors stripped and leapt into the sea, swinging from yardarms and such and, in general, seeming what they were: half boy, half brute; but this day they took precautions, owing, I supposed, to the rumor if not the reality of sharks. And I, standing astern, did let my shaded eyes stray over the bathing men—I admit it—as their ablutions proceeded apace; thusly:

Two men—sailors were ever in twos, it seemed, working in shifts and taking equal turns at everything—lowered a lesser sail into the sea till it bore a bellyful of water. They then raised it by boom to a shark-safe height, stripped and shimmied out to it—ever mindful of the "privates" they protected in a cupped palm—to splash in the sail like puppies in a puddle. The nonbathing mate—he who manned the boom—took care not to dip the sail down as sometimes they did when in less *active* waters, lest a leviathan leap from below, teeth bared.

As I watched, Cal came shuffling past me to stand further astern, not two feet from me.

I bade him hello. He nodded only, chin tucked tightly to his chest, eyes averted. And how I wished then to say that I'd witnessed his degradation the night before, to assure him he'd an ally aboard the *Athée,* against the devil Diblis. But of course I said nothing, only watched as the boy went about an odd chore, one which I supposed had something to do with our luncheon, which had yet to be served.

Tethered astern, the captain kept a fish car. A dinghy, essentially, outfitted to serve in the stead of a well, which the *Athée* lacked. Such wells are oft seen at the center of vessels, their bottoms bored through so that the flow of seawater serves as a filter, keeping their living cargo alive, and in health. Setting out from Savannah, we'd had several grouper in the fish car, but they since had slipped beneath Diblis's blades: cut for steaks and chopped for chowder. And since the seas had been so steadily calm, the car had been kept empty, bobbing behind us like a bottle; for, floating in close confinement within a stagnant well, fish might sicken, and in death draw—yes—sharks.

When it came clear that Cal intended to put the fish car to a new purpose, I asked, in a tone as light as I could muster, "A bath? Amidst the groupers?"

"No groupers now," said he.

"Yes, I know," said I, patting a tummy that was flat, despite what I wore: that damnable swaddling, blouse and vest that sweated me so. Stupidly, insensitively, I'd thusly complimented the devil's cuisine. I regretted the gesture the minute I made it.

I cannot recall what awkward acts or words followed, though surely there were some of both; but quite well I recall Calixto stripping down, shyly, his back turned toward me. Naked, he bent to draw in the buoyant, cork-cornered car, tying it tightly before taking a rope ladder down to it. When first I saw Cal straddle the taffrail and step off the *Athée,* I hurried to the schooner's side and saw with relief the aforementioned ladder. . . . Dark as my thoughts were, I'd instantly deduced that the bath had been but a ruse, that suicide had been the boy's true intent.

Calixto sat in the fish car as he'd sat in the cage, with little more room to move; yet he bathed. Hurriedly; for all the while Diblis could be heard calling his Duxworth to the galley, where chop of cleaver and clang of pot presaged the luncheon to come: Cold viands drawn from the locker—odd, it was, to have to dine on food prepared by one as detestable as Diblis—and sliced with that same knife he sometimes used to taper his nails. No surprise, I could not eat that day; and instead only drank from the biggin full of coffee as it was passed. But yes, I recall the meal well, as in seeing it laid out, I saw that Diblis was green at the gills and goggle-eyed; for already he'd retaken to his rum to fight the aftereffects of drunkenness. It was plain: by dusk Diblis would again be drunk.

As I stared down from the stern, Cal let out the line and the fish car floated back from the *Athée*. Whether we'd dropped anchor long enough for the men to bathe, or whether our progress was still so slow over the sea that it merely seemed we'd anchored, I cannot say. Regardless, I saw the last man in the sail clamber aboard, rinse himself with ladled rain water as his brethren had, and then retake to the sextant and wheel. Then came the captain's cry, "West, steady west with the Stream," which now was his refrain, and the only words heard from him. . . . Did I stare at the bathing boy? Doubtless I did, baldly, brazenly, such that no spectacles could disguise the act. But I shan't bother with apology now; and who, I ask, would willfully look away from such beauty as that, albeit in the shape of a sad boy bathing in a fish car? . . . As Sebastiana had once said on the subject of beauty— be it in art or in life—those who are not themselves adepts make the best admirers.

With Diblis calling his name ever more insistently, Cal began to draw the car in; and I, reaching down for the rope, helped him. Up the ladder he came, wrapped in naught but water. And when he took my proffered hand, I was again conscious of what previously I'd observed: the strength in his hand, his arm, and those broad shoulders that belied his boys' years. Standing on the deck, dripping seawater, he hadn't time to seek a rainwater rinse—"Dux!" shouted Diblis, "*Dux!*"—nor even to dry himself properly. Instead, he patted himself with his trousers, cursorily so, stepped into them, and knotted the belt of rope as he ran, hurrying down to Diblis with nary a word to me.

As I'd stood staring at Calixto, I'd grown conscious of something:

I was not aroused. Rather, not bodily—none of the slickness, the stiff-ness that bespoke desire—but . . . dare I say it? Here it seemed a ques-tion of soul, of spirit. That is: It was my soul, my spirit, *enfin*, it was something at once simpler and more complicated than lust that was roused by the sight of the boy. I neither desired nor coveted him now, whereas previously those had been my two reactions to beauty: to de-sire it, to covet it. Now the urge was . . . to protect, to parent; for here was a boy half my age and in dire need of my help. Make no mistake: I saw and admired his beauty, of course; it was just that his sadness, and the shame he could not shed moved me more.

This I'd never felt before: the need to nurture. But sure enough, as a glistening Calixto climbed aboard the *Athée* that midday, as he stepped into his stained trousers, as seawater sluiced down his back, down the sculpted strength of his arms and legs, as he shook out his blond locks as a mutt might, apologizing when he saw the spray from his hair hit me, and as he ran to answer his tormentor's call, all I could think was this: *I'll help the boy.* But how, *how?*

Night came quickly, as dreaded things do; and still I'd not struck upon a plan.

I'd drawn courage from the news of the day: The winds were up and the current was coming on. Now it was supposed we'd see our destined city late the next day. That landfall was near was good news indeed: I wanted off the *Athée*, and supposed I might need to take my leave; for though I did not know what the night might hold—I hadn't sufficient time, privacy, nor witch-things to try to divine such knowl-edge as that—I needed neither Craft nor induced dreams to see that danger depended, that soon it might, could, would come crashing down.

That news of Wind and Water gave me confidence enough to believe what it seemed I saw: yes, the winds were up, enough to ripple
the ridiculous cuffs of my second blouse—the first had gone rank,
and hung now in the hold, dripping dry—and the sea was blue where
before it had been green: and so here was the Gulf Stream. Cuba could
not be far off.

Calixto had kept to himself that afternoon, quiet and constant at
his work; and doubtlessly thankful for the distractions of his duties.
Or so I told myself; for the poor boy had more reason than I to dread
the fall of night, which would bring to him the prick, the burn, the
sting and stain, the shame of Diblis's needles and ink.

Few if any of the *Athée's* crewmen were free of tattoos. Perhaps the
captain was; but this I cannot aver, as he kept to his cabin, and
when—as infrequently he did—he deigned to come amongst us, he
did so in the full dress of a man aspiring to more than his present station. Yes, our shipmates bore varied designs done by inexpert hands,
perhaps even those of Diblis. Only a Scotsman, name of Everard,
showed skin art worthy of that word, *art:* a topless woman—of South
Seas origin, to judge by her skirt of swaying grass—writhed about his
right biceps whilst his left showed the piratical skull and crossbones;
both designs too trite to merit further detailing here. On his neck he
had a dog; rather, I thought it was a dog. Complimenting the Scotsman on same—a compliment being the only way I could excuse myself, once he caught me staring—I was corrected, coldly, and learned
it was a dragon. Others of the crew's tattoos I cannot recall, save one
which had been reduced to a scar: The Connecticut man hosted atop
the back of his right hand a patch of puckered skin, marking the spot
where he—with a blade that had doubtless been none too sharp, and,
presumably, the additional aid of aqua fortis and much, much
liquor—had cut from his *own* flesh (as not even the worst sawbones
would scar a sailor so) some unwanted design, and in that surgical

essay had rendered useless his thumb and forefinger by the severing of sundry nerves.

Tattooing was a sea practice so common that none save Cal and I were unmarked. And so it surprised no one when Diblis—still wallowing in the shoals of drunkenness, but soon to dive into its depths—began to set out his tools upon the table before our supper was even seen to. Still the men sat delecting the flour pudding with which our cook had favored us that night. But he'd have us be gone now, and said so.

With shaking hands, Calixto cleared the plates and serving ware, clankingly so, stacking them in a basin he'd take topside for a rude rinse. In their stead, upon the table, came Diblis's cakes of Canton ink and those saucers in which he'd mix the ink with water. Too, there were the needles: bamboo sticks to the ends of which he'd tied tridents composed of simple sewing needles, closely set. With these he'd prick and lift the skin, and set the darts of dye below, rather as a cook—*un cuisinier* far more adept than Diblis—might prepare a fowl for roasting by setting spices betwixt its flesh and skin.

With supper done and the sun down, each of us retired to our separate pursuits, the common mood of the crew somewhat improved. The *Athée* had not been a happy ship, indeed not, but now its men were near enough Havana to look forward to its fancies. Two men took to the watch, and two took to their bunks with books or lesser amusements: sketch pads, diaries, letters they carried and read, again and again and again. The captain was secreted away, as ever. As for Diblis, now it seemed he'd drink the kegs down to their dregs, as if by emptying them they'd be able to hold even more of the pure rum of Cuba. And Cal, poor Cal still had his scullion's tasks: Having rinsed and stacked our tin plates, he'd taken a seat at the taffrail, where, legs adangle, he sat peeling carrots drawn up from a bottomless kettle, more carrots than could have been consumed in the half day left to us if the

Athée had been the floating hutch of a hundred rabbits, and not the eight lonely sorts we were. Down went the orange shavings onto a sea cut, scarred by the *Athée's* passing. This was busywork, of course; and with it Diblis meant to occupy Cal until such time as he found in drink, in desire, courage enough to summon the boy down to their shared cabin. Which soon he did.

 ## Chapter Five

Will any man despise me? Let him see to it. But I will see to it
that I may not be found doing or saying anything that deserves
to be despised.

—MARCUS AURELIUS, *Meditations*

THE CALL WHEN IT CAME WAS CHILLING. IF BEFORE DIBLIS'S
voice had been coarse, grating, now it was a hiss—
slurred by rum—and meant for no one but the boy to
hear. "Dux," it came, the *x* bearing the sibilance of a sac
full of snakes. *"Dux!"* And this was followed, ap-
pallingly, with that *chuck, chuck, chuck* by which one might
call a chick to its feed, or a cleaver.

I lay waiting for this. Whilst abed, I had not had to
stave off that sleep to which the sailors surrendered; for
I'd Cal and events to come to worry me. And if briefly
that worry left me, others came: Havana was near, and
held I knew not what.

"Dux," came the call again; and when no answer was
heard, my heart verily seized as I wondered: Had the boy
indeed hurled himself overboard, choosing death over
shame? I swung my stockinged feet over the side of my

bunk, and was about to drop down and hurry topside in case I could save . . . But then, just then I saw Calixto descending the gangway—bare feet followed by calves and scarred knees, such that I'd time to leap back onto my bunk and retake a sleeper's pose before those duck trousers showed. Best not to be seen, surely. So it was that, feigning sleep, I heard him pad toward steerage, heard that plank door open and close with a creak.

Would I follow Cal into that compartment where an aroused and drunken Diblis awaited, all his implements in array? Though I had not heard it, surely he'd set the latch behind the boy. Would I then ram the door, or summon such telekinesis as I'd only ever used to amuse myself: causing untouched pianos to tinkle tunelessly, and slamming doors and windows in distant rooms? Still I had no answers, no intentions. Instead I waited. And when finally I could stand it no longer, I snuck topside.

I slipped past the snoring men of the watch to the post I'd taken the night before. I knelt down beside that grate which Diblis had left open, lest he and his Duxworth smother within that coffin-small cabin. Diblis had set the scene within. With relief I saw that Cal would not be caged this night. With upset I saw him offered a draft, which he downed (as was not his habit); and then there came the words with which the end began:

"The rump," said a seated Diblis, fingering himself absently at first, then angrily; for though the sot's desire was diamond hard, his cock was not. "Let's start by marking the rump cut, eh? What say you, my Dux?" No answer came, of course. "Drop them raggedy pants, eh?" But before Calixto could, Diblis jerked the duck trousers down. "Now kick 'em free. That's it now, boy, yes. . . . Turn. Good. Now bend and back up to me, eh? *Mais non!* Don't turn to look at me!" And he slapped the boy's buttocks, his hand cracking across them like a whip. "Or is it these you want to see?" Here Diblis brandished the bamboo needles with a sly smile. "Oh, but stare on, stare on, eh? You'd best not look, as I don't want my Dux fainting now, do I, at a drop of blood or a little bitty prick?" *A little bitty prick,* indeed. And I, too, hoped Calixto would not faint; for I cared not to contemplate the liberties Diblis would take in that case.

Up from beside his heel, Diblis drew his bottle of rum and poured it onto the small of Calixto's back; from whence it ran downward, between his slap-stung buttocks. With his hand Diblis smeared the rum; and—I'd not seen this coming at all, nor had Calixto, surely—he lifted his lamp's glass sleeve to bare its flame. I thought it was an inking instrument he held to the flame, a needle he—improbably—sought to sterilize; but in fact it was . . . *Enfin,* it was a phosphorus match, and when Diblis touched it to Cal's flesh, flames went *whoosh* in pursuit of the rum.

I fell backward, hand to my heart. *What would I do?* When I righted myself, I saw that so, too, had Calixto fallen forward. But—blessedly—the pain of the flame had been as naught; for Diblis had fast smothered it with a length of flannel. "Oh, my Dux," said he, "who'd hurt ye? Not your Diblis. The flame is for purifyin'," and he laughed as he slapped his knee, summoning Cal back into place.

. . . Diblis. If ever a devil deserved his due, it was he.

Seated still, and with a tiny worktable drawn up to his side, Diblis set his right, death-blue hand upon Calixto's hip. He kneaded the firm flesh, and splayed his fingers to fan down over the boy's buttock (no redder from the flames than the sting, I saw). Then, brusquely, he set that same hand to the small of Cal's back and shoved, shoved the boy forward and down such that he had no choice but to bend, to raise his rump high, as will a she-cat in heat. Now here was a sight for Diblis's delectation; and delight in it he did: Whilst Cal set between his teeth a length of rope—to bite down upon, more against the shame than the imminent pain of the pricking—Diblis put both his hands upon the boy's rear, kneading and spreading the flesh, and then slipped his left hand down, down to daintily take—as a milkmaid might—the boy's . . . oh, let no *délicatesse* slow this tale: . . . to take in hand the boy's cock and balls. With his feet he knocked Calixto's own wide, and wider still. Now he had him, fixedly. Cal would not, *could not* move as the inking began.

From off the tiny table Diblis took a quill of the olden sort, and not—fortunately—a more common stylus of steel; with this he'd mark his dashed lines in accord with the bloodstained butcher's chart he'd hung to guide his hand. "Let it be the rump we set first, eh? The tenderest, the truest cut . . ." And with that, Diblis set his pen upon my friend.

Now, if I knew one thing it was this: Not reason—reason had fled—not reason, but rather instinct would guide my actions; and so it would have at that very moment had I not been struck still by Diblis; who, thinking himself unseen, of course, and in total command of Calixto, leaned in to . . .

Holding hard with his left hand to Calixto's nether parts—and seeming to squeeze: so said Calixto's grimace—Diblis drew the boy back, back toward himself, whilst at the same time leaning in to take, to taste, to flick his tongue at . . . Oh yes: Diblis's tongue came flickering forth and ought, by rights, to have shown itself split, as every serpent's is, as it offered that chthonian kiss.

Here then was the *osculum obscenum*, that kiss by which witches of old were said to render their tribute unto the Prince of This World. But here was a devil doing it himself; for a sniffing, slavering Diblis leaned in to tease, to take the boy with his tongue.

Instinct, indeed . . . It was then I rapped, rapped upon the deck above Diblis's head; such that his face, withdrawing from its dockage, tongue yet extended, rolled up, up to see . . . Not me; for I'd taken care to fall back from view. In truth, *I knew not what to do.*

Silence. I crept nearer to see below, and just as I supposed, there sat Diblis, returned to his delights, doubtless having told himself the sound had been but a sea-knock, some flotsam hitting hard against the hull. So it was I had to rap a second time, harder, and as a human would: *knock, knock, knock:* thrice, in fast succession. No flotsam this. And this time I did not slip back from sight. And Diblis, looking up with those eyes of his—the right one shining like moonstone—saw me overhead and let go a gasp. I gasped in turn, seeing he'd slipped two spit-slickened fingers into his crying, cringing captive.

Instinctively, yes, I held his horrid gaze and stared down my dare: *Come up, devil.* And then I let slip my glasses and showed my Eye.

At first Diblis squinted up at me, wondering what or who he saw. Was I a sailor of the watch, someone he could cause to cower or make disappear. (Still those two dozed on and off—so said the saw of their snoring—and it was owing to the grace of the Gulf Stream that the *Athée* did not breach upon reef or rock that night.) So drunken, so deluded by desire was Diblis, doubtless he deemed the violation of his privacy the greater offense—greater than what he'd done, or was doing still to Calixto; for all the while he stared up at me he worked his fingers in his flinching charge. Oh, but then he saw it was me hovering overhead, and he said:

"Ah *oui*, the Fancy-man." I saw his anger change, verily saw his thoughts hie to the *when and how* of the revenge he'd take upon me. Seeing the sickly twist of that smile, I nearly withdrew. But no. Still I showed the Eye and stared down my dare: *Come up, devil, and receive your due.*

Diblis stood, shoving Cal from him such that the boy fell onto his own cot across the cabin. And whilst stepping into his trousers, and buttoning his flaccidity behind his fly, still he stared up through the grate at me. "Fancy-man," said he, following this with threats hissed in French (which words I'd recount, had fear not precluded my hearing them).

"Diblis," said I; and the name was salt upon my tongue. "Come up."

To this point, no one had heard us; or so it seemed. Or perhaps they knew better than to question such sounds heard in the night. But now I saw, and heard Diblis slam the steerage door behind him, and his tread was so heavy on the stairs of the gangway it seemed the schooner shuddered. Surely the men of the watch would wake, if not the others, if not the captain.

Diblis had left his Duxworth behind with a warning, which I'd heard: "Stay," he'd said, commanding Cal as one would a dog, "or I'll sing your secrets into every ear, like a sweet canary, I will." And last I saw Cal he lay upon the cot, his arms wrapped about his head: the pose of one about to be beaten.

As a ranting Diblis was not so strange a sight as to derange the ship, even at night, no one woke. Rather, no one came topside alongside the cook. So there we two were, face to face, with no option left but fisticuffs; so said the ridiculous stance Diblis assumed. At the thought of this I blanched a bit, it's true; for I'd never fought with my fists. Neither was I about to that night.

"*C'est toi,* Fancy-man, who calls me from my sleep?" Diblis stood not ten feet from me, fisted hands upon his hips.

"Sleep, you call that?" And I gestured down to the grate through which I'd watched him two nights running.

He was coming at me now, slowly, unsteadily; and thankfully I still had wits enough to lead him back astern, away from the men of the watch, whom I suppose had had their share of rum as well and suffered now its soporific effect. Carefully, I kept the distance between Diblis and me from diminishing. "Is it often you bugger boys in your 'sleep,' Diblis? I'd not be surprised. Indeed, the devil himself must deal out your dreams."

He'd closed, till now he stood not five feet from me. We were

---

✳

astern, with nowhere else to go but overboard. And as Diblis lunged to take me in his ham-like hands, I . . .

I saw Calixto, standing at the top of the gangway. He held his trousers in place, but by the moon's light I saw a half-drawn line of ink snaking over his hip, up from his *rump*. I wanted Cal to stay where he stood; away, safe. And I'd have willed him to do so—literally willed it—had I not had Diblis to deal with. Diblis, who was determined to strangle me. Breaking his grip—and in so doing surprising myself, quite—I thought to distract the devil; and did so by resorting to French. A full and rather florid French. Why? Perhaps the elemental things I was soon to express had lain too long suppressed, were buried too deeply down to be found with a foreign tongue. Perhaps I still thought I could conceal things from Calixto, who had only that portion of French that any Spaniard or Italian can comprehend. Or perhaps I'd read too often of inquisitors, *and would be one myself*. Regardless:

Diblis, said I as I swayed to further unsteady him, *I watched you working upon that boy, saw your . . . your ardor increase in proportion to his shame, saw you harden in time with same. You, Diblis*, and here I stood still and paused, not for effect; but rather to dwell for a moment on what I now knew to be true. *You, Diblis*, I pronounced, *are about to pay a price for such pleasure as that.*

What price? Certainly I could conjure innumerable punishments—of both the mortal and sisterly sort—to stifle, to stymie and forever stop Diblis from partaking of such pleasures again. Indeed, already my mind was racing: Hadn't I read the *Book of Shadows* of some far-flung sister who'd perfected certain . . . phallic punishments? No matter; for already I knew it: Diblis would die. He'd leave me no other option.

There he stood now, cursing me and Calixto in turn. Said he, "Your boy has an ass full of secrets, Fancy-man; but so, too, do you, I suppose. That's it, eh? You two are . . . *ensemble?* I thought it was Savannah lay behind us, but I see now it was in Sodom where we found you two."

Oh, clever cook, I countered, *I see 'tis true that the devil will cite Scripture for his purposes. . . . You'll resort to your rusted Bible, will you? Well, I assure you, I've read books far more cunning than that, and I can do things neither your gods nor devils can compass.*

I'd confused him. Perhaps I'd scared him; for I was calm, coldly so, and he was drunk. But soon he returned to that simplest of insults: He questioned my manhood.

If only you knew, said I.

Still I'd not struck upon a plan; but soon I'd no need of one; for as soon as Diblis laid his hands on me—which he succeeded in doing as I slipped on a coil of rope—I reacted. It was instinct, yes; but in making that claim, I offer no excuse.

Wanting no more of my wordplay, Diblis struck as best he could: as a brute, and by a brute's show of strength.

He had me in a stranglehold, and we two tottered toward the taffrail till naught but that separated us from the silver-black sea; into which *I'd not descend,* no indeed.

Now, this was . . . uncomfortable, shall I say? My throat hurt. My every breath I had to steal, and they were too shallow to long sustain life. I could smell the stink under Diblis's choking arm. And then, looking up through tearing eyes at the stars, the moon, I knew it: *I was being strangled.* I worried less about the strangling act itself, truly, and more about . . . *enfin:* Would it cause the Coming of the Blood? . . . Of course, I was not quite so calm then; rather, I have difficulty summoning *the fear of death* now, given what's come.

So: As often happens, the situation had devolved to this: Kill or be killed.

I'd have to act, rather *react* or die. And so I surrendered to instinct, spurred not by the desire to kill Diblis—though there was that, yes—

but rather by my wish to spare Calixto the sight of what would even-tuate—Diblis's death, my survival—and, moreover, whatever means I'd use to bring on both. This last—*the means*—was yet a mystery to me; until:

Cal came closer and I saw he had in hand the same marlinespike we'd used in tackling the Turk's-head. Creeping ever nearer, I saw he meant to drive it into Diblis's back; but I'd not have that crime fall upon Cal. Revenge may be best when served cold, as is said, but one as innocent as Calixto could never have savored it. I, on the other hand, *knew the dead*, had heard the suits of both the justly and unjustly murdered, and had already deemed Diblis deserving of death, if not a fate far worse. No one could say I was innocent. And so I was spurred to action, and killed Diblis so as to spare Calixto having to do it. . . . It played out so:

Calixto came on, ever on, whilst Diblis and I danced our strangle-dance. If we were to turn, just so, Diblis would see the boy, perhaps unhand me and tackle him instead. And that wouldn't do.

"Cal," said I, if the strangled, or strangling, can be said to speak; in fact, I may have willed the action, and wordlessly conveyed: *Throw it. Throw it!* Whereupon with all my might I turned, turned so that Diblis and I both faced the boy as he obeyed me. But instead of *throwing* the spike as I'd decreed, Calixto lobbed it toward me; for me *to catch* and put to purpose. But I'd not intended to catch the marlinespike. I'd no intention of driving it into Diblis myself, by main strength, no indeed.

Hélas, the die was cast; and so once the spike was airborne, well, I seized it with my witch's will, righting and steadying it so that it spi-raled toward Diblis and struck its mark with all the surety of a bullet. Not six inches from my face, Diblis's right eye gave with a . . . a pop and a slosh. Like the crack of an egg upon the lip of cup, it was. For, by dint of will alone, I'd sped the marlinespike through the salted night to find his eye, his right and now wholly ruined eye. His left blinked on a while longer: a most disquieting sight, in point of fact. Then certain parts of Diblis's body began to spasm, as if sparked. It was not long before twitches ceded to stillness; for the spike had splintered brain and bone both, and three inches of its steel stuck from the back of Diblis's head. The protruding tip of the marlinespike showed itself slick with gore, and clotted with . . . with whatever it was that twitched in time with the last movements of Diblis, by which he fell forward. Landing face-first, Diblis drove four more inches of the marlinespike through his skull. And it was then the blood came, from beneath as well as behind his head, to darken the deck.

Death . . . but I shan't accord Diblis's its due. All I'll say is he lay at our feet like a long-landed fish. Like a whale, actually; for well I recall the slap and shake of blubber as he fell upon that deck.

It was done. . . . And if I seem flippant, forgive me; but being dead myself, I find the state rather less fearful than the living do. Death, more so than dying, is absurd (though a marlinespike through the eye of a deserving devil like Diblis, well . . .). And the longer I'm dead, the more absurd death seems; for humor often arises in direct relation to one's distance from a given fact, *non?* And it must be said: Nothing beats death for distancing one *from the facts*.

. . . Calixto, of course, had been witness to more than I'd have wished; but it was too late to undo that. Now the boy stood at my side, stupefied and staring down at Diblis. And there I stood. Over a dead man. With a shocked boy—staring at me now—at my side, and a questioning captain and crew about to come up; for surely they'd heard the row, or leastways felt the dead-fall of Diblis. *Alors,* what to do?

As every murderer knows, the first problem posed is this: the body. And so, turning my back to Calixto and thus stepping betwixt him and Diblis, I acted—*acted,* I say—as though I were hauling the man, nay, *the body*, toward the taffrail. Toward it, then up and over it. Though I knew not what I'd say to the captain of the *Athée*, surely my story would benefit from not being told over a corpse not yet cold. In truth, Diblis was far too heavy for me to lift—heavy whilst alive, he was deadweight now: much the worse—so I willed him into the sea with a whispered, *Sailor, meet your mistress,* and with a splash saw that strange marriage consummated.

Turning back to Cal, I saw the captain at his side.

. . . Panic, just *un peu.* But first I'd had a moment—little more than a moment, surely—after conferring Diblis unto the sea, to hope that we—now a bit leaner of load—might find full sails on the morrow and achieve the Cuban port long before he bobbed toward it. Oh, but here again I jest a bit at Diblis's and Death's expense; and so let me apologize and say that in fact I never doubted we'd beat Diblis into Havana Harbor; for, if these seas were *rumored* full of sharks, surely there was, in fact, *one* shark at least, and surely that one would find its way to the bleeding, blubbery treat that was Diblis. But all I wanted then was for the corpse to quickly recede so that no one coming top-side—and already it seemed I heard that scuffle and shuffle, that ruc-tion that accompanies cries of "Man overboard!"— . . . *bref,* I wanted no one coming topside to see the star- and moonlit spike stuck through Diblis's skull. And no one did; or rather, none cared. Least of all the captain; who, standing beside a shivering Calixto, was typically mum as regarded *men overboard,* and instead said to Calixto, quite calmly, "Brushes, boy. Into the scupper holes with all this blood."

The captain said nothing more; such that I've often wondered what secrets of the captain's Diblis dragged down to the depths. The cap-tain never again mentioned the man, let alone mourned his loss, and cared only that the cook's blood not be let to stain the *Athée*'s boards. Had we done him a favor in dispatching Diblis? Or did he simply seek to quiet the matter, the murder, for convenience's sake? Had the captain and all aboard known of Diblis's abuse of Calixto, and deemed the former justly dead? Or would the captain keep his own counsel until we put in at Cuba, whereupon he'd turn us over to the authorities? I was left to wonder all this and more.

If all the crew had been roused, only two or three—the Scotsman among them—now stood astern, staring at the diminishing Diblis: like a tiny island, he seemed, what with his big belly shining some ways off to starboard. But these mourners took their cue from the captain, who eulogized Diblis with naught but a dismissing wave and this, his rallying cry, "To Havana." And when the captain retook to his cabin, the crew retook to the rum, deeming Diblis's death excuse enough to drink. . . . And that was that.

As for Calixto, well, I asked one of the salts to swap bunks with him, saying the boy had seen too much, had suffered too much to return to the cabin he'd shared with the cook. (Lest you think I succeeded in tapping into the sailor's store of sympathy, let me say it was a Spanish real that sealed the deal.) And so it was that Calixto crawled into the high bunk opposite mine; from whence he stared across the hold at me, stared so hard and fast I had to wonder how much of my witchery he'd witnessed. (Answer: All.) As dawn drew near, still he stared; till finally I said, "I'll explain. Someday. Now go to sleep."

And then finally I turned my back to the boy, feigning sleep and wondering if I would . . . Explain . . . Someday.

 *Chapter Six*

Why, then, take no note of him, but let him go; and presently call
the rest of the watch together, and thank God you are rid of a
knave.

—SHAKESPEARE, **Much Ado About Nothing**

I WOULD SAY THAT I SLEPT NOT AT ALL THAT NIGHT, SAVE
I remember, too well, being woken by the morning gun
of the Morro. And had I not heard that same salute
marking nightfall, I'd have thought we'd fallen to those
pirates said to frequent the southerly waters, and the
lesser ports of the islands that lay therein. As it was, I
sat up in my bunk with a start—and a *bang* to my head
that occasioned a bump—to find all the other bunks,
including Cal's, empty of sleepers.

Hurrying topside, I saw we were tacking toward that
narrow cliff-cut topped with what seemed châteaux of a
sort, and which soon I'd learn were forts; for, in addition
to the Morro—with its twelve guns named in heretical
honor of the Apostles—several other fortifications
guarded the entrance to Havana's harbor. . . . Havana:
Here we were. Oh, how my heart hammered.

But where was Calixto? Had a suddenly suspicious captain confined him, questioned him as to the details of Diblis's death? Though still I doubted Cal had seen enough to incriminate me in the *supernat*-ural sense, surely he'd witnessed a . . . *natural* murder: me somehow stabbing Diblis and hurling his body overboard. But how would Cal account for the marlinespike spiraling through the dark, far faster than he'd thrown it, and arriving not at the center of a bull's-eye, but rather Diblis's? And who'd believe the boy when he said that I—tall, lithe, and lean, but not so exceedingly strong—had cast the cook's corpulence out to sea with ease? Yes: It'd be best if the boy met with no questioning; for I wanted no trouble from any quarter, be it the crewmen, the captain, or the customs men who'd come.

I worried for naught: There was Calixto in the rigging, staring down at me. And if at first I supposed it was worry writ upon his face, soon I knew better: It was wonder. His countless questions had distilled down to wonderment. Might I even say it was *awe*? And there I stood staring up at him, having sworn I'd explain. Oh, but where would I begin? And how would I ever find words to match his wonder? . . . Luckily, a boat approaching port is a busy thing; and Calixto's duties kept him from questioning me that morning.

I breakfasted upon a bit of old biscuit and coffee, the bitterness of which elicited the sole condolence I'd ever hear regarding the death of Diblis. Said Everard the Scot: Were he to wake a second day to such syrup as this—whereupon he brandished a mug of the aforementioned mud—he might come to miss "the blue devil" who'd gone down. With that he smacked the tin cup against a spar and tipped it, and waited a long while for its tarry contents to spill. Other such dry-eyed commentary came as testament to what the crew held to be true: A drunken Diblis had disported with his Duxworth—again I wondered: Could they know of the sex-sick acts I'd witnessed in steerage?—till finally I'd come to the boy's defense; and in wrestling the drunkard, he, Diblis, had slipped and tipped his tipsy self over the taffrail, and down he'd gone to drink with Davy Jones. This, far from occasioning any concerns, seemed to amuse the men. That I, *I* of all people, had stood up to Diblis, amused them, yes. And far from being blamed or chastened, I was all but clapped about the shoulder, commended for a job well done. *Bref:* Diblis's coffee was missed more than he.

Still, wouldn't the captain have to render up an account of the missing sailor? Surely he'd have to reconcile the roll, just as he'd have to reconcile the manifest with the Cuban customs officers. And if so, how would he account for what I thought, nay, *swore* he'd seen, coming astern whilst Diblis yet bobbed in sight: that marlinespike shining in the night like a lightning bolt? Or hadn't he seen it? . . . As ever, it seemed wisest to keep from sight; and so, having breakfasted, I slipped back belowdecks to pack my haversack and otherwise ready myself for Havana and whatever attended me there.

With the *Athée* fallen still, I once again came topside; for I thought we'd arrived. It was with disappointment, nay, something rather more than disappointment, that I saw wharfage lie some ways distant. Still we sat at the far end of that channel, waiting. For what? I wondered.

I sat astern, where still some drops of Diblis's blood could be seen—these might well have occasioned *une crise de conscience* on my part, but not this day—and I distracted myself with Sebastiana's letter. Only when I'd read it five, ten, fifteen times—wondering did she await me in Havana, wondering who was Q., et cetera—only then did I see we were again under sail. Perhaps I'd missed a pilot's coming aboard to steer the *Athée* up the cut and into the crowded harbor. If so, I'd not miss the same again: Closely I kept watch for the approach of any boat bearing officers of the customs house or the Spanish crown. . . . Oh, but soon I grew distracted again; for:

The bay was so crowded with boats it seemed one could leap bow to bow, and gain land like a hopscotching child. I'd never seen such a show of sail. The masts seemed a floating forest, stretching from blue to blue, from sea to sky. And the flags! *Mon Dieu*, there were flags from the four corners of the world:

The red and yellow stripes of Spain, of course; and others from the lesser states of the Spanish Main . . . The blue, white, and red of France . . . The Union Cross of the Royal Commonwealth . . . The red cross of Saint George . . . The dark and double-headed eagles of Austria, Russia, and Prussia . . . Others from Holland, Italy, and Brazil. And of course, the Stars and Stripes (such as the *Athée* flew). This show of nations surprised me, I admit; for I knew not of *the centrality* of Cuban commerce.

Indeed, then as now, out from Cuba sailed sugar, molasses, rum, tobacco, cigars, coffee, and lesser crops. That much I knew. But I'd not counted on the island's *importation* of so much else: In addition to our Connecticut corn, there'd come rice from the Carolinas, jerked beef from South American states, wines from all the world over, and manufactures from England and elsewhere. Too, and most troublingly, I'd learn that certain of the boats surrounding ours had surely slipped into the lesser ports of Cuba carrying human cargo; for that island was, indeed *is yet*, engaged in that most infernal trade, and seems likely to remain so whilst she labors 'neath the thumbscrews of Spain.

Then—back in '37—the Mixed Commissions concerned themselves with that caste of liberated slaves, the *emancipados;* but still assorted treaties dating back to the teens—all of them imposed upon Spain by Britain—were toothless, and the slave trade flourished, if not in the port of Havana itself, then all along the coast, where Spanish officers were fee'd to allow to land those slavers who provided Sugar's labor and Spain's profit. . . . It is a Hell-born scheme, surely: slavery.

If slaves came clandestinely into Cuba's secondary ports, all other *commodities* entered its capital city as I did: by sailing into Regla Bay, properly paper'd.

Soon the *Athée* was surrounded by a flotilla of lesser boats. Representing neither customs nor the Crown, these were commercial craft: skiffs laden with cigars and oranges and such. The peddling stewards of these craft peered out from beneath striped awnings, calling up to us their wares. Others, with nothing to sell, solicited passengers seeking a ride ashore. This was of course illicit: No passenger was to debark before being cleared by the Health Officer—see him in his suit of whitest linen, a cigar stuck in his mouth and a red cockade stuck in his straw hat—who must satisfy himself as to the general health of the vessel, its cargo and crew; whereupon there comes the customs man, who secretes himself with the captain so as to reconcile passengers and passports, manifests, and, presumably, cash; and—himself satisfied—grants leave for all to land with their luggage.

Oh, but that day I'd wait for no such officers to board the *Athée*. Rather, having called Calixto to my side with the subtlest of gestures—indeed, I may even have willed him to come, sister-style—I told him what already I'd arranged; and soon we two descended onto a fruit boat beneath whose emerald awning we rode unseen to shore. As said, I'd risk no trouble aboard the *Athée*. (The captain's quietude concerned me, still.) And neither would I leave Calixto to risk it in my stead.

So it was I landed in Cuba without clearance: I'd not waited for the requisite passport, stamp, signature, or what have you. (In truth, I'd panicked.) Calixto's case was less complicated, of course, he being Cuban. But such matters were easily seen to in days to come—I had some coin, and Cuba is a crooked country—so that soon I was safely resident in the country; or so said papers procured for *dos pesos* and showing the signatures of those empowered by the Crown. Indeed, I'd the right to "transit in all directions" for one month, at which time my passport would require renewal. One month? If Sebastiana wasn't in Havana—and I had my doubts she would be—mightn't I need more than a month to find a man whom I knew only as Q.? I supposed so; for, to judge by the port, Havana was a quite populous place. Of course, what I didn't know, and could not have supposed, was this: He, this Q., would find me. . . . After all, he'd been searching for me all his life long.

Just as he'd boarded the fruit boat unblinkingly, so, too, did Calixto follow me into the city like a stray: devout, he seemed; such that soon I wondered why. I'd cast no spell over him. No, indeed: As said, I'd learned that lesson the hard way when once I'd compelled love. Neither had I reasoned with the boy, or solicited his company *in so many words*. True: I'd sworn to explain what mysteries he'd seen; and so I supposed it was that—that, and the fact that he'd nowhere else to go—that cleaved sweet Calixto to my side. . . . Of course, I minded not at all.

Up from the wharves we went, and owing perhaps to a lingering fear of discovery, the streets seemed thick to me, well nigh *aswarm* with soldiers. I could not distinguish between the Spanish and the English, and when I dared to approach near enough to hear their speech, well, there was no speech to hear: They marched in silence. Darkcomplected as they were, I supposed the lot of them were Spaniards; but if so, why were they dressed in the English style, with wide duck trousers, blue jackets, and straw hats that bore the name of their ships sewn onto the band? Others sweltered in seersucker uniforms, the cuffs of which were colored to mark some distinction of rank or duty. The officers, of course, were brilliantly conspicuous in their gilded suit parts and great, canary-colored plumage. But why, why this soldierly show in the streets? I asked Calixto, who responded with only a shrug of his shoulders. Doubtless the soldiers were off to preside over some ceremony or overly ornamental death; for soon I'd learn that such shows were common then in Cuba, with *all* Cubans—be they Criollos or Peninsulares, the former Cuban-born, the latter Spanish— drawn to the squares in the hope of seeing someone garroted, eye- gouged, or otherwise done to death.

We proceeded from parading soldiers to straggling ones; for we abandoned that wider boulevard and took to the shade of a side street. It was then my fear of discovery dissipated; but it was then, too, that I had to wonder: If we were not hastening *away* from the soldiery, where was it we were hastening *to*? Where was it we were going?

And it occurred to me that I'd do Calixto—and myself—a favor if I gave him the slip. Surely he'd family he wanted to search out. (Though he'd said no when I'd asked him this.) And surely those mys- teries he attributed to me would be forgotten, now the boy had re- turned to the city of his birth, et cetera. (They were not. He stood staring at me, expectantly, every time we stopped or even slowed in the streets.) Surely . . . *Enfin*, no: He stayed at my side and soon I'd no choice but to formulate a plan suitable for two. (In truth, I would not have, *could not* have left him; for, after so much solitude, I'd grown accustomed to his company. And, for better or worse, we were bonded: . . . Accomplices? . . . Conspirators?)

So: a plan . . . Yes: A plan was needed. A *literal* plan. A map, I mean. Of the city. Otherwise, we'd wander, and perhaps fall prey to chance, or the play of Fate. . . . What if, for instance, we were to stumble upon the planes of the dead, some graveyard from which might come—to my ears alone, *bien sûr*—the groan of the recently-gone? Yes, indeed: Best to keep from the disquieted dead, lest Calixto learn the effect they sometimes had upon me, equally unpredictable and potent. Quite potent. Mightn't the Cuban dead, if met en masse, rile my senso- rium—I refer, of course, to my five mortal senses *and* the witch's sixth—as the dead had done before? Mightn't they addle and drop me, rather as mortals suffer the sudden onset of fever? Mightn't they strike, cobra-quick, plying me with their prayers and suits? Such are the worries of a death-allied witch. . . . More: Hadn't I enough *to explain* to my companion? Indeed: It'd be best to avoid the Havanan dead.

It was off the Calle Obispo, I recall, that I stepped into a shop in search of said plan. Over a cold counter of zinc—whereon my perspiring hands left prints; for the weather was typically close that spring afternoon—I sputtered what Spanish I could muster. Surprised, I was, when there came from behind me a much more elegant, succinct request: Calixto, of course. In the rush off the *Athée*, in the confusion of the streets, I'd somehow forgotten he spoke Spanish; for shipboard I'd only heard his broken English, and not much of it. Now here he stood haggling over the price of a simple plan. . . . Haggling. Here, there, and everywhere it seemed no price was truly set, such that the casual shopper expended more energy than cash. I confess it: I would come to long for the simpler American markets, where one could shop in silence, in solitude. . . . Always and everywhere that was my preference as regarded interaction with strangers: *silence and solitude.*

Back on Obispo—a street so narrow I'd worn skirts in New York City, at Cyprian House, that would have swept its width—I unfolded the plan, turning it this way and that yet failing to find *North.* Calixto, quick with a compass, as every seaman is, smiled. Finally: something other than that wary awe. And when I handed him the map, he— staring at me, and smiling still—folded it and tucked it into a hip pocket.

"Tell me," said he; and I blanched, thinking he meant for me to speak of the night before. "Tell me: Where is it you want to go? . . . You tell. I take."

What could I do but shrug and surrender to his lead? What was I

※
---

to say otherwise? *I search out a nameless monk, and a French witch who may be a thousand miles away?* I thought not. More: It seemed Calixto knew I'd nowhere to go. So it was we wandered whilst I tried to come up with a plan of the other sort.

I knew how it felt to be pursued; and eventually I knew that we were not being pursued that day, at least not by humans: the occasional cur came sniffing round, of course; for dogs were drawn to me the more since I'd lain with the dead. . . . I knew, too, that the *Athée's* captain had not reported Diblis's death. He'd simply stricken the cook's name from the ship's records. This came to me as clearly as any divined dream. Somehow—owing perhaps to that sixth, sisterly sense—*I knew it*; just as I'd known, or *sensed* things similarly since suffering those . . . events, let me say, the surviving of which had strengthened me. Indeed, my sister-strength had been stronger, much, since I'd *all but died*, rising to find my Eye fixed. But once I'd returned to St. Augustine, I'd not put this newfound strength to purpose; for there, in the territory, on St. George Street, in a house as haunted as I, everything I saw I'd seen before, and to see, to sense *more*, well . . . it had seemed a waste. Witchery left me . . . wanting. As did life. But in Havana, I felt that strength again; and, strolling, well, I loosed my senses and took the city in.

I'd not have known it then, but here was happiness.

Q.? Sebastiana? If earlier I'd been hell-bent on finding one, the other, or both, now I cared not a whit who or what might come, as long as it was not a corps of soldiers with shackles. Why? Simply put: On the Calle Obispo, with Calixto at my side, I came alive. On the very same day *I began to die*; for Havana held . . .

Alors, see the city for yourself:

Chapter Seven

I speak truth; not so much as I would, but as much as I dare.
—MONTAIGNE, Essays

THE TOURIST, OR FIRST-TIME TRAVELER TO SAN CRISTO-
bal de Habana—for so the city is named, in honor of
Columbus; whilst the country itself has had to resist
the Spanish insistence on renaming her: first Juana,
after the daughter of Isabella and Ferdinand; then Fer-
nandina, after Ferdinand himself; and latterly, Ave
Maria; from all of which she has returned to her original Indian appellation of Cuba— . . . it is said that
the tourist is often amused by the names given Havana's streets and stores. And though it is true the
Cubans are profligate in their naming of streets and
stores, not to mention cities and countries, surely I—
a doubly-sexed witch who'd murdered a man not twelve
hours past, and who now wandered the walled city in
search of a nameless monk, my Soror Mystica, and certain promised "secrets" — . . . surely I was no mere

tourist; and yet I, too, was amused. And thankful for the distractions of the old city.

I had grown accustomed to that commercial tradition whereby a store often shows its owner's name, alongside some carved character or printed pictograph upon a sign that makes plain the trade practiced therein, i.e., the blinded Cupids seen above brothels; and so I did remark with amusement such establishments as Las Delicias de las Damas, La Cruz Verde, and El Leon de Oro. More amusing still were such street names as La Rectitud, La Integridad, La Probidad, and La Buena Fe: streets whose inhabitants, I supposed, aspired to something higher than lowly commerce. . . . But what I recall these long years later is a certain store upon a certain street:

The Calle Obispo. Calixto and I walked down its store-lined length to the wall separating the two Havanas, the old from the new. Putting the port at our backs, we'd discerned from our plan the city's primary streets; and splitting the difference, taking neither Obrapia nor O'Reilly (which Calixto dismissed with a wave of his hand), we walked the median route of Obispo.

As said, these lesser streets of the city were narrow, so narrow as to seem not thoroughfares but rather, and simply, the space between buildings. The houses on said streets were built close upon one another, perforce, and their upper stories seemed to lean out over the streets, staring down from beneath beetling brows and showing their wrought-iron balconies like scars, like black sutures sewn onto their sun-paled, pastel'd skins. So near did the houses stand that here and there awnings stretched between them, overspreading the street. These canvas panels—slit to let the rain sluice down—afforded shoppers noonday shade, quite welcome even then, in the midst of a mild spring.

Amidst the street-level shadows the stores were as caverns, cool and dark. Windows showed the city's wealth: wines from hither and yon;

dazzling, diamond-encrusted things set amidst the darker sheen of tortoiseshell accessories and the piebald display of Canary Island embroidery; and oh yes, there were hundreds of hats, sunshades, and other such tropical needments. Of course, I had no need of these; for, as ever, I sported my spectacles even though their blue lenses added unwanted depth to the shadows and I had at times to feel my way forward by foot, testing each step before committing to it; such that at one point, wanting better balance, I laced my arm through Calixto's, as a lady will, before fast recalling my outfit, my *manly mien*, and withdrawing, albeit not before my action seemed to spur my companion to sudden speech:

"Last night . . ." he began, halting only as I stopped—quite suddenly, yes—before a shop selling cakes of careful design: tiny squares born of chocolate, marzipan, almond paste, and such fruits as are common to Cuba but which I'd never seen before: sapodilla, guanabana, maranox, et cetera. Shamefully, I ignored Calixto—and his coming words—and lavished my attention *on the cakes*, as though they were so delicious-seeming as to preclude all thought. *Hélas*, the boy was not so easily put off, and again he spoke, nay *broke*, like a damn:

"Last night . . . with Diblis . . . it . . . you . . . I mean, *I saw you*—"

"*Oh, mon Dieu*," said I, grandly, nose pressed to the shop's window, "*ces gâteaux-là!* How delicious they look!" Though I could not stop Calixto's questions from coming—this I knew—still I hoped to stall my answers, *the explanation* I'd sworn to give.

Calixto, puzzled, and too polite to persist, fell quiet. Oh, but *le pauvre* seemed about to burst, and so it was I who spoke next:

"You are not wrong," said I in simple English; for simple English was our shared language then. "You are not wrong to think you saw something . . . to think you saw *strangeness* last night. You did." And there my confession sputtered to a stop; for I recalled what I'd long ago learned from Sebastiana, back when first she'd ushered me into the

Shadows: *There exists the inexplicable.* That had been fine, then, and had forestalled my own questioning; but hadn't I sworn to tell Calixto the truth, *to explain?* And, in fact, my murder of Diblis numbers not amongst the Shadow-life's inexplicable things: I could have explained the act plainly—as *murder most foul*—and without recourse to such words, such notions as sisterly will, telekinesis, et cetera. *Bref:* I could lie. . . . What to do? *What to do?*

I proceeded with caution, and with care, that's what I did; for when we sisters test the mettle of any mortal, we set their sanity upon a razor's edge. This lesson I'd learned.

Had Calixto strength enough to survive induction into the Dark? *The Books of Shadows* are replete with tales told by sorrowing sisters who rendered insane those they'd intended to save: Too much truth could do irreparable harm. . . . But what of Calixto? Perhaps he was different, more like Sebastiana's Roméo and the Duchess's Eli and other young men of whom I'd read, all mortal boys kept as consorts within the sorority. Wondering this, a second question came: Had Calixto somehow come as my consort? Was he . . . *mine?* And could I, despite the parental protectiveness I'd felt for him aboard the *Athée,* could I . . . *Enfin,* to these and other questions no answers came, not that day, not as we walked the Calle Obispo; for soon all reason, all rationale fell into recess, and I felt welling up within me that species of heart-speech better known as Truth. . . . Here then was trouble.

We'd walked the length of the street, till now there rose before us the olden wall of the city and the Puerta de Monserrate. I'd no intention of ambling on—never did I doubt that Q. waited within the walled city—and so I led Calixto to a bench set beneath a palm which swayed not at all; and as we sat in that still, sweltering shade redolent of the sea, I began: "There exists the—"

And then I stopped; for looking into Calixto's eyes, I saw the inadequacy of the line before I could utter it in full. He'd hear those words with as little satisfaction as I'd find in saying them, knowing it was naught but a preamble to more dissemblance, more lies. . . . Understand: All my life I'd been defined by my own lies. And even when I learned the truth of who I was—*man, woman, witch*—still I'd told those truths to no one, or rather to no mere mortal. Had I so tired of the lies, of the separateness and the solitude born of them, that now Calixto would be the first to whom I'd tell *all and everything*? Now, here, in Havana?

It seemed so. And indeed, then and there, I determined to tell my truths, *all* my truths, and let the consequences come. So it was I surprised myself by saying:

"Go. Go! Tell your family of your return and—"

"But I told you: I have no family here, none I want to see or tell or—"

"Go, please," said I, my words as simple as that: an imperative, followed hard by a plea. And surprising myself again, I added, "Meet me . . ." Where? Why? I suppose I could neither lie nor say good-bye, not then. "There must be a cathedral here, *non?*"

"*Sí,*" said he.

"Meet me there. . . . Tomorrow."

"But why? Why do you tell me to go when I have nowhere to go, no one to—"

"*Go!* Please." I was angry now; not at Calixto, of course: He'd done nothing wrong. I was angry at myself; for, having approached my truths, having crept up upon them like a thief, I'd fled from them, fearful. As always I had. "Go now, Calixto, please, and meet me there tomorrow, at the cathedral. At this same hour." Did I think another day would render my truths easier to tell? I don't know. All I knew, all I can recall is being grateful for those blue glasses: Calixto could not see that my fixed eyes were brimful of tears.

"Where will you . . ." he began, gesturing broadly enough to take in the city entire. And of course I shared his wonder: Where would I go? Where would I sleep? Would I search for Sebastiana, for Q.? . . . Or would I run with my truths untold?

As Calixto walked away, turning once, twice, I saw by his stoop, by the slump of his shoulders, that he supposed I'd disappear. And true it was: To disappear in a city like Havana would have been no trick at all, not for any man or woman and certainly not for a witch. (There are sisters resident in similar Shadow-cities—Edinburgh, Amsterdam, New Orleans . . . —who have never been seen by Strangers.) As I watched the boy walk away, cross the Calle Monserrate, and disappear into the Extramuros, I, too, thought I'd do it: disappear, that is. I could take my truths with me and lie my life away.

Oh, how I hated myself then! I sat on that bench dressing myself down in churlish French, and when the French failed me I resorted to the American argot I'd learned from the saltiest of the sisters at Cyprian House, in Man-hattan. Surely I'd have appeared crazed to any who saw me sitting there, cursing my cowardice, till finally I stood and said (aloud, yes), *"Plus jamais!"* No more!

It was an oath, I suppose, a promise I made to myself. I'd tell all. I'd lie *no more*. . . . Beginning now.

Hurriedly—so hurriedly I was nearly ground to dust beneath one of the tall wheels of those curiosities of Cuba: the horse-drawn *volantes* then crowding her streets—I crossed the Calle Monserrate to the city gate; but Calixto was nowhere to be seen. Standing there, I heard a clock tower sound the hour, and I began to count those twenty-four, nay *twenty-three* more that would compose my last day of lies.

Knowing no route but the one we'd come, I retook to it and walked back down the Calle Obispo toward that tolling bell. And when finally

I found myself on the Calle Ignacio, nearing what seemed a holy precinct—to judge by the surfeit of flowers being sold, and the veiled duennas crowding their virginal charges—only then did I unfold my plan to confirm the place of reunion.

Indeed, there it was, cornered on the calles Ignacio and del Empe-drado: that cathedral that houses Columbus's remains, its architecture and mossy, pocked facade telling eloquently of Spain's age-old hold over Havana. I would not go in. Instead I stood watching women milling around before the great portico on Empedrado—the white women wearing black, and the black women wearing white; and it was this simple scheme of costumery that set me upon a course of action.

. . . Yes: a dress; for, without Calixto—for whom I watched, as-suredly—the fear of discovery returned to me as I stood in contem-plation of the city plan and saw upon it how proximate were the port, the Plaza de Armas, and the palace of the Captain-General. Best not to be at the center of the city. Best not to risk discovery by the au-thorities—I yet lacked the proper papers—or any sailor off the *Athée*. And so: a disguise: a dress.

Oh, I suppose there was rather more to it than that. . . . I missed my feminine fripperies, I did; for I'd been far too long in pants. And surely seeing me in a dress would strike Calixto as the surest metaphor of . . . of my *self*, the true self he'd meet on the morrow. Yes, indeed: I'd determined to tell all, and now it seemed I'd show all as well. . . . What*ever* was I thinking?

Hélas, thusly decided, I returned posthaste to a store I'd passed where the calles Obispo and San Ignacio crossed. In La Diana I bought a bolt of that fine linen found in Havana, *bolan,* striped in blue and white, giving not a thought to the impracticality of the purchase. It was an impulse: I'd seen the *bolan* draped over a wicker mannequin in the window and saw, verily saw the dress that could come of it. (I refer not to sisterly, or witchly Sight, but rather to that of a woman shopping, *c'est tout*.) And when finally I felt the fabric, well, I forewent the haggling and paid the asked-for price.

From La Diana's proprietress I took the name of a tailor; or rather, a seamstress. And off I went in search of same, having located her address upon my plan: the Calle Oficios; a district wherein I found the seamstress resident alongside others engaged in related trades: milliners, clothiers, cobblers, dyers, and the like, the lot of whom I supposed to be freed blacks and mulatto Cubans. Soon, having encountered few difficulties, I found myself the owner of a suitable store of the previous season's fashions; for upon the démodé I insisted, the better to blend in amongst the masses and draw no envious eye. I bought some menswear, yes, but mostly I sought what a woman needs and wants: from unmentionables outward to a brooch which showed the sun's rays and would not have been amiss upon the puffed-up bosom of the Sun King himself. There were gloves of the smoothest kid, I recall. And shoes heeled so high they'd hurt; but I didn't care. I'd reaccustom myself soon enough.

When the seamstress asked where it was she ought to deliver the dress sewn of the *bolan* when she completed it, in two days' time, I stood before her in silence. Already I'd lied, in ludicrous Spanish, surely, saying I sought a dress as a birthday surprise for my sister, who, as luck would have it, stood to my same height; who, in fact, shared all, or *nearly all* my measurements; and therefore the seamstress ought to sew the dress as if it were . . . for me. Yet I did not let her take my measurements; and indeed backed from her tape measure as though it were an asp. "No, no," said I, *"no necessito."* In the end, the seamstress agreed. The requisite alterations could be seen to later. But what about delivery . . . ? "Ah, yes," said I, sputtering on about the aforesaid sister, who was staying with me at . . . who awaited me at . . . a hotel . . . somewhere down along . . .

And when vaguely I pointed toward the port, the seamstress spared me, saying, so matter-of-factly it seemed my sister and I *ought* to have rooms therein, "The Hotel de Luz, senõr?"

"That's not the one sitting just . . . ?"

"*Sí,*" said she, adding in English, "corner of Luz and . . ." And now she pointed outside in turn, meaning to name that same street—the Calle Oficios—on which her own atelier stood.

"Ah, yes," said I. "Luz and Oficios. That's the very one, indeed."

"Señora Almy?" came the final question; and as my interlocutor paired the name with a smile, so, too, did I smile in reply.

Thusly did I learn the name of my future *hotelière*. And when I regained the street—our transaction completed with payment on my part and promises on the seamstress's—I went in search of a few things more; for certain spells would soon be called for. Finally, burdened by both my newly acquired clothes and those sundries requisite to spellwork, such that a mule for hire would have been a welcome sight, I made my way to the Hotel de Luz; wherein I installed myself for what I could only describe to the redoubtable, stoutish Señora Almy as "a stay of uncertain length."

I turned a goodly sum over to Señora Almy; for my room upon the third, or topmost, floor of the Hotel de Luz had much to recommend it:

It was large, and its heavily beamed ceiling rose some twenty-odd feet from the white tile of the floor, up the even whiter walls. A suite of furniture hewn from black walnut had been carved and gilded to suit the tastes of old Spain. Above all the doors there spread fanlights of stained glass, churchly in their effect. Indeed, the sun's light came now through the westerly fanlight and transformed the room, coloring its whiteness such that someone more devout than I might well have been driven to prayer.

Rather than pray, I took in the views.

Tall windows doubled as doors, and through these I stepped onto each of three balconies in turn. From the first the prospect was of the bay, out toward Regla and the hills beyond. A second, smaller balcony overlooked a common, and the old city. The third—wrought of iron, like the others, but seemingly leafed in gold—clung to the hotel's inner wall, giving onto a courtyard crowded with potted palms. Up from the courtyard there came the play, the plash of a small, unseen fountain, its water-song a lullaby that turned me toward the bed and the solace of sleep.

The half-tester bed was laid in white linen which seemed now a patchwork quilt, the colors coming as they did. Two plump pillows verily begged for my head, so weary and weighted with worry was I, so wanting sleep. And indeed, within an hour of my arrival at the Hotel de Luz, I'd surrender to that most Latin of habits: the siesta. . . . But first I had some Craft to work: I would induce that species of dream that has naught to do with sleep, and in so doing stave off sleep awhile longer.

Upon the bureau I ranged those witch's wares I'd procured; and had anyone—a maid or porter in the employ of Señora Almy—seen this display they'd not have known themselves in a witch's warren, but would only have questioned the snacking habits of the newly come stranger; for what I'd found in a market near the Calle Oficios was simple; so:

Six eggs of suitable hue (dun).

Apples (two).

Oils pressed from both the olive and the palm.

A six-inch length of cane (which was, in fact, for snacking; for I'd seen a child gnawing on same, the juice trickling from her chin like rain from a long-bladed leaf).

And several herbs, et cetera, known to be conducive to Sight: bay, sage, poppy seeds, and rosemary. To no avail, I'd searched the market's stalls for mugwort, wormwood, and Syrian rue; but I'd make do.

With such whatnot as this—and instruments easily acquired: a spoon of bamboo, candles, a black bowl, matches, and a vase suitable for use as a beaker—I intended to cast simple spells of Sight; and thereby See who it was I sought: Q., and maybe even Sebastiana herself. If I Sighted them, my search would be simpler. Moreover: I'd not have to wait, wondering and worrying over what was to come. I'd Sight the future, and find Fate before it found me. . . . Leastways, such was my plan.

First, I lit a white taper and let fall its wax into water I'd poured into the black bowl. *Ceromancy,* this is, of course, by which one reads those sigils, or shapes, made by the water-hardened wax. . . . Understand: I might have Seen moonshapes and—by the application of an almanac—called into accord those shapes and the lunar calendar, thereby Sighting a day of some supposed significance. Or I might have Seen a sail: *watch for a ship.* Or a blade: *danger.* Or a bat: *beware the night.* Or innumerable other shapes portending this or that. . . . But this day: nothing. Neither were the yokes of the eggs legible in the water.

So it was I resorted to the spices, and burned bay leaves— *daphnomancy*—upon a table topped with sandstone, which I moved nearer the door that gave out over the city. This I did to see, specifically, what was to come of my confessing to Calixto. The bay leaves burning down to ash, fast, would not have boded well. A slow and crackling burn? *Beware.* But a slight breeze came and blew the bay leaves away; which occurrence I opted not to interpret at all. That same breeze queered the reading of the poppy seeds, which sat smoldering beside those leaves of laurel; for it rendered illegible their risen smoke. So it was I resorted to oracle sage, *Salvia divinorum,* burning it to open some soul-door within myself, as sisters have done since the days of Delphi; but neither did the sage speak to me. Finally, the day drawing on, the sun sinking, tiring all the while, I smothered all the herbs lest their scent draw Señora Almy to my door, and ate one of the apples whose spiraling peel I'd intended to toss onto the floor, where perhaps it would fall as an initial or something more.

Bref: My efforts at Sight were short-lived and found no effect—and not for the first time, *bien sûr*—ending, blessedly, in that mind-stilling siesta.

I was woken by the flutter and, yes, the *hum* of a hundred hummingbird wings.

The birds were no bigger than my thumb. From whence had they come? How had . . . ? *Enfin,* I woke in confusion—as who wouldn't?—and knew only what I could perceive with my six senses:

Into the room—dark now with dusk—there'd come fifty hummingbirds *so very bright* they seemed light itself; for they were white, as such creatures never are, and cannot be. Oh, but I knew not to dwell on "cannot"; for, indeed, *there exists the inexplicable,* and there it was in avian form, hovering over me as I lay atop the bed.

I knew a sharp pain in my hands and feet, and upon my face, and rightly assumed the bee-size birds had woken me with their needling beaks. So numerous were they, and so close, they caused the fabric of my blouse to flutter, my skin to cede to gooseflesh. Yet I did not fear the birds; for—strange as they were—they'd come as a sign, surely. A communication of some kind. But *what* kind? And who'd send such a sign? And however was I to read it?

After buzzing about the bed as bees would a hive, the birds dispersed into the room, lighting it lantern-bright. Worse: They fought, ferociously, dipping and darting and needling one another. Then they seemed to still, to coalesce, outside. I saw them framed by the doors of that balcony that overlooked the old city and . . .

The city. They'd something to show me *out there,* surely.

Up I leapt. The birds stilled the more as I approached.

The sky showed the hues of oncoming evening: The sun was near to sizzling into the sea. Yet still there was light enough to see the *cinquantaine* of birds—they were fifty, exactly: I could not have counted them, of course, yet I knew their number, and was right— . . . see them as they banked out from behind the Hotel de Luz and set out over the city: stitches of light darning the night. They were so bright I followed them with ease; for their whiteness was supernal, sidereal, yes, star-like to my sister-eyes.

There. I saw it. Saw what it was the birds would show me, *would have me see.* I'd only had to follow their line of flight, their line of light to a tower none too distant, atop which he . . .

I saw him, yes, *there*, in the gloaming. A man, old, bowed, black, and darkly dressed. It was a robe he wore, hooded. This I knew when he threw back the hood to show a bald or shaven skull. His face? I strained to see it, but it was too dark now for the discerning of detail.

Around him where he stood, there atop that squared tower—only three, perhaps four stories high, yet it seemed he and I were alone above the city—the hummingbirds circled; till he raised his hand. Was he waving at me? Impossible: He seemed somehow incapable of so simple a gesture. And then I saw how he—with that wave—controlled that odd flock of his: Suddenly the birds were gone from sight, flown off into some cage made of night; or otherwise extinguished. That wave. So strange. With it he'd . . .—absurd, this; but I knew Sebastiana would not have sent me in search of a *mere* monk, a man holy only by virtue of his vows— . . . with that wave it seemed he'd dismissed the very day; for, concomitant with it, the sun had set. Coincidence, thought I. Mummery and nothing more.

Now all was dark. So very dark and deep, that first Havanan night: black, in fact.

What next I did was this: I hurried to the hallway door and threw its bolt. I then slammed shut and secured the three *portes-fenêtres* and sank onto the floor, into a corner, shivering with a cold that came from within; for something about the monk and his oddly bridled birds had chilled my witch's blood.

In through the fanlights came moon- and starlight, passing through the variegated glass to stain the floor and walls. In a pool of silvered color I sat a long, long while. And somehow, in that pool of silvered color, I slept, shunning a bed on which white feathers, *light feathers* had fallen.

And when at first light the sun came to hone all the colors, and the colors woke me, well . . . I'd a day-lit truth with which to contend: I'd been found by he whom I'd sought: Q.

In full: the monk, Queverdo Brù.

※

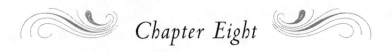

Chapter Eight

Go on through the lofty spaces of high heaven and
bear witness, where thou ridest, that there are no gods.

—SENECA, *Medea*

*I*F THE DIALOGUES OF SAINT GREGORY THE GREAT ARE TO
be believed—and I, who'd long ago abandoned all Belief, found myself free to believe in any- and everything,
even the testimony of saints, so famously suspect—then
the Devil himself showed himself to Saint Benedict in the
shape of a blackbird. Likewise there I lay, cheek to
the cool, colored tile of the floor, having suffered the
visitation of fifty alabaster birds the night before, having
"heard" the testimony, the flutter and hum of a hundred
wings. . . . But was it the Devil in aviate shape I'd seen?

Doubtful. Doubtful it was He whose name deserves
a capital *D*. In Him I had little store; indeed, I'd have put
the Devil on a par with his opposite, the former low and
the latter high, and both of them equidistant from us,
from me. To God and the Devil I gave scant thought.
What were such majuscule types to me? Concepts, noth-

ing more. What I'd come to fear were the lowercase soldiers of same: girls gone crazy in convents, papists roving in packs, and men—like Sebastiana's Asmodei—seemingly beholden to no evil but their own. Was this monk such a man? Already I had my suspicions; for, upon waking, I found upon my hands the marks made by his white, winged summoners.

Still, as is the wont of a rational being—and still I held to reason, despite all I'd seen down the years—I woke desperate to attribute it all to a dream. Hadn't I been engaged, earlier, before the birds had come, in divination? Indeed. And didn't the induction of Sight draw down dangers all its own? Were not the Books full of tales told by sisters who shuffled time and Saw to their great regret?

But no dream, this; for I saw again those feathers scattered all about me where I lay upon the floor, bone-cold and crooked, as if I'd fallen from a height. The feathers were so small they'd have fit upon my thumbnail. So many feathers, there were, and all still luminous, *white as light*; for they'd fallen from off those one hundred wings only hours ago. They were like shards of light, sparks struck from off a corner of the sun, or moon, or stars. This I remarked as I placed one upon my palm. And lest those feathers formed of light not convince me that I'd seen—and not dreamed—the hummingbirds, and Brù, well, it was then I found upon myself further proof:

Reaching to sweep the feathers from me, I saw in that pied light the wounds upon the back of my hands, and upon my forearms, and my feet, and, surely, my face: all the flesh that had been exposed when the birds had come. Though I had no mirror to hand, I felt upon my neck and face and knew, knew the birds' work there as well. These wounds were not deep, mind; indeed, they were all the more remarkable for *not* having broken the exposed skin, but rather for having . . . aggravated it so.

The tops of my hands showed . . . pustules. So, too, did the tops of my feet, down to the tips of my toes. Neither palm nor sole had been spared. Indeed, there were holes all over my skin, holes neat as the prick of a pin; and from these there seeped . . . I knew not what. *Enfin*, it was golden, slag-like, and viscous to the touch. And rough: It grated between my fingertips, as if sand were within it. It seemed a substance all the birds' own, set beneath my skin—as Diblis had sought to set ink beneath Calixto's—by fifty needling beaks. Creatures of the seas and sands were capable of imparting similar stinging secretions; and even some toothy trees and shrubs of the American South bite to similar effect. But this was different, quite.

I tasted the irritant from off a fingertip, but learned nothing of its source: It bore not the ferrous taste of blood, nor the tartness of berries, nor the toxicity of a man-made dye. And though my scratching at the skin brought little relief, I could feel the sting lessening. It had a course to run, this pus, this strange serum, and would do so regardless of what I did. Its effect? I'd have to wait and see. Fatal? Unlikely; for the monk, Q., had summoned me, had he not? He'd sought my attention; and now that he had it—and most assuredly so— . . . *alors*, he wanted to see me, to speak to me. He wanted me to come to him.

Sitting still—to move seemed to speed the irritant's effect—I sought something that might soothe its effect; but I saw nothing more salutary than the apple peels I'd let fall upon the floor, and which were juiceless and browning, dry and dead as the shed skin of a snake. Had I really tried the night before to read the peels of two apples? *Mon Dieu*. I'd been desperate, *non*? (And what I wouldn't have given, just then, to have those two apples intact; for I was famished, as sisters often are after a Sighting spell.) . . . And so, I sat through the lessening of the sting till it stopped. It seemed to fade fast—before my very eyes, in fact—as if I were succeeding in *staring it away*. And so I stared the harder, stared till my skin reverted to that sun-bronzed hue I knew as my own. Witchery? Eye-work? Perhaps. I cannot say; but soon the serum and its sting were gone. And whether the birds' work would have any lasting effect . . . *alors*, I'd have to wait to see. Or demand an answer of the monk.

I stood, shakily, wondering was I otherwise well. It seemed so, save for a light-headedness I attributed to that deep, deep sleep for which I'd only myself to blame: I'd been so very tired from the travel, and from the scene with Calixto, that I'd practiced the Craft far too sloppily, and the aftereffect of that—particularly where divination is concerned—is akin to having swigged from a bottle of tanglefoot: Thought is slowed, the tongue grows grimy and thick, and one hears sounds as an anvil might be said to hear the smith's hammer. And nothing but time will set right a sister thusly stricken. Indeed, regardless of whatever effect the birds' secretion had had upon me, I'd have been slow to wake that day. I was tired, suffering a lassitude that saw me curl upon the cooling floor—those tiles were ever cool, despite a sun that seemed to hover just above the frilled tops of the trees—once the stinging subsided. Though the bed seemed impossibly far away, sleep was still near.

I woke a second time that day.

Sleep had descended like a drape, all enveloping. It bore down upon me fast, unfreighted by dreams. It seemed I'd segued from the contemplation of apple peels to sleep; and, next thing I knew, I was waking again, only slightly less disoriented than I'd been at first light. The marks of the birds were gone, and that stupor that had eventuated in sleep was lifting as well. I stood, as unsteadily as a still-slick foal, and made my way to the window, thinking I'd peer through the shutters to see Q. in the distance, high atop his tower, or turret, call it what you will; but when I threw back those shutters I found a low sun, one fallen well west of its height. *Could it be?* Had I slept the day away? My rickety joints answered in the affirmative: I'd been *hours*, not minutes, upon that floor. Yes, hours had passed, and day was nearly done, and . . .

"The cathedral!" I cried aloud.

Calixto. Had I missed Calixto?

I dressed hurriedly; which is to say I re-bound my breasts, rolled the cuffs of my sleep-rumpled blouse down over my forearms, which yet were tender to the touch, and stepped into my boots. I stole through the common area of Señora Almy's hotel. No one was about. But as I made my way toward the cathedral—cursing myself for having slept away the day—the streets grew ever more crowded.

The city's citizenry were rousing themselves from their siestas, as were Havana's hundreds, nay, thousands of tourists. Through the afternoon and into the twilit hours, they'd ready themselves—the men dressing, despite the tropical clime, in the tyrannical attire of upper-bred Europe: black dress coats, long pantaloons, black cravats, and high black hats; the women in twists and puffs of tulle and such—for a ritual I would witness innumerable times in Havana: They'd ride up and down the boulevards *à la file*, holding to no destination, hoping only to see and be seen. And though their route—the Paseo Isabel Segundo—was, *is* indeed a grand avenue, sundering the old city like a seam and running from sea to bay and back, taking one within sight of the Morro, the Presidio, the Teatro de Tacon, and the gorgeous gardens of the city's bishop, the simple *routine* of the ride always struck me as . . . stupid. I thought so every time I saw it enacted; and from that show I took no joy, save in the livery, the bejeweled livery of the black postilions riding high atop those *volantes* and *quitrines*, the two-wheeled contraptions pulled by horse or team. Those outriders were resplendent in their galligaskins of black leather, buckled and cock-spurred at the heel, and rising from the top of their booted feet to some eight or nine inches above the knee, forming a shield of sorts when they sat, as rarely they did; for to sit was to hide the rest of that attire in which they, and moreover their masters, took such pride: scarlet jackets, say, set off by golden piping and lace; broad-brimmed hats of straw, festooned with feathers or banded ribbons; and pants so black and firm as to seem a second skin. So regal, those postilions seemed, as they drove Society hither and thither; yet still I'd blanch at imagining the inanities that rose to their ears as their passengers spoke of faraway courts, of *bals masqués* and this or that rogue marquis, all the while worrying that a snub or a fan-snap might damn them to some societal purgatory.

How it hit me that first afternoon: Here I was amidst Society after having been a sister in solitude for so long. I had no need of society, per se—disdained it, in fact—and would surely have wandered sooner onto some quieter backstreet of the city had it not been for the date I'd set with Calixto; and though I was hours late, *hours*, still the most expeditious route toward the cathedral was wanted. Why then did I tarry?

Fear, I suppose. I was fearful of realizing what it was I'd done, and what it was I'd lost:

Friendship? Love, and the end of loneliness? *Enfin*, if I'd had a chance at any good thing I'd lost it, surely; for, yes, hours had passed since our appointment, and doubtless the boy—deeming me untrue—had abandoned both myself and his hope of ever having the strangeness he'd seen aboard the *Athée* explained. . . . I'd been alone all my life. Prolonged solitude was not a state worth hurrying to. (Cowardice, this was, really.) And so it was I even *slowed my step* as I neared the cathedral, and walked, nay, *wandered* the widest, most crowded avenues; till I came upon the Plaza de Armas as the hour neared eight. This I know; for always the band struck up at eight. So it was I sat upon an iron bench and watched as musicians in martial attire primed their instruments: flutes whistled, reeds screamed, and drumbeats cracked the shell of oncoming night.

The Plaza de Armas—a square, really, set before the Captain-General's house, which I'd sought to avoid the day prior—was full of people. Society was in evidence, as were those men whose attire told of the island's primary trades: sailing and soldiering. Of course, I dwelled on none of this then. Blind, I was, so little did I care to decipher such cloth-coding, such pomp and . . . silliness.

The band played passably well, even as they bound the music with that discipline that had been bred into them; for they, too, were soldiers, all. There sat their commander— the Captain-General—high upon his porch, seeming pleased. He applauded; whereupon, the crowd followed his lead. Had he dozed in the warm night, I've no doubt that all those present in the Plaza de Armas would have bedded down as well upon its bricks and grass-blades; for so it goes in a state thusly policed: The people, like cattle, both fear and attend the prod. This is unpleasant to witness; and so it was that I watched instead the fronds of the palm trees; for they swayed in time, to the wind if not the music, though the two did sometimes meet, whereupon the palms did seem to waltz.

. . . We sisters will make our own amusements, will we not, when life is lacking, and the heart has fallen into arrears? Indeed. And so it was nearly nine when finally I found myself on the Calle del Empedrado, *devant la cathédrale.*

Though the sun was low, and near to setting, still the stone and slate surrounding the cathedral—pavers, steps, and such—gave off their heat in shimmering, spectral waves; so much so that my first thought upon entering the church itself was this:

From whence have these *inner* walls stolen such cold? For, though

———————————— ✳ ————————————

warm without, it was chill, very chill within the church. Only later at
night do such places grow warmer, when finally the heat of the day pen-
etrates their stone; likewise, being always a half day behind the sun in
its tour, those same stones hold to night's coolness at noon, and thusly
are worshipers drawn into them from under the broiling sun. Oh, but
whether the air of such sepulchral places be chill or warm, it is always,
always still. Deathly still, weighted with the dust of eons. Faith, too,
weights such places, as though all the prayers ever loosed by their parishioners—words unheard, wasted—rise to push against the arched roofs
before raining back down, unheard, upon the faithful. Such cathedrals
as Cuba's can seem verily *littered* with such palsied prayer.

Tomb-still and chill it was, within the cathedral; and appropriately
so: No less a personage than Columbus lay within. There, near the
choir space, under the alto-relief, behind a brief inscription of Spanish gratitude, were interred the bones of the discoverer. Or so legend
holds. . . . Oh, but be wary, witch, of tales telling of the deposition of
bones; for many a tomb sits untenanted. This I know.

Soon I acclimated to the darkness and the cathedral-cold, and for
once I was thankful for the swaddling with which I bound my breasts
when in men's attire; for, though often it made me perspire, and itch,
itch, *itch* in those tropical climes, now it gave a measure of warmth. It
was then—warming, with eyes yet adjusting to the shadows composed
of equal parts sun, moon, and candlelight, all of it off-color owing to
the great panes of painted glass through which it passed, as in my
room at the Hotel de Luz— . . . only then did I tell myself the truth:

He is not here.

And he was not. . . . Of course, I refer not to Columbus—I cared not
a whit about the carcass of the conquistador, fallen now to powder
wherever it might lie—but to Calixto.

Not knowing where else to search the boy out—surely he'd not gone back to the *Athée*, and if he'd sought welcome amongst his scattered relations, well then, I'd lost him to the city, too crowded for even the strongest witch to Sight him by spellwork or wander, against all odds, hoping, merely hoping to find one man in that multitude—I crept further into the cathedral. And I do mean "crept"; for I'd been taken unawares in such consecrate places before, such that now it seemed safer to *assume* the presence of the disquieted dead. But there I stood, listening, sensing, and . . . *nothing*. If there were souls in residence alongside Columbus, they lay in repose, heeding—as the vast majority of the dead do—that most common of eternal orders, inscribed so often on stone: *Requiescat in pace*. Indeed, the dead within the cathedral were quiet, resting in peace; however, to my dismay, the living were less restful. And there were many of them, surprisingly so, given the hour.

I know not the day or date in question, and neither will I stop to back-conjure it—for this borrowed hand has been stiffening this last half hour, such that now it scuttles along these pages crab-like, growing harder to control (to which fact this penmanship attests, surely)— but there were people enough in the cathedral for me to surmise, then as now, that a mass or rite of some kind had recently been read. Too, tapers had not burned themselves down, and incense yet bit at the air; indeed, I saw in the dark the gray swirls—like ash upon the air— made by whoever had lately swung the thurifer upon the altar. The Church calendar having grown so crowded with saints, I supposed one had been feted not an hour past, whilst I stood watching palms waltz above the Plaza de Armas; and still parishioners sat scattered upon the squares of black and white marble flooring—pewless, the place was— as though they were chess pieces, pawns all, in a game played for the amusement of God. No: No pews broke the plane of the cathedral floor, though sculpture, relics, and Romish whatnots ringed it.

Dressed as I was, I made myself one with the few men gathered along the back wall of the cathedral, till finally I found myself upon a prie-dieu, padded at the knees and elbows so as to ease the physical pains of prayer. Beside me where I knelt there burned a bank of red-glassed votives, each flame an offering. By this roseate light I took in my surrounds.

Church-bred, still I could lose myself in the grandeur of such places, and sometimes take solace in them—not in those metaphors for which the faithful pine, no, but in the base components of same: the stone of statuary, the flame of tapers standing tall as a child, the flaking paint of frescoes, et cetera. I sought such solace that night; for, if there was a disquieted soul in the cathedral that night, it was mine. *He's not here.* I said it again and again: a prayer in counterpoise. And on went this pitiable scene till I saw—nearby, standing in the reddened shadows—something, someone, *enfin* a statue that brought the past hurtling back, and in so doing spared me the pain of the present.

If there is a saint in whom Church and Craft meet, surely it is Sebastian—he of the martyrizing arrows, the deep-set and dolorous eyes, and the half smile speaking so eloquently of sufferance and transcendence; he of the firm and perfect (albeit pierced) flesh, so exquisitely rendered, whether by brush or chisel, whether by Raphael, Rondinelli, Reni, or Rubens, that he seems a boy-man, or man-boy, too beautiful *not* to suffer. . . . Granted: The historical Sebastian was an old, age-ugly man when martyred, but—as the priests and painters of the Renaissance knew—art must please in its particulars if it is to succeed at proselytizing.

Saint Sebastian had long been a study of mine, ever since I'd first seen him depicted in that tapestry that hung in a back hall of the convent school I'd fled. The tapestry might not have hung there at all, save

for what I suppose was its worth, its value in francs. To the dark it had
been consigned, yes, lest we girls see a man naked, in extremis, and exquisite. Of course, I—ever accustomed to the dark, if not yet the
Shadows—had found the tapestry and visited the saint regularly; for
I—and here I beg forgiveness, sister, for the excess sentiment of my
youth—I felt myself persecuted as surely as the saint had been, run
through not with arrows, no, but by the . . . the cruelty, the contempt,
the calumnies I knew amongst those convented girls and nuns. Then,
of course, there came the fateful day I met my own saint, or savior—
not Saint Sebastian, but Sebastiana d'Azur. For me she somehow
made bleed not her namesake but another tapestried saint—Francis,
who bled as he knelt in stigmatic receipt of Christ's Five Wounds—
. . . *bleed*, yes, though he was naught but dyed wool, artfully wrought—
thusly priming me for induction into the Shadows and showing me
that truth I hold to still (and *of which*, I suppose, I myself am proof):
There exists the inexplicable.

Whose Saint Sebastian it was in Colombus's cathedral, I cannot recall. What's more: It doesn't matter; for every Sebastian I'd ever seen—
whether in life or in libraries—had become mine of an instant, as did
he in Havana. Though no depiction—and certainly no statue—had
ever *drawn me so.*

This Sebastian took unto, nay, *into* his marble flesh the light from
those votive candles, such that he appeared . . . pink: quickened, animate, alive. The stony saint stood six, seven feet tall in his shallow
niche, and was turned to accommodate the wrought-iron arrows that
pierced his flesh; thusly: through the right biceps and into the chest,
pinning his arm to his side; down and through the smooth and
oblique muscle of his abdomen; through the right thigh and calf, the
arrowhead of the former lost within the flesh but that of the latter
reappearing, its tip gory with gold leaf. There were other arrows as
well. Of course, I'd seen worse-suffering Sebastians, some with pierced

necks, one wherein the martyr has suffered an arrow shot up, *up* through the jaw to protrude through the cheek, and isn't it Tintoretto's saint who's taken a shattering arrow to the forehead, an inch above his wide-staring eyes? But the Havanan Sebastian bore a grace all his own; and moved though I was, still I knew it to be a most artful depiction of those hours after Sebastian has suffered the worst of it and knows, *knows* that by some godly intervention he has survived those arrows shot into him by his fellow soldiers, those praetorians commanded by Diocletian, Emperor of fourth-century Rome and Killer of Christians.

Those soldiers (or so legend holds) had left Sebastian tethered to a tree, presuming him dead—a safe assumption, this, seeing as how they'd emptied their quivers into him. However, returning on the morrow, they found their fellow not only *very much alive* but seeming only slightly discomfited by the arrows bristling from his body. The emperor, who'd condemned Sebastian for his supposed conversion to Catholicism of certain aristocratic clans, sentenced the saint to die a second time. No arrows now: This time it was to be a blow to the head, delivered quickly and quietly, at night, atop the Palatine hill, lest any sect rally round the man who would defy death once but, *hélas*, not twice: His skull crushed, and the arrows ripped from his flesh, Sebastian was *disappeared* into a cloacal pool.

Oh, but perhaps Sebastian had not died at all. Perhaps he lingered on in life's mirror: dreams; for he is said to have appeared that very night to the widow of another martyred Roman. She—name of Irene—heard from Sebastian himself where it was she'd find his ruined body; and this she fished from the muck, the shit and stink of the sewer, conveying it out along the Via Appia for secret interment beside the bones of Peter and Paul, where it would be venerated from that day to this.

. . . *Enfin*, there I sat, sorrowing before this statue and wondering why, *how* it spoke to me so; but, dead though I am, *immortal*, Missy lets it be known I haven't the time to list all those things for which I alternately punished and pitied myself. Suffice to say that I found myself rootless and blue, destined, surely, to live out my days alone and without love. All that I was—a *sur*-sexed witch somehow allied to the dead—I wanted *not* to be; and all that I coveted—as embodied in Calixto—I had lost. Or so I thought.

And if I suffered an emotion then aside from sadness—my habitual melancholia—and confusion regarding the stony saint's *appeal*, it was anger. Not at myself. Nor at Calixto, who'd no doubt waited according to plan, and who now I'd have to find by whatever wiles and sisterly ways availed themselves. Sebastiana? Perhaps; for, once again— as she had in New York, with the Duchess—it seemed she'd consigned me to the care of another. . . . Q., then? Yes: He was the locus of my anger. How dare he use me as he had? Indeed, this Q., whom already I distrusted, had some answers of his own to give, *non?* To him, to said answers, I'd hasten, finding and following the flight of those birds of light.

. . . Anger, yes; for I'd hoped that day would be one of truth telling, of soul lightening brought on by the setting aside, the discharge of lies; but now, at day's end, here I was at the cathedral not with Calixto but alone, very much alone, and newly determined to search out some ill-met monk, another denizen of the dark, of the Shadows, a keeper of secrets I would come to wish I'd never learned.

Out I stepped into the night; and from the cathedral I wended my way back through the moonlit streets—redolent, I recall, of piss and patchouli—in search of my room at Señora Almy's and a locked door behind which to think, to plan, and to put to purpose what Craft I could in pursuit of both Calixto and Q.

———————————— ❋ ————————————

From that room, from that same windowsill from which I'd seen him the night prior, high atop his turreted lair, only from there could I situate myself and find Q. I'd tried, upon leaving the cathedral, to plot his whereabouts upon the city's grid. No luck. I'd have to see that strange tower, maybe even see him atop it, if I were to make my way toward it, toward him. I wondered, would there be another sign? Light-bright birds to descry against the night, like shooting stars? I'd look, yes, but I'd do so through closed shutters, lest those humming-birds come with their blistering beaks. (And thoughts of their sting-ing serum assuaged my anger not at all.)

I was but three, maybe four steps inside the Hotel de Luz when I heard the voice of my hostess:

"Señor," said she, as yet unseen.

I continued toward the stairs as if I had not heard her, but again the call came—"Señor!" —as if now she were offended; and I stopped with one foot upon the first step, by which pose I hoped to convey a disinclination to discourse. I looked this way and that, but saw no sign of the woman. It was then she appended to her "Señor" the name I'd given her not thirty-six hours prior; but still . . . *where was she?* The reception foyer was half the size of my room above, and— save for a profusion of palms and flowering things—as sparsely dec-orated, and . . . Ah, there she sat. A bangle upon her fleshy wrist had betrayed her; for I saw its glint in a small mirror affixed to the far wall. Yes: Too rotund to rise with speed, Señora Almy sat behind the high, bamboo-fronted counter, yet she missed not a trick owing to a spying system of mirrors quite carefully hung.

"*Oui, madame,*" said I, moving to peer down at her over said counter, upon which sat a small triangle of iron, which no one, I'm sure, had ever had to ring, so . . . solicitous, so watchful was the señora. "*Oui?*"

I repeated, hoping with a show of French to stanch the flow of words set to come from the woman.

Oh but wily Señora Almy soon had the advantage; for—fleetly, fluently—she answered me in French, saying that a package had arrived for me. This she handed over the counter—ever seated, she was—and I received it with a nod and a mumbled *merci*. Of course a *hotelière* in the heart of old Havana would have some French—had I not seen all the world's flags flying over the harbor? Doubtless she'd ten other tongues as well.

"*Eh bien*," said I, making a show of the seamstress's label upon the package, "*le petit cadeau pour ma soeur*." To which the señora responded with what seemed a knowing smile. . . . Indeed, I'd have to take care with this Señora Almy.

Soon I was upstairs, doors and shutters locked and latched, unwrapping upon the bed that dress sewn of *bolan*. A tug at the seams testified to the seamstress's talents. Oh, I was glad to have it, and grew giddy, verily giddy at the thought of seeing it upon my "sister," though there loomed the larger issue: How would I, how would *she* pass Señora Almy, who no doubt slept upright and wide-eyed in her espial station? No matter. I was a witch. I'd find a way.

The seamstress, artfully, had turned the *bolan* this way and that in sewing the ensemble; that is, the blue and white stripes descending from the shoulders to make the bodice of the dress were set perpendicular to those of the skirt. If it sounds . . . *busy*, it was not. "Brilliant," said I aloud. Too, she'd fashioned a type of jacket—more of a wrap—its stripes matching those of the skirt. Here and there, at the throat and cuffs, she'd added sprays of navy-blue lace. "Well done, indeed." Had I set out to sew myself such a dress, I'd have run all the stripes north-south, surely, and the dress would have seemed sewn of mattress ticking. Already I'd forgotten what I'd paid for the seamstress's time and talents, but it was worth it, and how I burned, *burned* to slip into *a proper dress;* for I'd been too long in men's attire and coveted a change. Too, it seemed wise to disguise *my manly self:* If someone sought me . . . *alors,* it was Herculine, not Henry, they'd see upon the streets.

I found my ewer filled afresh, and over its accompanying basin I stripped and washed away the sea-stench and the dust of the streets. Then I dressed, dressed from tip to toe. When the woman's shoes I'd bought gave a pinch, I traded them off for my well-broken boots. Comfort has its own imperatives; and besides, no one would see my feet beneath the bell of the *bolan.* Too, I'd some walking to do, if I were to find Brù.

Dressed, I sat upon the bed's edge hoping Señora Almy was otherwise occupied—how else to slip past her?—when I heard a hiss, a hiss that seemed to come from a candle I'd lit and set before my mirror so as to multiply its light. . . . A moth, its white wings singed, lay aflutter atop the bureau, at the candle's base. This being the province of proverb—moth is to flame as cat is to cream, et cetera—I gave the struggling creature little thought. Oh, but that hiss had been quite loud, had it not? More like a pitch-tipped torch being doused in a bucket of water than a moth catching flame. And now, there lay the winged thing, scorched and about to . . .

Stay. . . . I stood and moved toward the moth. Its spread wings were perhaps two, three inches in width, and as I watched I saw them . . . heal. The burn marks lightened, and the wings progressed from a cream color to gold, and finally—seconds later—to white. No: Not white, but . . . *light.* Yes: the moth had now that same strange luminescence of the hummingbirds; though I did not see it as such, not then. I took it onto my fingertip. Fine though its wings were, they were not truly translucent: Light did not pass *through* the wings, but rather they seemed light itself. And then, with a *whoosh* as faint as a whisper, it was up, up into the air of my room; where, for a moment, it swirled in eddies I could neither see nor feel.

Foolishly—or so it now seems—I thought little of this small resurrection and returned to admiring myself in the mirror. In fact, I
recall—and state without pride—that I then scoured the bureau's
drawers for a stray hair pin, something with which to secure the quick
chignon I'd twisted of my otherwise lank, tied-back hair. Setting such
vanity aside—in truth: I fashioned something suitable from a bit of
the twine with which the seamstress had tied up my package—I
turned again to the regenerate moth; for it had settled upon the inside
of the shutters of that same window through which the birds had departed. Though I'd not opened these earlier—forgoing what might
have been a most welcome breeze—I did so now, caring not a whit,
indeed *supposing* that Q. might be watching from beyond. I'd free the
moth; which still, stupidly, I did not associate with that bird-brigade.
I deemed it some strange species, *c'est tout,* and told myself the Cuban
night was no doubt replete with such strangeness. As indeed it was;
for:

When I reached to unlatch the shutters, suddenly—and I had not
yet touched the metal of the latch, nor the wooden slats of the shutters themselves—suddenly, I say, like fingers curling round one's
throat from behind, there came from the far side of the shutters,
through its slats, ninety-nine more moths, each identical in size and
brilliance to their fellow: the hundredth. (Queverdo Brù bred his
smaller creatures in *centeni.*) There they clung, till the shutters themselves seemed made of light. Panicked, I pushed at the shutters, and
thus at the moths themselves, such that my hands came away dusted
with . . . with light, I suppose, rubbed from off their wings. . . . Was
it the serum? Would it sting? It was not. It did not.

As the shutters slapped back against the hotel's wall, hard, a good
number of the moths lost their hold upon the slats and retook to the
night. None came toward me, into the room; but there they all hov-
ered, near the sill, expectantly. I stared, nay, squinted, despite my blue

spectacles, into the light made by the mass of them; and I cannot say how much time elapsed before I saw them all settle across the street, atop the sloped, slate roof of a house. There they all were, diamantine, or rather like raindrops of light arrested in their fall, in their slide down the roof to its edge. They were . . . waiting, yes. For me. As I stood, disbelieving the sight of a rooftop thusly lit, I saw that the walls supporting the roof had begun to . . . to blink; and it was this that recalled me to reality: I'd lived long enough in the dark vastnesses of Florida to know a firefly when I saw one. Typically they came in clans—though never in such profusion as this, nor shining so steadily—and could light a dark room tolerably well, either free-flying or caught in paper cages, the latter serving as lanterns. Once, shipboard, I'd seen a man take one by the wing and read by trailing it over the lines of a letter. And only then—reality returning at the sight of a species I knew—only then did I begin to tremble at the sight of one hundred fireflies blanketing the wall opposite my hotel, such that now the whole of the house was . . . alight.

It was some while before the moths and fireflies took to the night, some flying to the sill at which I stood as if to convey what already I knew: Here were more winged things come to summon me to Q., to lead me to him, as indeed they did.

Whether or not Señora Almy saw me quit her hotel that night, I've no idea; for I forgot about her, so fast did I descend to the street, fearing my light-guides might leave me. (Best to confront this Q. straightaway and be done with it, best to see if indeed Sebastiana had come.) If the señora did see me, or rather "my sister," she never remarked upon it— unsurprisingly, seeing as how a *hotelière* who presumes to judge the pleasures of her guests, be they what they may, is a *hotelière* soon put out of business. . . . Regardless, I'd descended fast to the corner of

calles Luz and San Ignacio to find, and follow, those illuminate creatures vaguely north, northwest, toward the monk, the man, Brù. Timorous though my step was at times, *I had to go.* And when I
faltered—and I did falter, indeed—I drew on my anger and saw my
booted step grow resolute.

Enfin, who was this Q.? Surely he was no more a *mere* monk than I
was a mere man-woman-witch. And lest I doubt he was Shadow-born,
I had proof of his powers, did I not, seeing how he commanded those
light-creatures? Whenever I'd seen such strange creatures in the past,
they'd been under the command of a sister. So it was I wondered if
this Queverdo Brù were some sort of wrong-sexed witch, a warlock,
and these light-bright beings *his* familiars.

Unlike the hummingbirds, whose beaks had bothered me so, the
moths and fireflies only guided me, clustering at each corner, making
known the turns I was to take. The moths mirrored the moonlight on
the fluttering planes of their wings, and the fireflies flashed. It was, despite the strangeness of it, a beautiful sight—a most literal *guiding light.*
Did others witness this? I cannot say; for, when someone approached
upon the darkened, night-desolate backstreets of the city, the moths
disbanded and the fireflies dimmed. Or so it seemed. And then, again,
there they'd be, star-bright. And I'd follow.

I suppose the season of my arrival in Havana is best deemed spring,
but all four seasons simmer in the Cuban capital. And indeed that
night, as rain began to fall, the streets were set to steaming.

I ducked from door to door, and stood beneath porches when the
rain poured down. I shooed the fireflies when the rain slowed, so
they'd fly the faster; and had anyone witnessed this, it must surely have
seemed that I cast sparks from off my fingertips, so near did the flies
hover. But it worked:

Soon I found myself standing before a great door. The moths had

gone I knew not where; but the fireflies ringed the door almost deco-
ratively. And there I stood, dry beneath the door's lintel, as the rains
came down; for here was the sort of door upon which one does not
simply knock, no.

This door stood to twice my height, and its two panels—which,
when opened wide, would have let a barge sail past—were black as
pitch; but into one of these great planks there'd been cut a smaller
door. Through this I stepped, finding that it gave way with a groan
when pressed upon. Finding, too, that not only did the door appear
black as pitch, it had been brushed with something similar to pitch.
Such that when the lesser door slanted open, and the moonlight
struck it, I saw upon its tarry planks hundreds, nay, thousands of
winged creatures stuck to it and seeming to . . . writhe, as if alive.
Worse: When several of the fireflies flew onto the door, stuck to it,
and fast began to dim, I knew this to be the case—they *were* alive.

The pitch, or tar . . . *enfin*, I'll refer to it as darkness. This darkness
was upon my fingertips, which now I raised to my nose, seeking—to
no avail—to identify it as I stepped slowly over the threshold and into
the dark beyond the door. Hiking high my skirt, lest it snag upon the
stickiness, I reached, reached with the tip of my boot and sought the
ground beyond. Finally, I found it, and stood astraddle the door, loath
to step off the street into a moonless courtyard in which I'd be truly
blind—both sightless and ignorant of all that lay beyond.

But this I did, and the door closed behind me with a slam, the
source of which I hoped was simply the rising wind; for it seemed a
storm was coming on. This slam resounded, such that I knew I stood
in a large, stone-walled place: a courtyard, perhaps; for I heard, too,
the nearby fall of rain. I suppose it was that same slamming of the
door that brought to my side those creatures I sensed but could not
see, save for the hip-height red of their eyes. I felt myself surrounded
in the soundless dark. . . . Stay: There *was* a sound, which I took to be

the rustle of wings, and another which worried me more: the scratch of talons upon stones. I felt their small heads at my waist, and something hard—doubtless a beak—worked its way up beneath my arm, toward my blessedly unbound breasts, whilst another tried to peck its way under the bell of my skirt. Thusly did I find myself standing in the dark, that utter and terrific dark, fending off fowl, and willing, *willing* a fall of moonlight, or something, anything, by which my turned Eyes might see.

✳

 *Chapter Nine*

For the priest whom you see seated in the stream gathering his colours, is not a man of copper. For he has changed the colour of his nature, and become a man of silver whom, if you wish, after a little time, you will have as a man of gold.

—Zosimos of Panopolis,
Ars nostra (On Our Art), c. A.D. 300

The house at which I found Queverdo Brù would have appeared typical to any passerby seeing it by sun- or moonlight: a three-story facade, snug to the street, its colorless shutters ever closed—not uncommon in the tropics—and its sky-blue paint gone pale and peeling away in places. Neither would the details of its architecture have distinguished it from five, ten others houses upon the same street:

Passing through the large porte cochere in which I'd been arrested by both the utter darkness and those peafowl that prowled it—yes, improbably, here were peafowl—one came upon an inner courtyard, a perfect square bordered by walls three stories high and showing balconies of grillwork and wood. The lowest of these three stories gave onto the courtyard itself, where a large, pear-shaped fountain sat center-all, water trick-

ling over its lip—driven by means mechanical or magical—and running down its glazed sides much as . . . much as drool runs down a
dummy's chin.

The paved parterre surrounding the fountain had been laid out
formally; but if ever its beds had thrived with fauna of a sort, well,
now they were but weeds, crisped and sere and cracking 'neath the
careless tread of the fowl. Beyond the courtyard, set beneath the balcony, were storerooms where previously a merchant might have kept
his coffee, sugar, or such; but these Q. had converted to stables. I saw
their Dutch doors, some standing wide and spilling straw, others having only their top, iron-barred halves open and showing naught but
shadows.

Above the courtyard, on the second story, sat the *entresuelo*, a warren of functional rooms whose walls rose seven, eight feet to ceilings
carved of oak. From these rooms, doors opened onto the lower balcony. Above this, in turn, sat a third story of larger, finer rooms outfitted for family life. Here the ceilings were twice the height of those
below, and painted. Frescoed, in fact; though by the time I saw those
ceilings, the painted plaster had fallen to the floor in great floes; and
there it had been left to lie—quite like painted ice, yes—upon that sea
of parquet.

In such houses as this there is sometimes a fourth floor of sorts:
rooms built upon the flat roof, or *assoltaire*. Typically, these are mini-
mally functional affairs, flat-roofed themselves and free of ornament,
reserved for the use of sons grown randy or guests who otherwise
might linger too long. Of course, Q. had made something . . . *more* of
his fourth floor.

Atop those boxy, adobe-like rooms of the *assolatire*, which ran the
length of his western wing, Brù had strung tents of varying size, accessible by means of ladders fashioned from logs and rope. A fifth
story, I suppose. At the end of these, as far back from the street as the

lot allowed, there rose that tower—part cistern, part pigeon cote—upon which I'd first seen Q. I looked up at this silhouette of *assoltaire* and tent, jaggedly black against the blue of the moon.

Yes, the moon had cast off her clouds, and now her lunar twin shimmered on the black water of the fountain's well. Those peafowl—whom already I detested for their red-eyed stare and their prying at my . . . *privates*—appeared bluish white as well, as if made of moon-glow. Indeed, aside from those ruddy eyes, they showed no color but this luminous blue. Or was it white? Even the Argus-eyed tails of the males were naught but . . . moon-colored. And still they surrounded me as I stood staring up at the strange roofscape, some part of which now began to wave. A pennant? A flapping black standard? Would that it had been. Instead it was the robed arm of the monk, summoning me *Up, up.*

As the four corners of the courtyard sat in deepest shadow, I knew not where to go, how to ascend.

It was the peafowl pushed me toward the far left corner of the courtyard. Were they sentient, these creatures? Were they acting upon the orders of their keeper? I think not; rather, they'd been domesticated, like dogs, and knew best that corner of the yard where their master—and thus their meals—most often appeared. There sat a knee-high trough of rough-hammered tin, with bowls ranged beneath it; bowls that I kicked with my shuffling step, such that from them something spilled. This was too viscid to have been water. From the sickening consideration of this substance—it pooled, and appeared . . . *mercurial*, yes, beneath the moon—I looked up to see a Moorish arch cut into the corner of the courtyard wall. Beyond this I saw the first stair of a curved and rising flight.

The stairwell was steep, and turned like the threads of a screw. The steps themselves were of stone, stone worn low in the middle by the weight of all those who'd used them in centuries past. Thusly did the stone speak to me of home, of France; for in America all steps are yet squared, and silent on the subject of Time.

So intent was I upon my climb—the thinner insides of the steps were slippery—I did not wonder at the dim light within the stairwell. I climbed, simply, content to leave the peafowl behind; for they did not follow. Oh, but worse, far worse it was when one such "light," as it were, fell with a *peep* and *squeak* upon my head, tangling its angular wings in my hair. I grabbed for a banister, but, finding none, braced myself against the wall, itself slick as that of a well. I then shook, *shook* my head fiercely, so fiercely I nearly fell; but only then did the bat come free.

Bats, yes. Brightly white and no broader than a hand span. They hung stalactitic from the undersides of the stairs above me, and it was their guano that slickened the surrounds. Fast, *very* fast I found the second-floor landing, but there I saw more bats, hundreds more, spade-shaped and pendant from the third-floor balcony. From its rotted wood they fell now, as one, and broke in a bright wave upon the black night. I heard the slice and flap of their wings, and felt the wellnigh infernal wind that rose from same. I knelt low, and hid the trap of my hair beneath my hands. In time the bats settled elsewhere, and I stood; for it was two more flights of stairs to the *assoltaire*.

There were bats in the next stairwell, too, but these were still: only a few fell, only a few flew. Finally there remained but one more flight of stairs. These rose straight to the *assolatire*. Ten, fifteen steps perhaps; and I'd have taken them quickly had I not seen . . . him. There. At the top of the stair.

He seemed darkness itself, but as I climbed—none too quickly now—he turned, just so, and the blue of the moon showed him in profile. Owing to his hooded robe, that Bedouin-like burnous he wore, here was a profile devoid of detail. Indeed, he seemed shadow-hewn as compared to his pets. Midway up this final flight, I heard my-self say—in a voice reed-thin from fear—" . . . quite the menagerie you have here, señor." Still I was angry about that band of humming-birds who'd come, and I hoped my words piqued, as had their beaks. If he heard my intent, Brù dissembled well; for he made no response save this: He reached down his right hand to help me.

His tendrilous, tar-dark fingers fluttered before my face. Against all instinct, I took his proffered hand, as a woman would: I set my fingers crosswise upon his pale and hardened palm. I felt his long and *very* strong fingers close upon mine like a clamp. Moonlight ran in the run-nels of his thick, untended nails. His knuckles were a range of bone-made mountains. And the whole of his hand was cold. . . . Here, on my part, was a pose of politesse having no practical purpose; for Brù neither pulled nor steadied me. And oh, how I wished then that I'd worn pants, *manly attire* that would have afforded me one of those heartier, albeit hated handshakes instead of this . . . dependency.

Soon we stood on a level, and I saw that—if freed of his stoop—this Queverdo Brù would stand as tall as I, taller even. Still I could not see his face, recessed in the flared hood of his robe. As he said nothing—what manners he'd shown in extending his hand had ceded to stillness, to silence—I asked, "Sebastiana d'Azur? . . . Has she come?"

It was then his face came forward—oddly, as a tortoise's does from its shell; and showing a neck just as leathery, just as sinewy—and he said, in a voice leonine in both timbre and tone, "Who?"

And so it was I supposed myself abandoned, again.

Queverdo Brù . . . I saw now that he was aged, quite. And bald. And blacker than the night.

He'd brought his face forward but then threw back the hood of the burnous as well, showing features that were still handsome; or rather, more *handsome* than not. Most markedly, he'd a wide mouth and ready smile; but his was a smile that never reassured me. It had, in fact, the opposite effect; for his smile disclosed wide-spaced teeth and a tongue both of which seemed, or *were* . . . golden. How better to say it? That smile of his seemed *to glow*, as had the gold overspilling the bowls below, and the guano on the steps, all of it . . . *elemental* in some way, at once natural and noisome.

"Ah, yes," said the monk when a moment more had passed, "you speak of the French witch." If his English were accented, no one word betrayed it. It was as though each word he spoke had been turned, tumbled in his mouth till it came forth clean, shorn of all ornament. It was discomfiting, that . . . that cleanliness. "She has not come, no, but I trust she will, *sí* and certes." And so certain, so *portentously* certain was he of Sebastiana's coming, he'd seen fit to utter affirmations in two tongues, adding a third when he said again: "*Sí*, certes, and *oui*, she will come."

Had I expected Sebastiana to be there? I think not. I knew better than to *expect* things of my Mystic Sister. But *I'd hoped*, yes; and something inside me sank at hearing she'd not shown, such that I blinked back tears as I said, apropos of I knew not what:

"Meanwhile . . ." It was a word, *c'est tout;* but had I not spoken, then, I'd have begun to cry, *si*, certes and *oui*. And this I knew: If a woman sheds tears when first she meets a man, she stands little chance of ever having the upper hand.

"Meanwhile," mocked the monk, "she has sent you."

"And why is this? Do you know where she is, or why she—?"

He held his hands out toward me, palms pushing at the air—great pale planks, these seemed—as one does to slow a horse or quiet a colicky child. Then, slowly, he tipped them palm up. "Your questions fall as fast as the rain," observed he; and indeed I was wet, though I'd not felt the fall of rain, not since climbing to stand beside Brù on the *assoltaire*. "No doubt you could match a query to each drop."

"No doubt I could, yes."

"But," said he—showing that most disconcerting smile—"if all the rain were to fall at once, we'd drown beneath its weight, would we not? You must hold your questions some while, as a cloud holds its rain." To which sophistic claptrap I thought to append, *Ah, but a cloud grown weighty with rain is a cloud inclined to storm,* non?

Instead, I said nothing; and when Brù sought shelter from that steadying rain, I followed.

Up a rope ladder we went, from the *assoltaire* onto the roof of one of those squat, daubed constructions and into the largest of three tents hidden high atop the city, well above any neighboring abode. These tents were five-poled affairs—poles at the four corners, of course, with a fifth giving the tent its pitch—and sewn of a colorless canvas seeming better suited to the Sahara than the heart of Havana. There were side panels which one could untie and let fall; this Brù did that night, against the rain, whilst I took in our surrounds by the light of oil lanterns hung at the corners of the tent and giving a glow to all I saw:

The canvas walls—billowing now, as the winds began to blow—bore black handprints; and by the uncommon length and splay of the fingers I saw that these had been made by Brù. (*Qui d'autre?* I rightly assumed Brù had no companions save for that light-bred brood of his.) Alongside these prints were words written in a language I recognized—Arabic—but did not know well enough to read: "*b'ism'il-lah ma'sha'llah,*" as it was written; and the purpose of the inscription was plain: They'd been placed there, along with the prints, for protection; more specifically, to placate the afreets. *May God avert evil,* were the

words. And Q. had hung skins, too, from the tent poles, as the patri-
archs of Israel and Assur had hung teraphim from the skins of their
tents. So: Was this Queverdo Brù a priest of African or Near Eastern
provenance?

I asked, of course.

"If a priest be he who labors at holy questions, then yes, I am a
priest"; which told me nothing at all; for all of us labor at questions
that might be called holy, *non*? But in fact, by night's end, I'd know
what Brù was, and know, too, that he was African.

This last fact he let slip when I asked about his favored burnous,
that unfitted, hooded robe that I'd only ever seen in traveler's sketches
of desert dwellers. Said he, such attire was commonly seen in the city
of his youth: Alexandria. And with his faded, sun-grilled robe and
sandals, Queverdo Brù did seem like a monk; or rather, *would have,* had
it not been for his various . . . *accoutrements.* Indeed, so accessorized was
he it seemed doubtful he dressed himself each day. Stranger, though,
to think he lay down to sleep in all that he wore; for:

Yes, he was well adorned. This I remarked as I watched him at
work upon the tent walls, tying their unfurled panels into place. I saw
now that his every finger of his left hand was ringed—some doubly
so—though his right hand was plain. The rings caught the lantern
light, and shone as precious stones will. Two golden, Moresque bands
glinted upon his thumb. And the belt which held fast his burnous,
this, too, was *jeweled* in its way: from it there hung crystals, ores, and
other talismanic trinkets, all of them spaced between short iron rods,
like ribs, that served no purpose I could discern. Too, there hung a
knife, its hilt and half its argentine blade showing above a sheath of
tooled leather. Holier things, requisite to the everyday exorcisms of
my own abandoned faith, were evident as well: a crucifix of carved
ebony; a Saint Benedict badge; and, of course, a rosary beaded with
balls of silver filigree, its Christ carved of jade. At the apex of this

rosary—rather, that point at which the circle joins—there was set the desiccate skull of a rodent. A rat, perhaps. Or a cat. Or the fetal skull of . . . of some higher species.

If Brù were a priest, he partook of no religion I knew. Doubtless his powers exceeded those of any standard priest—whose powers are, after all, *ordained* by the Church unto mere men; for something had led him into the Shadows and the acquaintance of us witches. Perhaps he was a priest of *all and no religions,* as it were: *bref:* a shaman.

"Are you . . ." I began; but I finished rather more emphatically: *"What are you?"*

Not turning from his work—the last panel was nearly secured, and the unvented tent now shuddered in the wind—he laughed, lightly so; and the sound might have soothed, had it not been for the accompanying smile. Regardless, a laugh was no answer; and so:

"Are you a witch-man, or warlock?" I'd never met one, but had heard tell of a very few. "Can you work the Craft?"

"Nostrum non est opificium, sed opus naturae; which means . . ."

"Yes, yes: 'Ours is not a craft, but the work of nature.'" I'd not be bested by this Brù. ". . . Are you a scholar, then?"

"If a scholar be he who studies poetry, parable, sophistry, and science."

Mon Dieu, how he frustrated me! And so I all but demanded:

"Tell me how it is you know my—" but I stopped myself; for the possessive pronoun would have told of my love, and my loss. I calmed, and the question came: "How do you know Sebastiana d'Azur?"

"I do not know her at all," said he, "save for a very few letters that have sailed that way and this." Here he turned to me, finally, hood down, and the lantern nearest where he stood showed eyes seeming too pale, and scars upon his neck, unhealed, set there as if by a rake of four tines. They were empurpled, leech-like; and—as the lantern light caught them before Brù could conceal them with his hood—

suppurating still. Here were new wounds. "When first I heard about you, I wrote her. I invited her here, but . . ."

"But she's not come?"

"No, she has not come. Soon, I should think," but his voice wavered on these last words, such that they were not at all the assurance he'd intended. "I await her arrival with an anticipation equal to yours."

This I doubted; but now there was a more pressing matter:

" 'Heard' about me, you say? From whom?"

The tent tied down, the tapers and lanterns all lit, he came to me where I stood. "Sit," said he, motioning toward two sofas set *face-à-face* beside the tent's central pole, atop a worn rug of Oriental origin.

"I see no reason to sit, to stay, if Sebastiana is not—"

"Sit," said he, again; and though the word was not the command one throws down at a dog, still—and I record this relieved of all pride—I soon found myself sunken deep into one of those downy sofas. So deeply, in fact, it seemed a trap; and I wondered if Brù hadn't stuffed those sofas with the feathers that fell so profusely from off his hummingbirds (of which—blessedly—there was no sign at all). To extricate myself from that sofa—still I worried that I might need to flee, somehow, though the tent was tied down now— . . . to flee, I say, would have required an effort more *athletic* than my sopping skirt would have easily allowed. Witch-work might be wanted; and so I sat at the ready. Still, from this new vantage point, I took in more of that tent wherein East met West: a hookah pipe rose to my right, whilst in a far corner there sat *un petit secrétaire* worthy of Versailles. Elsewhere, there was little art but much craft—craft of the ordinary kind—scattered about: masks and totems and such, all carved of hardwoods and with intricate inlay. . . . But it was that secretary that intrigued me most: Too easily I imagined Q. folding those long legs of his beneath its burnished wood to write to Sebastiana. How I burned, *burned* to know the nature of their correspondence. I wondered, might my sister's letters be near? If so, what would I make of their contents? Presently, it seemed Sebastiana had some explaining to do.

With rain slashing at the tent, with lightning illumining the whole rather too often for my comfort, Q. took the sofa opposite mine. Spreading his arms over the sofa's curved back and crossing his legs, he seemed to fill its span. And I saw now the truth of what I'd supposed: Brù wore nothing beneath the burnous. His legs showed bare to the hip, and the robe split to show a concavity of chest in which the business end of multiple necklaces sat, rather like treasure buried in an ebon chest of another sort. Ivory and gold, *much* gold, glowed upon his skin. Too, I thought I saw a monocle of thin-sliced emerald, such as Nero is said to have worn, the better to see those debaucheries done at his command upon the jeweled floors of the Domus Aurea, his house made *all of gold*. Gold, too, was Brù's house; rather, gold was everywhere.

Supposing my too-direct inquiries would be rebuffed, I took another tack and observed, "Your rings. They are . . . lovely." Vapid, yes; indeed, here was converse one might hear in the company of England's teen-age queen, Victoria, talk of whose showy ascension had filled the pages of the last newspaper I'd bothered to read, some months prior. *Mais hélas,* I was never one for parlor talk. But neither was Queverdo Brù, whose speech was more pedantic than polite; as per:

"You have read Philostratus Jarchus." Realizing this was a question, I said no, I had not. Further, I made the mistake of asking:

"Ought I to?"

"Philostratus Jarchus tells of the magus Apollonius, to whom, in the first century anno domini, a Hindu prince bequeathed seven rings inscribed with the signatures of the regnant planets."

"Indeed?" . . . I tried to summon patience; for here sat the only man in Havana who knew of my Sebastiana, whose letters—wherein I'd read of her whereabouts myself, *merci bien*— I imagined tucked in the

✻

drawer of that secretary across the tent. And so I said, "Tell me more," when in fact I longed not for information—certainly not information pertaining to Philo-who's-it or a magus other than he who sat before me—but rather the shuttered confines of my room at the Hotel de Luz. There I hoped to wake the next morning refreshed and ready to renew my search for Calixto and Sebastiana both. Oh, but now the rain fell heavily, running in rivers from the tent's center to splash off its sides. And storm or no storm, I was not ready to leave. Not truly. Not yet.

"These rings," said Q., stripping them from off his fingers, "these are the rings of Apollonius, who vowed to wear them in sequence and—"

"Surely those are not the same rings." Gold? Many hundred years old?

"No, witch," said he, "but I cast these myself in a similar spirit." And he stripped himself of the rings, one by one. Rings off, Q. leaned forward. No: in fact, he half stood with the help of a staff of entwined snakes, a caduceus I'd not seen leaning against the sofa's side. Reaching, *reaching*, he dropped into my cupped hands the seven very heavy rings. The largest accommodated my first and second fingers, and would have been a bracelet on a child. These were exquisite, indeed. Was he a goldsmith, then?

Q. continued: "Apollonius wore them in sequence, as directed by the prince; and in so doing he lived beyond a hundred years whilst losing none of his comeliness."

Q. was, to my eyes, rather less than comely—the more so as every second passed—but was he *one hundred*? Wondering this, I sickened deep inside. Had I happened upon another Shadowist bent upon immortality? I'd met such a one before, in the Never-Glade, and had no intention of suffering someone similar, here in Havana, no indeed; and so I stood to take my leave. Rather, *tried to stand*.

In struggling to stand, to extricate myself from the sofa with hands inutile—full as they were of the seven rings—I found myself seated upon the sofa's edge; whereupon I saw the floor of the tent for the first time since sinking into the sofa. And there, upon that rug of Eastern arabesques, there sat a snake. A python, light-bright and coiled, its tail tucked into its mouth. Lightning lit the tent. (Leastways, it lights my memory of the moment.) And Q., with his sandaled foot, pushed nearer the python's mouth a saucer full of shimmering milk. "Ourobouros," said he. This I supposed to be an introduction. "Fear not," added Brù, to no effect; for already *I feared*.

The snake would have stretched its whiteness ten, twelve feet. Uncoiled, it surely would have spread across the tent from corner to corner. It was still now, busy with its milk, but how had it come between us so stealthily, so silently? *That* was what frightened me more as I sat back upon the sofa, tucking my booted feet beneath the bell of my skirt. . . . *Bien*, I'd sit and listen. And so I did, holding all the while to those rings that had conferred a century unto Apollonius.

"I seek," said Q., "an elevated estate." I knew he referred not to that aerie, that rooftop tent in which we sat as a storm came ever closer; but it would be hours later before I understood. Moon and sun, Luna and Sol, would swap sky-heights before Queverdo Brù made it plain: The elevated estate to which he aspired was . . . *enfin*, it was Perfection. Or so he called it.

To explain: Brù was all I'd supposed him to be: equal parts priest, scholar, shaman, smith, and magus; for he was an alchemist. Which fact I would learn in the course of the catechism that followed.

Through the long hours of a stormy night and morn, we sat upon those twin sofas and Queverdo Brù spoke like a man accustomed to silence. And confusing words they were, too, as the age-old alchemical creed is, of course, *obscurum per obscurius, ignotum per ig-notius*. The obscure by the more obscure, the unknown by the more unknown. . . . They were a clan that did not prize clarity. Secrecy? Yes. Clarity, no.

Indeed, Q. urged my accession to an oath of silence; which I took, all the while staring at that snake which had let go its tail to lap, lap like a cat at its saucer of milk. Milk that was white, yes, but some-how . . . constellated: Something twinkled in the milk, and twinkled upon the split tip of the snake's tongue, too. But I did not wonder overlong at this: *Best not to peer down at the python,* I told myself. What's more: Already I'd raised my left hand to repeat that oath, so laughably prolix:

"I swear by heaven, by earth, by light, by shadow. . . . I swear by fire, by air, by water, by earth. . . . I swear by the height of the heavens, by the depths of the sea, and by the abyss of Tartarus. . . . I swear by Mercury and by Anubis, by the braying of the dragon Cher-courobouros, and the three-headed dog Cerberus, guardian of Hell. . . . I swear by the ferryman Charon, and by the three Fates, and the Furies, and the bludgeon never to reveal these words to anyone who is not my noble and charming son," et cetera.

At oath's end I could not help adding, "Had I a son—or daughter—I'd like to think they'd be both noble and charming; however, having no heirs, I suppose myself the lockbox of your secrets, señor." Further, as I wondered if Q. had been apprised of my . . . particularities, I ven-tured, "And, as I am unlikely to spawn or sire any offspring . . ."

He stayed me with a raised hand, pale as the in-curl of a conch. Too, it seemed he'd hissed. Or had this been his Ourobouros?

Alors, I took his strange oath. And here—upon this page, pen in this putrefying hand—I shall break it, forthwith, and spill those se-crets that would lead, years hence, to my own . . . Elevation? Perfec-tion? What else can I call it? Words can confuse things so. And the

---

✳

state itself is simple, or rather it was, *is* to one who . . . *lives* it, shall I say, though it be death I reference?

Having ascertained what Q. knew of Sebastiana (little, or so he said) and Calixto (nothing, of course), I settled into the sofa to listen, to learn, all the while watching for the angular head of a snake to appear . . . somewhere. Time pleasantly spent? Assuredly not. But here was the promise of secrets centuries old, and though I'd heard such things before—promises and secrets both—it seemed the wiser course to stay, to wait out both the storm and the snake, the former breaking overhead, the latter now gone from sight, having slithered . . . *where?* I wondered.

In truth, I had only a slight interest *in* and no urge *toward* the alchemical trades. Unlike the witch-lore I'd learned, I saw no application for it, no use suited to its cryptosecrets. More: My head began to ache as Brù spoke on; for alchemy is so deeply steeped in secrecy, *the sense of it* must be sifted for, its texts and treatises sieved for their metaphoric gold.

Gold. Yes: It was on that very subject that Q. began his disquisition.

He'd slipped from the tent despite the storm, leaving me in possession of those rings, and wondering should I, *could I* take my leave unseen, should I, *could I* slip across the tent to rifle the drawers of the *secrétaire?* But the presence of the python stilled me, and there I sat upon the sofa, as in a stockade. Brù soon returned, soaked yet seeming not to know it, and bearing a tray laden with a light supper of sorts. Such hospitality did not suit him: He looked like a simian charged with the care of a sheet of eggs. Nor do I recall those small courses served. However, I do recall the tray and utensils; for—and I knew this the minute I felt the balance of the fork, and the heft of the rudely hammered bowl—here was gold, unalloyed and true. Each piece was precious, surely. And Q., seeing me observing same, re-launched his lecture; thusly:

"It was Li Chao Kuin who advised the Emperor Wu Ti to sacrifice to the *tsao*—"

"*Attendez,*" said I, and rudely so; but this was too much to take in at once. And far be it for me to say, but Brù had no sense, no sense at all of rhythmic speech; such that I wondered when last he'd conversed with someone, *anyone*, be they Shadow-folk or no. "The *tsao* . . . What is this?"

"The *tsao*," said he," is a furnace." He stared at me unnervingly; for his pitchy pupils floated freely: dark islands in the jaundiced seas of his eyes. And now he was rude in his turn: "I have had letters from your Sebastiana in which she refers to you as *une érudite*. Surely you know I speak of the Han Dynasty when I speak of Wu Ti?"

Several well-salted responses rolled to the tip of my tongue, 'tis true; but these I swallowed back, saying instead, "If I've erudition, it is born of the West, as was I."

Resignedly, and with a sigh, he resumed:

"Li Chao Kuin, in his . . . *furnace* made such sacrifices as to sum-mon supernatural beings from the spheres; as—once this is achieved—the powder of cinnabar can be heated in the *tsao* and trans-formed into yellow gold." Standing before me still, tray in hand, he nodded down as if to say, *Take what you will.*

Again, the food was forgotten; but the fork, the bowl grew heavier now in my hands. I set the seven rings upon the tray, the better to ap-praise the weight of these implements. "Gold, then?"

"Yellow gold, yes," said Q., as if it were common to have house-hold goods thusly compounded. Then he motioned me to drink from a goblet, also of gold. Relieved, I was, to find naught but red wine within, heavy and tasting of cherries; but my relief was short-lived. "To drink, to eat from vessels thusly forged," said Q., "is to get the gift of years."

I nearly spat the wine. *"Mon Dieu!"* said I, having swallowed hard. "Is that all man seeks? Money first, and immortality after?"

The question was rhetorical, of course; yet Q. answered it, quoting words that would come to seem his creed: "Longevity, liberty, and gold . . . But gold—or money—is the least of it."

"Is that so?"

"It *is* so. Gold is not money. Gold is metaphor."

To which I made no reply, seeming to anger Q.; who continued:

"If one gets, truly gets the gift of years—and this is not assured— one may then see the *hsien* . . . the blessed island P'eng Lai in the midst of the seas. There the Immortals live. And if one sees the island, and if one makes the *feng* and *chan* sacrifices, then one . . . one will not die."

"Indeed? . . . Hmm." I set my goblet down upon his tray, heavily. My choice was this: mockery or madness; for ever since Sweet Marie, talk of immortality maddened me, quite.

"Mock not the magician Li Chao Kuin!" With this, Q. bent to set the tray down in turn, so heavily the goblet spilled to tip its contents onto the carpet—about this he cared not at all—and he retook to the sofa opposite. This he did suddenly, all the while staring at me.

"I mock no one," said I—though of course I had, and did—"be he magician or man. I simply wonder where this island is? Have you a map, señor? . . . And on this island, on P'eng Lai, what manner of immortals might one find? You see, I've met immortals of sundry sort— incubi, succubi, and such—and wonder if this P'eng Lai might be a haven for same." *And if so,* thought I, mocking no one now, *spare me the map upon which such an island is marked.*

Silence ensued. Thunder and lightning, too. Finally, this, from Q.:

"You disappoint me." It was odd, so . . . so factual did it seem, as if he'd said, *You are blond.* Or, *You are French by birth.* And his words stung; for an orphan is bred to please, and never loses that need.

"Is your mind not suited to metaphor? . . . I speak of the things *be-*

yond things. Mock not *my* words if it is you, *you* who are unable to hear
the meanings beyond meaning, the metaphors of the Art."

Suffice to say: I'd been admonished; such that now I can recollect
and record his words with ease, and without recourse to the Craft:

"I speak not of an island, by the common conception, but rather
of a place; and in that place, there is Perfection."

I was hesitant, but I had to know: "Immortality, do you mean?"

"*Sí*," said he, seeming pleased, nodding. In that inconstant light I
saw again the scars upon his neck and was reminded of my own: claw-
made, stripes set into each shoulder by that cat kept by Sweet Marie.
And before I knew it—maddened as I was by more talk of
immortality—I'd spoken that hated sister's name.

"You," said I, accusingly, "you and Sweet Marie both . . ."

"Whose is this name you raise?" I saw no lie in his wide-eyed stare;
but still I said:

"You know the name, surely."

"I do not," said he. "It resonates with rumor, is all. It seems I heard
it years ago, from fishermen who invoked the name in speaking of
Florida's swampland. Is it she of whom you speak? The same? A witch,
I presume? If so, I say again: I know no such witch. . . . I have been
alone a long while, and I seek no society."

"You sought me," I said. "Why? Who spoke of me? And why did
you write Sebastiana asking after me?" *And why,* I wondered to myself,
why ever did my Mystic Sister send me to Cuba in search of such a man as this?

Soon I had answers; and they stunned me.

You see, no less a sister than the Duchess herself had called me to
the attention of Queverdo Brù. *The Duchess.* Surely I blanched to hear
her name—Lenore—upon the lips of the alchemist.

Years, *years* we'd been without word from the Duchess. She'd disappeared upon the death of her poor Eliphalet, and the subsequent
dissolution of Cyprian House. Those of us who kept in contact as

best fate allowed—I refer chiefly to Eugénie, who'd returned to New Orleans—had never had a single word more from her. How odd, how deucedly odd to hear from Brù—of all people—that the Duchess had left New York, sailing from Society, from the Shadows, from sadness, and boarded a boat bound for the Cuban capital, from whence she planned to sail to an island sitting southwesterly. Beyond that, said Q., he knew nothing of the Duchess, least of all her whereabouts at present.

Enfin, it was the Duchess who'd first spoken of me to Queverdo Brù; whereupon he'd written to Sebastiana d'Azur—at that address the Duchess had given; whereupon Sebastiana, in her turn, had arranged this rendezvous. . . . Why? Why had Queverdo Brù sought me? Still I wondered. And once I knew, well, then I could only wonder why my sisters had betrayed me so.

Oh, but stay: They hadn't betrayed me; *for they knew not what they'd done.* So it was I was able to forgive them for all that followed.

lbedo

 *Chapter Ten*

Mercury and Sulphur, Sun and Moon, matter and form, these are the opposites. When the feminine earth is thoroughly purged and purified from all superfluity, then you must give it a male meet for its ripening.

—EDWARD KELLEY, assistant to John Dee,
court alchemist of Elizabeth I

GOLD AND METAPHOR, AND THE METAPHOR OF GOLD; THUS began my initiation into alchemy and its world of secrets.

Though I was no adept, neither was alchemy wholly new to me. I knew its most basic tenets; for I'd done enough reading in the Dark Arts, and at some point all such Craftwork converges, whereupon the metallurgist meets the magus, the sorcerer the shaman, et cetera, as in the person of Queverdo Brù. However, I believed, as do many others who've heard tell of the alchemical art yet have not studied down to its muddied depths, that its practitioners, from the smith-gods of antiquity to the present day, held to a simple, *lesser* goal than is the case: That, driven by sordid cupidity or a vainglorious desire to ape the creator—*bref,* greed and glory—they sought to forge gold from dross. This they did, yes; but there was rather more to it than that.

I knew that the alchemists of old—*alors*, the first secret I learned was that there were alchemists *of new*, such as Brù, men persevering into the present— . . . these alchemists, both old and new, sought to dig down to the core of life's mystery, the *mysterium magnum*, where they hoped to find the great animating essence, the *prima materia*, from whence all transformation proceeded. By "transformation," I refer both to that godly gulf that separates the animate from the inanimate as well as those states marking the progression from the former unto the latter state: birth, growth, death, putrefaction, and reconstitution. The agent said to effect this transformation is the *prima materia;* wherein all alchemical secrets reside, and upon which all alchemical successes hinge. Long ago, this came to be called the *filius philosophorum,* or Philosopher's Stone. Or, in Arabic, *al-kimaya* . . . Alchemy.

The Philosopher's Stone, however, is no stone at all. Not in the sense of, say, a diamond; though let it be said the alchemists sought and adored those sorts of stones as well. Thusly did Q. wear that Neronian monocle of his in accord with the dictates of Camille Léonard, who, in his *Speculum lapidum* of 1610, recommends that emeralds be worn to "bridle lasciviousness, dispel demoniacal allusions, strengthen the memory, and inspire rhetoricians." (And Q., as rhetorician, certainly was inspired: He talked rather like Italian tenors die; which is to say, slowly, *very slowly*, drawing the act out with drama.)

Indeed, I'd discover many other such tomes related to the alchemical study of stones, precious or otherwise. Some held that sapphires produce "peacefulness, amiability, and piety" whilst also having their uses against the bite of scorpions and serpents; and would that I'd known *that* my first night with Q., with Ourobouros slithering about, but I was yet some months away from finding Cardan, whose *De Subtilitate* speaks to the uses of sapphires. In time, though, that study begun at Brù's would lead to the acquisition of a jewel box to rival any Sebastiana might have seen in the courts of old Europe; for, though

I'd have deemed myself a skeptic, yes, still I was no fool, no tempter of Fate, and so I had stores of topaz to neutralize any liquid in which a poison might be present, and pearls aplenty—as they (powdered, and mixed into wine) are the sovereign remedy against headaches, and some forms of divination hurt, verily *hurt* the head—and rubies, too. Rubies, which are said to increase the gifts of fortune; and in my case, most certainly did. But more about rubies and riches anon.

Too, there were the lesser stones—such as Brù's crystals—which are reputed to possess efficacies of their own, particularly for a divining sister, and therefore seemed worth having. And so it was that my estate would later reckon tiny leathern bags of earth-art from all the whole world over: selenite, extracted from beneath the shells of Indian snails, which, if tasted, helps in augury; amandinus is said to help the Seer as well; so, too, chelonites, when drawn from a mollusk and placed beneath (not *on*) the tongue at moonrise. With such substances I had some luck, it is true; though I was never a Seeress to rival certain sisters of my later acquaintance. . . . Oh, but I stray, and speed my story, when the point I mean to make is simply this: The Philosopher's Stone is *no stone at all*.

What is it? *Alors* . . .

To quote Arnold of Villanova: "There abides in Nature a certain pure matter which, being discovered and brought by Art to perfection, converts to itself all imperfect bodies it touches." *Voilà*. But the difficulty, and the alchemical task, is this: How to discover it? And by what Art bring it to perfection? Therein lies the *opus magnus*, the great work of alchemy.

And though the Philosopher's Stone was understood not as mere gold itself—more rightly, it resembles rubies—it came to seem the substance *most capable* of transforming matter and sustaining life. Hence, gold-essay: That great, age-old effort to produce gold, to render it from lesser metals through a series of operations, the *opus alchymicum,* in which the metals were subjected to heat, acids, et cetera. More important than the production of gold itself, gold-essay came to represent something greater, in spiritual terms. Gold is wealth, yes; but *metaphorically,* gold is purity, that which does not tarnish or decay. In seeking it, then, the alchemist sought his own perfection.

And so gold came to symbolize immortality; for *perfected* man is he who triumphs over time, over death.

The Alexandrian alchemists, in particular, were ever aware that in pursuing the perfection of metals they were pursuing their own perfection. They worked upon themselves in their laboratories, as surely as they worked upon metals, removing the baseness of both. Indeed, the Alexandrians were amongst the first to speak of the *elixir vitae;* which, centuries later, Bacon himself brought to the West, writing in his *Opus Majus* of "a medicine which gets rid of impurities and all blemishes from the most base metal, can wash unclean things from the body and prevents decay of the body to such an extent that it prolongs life by several centuries." This notion of an elixir supplanted the myth of a miraculous herb or drink that could confer immortality, which myth was common to all European peoples and whose antiquity is certain. . . . Of course, I knew none of this that storming night; but I'd suspicions enough to say to Queverdo Brù:

"Tell me how old you are."

At which he smiled his golden smile, but said nothing more as he busied himself by slipping the rings of Apollonius back onto the fingers of his left hand; and so I pressed:

"Do you now deny your interest in immortality, the same you confessed moments ago?"

Seeming to steady himself, he answered me with words devoid of all personality, chillingly so. "The aim of the true alchemist is and has always been the isolation of the animating spirit, that which allows a thing or being to pass from a lesser state to one more . . . exalted."

"Eventuating in . . . ?"

"Perfection."

"And this perfection, as applicable to the alchemical practitioner is . . . ?"

A pause. "Immortality, yes."

"Ah," said I, triumphantly. So self-contented was I—a fool!—that I recall reaching out, oh so casually, past the python, coiled upon the carpet between us, to take from off the golden tray some sort of hors d'oeuvre. A pastry, it was, if I recall rightly: A layered, flaky confection covered in crushed nuts and honey, honey that I would try time and again to lick from my fingertips till finally I grew embarrassed and desisted, sitting back sticky and yet still thinking myself so very smart when in fact I knew nothing, least of all that I'd approached the edge of an abyss.

Alchemy is ancient, indeed. Born of the arts—both sacred and mundane—of Egypt, Phoenicia, Greece, and elsewhere in the Near East, its chief texts came to be called the *corpus hermeticum,* some fifteen-odd manuscripts that sprouted in the shadows cast by such men as Pythagoras, Democritus, Socrates, Plato, and Aristotle, all of whom came to be classed Masters of the Doctrine. Others—being of a more *fabulous* bent—held that alchemy and its texts were dropped upon us whole by the Greek god Hermes Trismegistus, Hermes the Thrice Great; who engraved this secret knowledge, the *arcana arcanum,* on a great emerald that fell from the forehead of no less than Lucifer himself on the day he was cast down. Hence, these hermeticists refer to the whole of the arcana, or *all ancient knowledge,* as the *tabula smaragdina,* or Emerald Tablet.

Regardless of whether it grew from Eastern obscurities or fell to us on the day of Satan's downfall, alchemy made its way from east to west, flourishing in the twelfth-century monasteries of Europe; and Brù began to scatter the names of certain "monks" before me like crumbs, as if I were a bird who'd peck my way through this lesson of his. . . . Zachaire, Lenselt, Fulcanellie, none of whom I'd heard of. Others, of course, I knew: Roger Bacon, the Swiss Paracelsus, Cornelius Agrippa, and those two alchemists who'd been employed by England's Virgin Queen, namely Dr. Dee and Edward Kelley.

Finally, when asked if I'd read *Les Merveilles de l'autre monde,* written by the Canon of Riez, I replied, rather bitingly, "I have not. . . . *However* have I missed it?"

I had further disappointed my self-appointed tutor; but I cared not a whit. All this yet seemed so abstract . . . so, yes, *arcane.* However would I apply it? What had it to do with me? What's more: I was tired. And with the storm having passed, and the first of the cocks beginning to crow, it grew harder to concentrate. I succeeded only intermittently in keeping from my mind thoughts of Calixto—lost in the city—and Sebastiana—lost to me in the larger world. And if there was one question that kept me attuned, and awake, intent upon Brù's words, it was, again, this: Why had Sebastiana sent me to him? My younger self would have waited for answers to that and other questions; but no longer: I hurried the alchemist on with prods and prompts, all the while mindful of a certain . . . menace, yes, which I could not ascribe to Ourobouros alone, as the snake had coiled again, rejoining tongue to tail.

"And so . . . ?" I would say. "Yes, and then what . . . ?" I would say. Whereupon Q. would set into place another piece of the alchemical puzzle.

I may have yawned at some point. I cannot recall. All I can say for certain is that I asked what all this alchemy had to do with witches, *with me.*

"But I speak not of witches," said Brù, with what seemed a degree of disdain. "I speak of no such *magical* types. I speak of men with naught but knowledge, mortal men in pursuit of . . ."—and he dared not say it again: *immortality*—". . . in pursuit of perfection. That is my point, precisely: I speak of those without powers such as you have."

"Have you no powers, then?"

"I have knowledge only."

"How then do you control your . . . creatures?" And I thought that with his answer we'd come to the crux of it all; but no:

"Control? Oh, no. If I control them, it is as a child controls a pup. They are trained, but only slightly so. If anyone controls them, it is you." Which made no sense at all. However was *I* in control of those light-bright creatures?

"Indeed?"

"Indeed. They heed few commands of mine, and need from me only . . . only the intermittent feeding."

"Explain then the hummingbirds—whose beaks burn, by the way—and the others, the moths and fireflies that I followed here, the peafowl and bats, this python whose company I've kept all night, and none too happily, if I may be frank."

"Ah," said Q., "to explain would require more time and, if *I* may be frank, more attention than you seem able to muster at present, if your weighted lids be any indication. And so, if my words are lost on you at this late hour, witness this"; Whereupon he rose with the aid of his caduceus, quit the tent, and came back moments later with a hummingbird in his right hand. Standing before me, Q. proceeded to wrench, *wrench* from off the tiny bird its two white wings; from which cruel show I recoiled. Upon his pale palm, there the bird sat, wingless, seeming a . . . a thrumming capsule, a cocoon. In his other, closed hand he held the wings, loosely, such that I could see them flapping still, and at that great speed common to the species. Which was worse—the sight of the larval body, or the sound of its dissevered wings flapping—I cannot say; but worst of all was what followed:

Brù bent to feed the bird's body to the python. And from the cage of his closed hand he loosed the wings to fly, to fly to the top of the tent, and to seek—blindly, dumbly—those corners where they remained, flapping, flapping, one here, the other there, neither slowing nor . . . dying through what transpired.

"Alive," said I, leaning carefully forward to watch over the sofa's end that . . . that peristaltic pulse by which the python ate. "Alive?" And then I looked to the wings, on high. "Still?"

"No," said Q., correcting me as though I'd misstated some lesser fact. More chidingly, he continued: "You surprise me, witch. I had thought you'd be better acquainted with the animate dead."

And indeed I was; but this . . .

"They are the deathless spirits of animals that were."

"Deathless? Again, you mean to say—"

"Immortal, yes. But how *tirelessly* you insist upon the word! . . . Yes, these are deathless—*bueno:* immortal—creatures who heed no command of mine. It's you they seek. It's you who stirs them so."

Unwelcome as this news was, I must aver that it was not a surprise. Hadn't I a long association with the disquieted dead? I had. And why would animals—*disquieted* animals; for surely their ends had been less than peaceable— . . . why would animals be any different from humans who'd met similar ends? What's more: Animals had long seemed drawn to me, the more so as my strength had increased; and this despite my disinterest in them; for, unlike many a sister, I had no affinity at all for *the lesser breeds* and kept no familiars. This then—in its way, in its oh so very strange way—stood to reason; but still I asked:

"How then did the birds find me at Señora Almy's, if you did not send them?"

———————————————— ✳ ————————————————

"I knew not where to send them," said Brù. "In fact, this is the first I learn it: that you stay at the Hotel de Luz. (Which place, by the way, you ought to quit: Its proprietress keeps well-oiled keys to every door.) Last I heard from your Sebastiana d'Azur, you may or mayn't arrive here. Spring, summer, or another season. But I knew those winged things would find you if loosed upon the night. . . . Spirit unto spirit. Like unto like, might I say?"

"You might, yes; save I am very much alive, whilst these birds of yours, this coterie of creatures, surely they . . . are not alive?"

"No, no," said he, "they are very much dead. Or rather, they are the distillate of life."

"The distillate of life?"

"Yes," said Brù, retaking to his sofa whilst still the python dined, whilst still the wings crowded the tent's creases, singly, and thus disturbing me even more: had they remained *two*, as wings ought to do, well . . . "But now we touch upon the topic of process. Very important, this. You'll sit some minutes more, will you not?"

What was I to do? Step over the snake, duck the dis-corporal wings, and bid the alchemist adieu? No . . . And so I did sit some minutes more, ever more intent upon Brù's words. As he promised to be brief, so, too, do I, now; for this Missy's mortifying hand seems to mock my memory of those ever-flying wings that knew not the rigor mortis that slows this pen so; *hélas* onward, onward I push, against nature and toward tale's end.

And so, if alchemy is the pursuit of perfection, and its manifestations are manifold—gold, yes; but also . . .

Alors, let me quote Queverdo Brù in asking:

"Is not nature inclined to her own perfection?" This is the chief alchemical tenet; for if nature is *not* so inclined, then no alchemist can hurry her to that end: perfection. "She *is*," averred Q., "she most assuredly is. Left in the womb of the earth, every ore would become gold but only, *only* after hundreds, even thousands of centuries. The alchemist merely precipitates the Rhythm of Time. 'In the hands of an adept, as much may be achieved in a minute as a century,' so sayeth Trithemius. It is an achievement no different from that of the smithgod who first forged tools from ores, from silex, by the Mastery of Fire, speeding processes begun in the Earth Mother. So, too, did man speed nature when first he fired pots from mud scratched from beneath the mother's skin. Do you see?"

"I do," said I; but in truth, still I pondered this principle of perfection from which all his philosophy progressed, and to which it all returned.

"Our aim is simple," said he. "We seek to speed Nature's processes. We seek to speed all things toward perfection."

I knew he was not talking about tools and fired pots now. "*All* things?"

He paused. He sat back upon the sofa; for he'd come forward whilst speaking, whilst preaching, whilst proselytizing. "You tempt me toward talk of immortality," said he with that sly smile, glittering now in the guttering light of late, late candles.

"It is you," I countered, "you and your fraternity who seem tempted not toward talk of immortality, but toward immortality itself. If gold is not your goal—and indeed, greed seems hardly reason enough to sustain such studies for several thousand years—then what is it? Gold is to metal as man is to . . . what? The one-word answer must needs be *immortality*."

But he would not say it. Instead: "Perfection. The Philosopher's Stone. This brings with it the knowledge of God."

"And how is this perfection manifested in man, if not as immortality? Is immortality not the gold standard of man, of *alchemical* man?"

It seemed I'd once again caught him out, disentangled the skein of his sophistry; for, as men will when cornered, he resorted to flattery:

"Ah, witch," said he, "your Sebastiana wrote well of you, and truly, too. You are both subtle and wise, and—"

"And you would not presume to compliment me so if I did not sit here in a skirt. . . . If you wish to speed something this night, pray make it your speech. It is late," I added, "and I've a nosy hostess past whom I hope to slip before first light."

"You will stay here," said he, so matter-of-factly I was taken aback. Barely stifling a laugh, I asked:

"Oh, really? Will I?"

"You will," said he. "I need . . ." And his words trailed away.

"You need what?"

No answer came. "Have *you* not need to quarter somewhere whilst here in Havana? Solitude suits you. This I see. And have you money enough to secure it, there, at your hotel, amidst strangers? You will need to pay for your privacy there."

Indeed, I had not brought much money; for it hadn't seemed that I was sailing *away*. But my sojourn seemed likely, now, to stretch out as I sought Calixto, attended S., et cetera. Still, was I prepared to bed down amidst parading, prying peafowl and bats bright as moonglow? Whilst wondering, I returned to my earlier question: "You. What is it you need? Or are you simply in the habit of hosting sisters?" I thought again of the Duchess, here amidst such . . . *splendor*? Hardly. Unless the house itself—all its many rooms as yet unseen—held surprises beyond my imagining (and indeed it did).

Surprisingly, the alchemist's answer was direct:

"I need you," said he, speaking the words neither as a lamenting lover, surely not, nor as a boasting businessman who says, *I need you, You need me, And together we* . . . No. He needed me. The words were plain, simple. Would that the philosophy underpinning them had been equally plain and simple; but it was not. "Yes," said he, "I need you. For I seek more than gold. I seek . . . success, elevation to—"

"Yes, yes," said I, "elevation to another estate. I know. But what . . . ? How might I . . . ?"

"I rival Nature, yes, in seeking to speed her ways; but it is neither gold nor immortality I seek, no. Rather," and here he hesitated, as indeed he ought to have, preparing to admit, finally, that he . . . *Enfin,* he said it in a whisper: "I seek the Mastery of Time."

"Immortality, you mean," and if I was growing impatient with his indirectness, his reluctance to admit what it was he sought, *in a word,* well, so, too, was he growing impatient with my persistence; and so:

"No!" The word cracked like the lightning that had come earlier. Beyond the canvas walls I heard the up-flutter of winged things. Again he came forward, to the edge of that sofa where now he sat with his ten long fingers entwined. His eyes were wide. The fallen hood of his burnous seemed to flare behind him, as a striking cobra's would.

"I have had success," he intoned. "I have not made gold, but things nearly as precious. I have approached the Stone. And I have . . . perfected living things." Whereupon he cast a glance toward the white wings, flying, flying still, and by association referenced his corps of creatures, which now I knew to be spirits. The animate spirits of animals. But however had he rendered them thus?

"Yes," said he whilst still I stared at the wings, "they are . . . inspirited." How many synonyms would he find for *immortality*?

And oh, how Brù would have loved to have met Sweet Marie. What deviltry mightn't the two of them have achieved? They'd either have ruled—like a double-headed Dis—over some earthbound *otherworld* of their own devising, or they'd have dueled to an immutable death, the one rising to wave the other's slackened skin in triumph. Truly, I shivered at the thought.

"To achieve this," I queried, "the Mastery of Time, as you say, you need me? How so?" I was curious when I ought to have been scared, very.

"Yes," said Brù. "Yes, I need you; for all the world is two. This the Emerald Tablet tells us." Was I yet intent upon the teachings of a Shadow-man quoting words from off a jewel fallen from the forehead of Lucifer? *Parbleu!* This Queverdo Brù could *need me* till Time's End; as for me, I needed *off his roof.* And so it was I determined to rise, to walk from his tent, leave his lair, and make my way back to the Hotel de Luz, led by no light but that of the rising sun, *merci bien.* There, I'd pack my few things, pay the spying señora, and secure my privacy elsewhere. Oh, but then—and would that I'd risen when first I'd thought to— . . . then the alchemist continued and I heard in his words . . . *sense.* And it stilled me.

"All the world exists in two. See how now the skin of this tent lightens as Luna cedes the sky to Sol." Moon to sun, he meant. "Does not the sea reflect the sky? So it is: All things have their twin and are linked, low to high, celestial to terrestrial.

"*Hieros gamos,* this is," said he. "The principle of the Two-Ever-Allied, Luna to Sol, sky to sea, mercury to sulfur . . . So it must be if the Work is to be achieved, if the true Stone is to be secured."

"The 'true' Stone?"

"Yes. The true Stone . . . I have succeeded in securing its lesser forms, but the greater, the *true* Stone, well . . . Some say the true Stone is a living being who possesses the *hieros gamos,* one in whom the two highest of high principles are one. I have long sought such a being. Rebus. Rebus is the name the ancients gave this one."

"I see," said I. His intensity scared me, I admit it. His smile, his eyes verily shone as if he were made of ore and stone, precious or otherwise. "And beyond sky and sea, sea and land, et cetera, these two highest of the high principles are . . . ?"

"The highest of the high are the female and male." I felt a coldness, a chill all out of keeping with the tropical night. "Rebus is the hermetic androgyne. Rebus is . . . you."

When I stood, shooting up star-like from deep in the downy sofa, it was to find I'd set my right foot too near the snake. Or did Ourobouros move to meet me? Regardless, the python—one long, lean, white muscle—now flexed her way up my right leg so that there I stood, snake-fixed and all too comprehending.

 *Chapter Eleven*

. . . He that knoweth not the principles in himself is very far from
the art of the philosophy for he hath not the true book whereupon he should ground his intent. But if he do chiefly and prin-
cipally know the natural causes of himself and know not the
other, yet hath he the way to the way of the principles of the Art.

 —Giorgius Aurach de Argentina, Prettiosissimum
donum Dei (The Most Precious Gift of God),
fifteenth century

W<small>HEN ONE DIES, ALL FEARS ARE FORGOTTEN.</small> T<small>HEY</small> <small>FADE</small>
away. And, as our fears fuel us whilst we are alive, the life
one lived fades away as well. Trying to recall, to recount
one's fears—be they terrors or trepidations—is difficult
for *the quieted dead,* rather like trying to graft leaves back
onto branches from which they've fallen. . . . Which is to
say: Though I recall the weight of that white python
wrapped round my leg, the fear I felt is long gone, and
I must summon *the memory* of the fear for this tale telling.
It is as though we dead see shadows more clearly than we
see the objects that cast them. And so: Onward, at
speed, lest more of the memory fade in time with the
hardening of these limbs not my own.

Snakes are slithery-cool, that much I recall, yes; and
this particular snake, Ourobouros, was weighty as sand
in a sac, weighty as a waterlogged body; but unlike sand-

bags or drowned men, the snake moved, moved as if it were one long, lean, well-trained muscle. And as it rose up my leg, to the knot of my knee and beyond—with its split tongue flicking, and seeming to search out my sex—I felt it flex. It tightened its grip, such that my booted foot began to tingle. Beneath the worn leather at the boot's tip, I saw—saw but could not feel—my toes, wriggling. When I could no longer cause that wriggling, well . . . It was then I said what it seemed I ought:

"I will stay." Or words to that effect. And only then did Brù say:

"I am sorry, truly," referring to the snake; but he was not sorry. Not truly. Not at all, in fact. And only after the alchemist spoke did I feel the snake slacken. Brù may have incanted some spell or spat some command—I cannot say; but whatever the cause—my saying I'd stay, or Brù's recalling the python, or some impulse of Ourobouros' own—the snake all but fell from my leg and retook to its coil. The blood rushed back to my lower leg and foot, needling it such that my laced boot came to seem a sort of iron maiden: a coffin-like restraint inset with spikes. I stamped upon the carpet; and the more I felt my foot, the closer my heel came to finding the snake's light-white flesh; but off it slunk, in search of its saucer of milk.

Doubtless I'd uttered those words, *I will stay*, under duress, whilst wondering what that constriction might bring to a witch whose blood was already troubled. And doubtless I knew I'd lied. Oh, but stay I did. Why? *Alors*, where else was I to go? More: We witches shy from Society's light, do we not, and take to the Shadows despite their depths?

And indeed Queverdo Brù—and his abode—were both deeply shadowed; but far better I'd be with him as my host than the prying Señora Almy, far better his odd domicile than the Hotel de Luz; or so I reasoned, then, having seen that Señora Almy had the Inquisitors' blood of her forebears.

I supposed myself safe, despite the snake; for hadn't Brù said he needed me? Wanted me? His hermetic androgyne, his Rebus. And if he'd not harm me, or otherwise cause me to suffer, then yes, I'd choose Shadow-life over Society proper. Wariness was wanted, that's all; and I was nothing if not wary.

What's more: Brù said he would leave me be; and true to his word, he neither helped nor hindered me in my search for Calixto and Sebastiana. . . . Yes: he let me be. Only later would I wonder if a man who keeps his own counsel, who is all but silent, can be said *to lie*?

I had the run of the house, from the courtyard up to the rooftop tents. Queverdo Brù kept no keys: No door was locked, not even that which gave onto the street; and I wonder now if this rictus, this stiffening slash of mouth belonging to my hostess isn't twitching toward a smile, such is my amusement at imagining someone, anyone, happening upon that tarry door of the alchemist's abode and pushing it back to find:

The porte cochere, dark no matter the hour of the day; but beyond it there spread that fountained courtyard in which I'd found, on the night of my arrival, those opalescent peacocks on patrol. That night I'd not seen much else: The dark and my dread precluded this; but daylight would reveal it all in detail.

The right-side facade, all four floors of it—a plane broken by daubed walls, balconies, and balustrades—bore a species of dark-leafed vine. This had grown thick, its tendrils long ago having leapt from banister to sill, having crept from sill to wall. It wove itself through slatted shutters. It braided itself round the iron bars of windows without panes. By daylight these leaves were the color of cinnamon, and shaped tiny tridents. And in my months of residence beneath the roof of Queverdo Brù, I'd not see the vine wither, but neither would it flower. Oh, but one day I saw it come alive. As so:

Surely I'd stumbled over something, in my graceless way—a paver loose as a hag's tooth, or a planter—whilst walking through the courtyard, up to that third-floor room I'd come to tenant; for all of a sudden, with that sound yet reverberant, I saw the vine's leaves flutter, shimmer as a tide pool will upon receipt of a single, slow-dropped stone, and all of a sudden . . . *Enfin,* they broke from the wall like a wave.

Hundreds, nay thousands of birds there were, big, little, but all blindingly white. Indeed, the shadowed corners of the courtyard sparkled, glistened as the roosting flock flew out from within the twining vine. There were the hummingbirds, yes; but also there were other species—merles, for one: blackbirds that were not black but white—darting through the dark and the light. The effect, the result was a chiaroscuro Rembrandt would have envied.

I fell to my knees, and crossed my arms over my head; for surely these birds would attack as the hummingbirds had. But no: The wave of light receded—I could feel the flap of their wings, hear it, too, but the birds themselves made no noise at all, no cry, no caw. Soon the aviate band retook to its common roost, and I watched as the vine seemed to absorb them, hide them save for what seemed a dim yet steady glow: Imagine the light of a small room wherein a lamp has just been lowered. Soon all the leaves had fallen still, and silence presided. It was then I felt upon my arms what at first I thought was perspiration; but it was—most disconcertingly—guano, golden, fine-grained guano that I washed away in the flow of the fountain. And I mention this grotesquerie for one reason alone: That effluent that had rained down upon me—I had it in my hair, and the shirt I then wore would have to soak for a full day—was not golden in the way a sunset is said to be golden. No: In the thin, odorless guano there shone gold, *actual* gold in the shape of flakes, some large enough to cover the nail of my smallest finger. It was quite like what the hummingbirds had secreted, though it stung not at all, being *upon*, not under, my skin.

Some nights hence, I caused that same exodus again. This time— wiser—I stood sheltered from the fall of precious . . . *shit;* and yes, down it came, glistening: a rain of gold. How odd, how eerie to see the birds in the dark, moving en masse, like a flag of light whipping in an unseen wind. When all fell still, there the courtyard lay, glisten- ing beneath the moon as the streambeds of California will be seen to do beneath the sun. But let me say: Never once did I see this scene and think *Value*, or wonder how I might gather the guano. No: It was all too weird for that. Moreover: Greed was ever low on the list of my many faults, and what riches later came to me came . . . not naturally, no, but . . . *hélas*, all in due time, all in due time.

Upon the right-side wall—and recall: access to the *assoltaire* was via the far left corner of the courtyard—this spreading vine formed a portico of sorts; and in the dank, shit-slick space beneath this dark- ening drape, upon the balconies, there'd been set potted roses. How they grew, I cannot say; for it seemed too dark a demesne for roses. (Doubtless the flow of fertilizer helped.) So grateful was I to see these roses—though they, too, were white, and contributed no color at all to that courtyard showing naught but blacks, whites, and the myriad shades between—I determined to drag a few of the pots out into the courtyard and set them center-all. This I did, only to wake the next morning to find their leaves fallen to ash, as if incinerated by the sun. Or the moon. And well I recall waiting to hear about this from Brù. Doubtless I'd fouled some experiment of his. But if so, he never said a word, though later I found those same pots returned to their places, the roses returned, fuller than before, *transformed*. If I were to admire them—revivified, as it were, the roses had rather less appeal—I'd have to do so in the dark beneath that living, shit-dripping drape. *Merci bien, mais non.* And so it was I came to fancy the cacti.

They were everywhere, and grew without regard to the light. (Yes, these, too, were white.) One, set in a stony pot, in the courtyard, was as big around as a barrel, with spines six inches in length ranged along its folds. Once, I was witness to a hummingbird battle, the which are brutal. A battalion of birds dipped and dove near this cactus, desperate for something I could not see, or did not know to be a hummingbird delicacy. Was it the dew that yet glistened on those spines? Could it have been a morsel of the cactus flesh that was sought? I knew not; and if my tale here lingers overlong it is only to say:

I saw one of the light-birds impaled upon a spine. By day, it was more easily ignored; for the bird itself blended with the sunlight. But by night, well, there the creature shone in its struggle, and in struggling impaled itself upon a second spine. You'll deem me cruel, perhaps—though you will agree: I owed no kindness to those creatures that had summoned me so—but I watched the bird in its throes for a week, maybe more. It was neither vengeance nor cruelty that drew me to that potted cactus each twilight; rather I came to wonder how long the creature could live, struck through and deprived of food or other sustenance. The sight of the bird became quite troubling and eventually I freed it, pushing it from the spines with a stick. It fell to the still-warm stones below, and I watched it where it lay, still, for no more than a minute, its color, or rather its light, undiminished. Was it dead, or . . . doubly so? Or was this like those swordsmen who survive being run through, only to die when finally their enemy's steel is withdrawn? . . . No; for up, up flapped the bird, and back it went behind that living wall of vine when, by Nature's laws, it ought to have *died* days prior.

But in Queverdo Brù's world the laws of nature were not laws at all; rather they were theses, tenets to be tested, and, often as not, disproved. As he'd disproved death. Or (as he'd have said) attained *Perfection*—leastways amongst his fauna and flora.

How was it I stayed at Queverdo Brù's Sinuessa, so like the abode of that name we know from Ovid, where flocks of snow-white doves dwelled? *Alors . . .*

When the nuns at the convent school first threw me away, discounted and discarded me—as indeed they did, having deemed me destined neither for God's glory nor the plainer purposes of man—they threw me—blessedly—into a library, yes; wherein I verily lived, at home in the ash of life, if not its fire. From that day to my death, I could make myself a home wherever a library were present. This I had done both at Sebastiana's Ravndal and the Duchess's Cyprian House, and this I did in Havana as well. I took to Brù's study, ever shuttered and lamp-lit, wherein were arrayed some several thousand volumes, some so old they may have been secreted from Alexandria before that city's library—the first of the world's great libraries—burned some fifteen hundred years ago when Julius Caesar set fire to the Egyptian fleet and flame leapt from ship to shore, taking the library and its store of ancient knowledge.

Brù's library was a large room needful of shelves, wherein I sat upon stacked books whilst perusing others upon a table made of, yes, more stacked books. It was dark, cool and quiet as a crypt, and I was told *in certain terms* to keep it that way; and so I read by lamp or candle, never daring to open a window to let sunlight tint the books or a breeze blow from them that dust-coat accumulated over the ages. (This I did not from fear of Brù, mind, but from love of books.) And I recall that room's earthy tang, an elemental admixture of earth and still, still air. Hours, *hours* passed as I sat in that library; or sometimes I'd take a tome to my room above it, a room equally dark, equally drear. How many hours? I never knew; for all the clocks in Queverdo Brù's home were stopped, as is the custom of his country (so said he), as guests ought never to feel rushed, or hurried from the host's home. . . . Indeed. Would that I had hurried from Brù's; but instead I descended once again into books.

Seated in that library, I'd sometimes draw back from a book and let my witch-fixed eyes refocus upon a ceiling painted with Pompeian murals, pale with age and peeling in places. No doubt an owner prior to Brù had commissioned such pieces; for—to judge from that ceiling crowded with toga'd *philosophes* and the Muses, clustered in its corners—the room had long been a library. Too, ringed round the door's lintel was the charge *"Ora, lege, relege, laborat, et inventis."* Pray, read, *reread, work, and ye shall find.* And this I did (minus the praying, of course). . . . Yes, when those books, and the sheer weight of all they held, pressed upon me, I'd toss a cushion onto the parquet and lie back to look up, to lose myself in a landscape over which Vesuvius loomed; and inevitably my thoughts would hie toward Sebastiana, in whose *Book of Shadows* I'd read descriptions of that volcanic pile, seen when she—*une artiste* of the first order, and bearing letters of introduction to the Neapolitan queen; which letters were signed by that queen's sister and Sebastiana's great patron, Marie-Antoinette—had gone south to make her way, much as she, many years hence, would send me overseas to do the same. But as it saddened me to think of my sister, my savior—*Wherever was she?*—I'd return to Brù's store of books, copying from them into volumes of my own; for to copy is to learn twice over, and knowledge was the water in which I waded, waded whilst awaiting . . . what? The coming of Sebastiana? The return of Calixto? Yes; but also the putting into place of those plans Queverdo Brù had for me, his long-sought Rebus; all of which plans he kept hidden from me 'neath a veil of hospitality.

 ## Chapter Twelve

For all we live to know is known,
And all we seek to keep hath flown.
—EDGAR ALLAN POE, "Tamerlane"

*I*F YOU, READER, ARE A WITCH WELL VERSED IN SIGHT, you'll wonder why I did not seek out Calixto as any Pythoness, any Sibyl, any Seeress might. Well, let this suffice: I was afraid to do so, at first, and thought it better, *safer*, to seek the boy by mortal means.

My search began the morning after I'd been *invited* to stay by Brù and Ourobouros. *To invite* seems not quite the right verb, no, implying as it does politesse and perhaps the gentlest persuasion, whereas the alchemist offered his home to me whilst his pet python threatened to squeeze the Blood from me and hasten my Red End. Was I then *impressed*? *Compelled* to dwell in so strange a place? Regardless, I agreed to stay, having first made it clear that I must, *must* be let to come and go as I pleased; for I'd *not* be captive.

Not much time had passed before I tested my host.

The streets of Havana were still wet when I set out over them by first light, having first climbed down from the tent atop the *assoltaire*. I was ever watchful for any light-born creature coming after me. None did. Not that I could see. And so wary was I of being followed, I soon was lost, having neither plan nor firefly to follow. Luck alone led me back to the Hotel de Luz, where I paid the prying Señora Almy in full, gathered my few things, and returned to take to my room beneath the roof of Queverdo Brù.

Later that same day, though it was not yet noon, I left Brù's house again. I wandered now, and heard the Havanan hours cut by bells into quarters and halves. It was the bells that would lead me—though none too directly—to news of Calixto.

Wandering, *enfin* searching the old city, I reasoned thusly:

Cal was a sailor. He'd been weaned on the sea. To it he'd return, as any boy-child might to his mother's breast. As I'd first confounded and later lied to him, it seemed doubtful he sought me on those same streets. Conversely, it seemed quite probable that he would seek passage out of the city as soon as possible, eager to put blue-green leagues of sea between himself, me, and my mysteries.

I'd worn the dress to elicit pity amidst the port's men: I confess it. But there was greater risk involved now as well, and I was fearful. Of detection, yes. Of molestation, too—corporal or otherwise—coming at the hands of a man; for, if faced with same, how would I hide from any witness or passerby my sisterly defenses? Understand: I did not fear for my safety—surely I knew suitable sister-work, and spells enough to thwart any thuggery—rather I feared *discovery* of the sort that had come from Calixto's witnessing the death of Diblis. Should bad devolve to worse, and someone cause me to strike, well, what would I say to a contingent of the city's thousand-odd soldiers come to stare down at some sister-slain sailor? *Alors*, soon I'd a mind full of lies, one for every conceivable occasion. . . . Oh, but wasn't it lies that had brought all this on the day before? It was. And, *in truth*, the thing I most feared was finding the boy I sought; for whatever would I say to Calixto, caught as I was between lies of little efficacy—he'd seen too much of my witchery to be dissuaded, this I knew—and truths which yet were unformed, were mere words which I could but toss at his feet, like so many dice, shaken and shot from the cup of my heart?

Fearful, I wandered; and—despite the fact that I'd recovered my plan of the city, and had it to hand—I ended up not at the port proper but rather at the cathedral. There I sat attending the hour of the previous day's appointment: noon; for this seemed to me logical. It was not logic, however; it was a lie I told to buy myself time. Calixto was not coming back to that cathedral: Gentle, graced though he was, still he had that outsize pride common amongst young men, pride that can seem a charade at times—I *must* do this or that, I *must* do what a fuller man would . . . —and whereby the heart is suborned to the mind, rather as a rabbit may be said to be suborned to a trap. And Calixto's pride—strengthened, perhaps, by the shaming he'd suffered aboard the *Athée*—would yet be too powerful to allow for his return to the cathedral *the day after*.

I sat a long while at—not in—the cathedral, despite the veritable call of my Saint Sebastiana—quite odd, this, *quite*—and watching the papists parading in and out. Rites were being read for the peacable disposition of the dead; and once a coffin came too near where I sat, in the plaza, and its occupant—or its occupant's after-soul, hovering near—caused my blood to course at that death-speed I so disdained, and sought to avoid at all costs. Again I determined to turn to the plan, lest I, in my wandering, wander too near the massed dead, a cemetery wherein they lay a-churning in their graves. But as I drew forth my plan, I heard two things in succession: the bells broadcasting half-twelve, and a man, coming westward up Empedrado—from the port, I presumed—calling out, in singsong fashion, the weather, as all the Cuban *serenos* do, or did, in another day, their own appellation unchanging even when the weather they sang of was less than serene.

The *sereno* had not come directly from the port; for as I set off in the direction from whence he'd come, I found, at the end of Empedrado, the fish market. I knew it by scent before sight. The sun was high, the day hot, and doubtless the fishmongers still there—at an hour late for marketing—were peddling the worst of their wares.

It stretched an eternity, that market; and I hurried from it, keeping as close to the coast as I could. In so doing, I came upon the Customs House, and the port proper.

In Spanish, in English, in French, I asked questions of any man who did not, on first sight, dissuade me from doing so. There were women portside, too, of course; but they scared me more than the men. Women require the slyest of lies if they are to be won over by another woman. Had I been wearing slacks and a vest, had I bound my breasts beneath my blouse, I'd have asked my questions of the women, be they sailors' mothers, wives, or treats. But, as I wore my dress of *bolan*, it was the men I approached, knowing that in their appraisal of my person they'd be so bald, so brazen, so showy and slow that I'd have time to appraise them as well, proceeding with my plan in accord with those instincts born of my . . . duality; for such instincts always served me well.

I'd bought a pearl-handled fan at a wharfside stall. Expensive though it was, I'd learned at Cyprian House just how efficacious a fan can be when dealing with men whom one must approach (as a woman) alone, and without benefit of introduction. Of course, if it's the man who approaches the woman, the fan must be fluttered in accord with a wholly different set of rules, and one can be less coy than I was, then, saying, to a stevedore who, despite his bulk, was whistling the gentlest of airs, one whose words, I knew, were English:

"Sir . . . Sir?" Speaking the word a second time, I curled it at its end, the way one curls a ribbon with a blade to render it a bow. When this furthered my cause not at all, I made so bold as to snap tight the fan and with it *tap, tap, tap* at his muscled back; his shoulder, more precisely, which already he'd bent toward a barrel on which was written, or stenciled, characters I could not read. Had any of the Cyprians been present to see me at my game, they'd have descended into hysterics; for here was harlotry, the which I quickly fled, saying, pathetically:

"Please, oh please, sir, *do* say you speak English."

He said nothing. But when finally he smiled, I redoubled my efforts, smiling up at him—*up*, I say, as I'd taken care to choose a man taller than myself: No mean feat, this, but a necessary one, as shorter men sometimes grow skittish when made to look up to a woman— and I began to spin a story the particulars of which are of no import now. The gist was this: What ships had left in the last half day, and which were preparing to leave in the next?

Saying nothing, the stevedore returned to his barrels; which now I saw bore alliterative labels in Roman script as well as those characters I'd seen earlier. *Pepper. Poivre,* they read, *Palau-Penang.*

I repeated myself. I pressed. Finally, flinging a fleshy finger outward—as one would fling scraps to a cur—he directed me toward a house, nay a hut, a shingled lean-to over the open door of which there hung a sign: *Port-Master.* This I approached, leaving no thanks in my wake.

Therein I found not the port-master but rather some fat, jowly minion of his from whom I learned the disheartening fact—muttered in a Spanish slurred by the tobacco he chewed, and showily spat—that nearly two thousand ships put in at Havana in a given year. "Señor," said I, in Spanish—and only when angered can one *truly* gauge one's knowledge of a studied tongue—"I am not interested in the traffic of this or any other year. I am interested in ships that may have sailed in the last twelve hours, as well as those readying to sail *as we speak.*"

In truth, I cared little about the ships soon to sail; for already I knew it: *Calixto had sailed.* Witch's or woman's intuition? I cannot say; but as I benefited from both, and sometimes a bit of Sight, *en plus,* my suppositions were rarely wrong. He'd sailed, yes. The questions, then, were these: With whom? To where? And when oh when would he return?

The answers to these questions were to be found amongst papers filed onto the business end of a nail driven into the port-master's hut from behind. From said nail the fat man tore two manifests, or bills of lading, or whatnot, frowning all the while. There I stood, fully expecting this *officer of the port* to turn his palm upward, or otherwise hint of a trade: his information for my coin. This he did not do. Wisely; for already I sought to recall the spellwork of a sister from Bahia who'd severed the hand of a man with words alone. Or had it been his phallus? I could not recall; nor did I need to: Soon I had what I wanted, nay, needed, and it had cost me nothing at all. . . . Understand: thinking my sojourn would be a short one—I'd search out the monk, rendezvous with Sebastiana, ascertain her "surprise," and return to my life, such as it was, on St. George Street—I'd carried limited funds from St. Augustine. If I were to linger longer in the Cuban capital, I'd need what money I had, and I'd not have welcomed an invitation to fatten the fat man's accounts, or grease his already greasy palm.

. . . Information. Yes. And so:

If Calixto had indeed sailed off at the earliest opportunity, the afternoon prior, his options—*legal* options, as I doubted he'd have signed onto a slaver or a smuggling ship, no matter his state of mind—would have been three:

Worst of these would have been the *Bashaw*, a Medford-built ship running the Chinese route. She'd left at first light, bound to round Cape Horn for Coquimbo, Chile, there to take on a cargo of copper and proceed to Canton. A voyage many, many months in the making. Would she return, *ever*? In response to this question, the portly port-officer could only shrug. Neither did he know if or when a second ship—the *Woodstock*— would return to Havana, having hours earlier resumed her run betwixt Philadelphia and St. Salvador with flour in her hold. So it was that my hopes soon rode the seas with a third ship:

The *Halcyon* had put out at dawn for Barcelona. If the winds were fair, the waters kind, she'd be sixty days at sea achieving Spain. There she'd spill her bellyful of "sundries"—so the manifest described her ballast—whereupon she'd take on casks of wine and other wares, and, laden still with three-hundred-odd boxes of Cuban sugar, proceed on to Antwerp. Blessed be, the *Halcyon*'s owners—Burnham & Co.—were housed in Havana, and so the ship *would* return. Someday.

I left the port-master's hut holding to little hope and one name: Burnham, as in Burnham & Co. Calixto may have felt forsaken, not to mention confused by what he'd witnessed of my witchery, but he would not so readily forsake me. I knew this. Rather, I wanted to believe this. He would come back to Cuba. *He would.* And only the *Halcyon* could have offered him both time away *and* a timely return.

Burnham & Co. operated out of a house not unlike Brù's, save that it was clean, well lit, and its inhabitants were rather more alive than . . . otherwise.

Within the office's warren of rooms, Burnham's advocates and foreign agents argued the finer points of the sea trade. In a quiet parlor upon the third floor I found a room of suited, sweating men, sitting as still as their nervous states allowed: Owners and insurers, these were, with naught to do but wait whilst their wealth was yet upon the waves. They sat on creaking, cane-bottomed chairs arranged along the room's walls. Center-all, like a bursting star, there sat an oddly fashioned, octogonal desk. At three of the desk's eight sides there sat secretaries, men whose pens chased numbers up and down the leaves of black ledgers, rather as if they were corralling ants. I cleared my throat at the room's threshold. I readied to speak, to ask if . . .

Before I could essay a word, one of the secretaries sprang up, quick as a shot, and ushered me backward into the hall, so smoothly and so swiftly I hadn't time to take offense. But it was from this fellow— handsome, with black hair so precise it seemed painted upon his pate—that I had my answer.

I asked, Had a boy of Calixto's description—and the secretary took pity on me, or perhaps Cal, when thrice I repeated the word *pretty*—signed aboard the *Halcyon* for its run to Barcelona?

Without recourse to any ledger, any letters of intent or contracts, the secretary said, *"Sí."* He'd signed up Calixto himself. It was a six-month consignment. To Barcelona, Belgium, and back. And lest I doubt him, the kindly secretary offered a description of Calixto so accurate I felt my throat constrict and my cheeks grow warm from the first of my fallen tears.

"Six months? . . . Are you certain?"

"Señorita," said he, "we speak of the sea—nothing is certain."

By now it was too late to sail after the *Halcyon*. Even if I could have found a willing carrier, the winds might never speed us to her side. And if they did, and we weren't shot at, repulsed as pirates, what then?

We'd pull up alongside her hull and I, jolly as you please, would scramble onto the ship in search of a boy who might well want nothing to do with me? *Absurd.* No sister could have rendered that scenario less than absurd.

What was there to do but wait? . . . Had my heart been an anchor—and not merely heavy as one—I'd have hurled it out to sea to see it sink with speed and drag me down behind it.

Just where I wandered from Burnham & Co., I cannot say. But eventually I came to the corner of calles Mercaderes and O'Reilly, and found myself before the tall doors of La Felicidad: A restaurant that was all glass and white tile and fans slow-churned by boyish Cubanos, its doors open to the hot, dusty street. This was a haven, and I'd come to spend many a long hour there in its sweet-smelling, cool confines. La Felicidad was renowned for its ice creams, its sherbets of guava, guanabana, and every other fruit found in the tropics. I ordered one that day—the guava—and ate it as it glinted, like pink glass, with a spoon baked of brown sugar. Only when I followed the ice with coffee—poured simultaneously from two pots, the one of coffee, the other of hot, salted milk—well, only then did I give in to those tears that caused my waiter to back from my tiny corner table with a sad smile.

I sat at that marble-topped table crying as quietly as I could. It seemed life was a game, one at which I was destined to lose. . . . Perhaps it was then, and only then, that I admitted to myself how I'd come to love Calixto, how I'd come to harbor hopes of *him and me,* the entity we'd be.

Having sought and found Calixto by mortal means, soon I fell to wondering what role witchery would play in my pursuit of him. I knew no Craft could call him back to Cuba, just as none could speed me to Spain. Neither could Craftwork shear the days, the weeks, the months from off the calendar. . . . But there was one thing I could do, where I sat, in a crowded La Felicidad. I could gain *certainty*. Certainty that would spare me six months waiting in Cuba, watching the sea as pointlessly as a widow in her weeds. Would Calixto come back? Yes or no?

I was hesitant, as always I was when using Sight. Though it was a simple yes or no I sought, what might a no portend? Calixto's choosing to stay in Spain? His never arriving there, or never returning hence, the *Halcyon* lost to the sea? Still, crying, I divined; thusly:

I called for oil, telling the sympathetic waiter any oil would do (though that of the walnut is preferred, olive oil works as well). It—olive oil—came. I poured it onto a white plate, and mixed in pepper (ash is preferred, but any blackening agent will do). Then, with the corner of my napkin, I rubbed the oil onto the nail of my right thumb. (A virgin is preferred, *mais hélas,* one makes do . . .). Then, having made certain I faced south—as this was divination pertaining to a person, as opposed to money (face east), crime (west), or murder (north)—I smoothed the peppered oil over the nail, asking all the while, sotto voce, Will Calixto come back to Cuba? Will Calixto come back to Cuba? Will Calixto come back to Cuba? (Others hold that a recitation of the psalms lends greater efficacy to such Sighting as this, known as *onimancy,* but I'd long since quit traveling with a Psalter.)

It is said that if the spell shows no effect on the oiled nail, the answer to one's query is *no.* If the blood beneath the nail is so agitated as to turn the nail blue, one has an answer in the affirmative. No more than a minute passed whilst I sat mumbling in a corner of La Felicidad; and then I had my *yes:* My thumbnail went beyond blue to purple, and progressed further to that black-purple common to nails that have found themselves slammed twixt a door and its jamb, or hit with the harder end of a hammer. I wondered would I lose the nail? But I didn't care, not really—and neither did I lose the nail: It cooled to its normal color by morning; for I was happy, happy despite learning *with certainty* that I'd six months to wait before I could undo what I'd done and tell my truths to the boy I wanted in my life till its last day.

I hurried from La Felicidad that night, having determined to return to Brù's and write Sebastiana. I'd cast the ciphered letters out wide, anywhere my sister was likely to be looking for me. (Still I believed she sought me, somewhere. I believed it in my witch's Blood.) My thinking was this: Yes, I sought my sister and that surprise she wrote of, but moreover: If I'd six months to spend in Havana, waiting, I'd want better company than that of Queverdo Brù.

Dearest S. (I wrote),
I am here, in Havana. You are not.

I cannot say I am surprised; for to do so would be to lie, and I have forsworn all lying. Of course, I never lied to you, sister: I hadn't the need: You knew me, know me as so few do. And that makes your absence here harder to bear.

Oh, S., where are you?

Receiving your letter——and was it the last you sent, that one directing me hence and telling, teasingly, of a certain surprise?——I set sail. I owe you, sister. I do as you bid me do. But I ask again: Did another letter follow fast upon that last? A letter explaining, or at least excusing your absence now, here, from Havana? If so, I never received it, and so I wonder: Where are you? And why am I here, when to be here seems to serve not me, not you, but rather this Darkman, Brù? To whom you, in collusion with the Duchess——yes, I will call it collusion, and let stand that measure of anger that weights the word——sent me. Why, why, why, if not to serve this ancient alchemist who wants and needs me (so says he)?

To explain:

I'd found an uncut copy of *Paul et Virginie* at a stall beyond the city walls, and so was able to retake to our cipher of old. It was simple. Numbers, set onto the pages of my letter without punctuation, would direct its recipient—and how I hoped this would be Sebastiana alone, and not that dread, pseudodemonic consort of hers, Asmodei—to letters, and sometimes whole words, on the corresponding pages and lines of the French novel. If it sounds complicated, it was not. Or rather let me say, we witches were accustomed to cipher, to reading and writing it; most sisters are. Indeed, a parlor game of sorts, at Cyprian House, had involved the deciphering of long excerpts from certain *Books of Shadows* that had fallen into the Duchess's care and which comprised—then, before the house's dissolution and the Duchess's disappearance—a wealth of witchery: the secrets of sisters from this or that century, this or that country. . . . Secrets, yes. And now I'd a few of my own and these I confided to Sebastiana with care; thusly:

I wrote you of Sweet Marie, did I not? I'm certain I did; but I am less certain you received said letter; and so, concisely:

Sweet Marie was, is, a sister in solitude. More: She is a witch unlike any other I've read or heard tell of. Leastways, I hope there is no other sister as demonic, as deranged as she. She rules an empire all her own deep, deep—I know not where, exactly, despite my long captivity there—in the Never-Glade, that tract of scrub, swamp, and bladed grass that spreads over the southerly part of the Florida peninsula and approximates the very scape of Hell. Glass Lake, this is: an island, in fact, surrounded by the eerie blue waters of a lagoon the source of which—so sayeth Sweet Marie; and I'd not have believed her if I'd not witnessed the waters' effect with my own eyes—is that legended spring sought by Ponce de León and myriad others. De León died leaving the fabled fountain unfound. Or so the world supposes. But Sweet Marie keeps it, or kept it—I may have blasted her waters with my Blood; but that's a story for when next we meet—and keeps, too, a corps of men on whom she tests its effect. . . . Too hideous, the details!

And I may or may not have written you of the Cyprians, but you know of them; for it was you who consigned me to their care, you who drew me northward thinking it was you I'd meet in Man-hattan. Sly sister! How I despised you for that petty de-

ceit! (*I know you have not done the same again, S., as cruelty does not become you.*) But in time I came to love the Cyprians, and by their . . . *titillating tutelage* I learned, yes, as you'd supposed I would. Thereafter, though, I left Gotham, going south again in search of my Celia. You may not know the particulars—I am fairly certain you do not—but I must spare myself the reliving of the pain pursuant to that period, and here will offer naught but these few nouns and let you, sister, if you choose, forge the links between them: love, of course, and loss; but between these two words I must place spellcraft, too sloppily done, and this death-alliance that has come to both weigh upon me and strengthen me so; and sadness; servitude, nay, slavery, for I ought not to demur at this late date; and longing, lies, and life, this last being the thing I no longer wanted once Celia was lost to me. And lost she is, lost she long has been, having set off for the Mexican territory alongside some members of her adopted tribe, the Seminole. I haven't dared to divine her life in detail, but I have Seen enough to show me she is happy, or happier than once she was.

Once I'd returned to Florida, and sought and found Celia, I found myself horribly, horribly alone. I drew back, deeply, and tried to lose myself in the Craft. (*I never could. To this day I work it only as I must.*) It was a living death, even though, as a witch, I was wondrously strong, owing to an encounter with a hundred massacred men. (*More details over which I cannot dwell, not now.*) . . . Perhaps I ought to thank you, sister—even as I am inclined to do the opposite, it is true—for writing, finally, and directing me here; for otherwise I'd have withered away in St. Augustine. And, what's more: In following your directions I found a fellow.

He is called Calixto. A sailor-boy half my age. Is he my boy, as Roméo once was yours? (*How are dear Roméo and his Derrich? Do they accompany you still? Will we all meet again when finally our paths cross?*) If so, I fear I have complicated said pact, may have precluded it even, by letting this Calixto witness my witchery before he was ready. (*I killed a man, albeit one deserving of death, by kinetics: a flying knife to the eye. This, Calixto witnessed.*)

And now he is gone; for I failed him.

With no family of his own, Calixto wanted my company. Had chosen it. This I know. But I let him go. Yes: Unwilling to lie yet unable to tell my truths—and you *know, sister, that my witch-ness is not the weirdest of those truths—I failed the boy, failed to keep that rendezvous at which I ought to have spilled my sisterly, my sexual truths. . . . Oh yes, I hear you, S., stating that it is counter to custom to speak our truths to mortals till we are certain they've come as consorts; but here let me counter your complaint thusly, asking:*

Where were you when I needed you?

Nowhere, as now. Neither in person nor by proxy, nor pen.

Where are you? Did you not say you'd come? Where are the letters you ought to have written me? If you know this Brù, surely you know how to get a letter to his abode?

Oh, S., seeing now that I ramble and lambaste you at length, I shall desist. I love you, sister. I always will. In you I found a savior and a sister, friendship and family. This I shan't forget. Neither can I stop supposing what might have happened to me at the convent school if you'd not shown. Many a night I've given thanks—to the goddess, to the moon, to you—for the fate I did not find there. And these words notwithstanding, I do not blame you for all that has transpired since you saved me. Yes, you saved me; but thereafter my life was mine to lead. I did what I knew how to do; and if someday I know better, I will do better.

But what of now, S.? Again my heart aches. I want you. I want this boy Calixto, who has sailed to Spain and beyond, and shall not return till a half year has passed. He will return, it's true. I've seen it. But what will I do for a six-month here in Havana, with no company but Brù's? Tell me. Write, please, from wherever you are. Better yet: Come!

I signed the letter *Amitiés, Amour,* and closed with my single initial—H.—whilst regretting that I hadn't Sebastiana's talents; for she signed her letters grandly, her wavering *S* seeming a pennant pulled this way and that on the wind, and sketched in its lower loop a toad. Oftentimes this was no mere sketch, but rather a depiction worthy of her former repute as a portraitist. Those toads marked her Book and every letter much as they, or rather an image resembling their globe-toed feet, marks the Eye of every witch. . . . Too late I realized that I hadn't told Sebastiana that my own Eye was now fixed, that I'd woken from *my first death*, if you will, amidst the men of Dade's Command, with my Eye holding to the Toad; which strange feature I had since concealed, as necessary—that is: when in Society—by sporting those blue'd sunshades.

Finally, having folded the three sets of twinned letters—letter the first pointed Sebastiana toward the cipher, or *Paul et Virginie*, whilst letter the second was itself *in cipher*—I mailed all six, separately, to those places I thought she might be:

Set the first to France. To Ravndal. Though woe betide her if she wrote back from there whilst here I sat in Havana, head half-cocked and listening for the creak of Queverdo Brù's door, or some lesser sign of her imminent arrival.

Set the second I sent to St. Augustine. Perhaps, thinking I'd not heeded her command to sail for Havana, and to Brù, Sebastiana and company had gone there to search for me. If so, two letters would await her poste restante, in the *S* cubby of that same storefront where I'd long awaited word from her.

Finally, the third set of letters I sent to New Orleans, into the care of the witch Eugénie, a former Cyprian whom S. knew from my earlier letters. I hoped Sebastiana would seek out Eugénie if somehow, for some reason, she'd sailed to the mouth of the Mississippi, drawn thither by that city's French and its surfeit of sisters.

Off the letters went. Now there was naught to do but wait. Wait for replies. Wait for Sebastiana to show. Wait for Brù to make use of me. Wait for Calixto to come back. . . . *Enfin*, wait for six months to pass as slowly as syrup from a hand-wrung length of cane.

 *Chapter Thirteen*

The alchemist should be discreet and silent,
revealing to no one the result of his operations.
—ALBERTUS MAGNUS, *Libellus de alchimia*

*A*ND PASS THEY DID, THOSE SIX MONTHS PRIOR TO CAL-
ixto's return to Cuba. In point of fact—and let *fact* con-
strain this narrative, if not its narrator—the boy came
back to Cuba inside of a six-month; and arrived not a
moment too soon; for . . .

Stay. . . . The temptation to speed this tale is great,
as I'd like to not have to search out a second host, another set of hardening hands with which to tell this tale
to its end; for this Missy serves me as well as any other
corpse could. Of course, a *living* hostess . . . ? *Alors*, if
only it were possible. Gladly, quite gladly, I'd trade this
unsought immortality of mine to once again *feel*, to
once again *hear* my heart hammering as my beloved
draws near. And oh, how I miss, too, the taste of tears,
and the heaviness of plaited hair; . . . miss even the
sourness of the mouth after sleep; . . . miss all the

tastes, the sounds and sights of things mortals know and take for granted.

Hélas, listen and mark me well, sister: You will one day die. Likely it will be the Coming of the Blood that renders you Aether (call the After-state what you will). And all that was, *is* you, will distill down and join the essence of all those others etherealized by death through the ages. That's if you're lucky. If not, if you have *talents* such as I had, well . . . Read on. Manifold and multiform are we who mutate under the press of death. Oh, but meanwhile, sister, live. *Live!* And believe me when I say that none of what the dead know can compare to all that passes through the mortal sensorium.

As regards this child I inhabit, and use: She is but as a well, and I the water within; for her quieted soul has ensilvered and ascended. Indeed, she lessens even now, diminishes further unto death even as I digress. And so, onward: I shall leave off mourning my mortal self forthwith and resume the story I've proposed to tell: *How I came to die.*

As I recall it now, my sojourn does not self-divide into its component parts: neither seasons, months, weeks, days, nor even hours. Rather, I recall that time as divided into days, and nights, each distinct from the other for reasons beyond the obvious.

By day I sat in Brù's library, or my room, reading, reading, reading. And if his interests had inclined toward any topic other than alchemy, it may be safely supposed that I'd have become expert in *that* field as well; for I found refuge not in the study of alchemy, per se, but rather in study itself.

At night, I wandered, and only by moonlight did I do what had to be done: I arranged for the posting of letters, sought information from the port-master's men pertaining to any ship due to arrive from either France, Florida, or the mouth of the Mississippi, despite being told, time and again, "Ships don't come, señorita, to speak of another ship's coming. They simply show." Too, I would visit Burnham & Co., to ask (in vain) what news they had of the *Halcyon:* Had she arrived in Spain, or set out again for Antwerp, or, perhaps, turned her sails toward home? Only at night did I sup, as well. I kept a simple store in my room, replenishing it at market stalls that stayed open late or opened at first light, that hour at which I'd often hurry home like some vampiric creature dreading the dawn; whereupon I'd sleep away the hotter hours of the day. . . . Why?

I lived as I did, shying from the sun, from light, for one reason only: At night I could see the light-creatures sent by Brù to track my every move. I cannot say *he spied upon me* by such means; for I don't know how those illuminate assemblies of his—be they composed of peacocks, cats, bats, rats, or his hundreds of hummingbirds, bees, butter- or fireflies—might have reported back to their creator. Perhaps he somehow accessed their sight, as Sebastiana once had done that of a crow, or raven, when, long ago, she'd had the bird fly above the coach in which I traveled south from Ravndal in the company of those elementals whose bidding I would do, Father Louis and Madeleine de la Mettrie. She, Sebastiana, had effected this trick by melding witch-work and dreams. Had Brù the same ability? I doubted so; and cannot say if he saw my actions *in the particular*. More likely he *read* the birds and other creatures and by their state of upset knew what I did: Did I sit in my corner of La Felicidad, or did I prowl the port in search of a sea passage? What might the flock have done in the latter case? I wonder. For Brù would never have let me sail. I came to suspect as much, and soon enough I would have proof.

Alors, Brù said he'd no powers, only knowledge; but still those creatures came. Of course, when questioned, he denied sending his creatures after me, said they came of their own accord, that it was I who drew them. Regardless, not long into my tenancy I determined it would be best *to know* when they were about. Far worse it was *to feel* them near, and yet fail to find them against the daylight. Worse still was feeling the fall of that gold-flecked feces—its source unseen— and having to wipe the grain, the grit of it from my skin, my shirt, my hair. So it was I donned hats both day and night, broad-brimmed and lacy, which luckily were the fashion then; and thusly did I spare my- self both the falling gold-shit and the censorious glances of the more fashion-conscious Havanans.

Of course, as Brù's library was large, quite, I read by night as well. I'd choose two or three books, place them in a canvas satchel bought for that purpose, and set out—my light-guard above—for La Felici- dad. There I would linger over a dinner: some dish done up with onions, garlic, and peppers, the like of which set my palate aflame; for I'd become accustomed to duller, Floridian fare, which is to say: fish, poached in pockets of palm leaves, or grilled, dully, by *moi-même.* Too, I'd further tarry over one, sometimes two of those wondrous desserts featuring fruits such as soursop, and nuts whose names I'd never learn. Yes, there'd be dinner, then dessert, and still I'd sit at my corner table—it became *my* table owing to coin, and that same kindly waiter, named Joachim—with a bottle of Catalan wine, or perhaps coffee, depending on the hour and my interest in whatever text I'd spread be- fore me. If it bore on prophecy, for example, I'd call for more of the wine. Theology? That would require coffee, as black and bitter as the text itself.

Only once did Brù—who had a most disconcerting habit of ap- pearing unannounced by any noise: There he'd suddenly be, behind me, staring out blankly from the full hood of his burnous— . . . only once did Brù balk at my bringing a book to La Felicidad. I forget its title; but Brù cared not a whit about the book's contents. "Too frag- ile for transport" was all he said, pulling the book from my rucksack so rudely he damaged it more than I would have if I'd *flung* it toward

La Felicidad. As this was early in my *apprentissage,* I supposed, then as now, that Brù simply wanted me to know that *he* knew what I was up to: That I'd carved into his library as a starveling would well-salted meat, and walked about the city at will.

Though I was some months under Queverdo Brù's roof, and found a measure of refuge in his library, he was hardly a companion and his house was hardly a home. I spent as few hours in the alchemist's company as I could, in fact; and even fewer when, midway through my stay, I grew more suspicious of his intentions. Never would he say *why* he wanted me near. Was I scared? No, not really. *Wary* is the better word. Should I have been scared? Undoubtedly so. Mostly, I was confused; and those rare occasions on which I sought Brù's company were spurred by this confusion. I'd go to him atop the *assoltaire* with my questions. Answers? Surely he had more than he gave; for he spoke in riddles, half-truths, and tautologies. And—I'd learn later—lies.

And so, no: Brù was no companion, and neither was he what I'd hoped he'd become: a teacher. Little surprise, then, that I came to forgo his company—not to mention his confused and confusing catechism—choosing solitude instead. Too, I took to retreating to a room, a sort of study I let elsewhere in the old city, a place where I could shutter back both Brù and his espial brigade; for it stands to reason, does it not, that a witch such as I was would value her privacy? The more so when she is *under watch.*

What did I learn, reading at Brù's by day and, by night, in the quietest, lamp-lit corner of La Felicidad, or in my secret study? *Enfin,* I learned about astrology, and astronomy, and tried as best I could to attune my ear to the Music of the Spheres. I studied mathematics, but only as was meet *and no more* (as too many numbers could make my turned Eyes roll). Chemistry, too, as there was much in Brù's library treating of that subject, it being the spawn of all the alchemical arts.

Bref: I roamed all those texts searching for where the roads of Craft and Science cross; for there—at that crossroads—one finds alchemy. . . . Sadly, I know whereof I speak; for it was upon a metaphorical cross of another sort, the arms of which were indeed Craft and Science, and the whole of which was Alchemy, that I'd be crucified. Oh, but that was yet years in the offing, despite Brù's best efforts. And so let me retreat from such end-talk and return to particulars; as per:

"Speak of the Rebus." This I commanded of Brù one day at dawn, some while into my stay.

I had just returned from my study and met the alchemist in his courtyard. (Brù knew about my refuge. I'm sure of it.) I'd been frustrated by the prior night's chosen texts, still tucked in my satchel. Each had proved more abstruse than the last.

"I read and I read," said I. "I read till my eyes seem *to swell*, and still . . . nothing! So tell me: What of this hermetic androgyne whose name you'd have me bear?"

Indeed, Brù referred to me as Rebus if he referred to me at all, but he'd not said any more on the subject since the night he—and his pet python—had *persuaded* me to stay. And since that strange invitation, Brù, learned though he may have been, did naught but confuse me further, as did his collected texts; which confusion I attributed to my own obtuseness, though—truth to tell—I'd never before found myself inadequate before any teacher or text. Thusly frustrated, I redoubled my efforts, reading through some texts twice, even thrice. Now, of course, I know that *to confuse me* was the alchemist's aim.

Brù stared at me when queried so directly that long ago dawn. I stood before him in expectation of that sly, golden smile, or a cold laugh, or something equally dismissive; but Brù seemed somehow pleased, impressed to see that I was applying myself, studying deeply enough to have become dismayed, angered by that sophistry with which all the texts were stuffed. Of course, I was assuaged not at all when Brù answered, nay, when he simply said—for it was no *answer* at all, and indeed it'd be a long while before I'd learn more of the Rebus—this:

"Nec scire fas est omnia."

"Oh, please," said I, too tired for an ancient tongue, "speak a *living* language."

Brù indulged me. "Horatius, that is."

"Good. Horatius. Who says . . . ?"

"Who says, 'We have not been ordered to know everything.' "

"Haven't we? Haven't *I*, at least?"

Brù said nothing in response, and I spoke on: "Haven't *I* at least to learn why I am here? Why you three"—and I spoke now of Brù, the Duchess, and Sebastiana d'Azur—"have conspired to bring me here?" I was right to speak of conspiracy, but wrong to implicate my sisters: As said, they had acted innocently, and had never meant to *offer me up* to Brù.

Perhaps the alchemist pitied me. (I thought so then, though I know better now.) Perhaps he thought me ready, after weeks, nay, *months* of book-work, for what he'd reveal next. *En tout cas*, he led me up to the *assoltaire* that morning, and further:

Into the largest of the tents we went. This was next to that tent in which I'd been received, when first I'd come. I'd not been in this tent before—I'd not been forbidden it, but neither had I been invited; and though I saw it was crowded with the accoutrements of Brù's study, as I'd supposed, the first thing I did was cast a glance into each of the tent's corners, looking for Ourobouros. And sure enough, there lay the python beside a black bowl of milk, its surface shimmering where the flaked gold was afloat. Odd as it sounds, I wondered not at the gold within the milk but at the milk itself. From whence did it come? Queverdo Brù rarely if ever ventured out—in fact, I'd never known him to leave—and if anyone came bearing comestibles of any kind, well, again, I never saw such a delivery. Too, neither did I see Brù eat. Ever. And so it seems likely that what I saw his slithering, strangling pet lap at was not mere milk, but rather something concocted by Brù in that *sanctum sanctorum* high above Havana, which now I took in for the first time.

Immediately I saw that it served a twofold purpose: laboratory, of course, but chapel as well; for in a corner of the canvas room there sat an oratory of sorts, anchored by an altar of carved hardwoods. Did Queverdo Brù pray? If so, to whom? To what? I'd no care to ponder the alchemist at prayer. Far easier it was to focus on Brù not as *priest,* but as *practitioner;* and so it was I turned my attention from his oratory to the more practical aspects of his work, as set out in his laboratory.

It seemed more a smithy or potter's shed at first glance. Center-all there sat a furnace—called an athanor, from the Greek *athanatos:* "immortal"—wherein the alchemical fire was tended with bellows and tongs, *and never let to die.* Its heat rose visibly to a hole in the tent's top: a sphincter of sorts, to speak plainly, plated round with sheets of tin, lest the whole tent be sent up by a wayward spark. This athanor clearly had pride of place over the oratory. So, too, were the surrounding tools intended to serve *it,* and not the altar. Arms came off the athanor—rather as legs come off the carapace of a cockroach—and to these adjustable arms of iron were affixed hand-like clamps to hold heated vessels. Vessels, yes; there were vessels of every conceivable shape and size: alembics, cucurbits, crucibles, flasks, beakers, and simpler tubes. There were vessels blown of glass, and pots made of porcelain. The many bowls scattered about, and stacked lopsidedly, seemed hewn from the same wood as the altar; but these were rudely fashioned, whilst the altar, surely, had been someone's life's work, so detailed was it, with stories told in layer upon layer of relief. At the foot of a long worktable, there sat an iron contraption built to display pestles, and therein some fifteen or twenty were arranged on end, ascending in height: from tiny ones of wood to the largest, seemingly sculpted from a single block of basalt.

Upon lesser tables I saw scales of balance, compasses, sextants, sieves, trowels, and tongs . . . tongs everywhere, some with rag-padded handles that told that fire was the tent's presiding element. Best not to touch anything, lest it burn. And there were timekeeping pieces of every kind, some upon the floor, others hung from the tent's iron frame. Clocks, yes, some square-faced and others circular, but all with arrested arms, like those of the library's clock; but the laboratory's clocks had not been stopped owing to some ancient notion of hospitality. So I supposed; for here, too, were hourglasses, all of them emptied of sand.

Queverdo Brù came up behind me where I stood, staring at one such stopped timepiece. He'd come too close, and done so too quietly, and too quickly, such that it seemed his words were not so much spoken as set within my ear. "Time is a despot," said he; and proceeding ever more excitedly, he added, in what seems now to have been whispers, "but together, as one, we can slip its constraints. We can be done with it. We can . . . discard it."

I heard his words, but their sense escaped me. No doubt I conveyed this, staring at his hooded face whilst backing away from him with what subtlety I could muster. I'd had enough puzzling philosophy of late. So it was I made show in withdrawing from my purse a watch, the same watch I wore upon a chain fastened to my vest pocket when dressed as a man, and said, "Luckily, I carry a watch of my own, señor. And now it tells me that it is time to . . ."

"Yes?" said a leering Brù. "Time to . . . ?"

I'd flipped open the watch's case to find its face dumb, dumb as mine must surely have been; for its arms had slackened, had fallen to half-six, and its hands seemed clasped, pathetically, in prayer. Oddest of all: I'd had recourse to the timepiece that very morning, when, in

❋

leaving my study, I'd sought to identify the exact hour of the sun's rising. And now here it was: silent as all its ancestors in Brù's timeless tent.

"Well?" said Brù. "What does your watch tell you, my Rebus?" His was a face that recast itself in smiling, as do those of some men I'd met. Such metamorphoses can seem evil, eruptive, as if a second face rises as a palimpsest of the first.

"That it is time to retire," said I. And this I did, descending from the *assoltaire* with Brù's laughter behind me, ringing out over the Havana morn.

Back in my drear, despised room—naught therein but a cot, an oil lamp, and the consoling thought that the Duchess had slept there before me—I wound my watch to no avail. If time were indeed a despot, it had decreed death unto that particular piece. And there was nothing I could do but . . . discard it. As Brù had said I would.

When next I went to Brù's laboratory, it was to seal my fate; for I asked if I might stay till the end of the six-month. More: I made the mistake of telling Brù that I'd determined to await the return of Calixto, and still hoped for Sebastiana to show. "Wise" was all he'd said when I'd told him of my plans and asked—to my *everlasting* regret—if I might stay. "Wise indeed."

I did not linger overlong in the laboratory that second time, nor ever; for it was hot as Hades, with Brù stoking the fire in his athanor. Too, the alchemist was always there. I assumed he slept in one of the lesser tents nearby. Why he kept so large a home . . . well, I saw no reason. Most of its rooms were unused, or so it seemed, save for the library and my bare-bones *suite* above it, and the menagerie kept to its periphery: peacocks in the courtyard, birds of every species nesting deep in the cinnamon-colored creeper, et cetera. (I never delved too deeply into those stalls.) And that was another reason I preferred being elsewhere once the sun set: It was eerie, unspeakably eerie seeing those luminous creatures beneath the moon, crowding into corners of the courtyards, and ever silent amidst the white roses and cacti. Yes, better by far to be out on the street, or in the populous safety of a lamp-lit La Felicidad, or, best of all, in my study, and having to suffer the sight of those creatures only as I came and went, seeing the avian ones near but not too near: a fallen constellation of sorts.

It was on that second visit that I spied the alchemist indulging in a strange habit of his: Before he knew I was near—and standing at the top of that ladder from which I could see him in his tent-cum-laboratory, the sides of which were folded back—I saw him lick the four fingers of his left hand, press them into a black bowl he held in his right, and then return the fingers to his mouth, as though the bowl were full of *chantilly*, or some such delicacy. Of course it was not.

Doubtless I stood staring too long. Regardless, soon I knew from the tilt of Brù's hood that he'd seen me; . . . whereupon he dipped and ate again. As I came nearer—he'd beckoned with those same, sun-dipped fingers—I saw that the black bowl was brimful with flaked gold. *Queverdo Brù ate gold*, as casually as another man might snack on nuts, smoke his cigars, or sip on his Scotch whiskey. As to what cellular process this precipitated or perverted, well, I asked and had only this as response: "Perfection. Ever and always, perfection."

Before meeting Queverdo Brù, perfection had seemed a worthy if unattainable goal. Rather like piety, I suppose, before I forfeited it along with all the lesser, external trappings of faith. But now, with Brù, perfection of the alchemical kind seemed all about . . . well, burning things. That's all Brù seemed to do: *burn, burn, burn*. Of course, he and his brethren wouldn't have called it burning, but rather cineration or something equally elevated (if not beyond English altogether, and on to other languages, both living and long dead); for they had such whole-dollar words for all the processes through which matter passed, supposedly, in its ascent toward perfection: putrefaction, coagulation, calcination, fixation, digestion, distillation, sublimation, multiplication, mortification, conjunction, dissolution, corrosion, ignition, precipitation, liquefaction, exaltation, purification, and yes, finally, perfection. All of which alchemical processes are grouped into *four stages;* which stages the alchemists—adopting that nomenclature coined by no less an adept than Heraclitus—refer to by *their representative colors:* Nigredo (for black), Albedo (white), Citrinitas (yellow), and Rubedo (red).

Still, it seemed to me that the practical alchemist was, primarily, pyromaniacal: *He burned things.* Why? Well, the alchemical adept concerns himself with matter as it changes state; and, I suppose, cineration— the rendering down to ash—is more easily attained than another of the above, multisyllabic states. *Throw it in the athanor and see what happens.* And if I simplify said processes, and the alchemist's intent, so be it: Alchemy and its practices benefit from *my* preferred process: *simplification.* This pyromania has its purpose, it must be said: Throw it in the athanor, yes, but watch, see if the substance reveals itself; for, said they, it sometimes—though rarely, *very* rarely—did, and the lucky puffer standing fireside, his bellows at the ready, might just benefit: If the burned thing should render down to something more than ash, i.e., *the sought thing, the Philosopher's Stone,* thereby ascending to purification and perfection, so, too, would the practitioner be purified and yes, perfected. Though perfection—manifested as immortality, of course—was so rare as to be *unrecorded* in ten-plus centuries of alchemical texts. That is, until now. Here. Upon these pages.

At first I'd thought Brù only wanted me near, the better to effect his . . . science, such as it was. Hadn't Sebastiana once said the same?

———————————————— ❄ ————————————————

That I—as a new witch—could effect certain aspects of the Craft that she could not? Indeed she had; and so it seemed sensible to me. I thought I'd have nothing to do whilst waiting out the six months but sit at Brù's side, or as near to his side as I could bear to be. (No perfume could hide the stench of that sweat-stained, ragged robe of his, not to mention the unwashed body beneath it.) And so I suppose I consented, albeit tacitly, to be his Rebus. Of course, had I known what the Rebus was—or what Brù supposed it to be—I'd have slipped from his side, run from his home, and swum from Havana if need be, leaving both Calixto and Sebastiana unfound.

. . . *Enfin,* the Rebus . . . Onward, at speed, and in terms as plain as all this odd philosophy allows:

The Rebus is said to represent the twofold substance, the conjunction of opposites, the *coincidentia oppositorum* so prized by the alchemists. Brù had spoken of this when first we'd met, before that snake of his had wound its way up my leg: the notion of opposites-in-affinity, of *hieros gamos:* Sun and Moon, Earth and Sea . . . Male and Female. . . . And what, or rather who, represented the conjunction of opposites better than me?

Me: the hermetic androgyne; whom Brù had thought of only in metaphoric terms until that day he heard the Duchess speak of a witch both male and female. *Metaphor made flesh.* It seemed he'd found his Rebus; whereupon Brù sought me, in time convincing both the Duchess and Sebastiana that he did so for purer purposes than were true.

Brù's true purpose?

Alors, first allow me a few words more about metaphor, lest you, sister, grow as confused as I was. Rather, as Queverdo Brù was; for it was he, the alchemist, who could no longer distinguish between metaphor and, well, me. . . . *I was what he wanted me to be.*

Understand: The alchemist saw the earth as *uterum universalis;*

wherein all substances, if left to Nature's processes, and a gestation many millennia in length, will—because all things Natural aspire to Perfection—perfect themselves. Or, become gold. Rock, diamond, silex, silica, mud, no matter: The earth, over time, will render everything gold. The alchemist's problem was that he, being mortal, hadn't time enough to wait out this earth-work; and so he sought some means to speed her processes. . . . As said: It was never gold-essay, the derivation of gold from dross, that Queverdo Brù held as his end. *That* he could do, more or less, achieving, if not gold or the Stone itself, its alchemical surrogate: *lapis ex caelis:* a lesser species of the Stone. No, Brù's truer goal, the end-work of all his alchemy, was simply this: the subjugation of Time to his strange Science.

Whereupon I return to the uterine metaphor and Brù's plan, that ill-fated *What if?* that led to my perfection, or perdition:

What if I, the Rebus, male and female, *uterum universalis,* were somehow to conceive a stone at speed? Mightn't it be the true Stone? If so, wouldn't it confer upon he who'd drawn it forth the much-prized perfection. Immortality . . . Of course it was he, Brù, who was supposed to triumph over Time, not me.

Hélas, in supposing me to be the ultimate uterine tool, Brù supposed amiss. I had a uterus of my own, yes; or so *I* supposed, when in fact I'd never had proof, never suffered those much-cursed monthlies. And so it seems doubtful I could have borne a child, let alone the true Stone; leastways not by those commoner processes known to women, midwives, and medicos since Adam first winked at Eve.

Months of study in Brù's library had been enough to show me the absurdity of his plan; but a lifetime of study, of longing, had led Brù to see it as logical. Insanity? Perhaps. Surfeit of study, solitude rendering a wise man dumb? Indubitably. But regardless of the reasons, there we were:

Brù, an alchemical maniac incapable of discerning me from

metaphor; and me—a melancholic, super-sexed witch waiting, *willing* six months to pass fast as a summer rain. And somehow I'd come to seem, to this other, to Queverdo Brù, capable of supporting, of either *conceiving or siring, or both,* the true and long-sought Philosopher's Stone, thus conferring unto him Perfection. I was no *mere* savior, as far as the alchemist was concerned: I was *the.*

※

 *Chapter Fourteen*

He, therefore, who now hears my words, let him search into them; which are to justify no evil-doer, but to benefit the good; therefore, I have discovered all things that were before hidden concerning the knowledge, and disclosed the greatest of all secrets.

—HERMES TRISMEGISTUS,

Septum tractatusseu capitula Trismegisti aurei

. . . WHICH IS NOT TO SAY THE PHILOSOPHER'S STONE IS *wholly* metaphoric; for Brù produced lesser, albeit similar stones in quantity. That *lapis ex caelis,* referenced above; the which I would discover, much to my dismay, on the day I began to die.

I'd been in Havana five months or more, perhaps. Sebastiana had not written, neither through Brù nor to my let study on the Calle Lamparilla, which address I'd sent her once Brù's behavior had become odd, suspicious— though still I knew nothing of his plan—and it seemed I ought not to count on his forwarding any letter that might arrive addressed to me. Nor had the agents at Burnham & Co. had any word of the *Halcyon.* Indeed, it'd be a month or more before they'd even look to the horizon in expectation of the ship. With my contact there—that black-haired secretary whom the others called Manolo—I left a note addressed to Calixto, one which I hoped he'd be handed the minute he returned to Havana. . . . So: stasis, this was. Nothing to do but read, wander, and wait for those winds that would carry Calixto back to Cuba, as slowly or as speedily as Aeolus pleased.

And so it was that one day I rose from the library floor to stretch, to smooth the kinks from my back and legs, and found myself moving toward a door, as yet untried, which sat beyond the library's, beneath that drape of vine that darkened the *entresuelo*. What had stopped me from exploring every room of Brù's abode? I cannot say; but in the few I'd explored I'd found nothing of import or interest, and I'd stood at their opened doors not as Pandora but rather . . . bored. And boredom it was that later drove me to another of the untried doors; and so:

Off I set, bending beneath that vine—it clung to the wall to my right, and like a sheet hung out to dry, strands of it ascended, on my left, slanting upward from the banister to the balcony above—keeping low, and moving quietly and quickly, lest I rile the roosting birds and suffer a sudden rain of shit. Golden or not, alchemized in the guts of a raven or merle, still it was guano.

These rooms—plural; for this was the strangest of suites—sat, as said, upon the *entresuelo*, above those storerooms or stables that opened off the courtyard, beside the library, and below my high-ceilinged room. Such rooms—smaller, their ceilings too low to let the rooms cool—would have housed servants, I suppose, in a former day, when the house had been lived in, *alive*. What Brù did with them, well, that is what I discovered that same afternoon.

It was late in the day, yes. Too well I recall the light; for I'd studied to that point where typically I'd have lit a lamp to take me through twilight and into night proper; whereupon I'd pack a book or two— I'd been poring over some untitled arcana, the author of which was one Basil Valentine—and set out for La Felicidad. I'd hurry home hours later, beneath my light-guard, or I'd stay away till dawn, or perhaps seek my study.

Of late I'd taken to sleeping in that tiny room I'd let from a merchant on the Calle Lamparilla. In that room, two stories above a cobbler's storefront, I could be alone. Stay: I was always alone in Havana; but only in that room could I find an approximation of privacy, of peace. Of course, to achieve this I had to slip into the stairwell off the street and make sure no light-creature came behind me; only then would I ascend to my room, which, perforce, I kept sealed tight as a jar. Therein I'd swelter whilst I studied or slept; but at least I was alone, in privacy and relative peace.

Not surprisingly, Brù cared not at all for this habit of mine. He did not say as much, no; but one day at dawn I returned to find a note set upon my cot. It was written in charcoal upon a piece of parchment, folded twice and tented upon my pillow. *Sleep here,* it said. Nothing more. And the penmanship—as scraggly, sharp-edged, and tight as a charcoal pencil would allow, and not at all what one would expect from a man as erudite, as seemingly sure of himself as Queverdo Brù—deepened my suspicions and caused me to wonder, more pointedly, how old the alchemist was; for the hand that had written the note had shaken, markedly so. This edict of Brù's I disobeyed one night more, to prove I could; but then I surrendered to it—surrender seemed the wiser course, somehow—and again I began to return to Brù's from La Felicidad, birds bright above me, rats and cats aglow in the gutters, seemingly visible to no one but me.

Alors, on the day in question, I set out to explore by that late-day light, and tried doors I'd not tried before.

Behind the first: nothing. Rather, I found all I'd expected to find: A window gave out onto the street, was shuttered, with each of its time-loosened slats letting in strips of sun. The room itself was devoid of all but dust. Dust, yes, eddying in the late-day light. And there was a smell I knew too well: that of maggoty meat. But from whence was it coming? Up from something fetid, something dead down on the street? Or from the sea? I backed from that room expecting to find more of the same in the sibling-room beside it; but in progressing from that room to the next, I was glad for those pots of white roses upon the passage, glad for their aroma, which offset, somewhat, the rot that rose to my nose: It was as though someone had bade me sniff an iron rod wet with rain, and redolent of rust and turned earth.

The second room. Well . . . Ducking in quickly, lest a bird or bat above the balcony let go its . . . its preciousness, I hit a wall of scent—the rot, yes, but something sweet as well—that was second in its effect only to the room's light. The light was not blinding, was not white, was not even bright; but it was, well, to speak of preciousness is apt, as the walls of this room seemed lined with rubies, *rubies,* and the scanty daylight ricocheted here and there: a prism of red, all the shadings of red from ruby down to the palest pink. . . . But the strangeness of the space was attributable not to those rubicund walls alone, no.

Since the permanent turn of my Eye, I'd found I was sensitive to sudden, sparkling light, such as that of the sun reflecting off a still lake or . . . or refracted through rubies. Surely the sunshades I wore to hide my Eye had further sensitized my sight; but I was not wearing those sunshades now—no need to hide my Eye from Brù, and who else would I happen upon in his library?—and so it was with my naked eyes that I saw the rubies, saw the white roses and slivers of cacti upon the walls. Surely it was so: Rubies and white roses and spiny succulents, all affixed to the walls in swirls and lines, *enfin* in designs. It smelled sweet within this room, roseate sweet, as opposed to the other room: so yes: roses, surely. And as my eyes adjusted, I saw those walls for what they were, and suffered these two, most unsettling thoughts:

There is no wind herein to cause the leaves of the roses to ripple so.

And: *These are not all roses.*

Yet I'd seen such whiteness before. It was familiar. . . . Here were, yes, hundreds, nay, *thousands* of wings torn from off the bodies of birds and beating still. Beating still! All were light-white, but they were of varying size. They'd come not just from the hummingbirds. And neither were they all wings. Here was all manner of light-flesh. I saw lizards' tails, and the jittering, crooked legs of hares. A tongue, large as my hand—and torn from what: a goat, a horse, a cow?—wriggled as if to taste the sweet air. I saw claws, and heard, *heard* them scratching at the wall to which they were tacked. Yes, all the whiteness was nailed or tacked to the wall amidst the red stones. The stones, too, were tacked up; but how, *how* had someone—Brù, surely—driven a nail, no matter how sharp or fine, through rubies and secured them to . . .

But of course those were not rubies I saw amidst the deathless flesh.

Here were walls—and the ceiling, too—adorned in that lesser species of the Philosopher's Stone; which, being yet imperfect, takes all shapes and sizes and ranges through all the shades of red. Scarlet unto crimson, and deeper down to garnet. And ruby, yes. I'd learn that it is quite malleable, and most forgiving, the *lapis ex caelis*—not at all stony in its attributes, or aspect; and so it was that Brù had been able to affix, to nail and tack, these innumerable stones to the walls. In fact, he'd arranged them most artfully, in swirls and all sorts of geometries; but he'd also used the stones and flesh, the roses and cacti, to depict things—symbols, signs, sigils: various *arbres philosophiques;* pentacles; and designs bespeaking things zodiacal and astronomical. There was even a well executed portrait—well executed, given the relative crudity of its parts—of the double-sexed demon Baphomet, its phallus a wiggling wing tip, its breasts two bits of rounded stone set in scapulae.

From the ceiling, similarly adorned, there hung several lanterns that were, well, skeletal in composition: Bones had somehow been sewn end to end, or tied with twine, and formed into lanterns of a sort. Within these sat candles, dully white and unlit now, though wax had dripped and now depended from the lanterns' bases like white rain, arrested in its fall.

Into one of the adorned walls an arch had been cut, rudely; but I did not need to pass through it to see, beyond, a second room similarly done. Room the first was full: not an inch of wall or ceiling was *undecorated;* but not so the second. Here, hideously, was a work in progress.

As night fell, I backed from the archway, and backed, too, from the first room I'd found. I felt cold, cold to the bone. How long had Brù labored to adorn these rooms so? How long had he waited for me to wander into them, and wonder this? And though I wondered *Why?* there was no need to wonder *How?* The nails were evident at the heart of each soft stone, and showed, too, through the luminous flesh and flowers. Neither did I wonder *What?* For I'd heard and read enough about the Stone. Indeed, Basil Valentine himself writes of the imperfected Stone, red and pliable. I knew what it was I saw.

Had I missed something, somewhere, a text that ordained that the adept create such a room? A chapel of sorts, adorned in reds and whites, those colors said to represent the *hieros gamos,* the opposites-in-affinity? Testifying to the diminishment of whatever trust I'd had in Brù, I did not even think to seek out and ask my host. Instead, I did what always I'd done when wondering something, anything: I returned to the library. I lit a lamp. And I looked for words to explain what I'd seen. No: I'd more than *seen* it: I'd taken in those rooms with my every death-strengthened sense.

———

I was two days into my search for the alchemical origins of such rooms as those. I'd found nothing but further descriptions of the Stone in its many, lesser states, such that I wondered how Brù had managed to harvest such a quantity of stones. It seemed he was onto something, surely: All the texts spoke of the difficulties in distilling the true Stone, yes, but they spoke of how hard it was to harvest the Stone in any of its preliminary, or imperfect, stages as well. Brù had done this. Again and again and again. I was left wondering how, and knowing the answer was too strange to seek it from the alchemist himself. And so: more research.

I, like a magpie, had made a nest of sorts for myself upon the floor beneath the library window. It was composed of an old blanket I'd found and several pillows I'd purchased on the Calle Mercadero (and which soon were redolent of the *entresuelo*'s strange stench, *everywhere* now that I knew its source). To this nest I retreated, with relevant titles piled close at hand.

The Book of Quintessence.

A Letter to the True Disciples of Hermes, by Sieur de Saint-Didier.

Others by Macar, Dioscorides, De Vigo, and Galen.

One such tome had closed and fallen upon my chest, in seeming imitation of my eyes; for I was tired, and needed a nap before I could resume reading. Waking from same—minutes, or maybe an hour had passed—I wondered, indolently, *Why rise?* And so I did not rise. There I lay, looking sideways at books piled upon the library floor. Not the ones I'd arranged and planned to read. These were others. Books I may or may not have perused already, whilst in Brù's library; for, with that disinterest born of my not having chosen my field of study, I'd piled the books and read them *par hasard*, never trying to catalog or categorize the lot of them. And I suppose it was owing to that change of perspective—still I lay curled upon the floor—that I saw it. *There.* At the base of a book tower twenty, thirty volumes high. A large, thin

book covered in blue-dyed kid. Azure-blue kid. And its spine, alone
of all the volumes atop it, was turned toward me, toward the wall and
the window beneath which I lay, such that I could see now its golden,
gilded script, and the words written thereon. Not words. A name: *Adelaide
Labille-Guiard.*

At first I thought little of this, and lay awaiting energy enough to
rise and resume my reading, to return to the text that had slipped from
my chest as I'd slept. But something within me held to that name. I
stared at it, read it time and again. It was French, *bien sûr*. Was that the
sole reason it seemed familiar? A memoir of some Court-kept type?
Doubtful, as to judge from the folio-size shape of the book it probably
contained plates, and the scripted name was perhaps not the authoress
of the work but rather its subject. Perhaps an artist who—

An artist. A flame held to my heel could not have righted me faster;
for suddenly I knew, *knew* that name as though it were my own.

Adelaide Labille-Guiard was, or had been, an artist, indeed. More
precisely: "despicable" Adele had been Sebastiana's chief rival. Theirs
were the two names sure to be on the tongue of anyone in the courts
of old Europe seeking to commission a portrait. Indeed, the two
artists had gained admission into the Académie Royale on the very
same day in 1783, "despicable" Adelaide thereby spoiling Sebastiana's
day (so she'd written in her *Book of Shadows*), and the two of them causing
the academy's members—all men—to redraft the rules of admission,
such that a third female member was destined to wait a long,
long while. (This, too, Sebastiana had blamed on Adelaide.) Yes, I'd
read of Labille-Guiard in Sebastiana's Book, surely, and now here was
her name scrawled down the spine of another book. Coincidence?
Perhaps; for Brù's holdings did include a few monographs on artists,
sculptors, and the like, though not many, and not without their being
allied—somehow—to alchemical study. Or perhaps . . . ?

I neared the book on all fours, such that I must have appeared for all the world like a bitch warily approaching pond's edge, whereat she's spied a turtle, and wonders now if it is the snapping kind. Slowly, slowly I approached, lest my hopes be dashed too soon and I feel foolish; for however could S. have . . . ?

Nearing, I saw that the dust upon the topmost books of that pile—none of which I could recall reading—had not been disturbed. But there were prints, here and there. Slender, delicate prints. A woman's? Moreover: I saw but the faintest coat of dust upon the blue leather cover of the monograph in question. It had lain there less time than the other, smaller books atop it. Most strange, this. Had someone placed it there, and turned those books above it so that only the one spine showed to any who might see it from beneath the window? And if so, who'd know the name of Labille-Guiard? . . . *I would.*

My heart, how it hammered. The more so when, in reaching for the volume, I caused to crash all those that had lain atop it. So loudly I might have pulled down the Tower of Pisa. . . . I waited. Had Brù heard? Too: What if I were wrong? What if . . . ?

Indeed, I was wrong. I saw a contradictory title now, impressed upon the book's front and confirmed within: It was a treatise derived from Delphinus's *Secretus Maximus.* But how? Surely . . . And when I turned the book on its side, there it was again: *Adelaide Labille-Guiard;* but the name was not, as first I'd thought, worked into the leather. Rather it was written in white upon a length of azure ribbon, and somehow adhered to the tome's side. Stranger still. Who would do such a thing, and why?

I could think of one person only.

Slowly, slowly, I opened the book and . . . and . . .

The actual, bound pages had been excised. Rather, a square had been cut into those pages, and at the center of that square sat a second volume, snug within the first. A book within the book. And upon the cover of this second Book, also of azure blue kid, there was embossed—how I felt it, caressed it with my fingertips!—that large telltale *S*, a toad sitting fatly in its lower loop. . . . Sebastiana!

Had she been to Brù's already? If so, how . . . ? Oh, countless questions came as the tome trembled in my hands.

As was my wont—I'd read too many *Books of Shadows*, and been too disappointed in the sad fate of so many sisters—I opened the Book not to its first entry but rather its last; and read:

> *Oh, H., oh, my heart, what have I done?*
>
> *If perchance you find this Book, at all costs keep it from the monk. Read it not in his house, but take it and run. Run, my heart!* ·

But if I'd done as directed, if I'd upped and run, I'd have been blocked by Queverdo Brù, who stood now in the library's doorway, his face drawn back deeply into the hood of his burnous, his expression unseen.

 *Chapter Fifteen*

When the alchemist expects the rewards of his labors, births of gold, youth, and immortality, after all his time and expense, at length old, ragged, rich only in misery, and so miserable that he will sell his soul for three farthings, he falls upon ill courses.

—CORNELIUS AGRIPPA, The Vanity of Science and Arts

"*B*UENAS TARDES," SAID BRÙ.

I was shaking and could not stop. "Monsieur," said I, ridiculously, "you frightened me." There I stood, the fingers of my right hand fluttering over my heart; fast, my fingers fell to tapping, tapping upon my chest, mimicking the beat of the organ within. In my left hand—and low, half behind my hip—I held, or rather hid Sebastiana's Book. More accurately: I tried to hide the larger volume in which hers lay.

"What is that you read there?" asked Brù. Had he seen? Did he know? Surely not; for if he suspected Sebastiana had left a note—let alone a Book, the last page of which advised me to run, *Run!*—he'd have sought it high and low. Then again, Brù could not have known, as Sebastiana had, that, if given enough time—and by now I'd had some five months' worth—I'd take up every volume in any library in which I was let to roam. Too, it was doubtful Brù knew the name of Sebastiana's rival. Oh yes, my sister had done well, hiding a message for me in plain sight. But if only I'd found her Book earlier! What could be worse than finally having word from Sebastiana—*a warning*, no less—and not being able to read it, as now I was not, with Brù standing in the library door, backlit by the dying light of day? If asked that question, I would have replied, *Nothing could be worse;* . . . but I'd have been wrong.

"It tells of Delphinus," I answered, bringing out the blue book from behind my hip and showing its front, not its spine. "His *Secretus Maximus.*"

"Ah, yes," said Brù, "*Secrets* . . . Worthy, worthy indeed." And he stood there, still as statuary. How I burned! Was he staring at me, or at that treatise that hid my sister's Book? I had no way of knowing; for the hood of his burnous yet overhung his face, and I could not gauge the angle of his regard.

Finally:

"Come," said he. "Onto the *assoltaire.* I've something it's time you see."

All I had to see I held in my left hand: Sebastiana's Book. . . . She'd been here, in Havana? When? With Asmodei? Were they, was *she* nearby, still? Doubtful; for I'd have known if she were near: I'd powers enough to know, *to sense* when sisters were near. It was that same frisson that the mortal men, the sparks who'd visited Cyprian House, had sensed, and pleasured in; for there, with thirteen of us sisters living in sorority, it had been plain and the Duchess had deemed dissimulation a waste. "If it draws them," she'd often said, "then let them come, and come again." Now I wondered, had the Duchess *and* Sebastiana been here, in Havana, together? If so, surely S.'s Book would hold some word of the Duchess as well, she who'd all but disappeared after cholera had crawled across continents to decimate her city and take her beloved Eliphalet from her. *So much at hand,* and now I was not at leisure to read it! Of late I'd suffered more leisure than the finest of ladies could put to purpose; but now, when I needed it most, I'd been invited onto the *assoltaire* by the very man Sebastiana had warned me of. But this was no invitation; rather, it came as a command. Neither could the timing of it have been coincidence.

"Now?" I tried. "It remains so very hot up there, even after the sun has begun—"

"Now. Yes."

What to do? I could not bear to set the Book down; and so, saying that I was on the verge of finally understanding the Delphinus, I stuffed it and another book into my satchel, slung it over my shoulder, and stepped past Brù, out of the library and onto the balcony that overhung the courtyard. A left would lead me round to where that stony, shit-slickened staircase spiraled up to the *assoltaire.* To my right, *our* right, lay the red-and-white room I'd discovered two days prior; and so, boldly:

"That room there," I said. "What part of the Art is that?"

Brù's dirt- and sweat-stiffened hood fell back, such that finally I could see his face, his golden half smile. With a tip and jut of his chin he sent me toward the left, *Go.* I stepped in that direction, toward the stairs, toward the *assoltaire;* yet still I observed—words cast back over my shoulder—"It seems a sort of shrine."

"*Sí?* Then tell me, witch, what do you suppose I would worship at such a shrine?"

"Some aspect of the Great Work, I suppose," said I; for I'd learned the alchemical lexicon, those words and euphemisms the puffers all seemed to revere. And then I stopped, turned, and even stepped back toward Brù; for I wanted to see, to read his face when next I spoke, saying, "Stones. Those are stones upon the walls and ceiling, are they not? Stones and bones and bits of flesh from off—"

※

"They are," said he, with a nod that I'd have read as respectful had I received it in a situation less dark, less dire. His face showed no expression at all: gone was the golden smile. I held his stare. And it was then Brù betrayed himself, tugging at his hood so as to hide those four thickened stripes of scar on his neck, scars that had healed to the purpled black of well-blooded leeches.

"Then those stones are of great worth," I went on, "*non?* Surely you have achieved what many labored lifetimes to—"

"It is *the* Stone I seek," said he, straightening, so that now his face was too near mine; and what next he spoke was twinned to the sourness of his breath: "The pure, perfected final-form Philosopher's Stone. Such imperfect, red-shaded . . . *spawn* of the processes are as nothing to me, *nothing.*"

"Still . . ." said I, stalling; for I hoped somehow to spare myself hours upon the *assoltaire,* in a stifling tent, beside Brù, watching him work at I knew not what. Perhaps an exasperated, bothered Brù would think better of his plan. Perhaps he'd quit me, or let me leave for La Felicidad or my rented room to read—*to read and run,* as my sister-savior bade me do. "Still, even some lesser species of the Stone, well, I read that this is not so easily achieved."

By now we'd shuffled nearer the stairwell, me walking backward, talking, stalling, with Brù coming steadily on. It was darkening in the courtyard, and the world seemed lit neither by the sun, nor the moon, nor stars. Rather, here was that eerie light that rose each day at dusk as . . . well, now the birds were on the wing, the peacocks were parading, and the bats overhung it all, the lot of them growing ever more luminous. The effect was comparable to that of the new lime lighting I'd seen in the theaters of Man-hattan; except there, in that box of stone and timber and wrought iron that was the theater of Queverdo Brù, the light was more diffuse, was not channeled into cylinders and shone upon sopranos, jugglers, or others of sundry skill. Oh, but that diffuse light was bright enough for me to see what next Brù would do:

From some pocket of his burnous, Brù drew forth what appeared to be a silver thimble, thick with symbols I could not identify; but when he placed it upon his left thumb I saw that it was tipped with a blade, no longer than an inch, the edge of which was serrated, the tip of which was at once sharp and scooped. Fast, he shot the right cuff of his burnous, and with his bared, black arm reached down a bat from where it hung overhead. The creature bit into Brù's right thumb, but soon it struggled not at all. In fact, it unfurled its white wings and spread itself over Brù's pale palm, as if to expose itself to . . . to take . . .

With the bladed thimble Brù cut into the bat. No blood came. No cries, no recoiling: The bat seemed impervious to what, certainly, was a most painful process.

Into an incision thusly made, and less than an inch in length, Brù inserted the thimble's scoop-like tip, turning it this way and that; and when he retracted it, he dropped into my palm, *mine*, what first I took to be the bat's beatless heart. Now there was recoiling, assuredly: *mine*. But it wasn't the bat's heart I had in hand, no. It was a button-small piece of stone, imperfect stone; which, when Brù took it from me and wiped it free of viscera, lifting the hem of his robe to do so—and in the process, parting the robe's halves to reveal, with what seemed to me to be intent . . . to reveal a generative organ large and pendulous as a papaya, and colored a dusky, grayish blue— . . . *enfin*, when smoothed on the hem of Brù's burnous, the stone shone ruby-true, and was soft, yet seemed to harden as I held it.

"Bats," said Brù, tying tight his robe, ". . . bats breed a dark stone."

"However did . . . ?" I began; but then my attention returned to Brù's hands at work. He had now a length of blackened twine—it seemed charred, or otherwise cured—and wound this crosswise round

---

✳

the bat; which, it seemed to me, sought flight despite the surgery it had just suffered. Bound, still the bat was moving when Brù dropped it into his pocket alongside the thimble with which he'd killed it. Or not.

"Why doesn't it die?" I thought Brù would say the bat was already dead; but no:

"Because it, because *they* have been perfected," said he, fanning the ringed fingers of his left hand to take in *all of his creations*. Upon reflection, he amended this: "No: *nearly* perfected."

If that be perfection, thought I as we continued our climb to the rooftop tents, *then, please, let me pass from this world imperfect.* And I did a quick calculus, too: How many light-bred *creations* had Brù had to cut into in order to adorn the Stone Room as he had? True, I'd never had a great affinity for animals—despite their seeming to be drawn to me, somehow—and had failed, miserably, in the training of a few familiars; but still, how hard was the heart of the monk, the madman, the murderer whose house I was in? . . . Some hours later, after a sleep too deep, too dreamless to *not* have been induced by drugs, I'd wake to an answer of sorts:

Brù's heart, let me say, was as hard as those steely shackles that then held me flat upon my back, immobile upon my cot—which somehow Brù had dragged into the red-and-white room—and which bit into my ankles and wrists rather harder than that bat had bitten my captor's thumb.

Waking, the last I could recall of the night prior was—fool!—taking a golden goblet proffered by Brù, and drinking deeply. It had been hot atop the *assoltaire*, with the late-day rain so common to those climes still steaming off the tiles and tar. And the drink had been cool, milky, and infused with fruit: mango, a bit of banana . . . Tempting, in other words. As Brù had known it would be.

❋

When first we'd ascended, I followed Brù into a lesser tent, one I'd not been in before. Beside this sat the larger laboratory, the canvas sides of which were tied back such that I saw Brù was building something within it, something of clay and iron and carved hardwoods. Though it was not quite complete, I knew from its shape what it was; but asked the alchemist anyway, "What is it you're building there?"

"An athanor," said he. It was as I'd supposed.

"Ah," said I, false and chatty, as though words alone could distract Brù from the contents of my satchel, and the Book within that weighted me so, that I wanted, *needed* so desperately to read. "But I've not read anything stipulating that the alchemist have more than one athanor. In fact—" But my words went unheard as Brù walked away, walked from the smaller to the larger tent, a route that required him to use steps (down), a ladder laid lengthwise over the tarry roof, and more steps (up), though the tents were separated by no more than fifteen, twenty feet. Brù now stood before the athanor of old; and taking the bound bat from his pocket, he tossed it, *whoosh*, into the furnace. "A *larger* athanor is what's needed," said he a moment later, returned to my side.

Blessedly, I did not linger overlong on Brù's words, not then; for this new tent, well . . .

This was not quite a laboratory, nor an oratory, nor living quarters of any recognizable kind. Was it a combination of the three? Not quite, no; but I knew what it recalled: a taxidermist's den. I'd seen such a stinking place once, in the Florida Territory. The proprietor had been a tanner by trade, a taxidermist by . . . what? It seemed a strange, rather sloppy *hobby*, but who was I to say? There'd been blades of every size and shape, and skins spread upon the walls—skins yet to be scraped lay piled beside the man's door: a feast for flies—and he'd even shown me (*unsolicited*) his boxful of glass eyeballs. Yes:

This smaller tent of Brù's bespoke taxidermy, or something similar. But what, I wondered, is *similar* to taxidermy? . . . Surgery? . . . Torture?

Within that tent death knew no *inordinate* dominion. I'd have sensed it if it had. Still, how then to account for the stench, which was considerable, as bad as any shambles, charnel house, or cemetery I'd had the misfortune to find in years past? Could Brù's creatures, though not dead, precisely, still take on the characteristics of the dead as he sought to preserve them in this space? For that is what he did. *Enfin*, it was not *preservation* per se, but rather . . . disposal.

. . . Admittedly, I was not overly dismayed to soon find Brù's focus fixed upon the white python, Ourobouros. That said, I did not yet know what he'd do to it. Oh, but when I did, *mon Dieu* . . . : If the alchemist had so little affinity, so little affection for that snake of his, well, that did not bode well for any other creature coming betwixt the alchemist and his Art, such as it was.

The snake lay at full length upon two tables of deal set end to end. Beside the tables were skeletal-like stands of iron, with arms holding glass-bellied lights in which scented oil burned; burned, yes, but not strongly enough to displace the death-stench issuing from I knew not where. Leathern strapping secured the snake in two places, such that when Brù raised his cleaver—oh yes—and chopped the python into four seemingly equal parts, two sections were secured beneath said straps whilst two others lay center-all atop the tables, wriggling, writhing. Granted, I'd never seen the . . . the insides of a snake—their outsides had disturbed me sufficiently down the years, *merci bien*—but I'd read enough of Galen, Vesalius, and other anatomists to know that *a living creature,* thusly abused, *ought to bleed.* But, as with the bat, there was no blood. Too, I'd have supposed cleaved flesh—snake or otherwise, alive or . . . not—would show itself grayish red, pink in places; but the snake's did not and was, instead, colorless, or rather dimmer than the snake's outer skin, which yet was white, albeit not sun-bright, as earlier it had been.

I watched Brù work at this autopsy, or necropsy, and said nothing—the circumstances seemed not quite conducive to converse—all the while feeling the weight of the found Book upon my back and wondering why I'd had to climb so high above Havana to see this stomach-churning show; which fast progressed from bad to worse.

Stay: That is untrue: *worse* had been the surprise of seeing the snake chopped into four parts. *Less worse* it was watching Brù gather up those pieces—each as long as his arm—and lay them lengthwise in a rush basket, as if he were out in a wood collecting kindling. Yes, into the basket went all four lengths of snake, the last and topmost being that piece which bore its head, from which the split tongue yet flicked, flicked as if the snake sought its milk-snack. Horrid now—and off the scale of *worse to worst*—was seeing Brù take up the head-length of snake, kiss it upon its scaly snout, and, when again the tongue came, *striking*, fast as a mongoose might, to seize the tongue with smallish tongs and tear it, *tear it* from within the convulsing white-flesh.

Setting the snake's tongue upon the table—where it moved like a scribbling stylus—Brù turned to me and said, as if I'd *needed* the act explained, "For the wall of the Stone Room."

"I see," said I, swallowing back the bile that had risen to the back of my throat. . . . I clutched the Book in my sack. *Run!* And oh, how I longed to.

Brù threw two parts of the snake into a barrel in the corner of the tent. Would that I could say I stood too far from said barrel to see its contents; *mais hélas* . . . Inside, piled three-fourths up the barrel's sides, was . . . whiteness. Shuddering, alive-dead, animal whiteness. Flesh slowly ceding to bone. All of it adornments-to-be. From that barrel and another beside it there rose the stench earlier described.

The rest of the snake—its head and tail parts—Brù carried across

※

the rooftop to his laboratory, bidding me follow. He'd stoked the athanor earlier, as evinced by the wavering air around it. Now he dipped the snake parts into a *tinajone,* or reservoir, kept outside the tent, such that I heard the rainwater hiss from off the fired snake flesh as Brù flung into the flames the last of Ourobouros, a snake he'd trained to sip milk, kitten-like, from a saucer.

Returned to the smaller, taxidermic tent, I wiped the sweat from my brow with the sleeve of my blouse. In a word, I was *queasy;* and grew more so as I watched Brù arrange his instruments—wiping the whiteness from off the cleaver, et cetera. And only then did I realize what part of the strange process I'd thought would follow upon the snake's being cut into quarters: Brù taking up something similar to but larger than his thimble and cutting into the snake flesh, slicing, scooping, poking, and prodding until he'd found his stone. But no: Too much meat to search, I supposed. And I understood, too, what it was he'd do instead: He'd render Ourobouros down to ash—*burn it,* as was every alchemist's wont—and later comb or sieve the cooled ash for stone.

Now, as to whether Brù ever culled any stones from the snake's ashes—and a creature as large as Ourobouros might well have produced more than one stone, albeit each imperfect; for, as Brù said, or warned, "Perfection seeks a higher species, *the highest species . . .*" —well, I cannot here record; for by the time the athanor had cooled enough to be combed or sifted, I was already . . .

Oh, but stay: First let me say why I did what only a fool would do:

Though darkness had come, still it was steamy hot atop the *assoltaire;* and further, as I wanted, desperately, to slip from Brù as soon as I could, to read what Sebastiana had written, I thought it best to do as he bade me do; and so:

Yes, I took that goblet and drank it down to the dregs. Its sweetness I attributed to the fruit within whatever Brù had concocted; and mind you, Brù drank, too. Of course, he'd not drugged his drink, only mine. With what? Herbs, *populeum,* an elixir or potion bought from off some unscrupulous sister? I cannot say. I do not know. I know only that it was a soporific so strong, so . . .

Soon everything began to waver like the air around the athanor. And whilst I don't remember sitting—the act of it, I mean—well I recall leaning back upon a divan, Sebastiana's Book hard beneath me, and asking, stammering, "Why? . . . What species?"

I feared Brù would say *Homo sapiens,* was sure he would. Mad, he'd progressed through the lesser species, breeding them to the Light, let me say, and now he sought a human in which to plant his stone-seed, somehow alchemizing it within said host until it, until he or she, rendered the one Stone. Hence the need for a larger athanor.

". . . species," I was saying, ". . . Stone . . ." I was flat upon my back, flat upon the Book. The birds, all the birds had risen to circle and swoop, diving down to the level of the tents, such that it seemed Havana feted itself with silent fireworks. So intent was I upon my answer—though I could hardly form the question, the muscles of my mouth being the first to fall slack—I was neither scared nor surprised by the birds' flight, though surely it presaged nothing too . . . auspicious, as far as I was concerned. I wanted to know: *Was it a human Brù would use?*

Somehow I got the question out, evidently; for Brù came nearer, to kneel beside me. I saw two hoods, two heads, two faces of obsidian with inset golden smiles. No, said he, it was not a human he'd use. He'd tried that. And he repeated himself, such that I heard again, ". . . *the highest species.*"

Did I somehow ask another question? Doubtful, as my head now lolled side to side, and my left hand had fallen, open-palmed, onto the floor, from which I could not raise it. Still, I heard that explication I may or may not have sought with further speech; for Brù said, "The *highest* species, yes . . . You: the two-as-one. The Rebus."

It was then I surrendered to sleep.

 # Chapter Sixteen

. . . because Nature produces all metals out of three things, salt, sulfur and mercury; . . . and that which has been left by Nature might be completed by Art, since Nature herself is always inclined toward her own perfection.

—MARSILIO FICINO, Liber de arte chemica, 1518

*H*OW BRÙ DID IT TO THE LESSER CREATURES I CANNOT say; but it is safe to suppose the processes were the same as those he used on me whilst I lay for weeks in the Stone Room. *Weeks,* yes.

Waking from the soporific—a day, or perhaps several days after being drugged: I'd no idea—I saw I was naked, and restrained. Cuffs and chains held me, cruciform, upon the cot. Strange though it may sound, I was not surprised. Horrified, yes. Surprised, no; for immediately I recollected that cup and the long draft I'd drunk from it. I recollected, too, the *perfection* of the python and my falling, shortly thereafter, upon the divan; whereon I learned of my own impending *perfection.*

At first, I fought, fought as best one can who lay naked, cuffed, and cruciform upon a broad canvas cot, captive to a madman in a cell the walls of which are alive.

My restraints were slack enough to allow me to lift my shoulders from off the sweat-slick canvas of the cot, to turn my head and . . . and retch. My throat felt coated. Doubtless this was the aftereffect of whatever drugged drink I'd been given by Brù. It had tempted me, then, that drink—so cool, so smooth and aromatic, sweet-seeming yet tricky as the legended apples of Sodom, said to turn to ash upon the tongue. . . . *Enfin*, mercury was what I tasted, and mercury was what I sought to spit from deep in my throat. That retching turning to a choking cough; for the Stone Room was thick with smoke. In the four corners of my cell, Brù had piled and lit, and caused to smolder, cones of sulfur. And if that infernal smoke caused a cough to rise from my lungs, so, too, did it bring the Stone Room alive in ways I'd not seen when first I'd found the room.

Then, I'd seen the white-flesh writhing upon the walls, but now, as seen through the scrim of smoke, and by the light borne of those bone lanterns, the . . . *things* upon the walls and ceiling were frantic. Birds' wings blew the smoke this way and that. Tongues lapped at the curing air. Other flesh which I could not identify—though I saw the two lengths of python, newly nailed above the arch that led into the secondary room— . . . other flesh was wildly alive now as well. Rather, *it was all dead* yet manifesting the attributes of life. It was all *animate*. So, too, were the myriad pieces of red-shaded stone tacked to the walls: The stones moved as stones will when seen through water. They wavered. They shape-shifted. Was it the smoke that made the stones *seem* to mutate so, or was it some other elementary effect that actually caused them to do so? All I know is that all imperfected stone is mutable. As for perfected stone, the one Stone, well, that is something else entirely.

That white-and-red, smoke-choked, and stinking room seemed a bad dream; or, more specifically, that dreamscape in which I would die, as had all those creatures that had come before me: The less lucky of Brù's creations who'd not been rendered down to ash and had their stones sifted out, but rather those that had had their stones removed by blade, by the prying fingers of Brù; who'd then made of their remains these bicolored mandalas, these tridents, these Sephirotic Trees, these alchemical talismans on the walls all around me. Here then was my living crypt.

Oh, but how would I be disposed of? By athanor or autopsy? By flame or blade? Or both. As had happened to Ourobouros.

And when would it happen? When would Brù harvest whatever it was he'd sown within me in the hopes that I—the Rebus, the long-awaited, androgynous Vessel of the Great Work—would bear the one, true Stone? I'd heard and read enough to know his end. Heard and read enough to know what he'd done to those creatures whose remains I saw arranged about me. Heard and read enough to know what it was he'd do to me and . . .

Read enough? I sat up straight, only to have the leather-and-chain leads of my cuffs pull me back down upon the cot. *Where was Sebastiana's Book?* Had Brù found it? Oh, where was the Book? Where was the satchel which . . . *There.* To my left. Upon the floor. Midway down a wall at the base of which were lain, lengthwise, bones drawn from animals larger than any I'd seen in the courtyard or stables. Bones so large as to call to mind the shinbones and forearms of . . . of humans, yes. Beneath these horrid souvenirs of all whom Brù had done unto death—Sebastiana herself? Or the Duchess? . . . *Please no*—I saw a pile of striped cloth: my dress of *bolan.* Having stripped it off me—and need I recount the feelings *that* thought occasioned?—it seemed Brù had folded it, neatly, so squarely it seemed my satchel must lay beneath it. But of this I could not be certain.

I hesitate now to dignify Brù's misdeeds with more alchemical clap-trap; for my hostess's hand hardens toward inutility, and why should I waste precious body-time talking of a pseudo science, one that is half philosophy, half sham? *Enfin,* for one reason only: It is true, incontrovertibly so, that something there was that fired aright, literally, when finally I died a decade later; such that here I am, the Rebus, Risen, Returned, pushing this pen with a hand not my own. And so, sister, let us indulge a millennium of dead men for a few paragraphs more. As said indulgence, I offer this distillation of what was done to me in the Stone Room:

None of the aforementioned dead men—true it is, too, that women dabbled in alchemy, most notably Mary the Prophetess, whose veneration of the *vas mirabile,* or male ejaculate, rivaled that of the Duchess, who attributed her sister-strength to same— . . . I say, none of those alchemists sought the Stone in *precisely* the same way; though, if the particulars of the processes differed, the principles did not.

All, *all* alchemists—from Roger Bacon up to and through Queverdo Brù—believed that the *opus alchymicum,* the Great Work, the search for the Philosopher's Stone, and Perfection, began in the union of *three basic substances:* salt, mercury, and sulfur. The contradictory qualities of two of the three—any two—were countered by the third; and therefore all three composed the *prima materia.* . . . *Bon. D'accord.* But what of those processes the *prima materia* ought then to be subjected to? "Aye," sayeth Shakespeare's Dane, himself as confused as any alchemist of old, "there's the rub."

In the interest of time—which is to say, rigor mortis—let me here side with Albertus Magnus—he of the thirteenth century, and as eloquent as any of his brethren—who spoke of the hoped-for progression of the *prima materia* succinctly; rather, as succinctly as any adept ever did, succinctness not being a striven-for attribute of the adepts. Thusly, according to Magnus the Magus, here is the progression unto Perfection:

First the three substances—again, mercury, salt, and sulfur, as commonly denominated—are combined in a suitable vessel. No mean feat, of course, the finding of a suitable vessel. (Hadn't Brù thought *I* was such a thing?) In said vessel, the three substances combine to form the *prima materia;* whereupon the mercury and sulfur are extracted as slag, and the salt is left to purify. Oh but how so? What is the *magisterium,* the catalyst that causes the salt, mercury and sulfur to combine? *That* is the question. (Some said the *magisterium* was water; and I can here attest: *They were right.*) . . . At last, purifed, the salt is "like unto rubies;" i.e., Brù's imperfected stones. Further alchemical progression—which is to say, *more burning*—was done in the hope of rendering these down to the *white elixir;* which the common man calls gold, but which, to the Practitioner who made it, and *perfected himself* in the process, is the one Stone: The Philosopher's Stone: That which grants eternal life. *Et voilà!*

I jest. . . . Understand: Alchemy was a lifelong pursuit, as it can take a half day to read and distill sense from a single paragraph of its canon; and I do not mean to conjure the image of alchemists roasting ruby-like stones in their athanors and, *poof,* pulling out the Philosopher's Stone—white as light—in their stead. No. Perfection was *a process made of mysteries,* and one which they all pursued, many unto madness.

Like Brù.

He had red stones aplenty, Brù did, but what of *the precious white* said to be akin to both gold and light? No. This he'd never harvested. Had he, he'd have already been perfected. And I'd not be . . . Oh yes, it was via some perversion of said processes that I'd be perfected, years hence, if perfection this be.

By the time Brù came to the Stone Room, well, yes, I'd grown despondent—to understate, terrifically, my tenor of mind—and might well have welcomed death. Oh, but all that changed when I opened my eyes and saw the hooded Brù before me, wreathed in smoke and dimly lit; and it changed further when that hood was thrown back and Brù let his burnous slip to the floor. Did he think he'd . . . *use* me somehow, in a way warranting his nakedness?

I was naked, too, of course; such that now I suffered the alchemist's appraisal, and not for the first time: Doubtless he'd spied upon his Rebus whilst I slept.

He nodded, as if pleased. *Pleased?* With what? It was that one gesture—naught but a nod—that caused my sadness, my despondency, *to alchemize,* yes, into a thing so pure, so perfect, it hasn't a name, hatred being but proximal to it.

When I saw Brù approach through the smoke and strip, when I saw his cold, appraising eye and that nod, well . . . I sought to strike.

But how? I hadn't the means.

I'd the strength, yes, but not the . . . stillness, the calm requisite to Craftwork. I wanted to bleed him, to cause his every breath to blow as blood from his nose, to bubble from his mouth as ours does at the Coming of the Blood. I could do it. Rather, I'd done it before, as a girl seated in an Angevin café—I recall it was La Grosse Poule—when I'd ensorcelled an innocent man; but that had been clumsy, done more out of curiosity than crossness. Still, why couldn't I do it again now, *now?* . . . *Hélas,* I could not.

Neither were there any tools or weapons present, nothing I could raise by dint of will and hurl at Brù the way I'd sent that marlinespike at, nay, *through* Diblis. There was nothing in the crypt but my cot, in fact; and though there were weapons upon the *assoltaire,* in the tents, I found I could not Eye-seize something I could not see. Lucky for Brù. If he'd have bound me in one of his rooftop tents I'd have found, I'd have *seen* countless ways to kill him, and may well have chosen several, killing him once for what he was doing to me, again for what I was sure he'd done to Sebastiana, and once more on behalf of the Duchess. Yes, I could have killed the alchemist thrice over: by blade, by bludgeon, or by hurling, handless, some sharp-tipped thing at his heart, or rather that chest-high hole where his heart ought to have been.

Perhaps I'd have been able to effect this had I found the aforementioned calm. I did not. Could not. Not that day. Oh, but the next— or the next after that: I cannot recall: not knowing how long I'd slept, I lost all sense of the calendar, and even now the days of my captivity are confused to me— . . . soon, let me say, I did indeed strike.

Brù, naked, his sex darkly pendulant—and flaccid, blessed be— came to me with something white in his hand. In the other hand he held a beaker, a glass beaker brimful of a silver-gray liquid. Of course, I know now that it was the elixir, the largest part of which was liquid mercury; not *mere* mercury, mind, but rather mercury Brù had somehow alchemized in his laboratory, such that it tasted, too, of salt and sulfur. As he closed in on me, I caused—by simple motion, or kinetics, I cannot say—the cot to judder and shift, or perhaps Brù simply tripped; regardless, the effect was this: Two or three drops of whatever it was he'd decocted spilled from the beaker onto my skin, and did not roll off as they ought to have. Cold, it congealed, and seemed like bullets that had skidded to a stop *atop* my skin, as if fearful of my flesh.

Oh, but when I drank the balance of the liquid in the beaker, it was warm, only turning cold as it slid to coat my throat with a texture, with a taste, that told me I'd drunk it before. Here was that taste I'd woken to and had tried to spit away; but now it was tenfold stronger, and as I swallowed it . . .

Stay: I cannot say *swallow*, or *drank*; for such words imply a measure of willingness. I did not choose to drink, and if I swallowed the elixir it was only so as not to choke.

Brù, you see, administered his potion by means of a large porcelain funnel, the lesser end of which tapered to its tip ten inches on. This he'd greased, or somehow slickened, such that when he succeeded in tipping back my head—he'd set the beaker down upon the parquet floor, trading it for a fistful of my hair, at which he tugged—he succeeded, too, in inserting the funnel; for he held my nose, and I'd little choice but to submit, opening to the funnel and the choking flow that came.

Whereupon I, summoning what calm I could, cast my keen Eye about the red-and-white room, certain, *certain* there was something with which I could . . .

And indeed I found something with which to strike. *Things,* plural; for I seized with Sight alone as many nail heads as I could, prying them from the walls—white-flesh, bone, and stone fell, audibly—and shot them toward Brù. They came quickly, the nails and smaller tacks with which Brù had pinned his odd work to the ceiling and walls—rather as a deranged lepidopterist might pin living butterflies to velvet—but they barely pricked at Brù; for they came weakly, having neither heft nor speed behind them—Craftwork is one thing, the laws of physics quite another—and only a few found purchase in his flesh. These he removed. They bothered him no more than nettles or the sting of his hummingbirds might have. And as a result of this failed essay, I surrendered what edge I might have had; for blindfolds followed. Brù learned of my witch's will, and saw, too, that he had to watch my Eye. And that was that. Thereafter, I'd no choice but to submit—blindly, yes—to the concoction delivered at Brù's whim, and in the stead of anything substantive.

Which is to say, I starved. Not unto death. Not yet.

Indeed, I knew I'd not die. Brù knew it, too. Nothing short of gross, bodily violence—bullets, dissevering blade work—could kill me. The Blood and nothing but kills us witches, and it does so at will, taking us when and where it wants. No process, and no elixir, no matter how magical, could displace this as my fate. I was certain of this. Oh, but neither could I hasten said fate; and, yes, wanting to die in the weeks that followed, I tried. I envisioned my Red End, but no . . . Nothing. So: What could I do but lie for days, for weeks, naked, in my own filth, wondering what changes Brù was effecting within me— me: accursed Rebus—and willing the Blood to come?

Thusly did I grow crazy in my turn. . . . And all the while a Book, *the* Book that might have spared me all this, that might have saved me, but that I'd found too late, lay ten feet from me. . . . Crazed, yes. And as the weeks crept slowly over that confused calendar and I grew ever sicker—that alchemical cud rising to my mouth, well nigh tidally—I grew so crazed, so delirious I nearly missed hearing my name— *Henry!*—when it was called up from the street below. By Calixto.

 *Chapter Seventeen*

Mercury is the permanent water without which nothing takes place, because it has the virtue of spiritual Blood which, when it is joined with the Body, changes into Spirit by this mixture; and reduced to one, they change into each other, since the Body incorporates the Spirit and the Spirit changes the Body into Spirit, holds it and colors it with Blood, since everything that has Spirit also has Blood and Blood is a spiritual humor which strengthens Nature.

—DARDARIUS, Turba philosophorum, twelfth century

I'D ADDED AN ADDRESS—NAUGHT BUT THE NAMES OF TWO intersecting streets—to the note I'd left for Calixto at Burnham & Co., handing it into the care of kindly Manolo. Had it been too precise an address, or directions—*Knock upon the tar-black door*—we'd have involved Queverdo Brù; and this was something I'd not wanted to do, not even then, a month or more prior to my . . . alchemization.

I know now that the day in question was a Tuesday, a typically sunny Tuesday that otherwise was of no consequence upon the calendar. How long I'd lain in the Stone Room, that I cannot say. Similarly, I cannot say what time of day it was when first I heard my name— no: not my *given* name, but rather the name I'd long used when meeting people as a man: Henry—though, to judge by subsequent events, it must have been late day, and darkening unto dusk. . . . I'd lost all sense of the cycling days, blindfolded as I was. Moreover, whenever Brù had deigned to untie the fold, still I'd find the room, the crypt, ill lit, and horribly smoky; for he'd sealed the one window somehow, lest that transubstantiating smoke escape it and slow the Great Work he'd set in progress. And as he . . . *fed* me at whim, I grew further confused, and could not equate those feedings with the meals typically termed breakfast, lunch, and supper, nor with those hours at which said meals are typically taken. Time was of a piece. And though I was not dying—how hard it hit me, this revelation that Brù could not kill me by his poisons, his potions, his Art—certainly I'd devolved from health, and was now emaciated and delirious. Yet through the cracks in my delirium there came that called name, *Henry*, as if from another world. Angel-song, it seemed. And was.

. . . Reader, begrudge me not a hastening of these details. That is, those related to my captivity. Surely they are no more pleasant for you to read than they were for me to suffer. That said, the tenets of taletelling insist that I tell here why it was I could not call out in response to Calixto, once I knew it was he down in the street.

Brù, you see, had gagged me. My cold-eyed, oh so efficacious captor had tired, it seemed, of struggling with me each time he came to the Stone Room, stripped and tried to . . . Horrid, horrid this! . . . For Brù began to lick me. Naked, he'd take to a knee beside the cot and lick me, yes, upon the hip, heel, breast, neck, et cetera; and, blindfolded, I never knew where his infernal kiss would fall. He did this, I suppose, to ascertain, by the taste of my sweat, how far I'd progressed to the desired state, that white-state that would show I was ready for either the athanor or autopsy; and, of course, the concomitant harvesting of whatever stone he'd sown within me. He could see me, of course; and yes, I was changing. Indeed, the blindfold would later seem a blessing; for had I been able to see the changes coming over me as I lay in that smokehouse like a piece of curing meat, well . . . But taste was the truer test, truer than sight, I suppose; and so Brù tested, with his tongue, the salinity from off my whitening skin each time he came to administer that silvery, liquescent elixir of his.

. . . The gag, yes. It was a leather strap that buckled behind my head—such that, perforce, I lay with my head crooked to the side, lest the buckle bite at the back of my skull—and into my mouth went a rubbery ball through which a hole had been bored. Through this hole Brù could slip, easily, that greased and down-snaking funnel so as to deliver his deathly decoction deep, deep within me.

I'd learned to still myself for these ministrations; for to move made them worse. Once I felt the funnel snag upon the sides of my esophagus, and cut me. What's more: Why struggle when I'd no recourse, when I was blindfolded and unable to work any Craft upon my captor?

So it was I could not call out in response when my name, as called by Calixto, came to me, and I heard it as one might see the tail of a shooting star: so bright, so distant, and yet so fast-dying one is not certain one has seen it. But then it came again. Indeed, later I'd learn that the boy had stood further down the street calling—*Henry, Henry,* progressing from a whisper to a cry—all the day prior, Monday, when first he'd returned from Barcelona to the offices of Burnham & Co., where, along with the balance of his pay, he'd been handed my note:

Calixto, I'd written, *forgive me.*

If you receive this note upon the Halcyon*'s return—and how I hope you shall!—please know that I have stayed in Havana to attend your return.*

*Call my name at the corner of the calles . . . —*and here I named the two streets in question—*and I will come, explaining this strange protocol and much, much else. All else.*

And I signed it *H.*

But in the six months Calixto had been at sea, that *H.* of mine had reverted to Herculine from Henry, and surely this—along with so much else—accounts for his surprise when . . . *Enfin,* what a surprise, what a fright I must have been when found! Stranger than any name change could account for.

Oh, but blessedly Calixto had come to me! And as soon as I knew as much, as soon as I sensed it, I drew up my Blood, my witch's will, my every talent, and I called to him. Not literally, not vocally, no. But in my mind's eye *I saw him,* saw the street where he stood, saw from his perspective the window behind which Brù had sealed me away; and I reached, reached for his mind, his heart, and in so doing, I drew my savior to me. I had to. Now, whilst I was lucid—something in that silvery soup of Brù's brought sleep, a deep, stupefying sleep—and Brù was busy upon the *assoltaire:* I could hear him hammering at the new and larger athanor, readying it for my perfection.

Yes, I heard the echoing hammer-shot down in the street in which Calixto stood, calling my name to a window very near the one behind my head. It might well have seemed a serenade. . . . Oh, but stay: I romanticize the moment when, in truth, the voice I heard was tentative and thin, scared. Later I'd learn that Calixto had almost not come, that he'd thought instead to sign onto a Burnham boat running the sea route to Rotterdam. And who'd have blamed the boy if he had? No doubt what he'd witnessed aboard the *Athée* had bedeviled six months' worth of his dreams. Oh, but blessedly, yes, he'd come. And was near enough to save me, if only we could hurry, if only I could keep Brù from coming before Calixto did.

There was one image I took care *not* to conjure, lest Cal see it as well: Brù's blackened door. Pointedly, the problem was this: How to draw Calixto to that very door but have him neither knock upon it nor call my name? He'd have to push it open and enter—*Do not call my name, Do not call my name . . .* —and come to the Stone Room unseen.

I thought back to all I'd read in the *Books of Shadows* about *the willing of deeds to be done;* and somehow I succeeded, and achieved all but one of the aforementioned points. Which is to say, Calixto came to the tarred door—and here I cannot discount luck, and chance; for doubtless the boy, ever more determined owing to what *I was showing him*, tried every door on the street—and pushing, not knocking, came into the courtyard; oh, but there, ignoring the peafowl or whatever albino creatures came, Calixto again called my name.

Brù's hammer fell still.

So panicked was I, and so very, very weak, I lost hold of the boy's mind and left him to his own logic: He called up to whomever it was he heard hammering upon the roof.

I tried my best to make a noise, a summoning noise of some kind, but I barely had strength enough to raise my limbs to the limits of my restraints, let alone rattle the cot upon the parquet floor. And of course I'd no literal voice, owing to the gag. In fact, though I did not know it then, I'd no voice at all: The mercury, I suppose, or some other ingredient had had a corrosive effect upon my vocal cords, or perhaps they'd fallen slack from disuse, or been damaged by the down-going funnel.

As Calixto called up from the courtyard, the white-flesh upon the walls of the Stone Room grew ever wilder, as if cognizant of the conflict to come. The wings blew the sulfuric smoke—like that said to seep from the very fissures of Hell—into tiny, ever-blackening tornadoes. Or perhaps my eyes deceived me, as did my every other sense, then. Save for my hearing; for:

I heard in the courtyard Calixto's booted step. Heard, too, "Henry? . . . Henry?"

I calmed myself as best I could, and I sent the boy images of books. *Books, books.* And a door. And a second, sealed door beside the first. Sent him, too, a most fearsome image of Brù; who'd no doubt begun his descent from the *assoltaire* to see who it was dared intrude upon him, upon the Great Work at hand. What I did not, could not send Cal was an image of myself, as I was; for I did not yet know what had happened to me in the course of that alchemizing month. So it was that Calixto was the first besides Brù to see me so . . .

Stay: First, before he found me, I heard his footfall on the balcony beyond, heard it stop. Then there came the creak of the library door. *He was in the library.* So near.

. . . Sebastiana's Book. Again I wondered, *Where is the Book?* Last I saw, my clothes, my dress still sat beneath that bone-adorned wall. Surely, surely the Book was there, too. *I needed the Book.*

Calixto's coming back out onto the balcony roused the birds from the creeper, and now their wings could be heard, aflutter. Above the din there rose the voice of Brù, itself rusted from disuse: "Boy?" called he from down in the courtyard. "Boy!"

Oh, but Calixto already had his hand upon the latch of the Stone Room's door, the door behind which I lay *working my will* as I never had before. *Come, come.* And luckily he'd not been dissuaded by Brù; for I heard the latch turn, heard the sealed door open with a sucking sound. And though I felt the flood of light coming into the room, seeping through my blindfold, still I could not see. And so what now I report came to me from Calixto himself, later; and as I find it discomfits me still—how very strange to sense such a thing, now, dead, and see it give rise to gooseflesh upon *cette pauvre petite*—I shall speed the present telling; and say:

Calixto found himself standing in a darkened, stinking, smoke-choked chamber. More precisely: He stood coughing upon its thresh-old, trying to wave the smoke away. At first he supposed a fire burned within. But no: Soon the smoke cleared through the opened door. Cleared to show me where I lay. *As I lay:*

Naked. Skeletal. Bound. And well nigh opalescent; for the *prima materia* was at work within me, as were its component parts. Excess of salt had shriveled what flesh still clung to my bones, and mercury, too, had done its work. I'd sores, and—when freed of the gag—I'd find my gums had drawn back from my teeth such that I appeared fanged. My smile—had I been able to smile—would have seemed a snarl. As it was, my chapped lips split when I tried to speak. A sight, a fright, indeed. But let me say again: *I was naked*. There, before Calixto. I could not see his reaction—his revulsion, surely—neither to my tortured nor my true, doubly-sexed self.

What next *I* saw with my own eyes was this:

Brù, in his burnous, the hood of which had fallen back to show the sheen, the sweat-slick top of his shaven head as he bent toward me. He'd removed the blindfold, yes, and was at work upon the cuffs. And as Brù bent toward the cuffs with a key, I saw Calixto standing close behind him. Calixto; whose blondness—how his hair had grown, untended, at sea!—gave him an angelic cast, an appearance aided by the play of light and smoke. A saving angel he was, yes; save that in art, in the painted and passed-about plates and panels of old, angels rarely brandish blades, rarely hold them to the throats of the world's tormentors.

Calixto had matured, physically, those six months at sea, such that now he stood strong, broad and blond, and beautiful; but not only had the boy strengthened—it had been hard going aboard the *Halcyon*, and his body had responded as those of boys will: *it grew*—but also he'd come upon a core of self, an *inner* strength he'd not had recourse to aboard the *Athée*; such that now he held a knife to the neck of Brù and looked through the smoky dimness to me, *me*—however did he see past the stranger, *the strangeness* that lay before him?—seeking only a nod, a wink, some signal conveying, *Yes, kill him.*

I could not give it.

I shook my head, *No.*

Calixto was confused. Surely I was not as he found me owing to any . . . willfulness on my part? True: The boy would have been able to list any number of sexual predilections or peccadilloes—a night, even an hour in any portside sink is . . . erotically edifying, let me say—but surely I'd not chosen to be subjugated so. Was Brù then *not* to blame? The boy must have asked himself this very question; for I watched with horror as he backed from Brù, as he withdrew that finger-length blade he'd no doubt drawn from a seam in his boot.

No. I shook my head again, this time to say, *Don't let him go. Don't listen to him.* For indeed Brù had begun to speak, just as I discovered that I could not.

With those long, dark, spindle-like fingers of his, Brù had taken the gag from my mouth; but I found, owing to several factors—a jaw yet immobile, and sore; a throat coated in that quieting, silvery syrup; and a mind in which thoughts, like sea grass, swayed—that I could not explain, could not accuse, *could not speak.*

Fear. I was fearful then. Not that Queverdo Brù would, or *could* harm us. He could not. He hadn't powers of that sort, had only his knowledge; and moreover, he'd lost that element of surprise that had enabled him to trick me, to use me as he had. Now, kneeling still, like a supplicant, beside the cot, before Calixto, he seemed but an old man. Doubtless he played the role for effect: stooping, shuffling when finally he stood and moved toward the boy, hands cupped like a beggar's, and spoke so intensely, so urgently, so intimately, that, even though I could not hear his whispered words, I knew to intervene. Summoning what little strength had returned to me, and my atrophied limbs, I raised my right hand and pointed—with a long-nailed, foul finger: the flow of filth from my person had coated the cot, and all, *all* that lay upon it— . . . pointed to my right eye.

Calixto saw and understood: *Diblis,* was my meaning. *This man has used me as Diblis did you.*

So it was that Brù, stunned at having come so near his project's end—I believe he'd have harvested the Stone within a fortnight, offering my remains to the flames of his new athanor or the life-clotted walls of the crypt— . . . soon Queverdo Brù found himself seated upon the floor in a most active corner of that crypt, cuffed, and seeming as desirous of death as I'd long been.

Though I felt no sympathy for the alchemist, none at all, still I'd never have chosen to stain my or Calixto's soul with his blood. Leastways I like to think I'd have refrained from doing so. As it was, I hadn't time, then, to worry about Brù crying in his corner: Before me stood Calixto, looking down, stunned at the sight of me.

He owed me, felt indebted because of Diblis. This cannot be discounted. Otherwise, surely, the boy would have run from who, *from what* he found before him.

And what was it, I wonder, troubled him the more? Was it the stink of my filthy, sulfur-infused self? A month untended, and deprived of sustenance—of the *non*alchemical kind—does a body no discernible good, to be sure; but Brù had worsened things by his work, or Work, as he'd have deemed it. The *prima materia* had silenced and blanched me as it had the lesser, or simpler species he'd worked upon, though I'd not brightened unto an albinism akin to theirs. I was pale, yes, perfectly opalescent, but I'd not yet alchemized unto the animals' light-state.

Alors, filthy, unkempt, seeming a revenant come back from Beyond, there I lay looking up, pitifully, at my beautiful, beloved Calixto.

And blessed be that boy, forevermore; for he did not disdain me, no. Indeed, he helped me to sit upon the cot, though once, twice, I caved in the middle, collapsed—*con*cave I was, my ribs prominent as barrel staves—splashing back onto the cot, into my own waste. All the while Brù sat watching from the corner. Calixto had cuffed him at both the wrist and ankle such that he'd have had to hump his way toward us, worm-like, to cause us any concern. More: I saw that Calixto had fastened onto Brù that gag I'd long worn, such that its fetid, chewed ball precluded any speech, any more crying coming from that corner.

When finally I could sustain an upright state, yet still was unable to speak, I motioned Calixto toward my clothes, not seeking to cover myself—rather late for that—but desperate to know if, as I'd supposed, Sebastiana's Book lay beneath them.

It did.

And though that news gave me strength, still I hadn't strength enough to open the Book when Cal carried it to me. I sat there staring at it, not knowing what to do, too soiled to take it, to touch it. I wondered. I worried. In fact, the alchemists of old had a word for my present, as yet *unperfected* state: *massa confusa*. Confused I was, indeed. Cal and I both were confused, though the boy's confusion was soon to deepen; for he'd not yet seen, or understood . . .

Bref, Calixto, like a gallant, took me up and carried me from the Stone Room. Here, surely, was the strangest of pietàs. Down we went to the courtyard, to that fountain with its rounded, shallow pool. In this he set me down, like a babe in its bath. And he washed me clean. Only then did he remark my . . . particulars; for, with his hand wrapped in his torn-away shirt, he wiped my fouled flesh, rinsing and wringing out the cloth onto the pavers of the yard, until finally, delicately, detachedly, he slipped his hand down to . . .

Fast, so fast I surprised us both, I grabbed Calixto's wrist. Too late: already he was on me, in me; for he'd let fall the shirt to . . . to explore, innocently, what surely, *surely* was not possible. Had he felt . . . ? Had he found . . . ? He'd seen my smallish breasts already, but somehow it seemed he hadn't . . . *Enfin*, it was finding *all* that I had stowed below board that tipped the boy toward inquiry.

Stunned as he was, he was neither rough nor rude, but proceeded with all the practicality of a physician or midwife, cold, yes, but primarily . . . inquisitive. Pointedly: *He had to know*. And so I let go his wrist. I let him learn.

Having handled my member, having found a vagina in the same precinct, he stood up and fell back from the fountain, staring at my breasts as though they'd eyes to hold his stare. 'Twas then it all went *click*. . . . Now I'd not sufficient strength to demur, to dissemble, even if I'd wanted to. Nor did I have a voice with which to explain—I'd have referenced, high-handedly, Hermaphroditus, spawn of Hermes and Aphrodite, et cetera, and done so coldly, braced for the boy's disdain— . . . and neither had I whatever is needed to lie. It is not strength the liar requires, but rather its opposite—not weakness, but a sort of *inverted virtue*—for which no single word I know suffices.

Lies . . . Six months prior I'd lied, not wanting to. And though I'd since determined I'd tell Calixto the truth if ever I could, if ever I saw him again, if ever he'd sit and listen long enough to one who'd deceived him so, who'd confused him with a show of Craftwork only to abandon him to his questions, to abandon his very person, leaving him to sit before the cathedral, to stew beneath a noonday sun . . . No: *No more lies.* Those three words I'd said to myself time and time again in Calixto's absence, till finally, rendering them mantric, *I'd heard their worth.*

Oh, but now I had no voice.

But Brù, in stripping me, had stripped me of my lies as well. (*For this* I came to hate him. *For this* I came to not care about whatever fate he found at our hands.) There I was, naked. For Calixto to see, and consider.

When next the boy spoke, though, the surprise was mine. "Your eyes," said he.

Calixto was seeing much, *much* for the first time; yet he chose to ask about my un-bespectacled, turned Eye; for, ever since meeting the boy,

I'd hidden my eyes behind blue-lensed sunshades, and had told him that same lie I told anyone who questioned me—few did, as few were met: that I'd a congenital aversion to the light, be it from the sun, moon, candle flame, or whatnot. . . . Lies.

But now, to Calixto, I nodded. *I'll explain.* And indeed I tried to croak out a word or two—pardon the pun—upon the subject of my toad-turned Eye, but I could not. Still I'd no voice. Would it ever return? All I could do was nod again, this time conveying, vaguely, *Up.* What was it I meant? *Take me from this fountain? Up to the Stone Room? To the library? To Brù? To Sebastiana's Book?* Or all the aforesaid?

I cannot say; but soon we'd returned to the library, through a courtyard eerily quiet and unbrightened by any of Brù's menagerie—where had they gone? . . . had the winged things flown away? . . . why had the peafowl crowded into a shadowed corner?—and I came to sit amidst the piled volumes with Sebastiana's Book before me, daring not to open it, doubting I'd the strength to read it. What might I find? What had happened to Sebastiana, and whatever company she'd come with? Truth to tell, I gave no thought at all to "the surprise" by which she'd lured me from home, over the blues of the Stream to Brù. Surprises and lies seemed cut from too similar a cloth.

In the crypt, Calixto further secured Queverdo Brù. And when he returned to me in the library, saying we were safe, he, shirtless still himself, bore both my dress and a lamp, by the light of which he found me curled beneath the window, on my nest, crying.

He came to me, Calixto did. He unfolded my dress, impregnated with sulfurous smoke, and shook from it whatever vermin had taken up residency in its long-still, striped folds. And then, gingerly, dare I say lovingly, forgivingly, he lay the dress over me; not to cover me, no, but rather because I was shivering from something worse than cold.

Then, as I lay on my side, raised upon an elbow sharp as a stake, only then did I open again Sebastiana's Book. I saw she'd not filled many of the pages before she'd . . . stopped. For whatever reason. And, turning to a blank page, I tipped my chin toward a pen and inkwell sitting near, though they might have been upon some satellite of the moon for all I could reach them myself. Calixto set them before me, put the goose quill in my hand. I dipped its clotted tip into the well— so slowly, so deliberately, with what little speed and control I could summon—and finally brought it up blue with ink.

Slowly I wrote, for Calixto, three words. The first two were a plea:

Keep me.

And the last told of a place, a location where I might revivify, seek out strength where no one but I could hope to find it. I wrote this third word in French, though I cannot say why; so that when I tilted the Book toward Calixto, what he read—in a spidery scrawl—was:

cimetière.

 *Chapter Eighteen*

Poor themselves, the alchemists promise riches which are not forthcoming; wise also in their open conceit, they fall into the ditch which they themselves have digged.

—Pope John XXII, Edict Condemning Alchemy

*H*E KEPT ME, AS I'D ASKED HIM TO. HE COULD HAVE RUN. He'd every right.

But Calixto felt indebted, as no one but me had ever protected him before; and now it was his turn to protect his protector. Plus, his life would have been moored on sand if he'd turned from me, his questions unasked, unanswered. . . . So it goes with the sisterhood and the few mortals—boys, mostly—with whom they share, to whom they deign to show their true selves: The bonds forged prove to be indissoluble. The boys believe—*Credo quia absurdum est,* said Tertulian: I believe *because* it is absurd—or their minds devolve to jelly in the face of *the seemingly inexplicable,* and they walk raving from their witch.

Calixto had asked no questions when I'd made that strangest of requests: *Take me to a cemetery.* All I'd had to do was assure him that I was neither dead nor dying. *I need it,* I'd written. *Five days among the dead, no more, and I will rise revivified, stronger,* this last conveyed with an attempted smile—my jaw yet ached from the ball-gag, and my split lips still bled—and the faux flexing of a biceps, which act must surely have called to mind naught but an egg being swallowed by a snake.

Enfin, he did it. He brought me to the dead, Calixto did. *He kept me.*

Having left Brù's sometime earlier—he was gone but a few hours, I suppose—Calixto came back with not one casket but two, proud to report he'd roused from sleep that Irishman who tended Havana's non-Catholic dead, paying the man X amount of money for the casket he'd keep and half as much for the one he'd return in time.

I knew the Irishman in question, as he was ever at the port, waiting for word of fever or some other pestilence by which to profit. He was vulturine, truly, in his baggy black coat, leaning upon a shillelagh into which he'd cut a rule of inches and feet so as to be ready to size up anyone on whom the Reaper had trained his eye. But why Calixto had gotten two coffins from the man, I'd no idea. If he'd a plan, I'd played no part in hatching it. I'd asked only to be taken amongst the dead, hoping there'd be disquiet enough to draw upon.

Along with the coffins, he'd rented a dray—how else to carry the coffins to Brù's?—which came rattling behind a horse so swaybacked, so shabby, it seemed to be searching out a plot of its own. Into the courtyard horse and dray came, that same night, through those tarred doors opening wide for the first time in a long, long while (so cried their rusted hinges). On the bed of the dray lay the caskets. They were identical, and each had been disinterred of late: Soil was caked in the heads of the screws. Straightaway I had a sense of the coffins' previous occupants—death is typically *for keeps,* but not so its accoutrements: In Havana, as elsewhere, coffins were let time and again, and priced according to their tenants' tenure therein— . . . yes, I sensed them as the living sometimes sense *my* presence, nowadays, whether I be embodied or not, as a perfume, rather strong and redolent of violets, lingering like (I once was told) the scent of a harlot who's just left the room. The difference being, of course, that I suffered not just the scent but *the effect* of the proximate dead; or rather, I had suffered it before. Of late the death-alliance had been more . . . *beneficent*; and already, standing in Brù's courtyard, I felt the first signs of . . . renewal, shall I say?

Still I hadn't all my wits about me, not by any stretch. If I had, I'd surely have asked Cal how it was he'd keep from confusing the two coffins—one for me, the other (I supposed) for Brù—and their contents; but, again, I'd neither my wits nor a voice to work with.

If Calixto had handed over cash for the coffins, well, *tant pis*; for I'd no need of a coffin. And I hoped he hadn't paid to secure a plot, or purchased those passes required by both the city's priests and its guardians of the gates if one hoped to inter someone—a Catholic, of course—in consecrated ground beyond the walls of the old city, all proceeds from which passes fell, *clink*, into the coffers of the Church. Non-Catholics one could dispose of as one pleased, though that was an end no dog deserved. Without evidence of Catholicity, licenses for burial on the island were denied, and the dead had either to set sail or settle themselves in unfenced, untended cemeteries dug in desolate locations. Uncoffined, unshrouded, there the non-Catholic dead were contended for by the vulture and the worm; and when sufficient time had passed, and they had devolved to dust, their graves were reclaimed, the contents turned out, the bones let to blanch in the sun and shift, reshape themselves into the oddest of skeletons, owing to rains that made muddy ossuaries of the lots. Skulls were harvested, more often than not; hence the grinning piles I'd see stacked in the corners of the yard as if they'd been set up for a game of skittles, or ninepin. . . . Oh yes, it was to such a charnel yard that Calixto carried me, as directed.

As I was no longer a Catholic in practice—nor, for that matter, *dead*—it was with relief that I heard from an abject, most apologetic Calixto that we'd have recourse only to a potter's field, if, indeed, it was a cemetery I sought. (Here was the boy's last chance to ask if he'd heard me aright.)

It is, nodded I, relieved at the boy's obedience—having seen what he'd seen in the Stone Room, in the fountain, and aboard the *Athée*, he believed in me: *He had faith*— . . . relieved, yes, as his obedience spared me having to explain, with neither voice nor energy enough to write at length, why it was I preferred to lie in a potter's field: Consecrated soil calms the souls of Catholics, you see, and those prettified precincts of theirs do not produce the disquiet I sought, or rather required for my recovery.

Wasted as I was, poor Calixto had to help me dress—never did fingers dance so deftly, never did eyes so avert themselves—and climb into my coffin; whereupon I showed him five fingers, meaning *Let me lie five days, no more*, and beckoned for Sebastiana's Book. I could not, *would not* suffer being separated from it a moment more. And when finally it lay atop my chest, and Cal had helped me cross my arms over it, well, I suppose it is simplistic to say I closed my eyes and slept, but I did. Essentially. And so, when I woke, I'd have to back-conjure what then came to pass by casting a simple spell of Sight widdershins—counter to clock and calendar; and this I did, such that now I may report the following particulars:

We went by dray to the port, where—and this surprised me, when I saw the blue water in the blue dream I divined—our party passed onto a barge bound across the bay for a boneyard on its far side, at Regla. There, a trembling Cal proved his trustworthiness in arranging for not one, but two interments. This was a delicate matter, as neither one of his charges was dead, and the sexton—too dignified a term for one such as he—with whom he had to deal was a brute, the sort of man who pries open the mouths of the dead, running the scabrous pads of his fingertips over their teeth in search of gold. Having learned well from me, Calixto offered an excess of coin to guarantee the sanctity of our two coffins; for he sought to protect me whilst I underwent what processes I would, but had also to hide the fact that he was about to bury Brù against his will.

Oh yes. Calixto had gotten a bound, gagged, and cuffed Queverdo Brù into his coffin—there the alchemist lay, shrouded in his burnous —and lest he smother, Cal had cracked the lid just so, using a bone brought down from off the wall of the Stone Room. It seemed the boy shied from his deed at the last, and though I'd done Diblis unto death for him—which favor he sought to repay— he took pity upon the alchemist. He hired for him a tilting, about-to-tumble tomb that sat aboveground. In this Brù would be able to breathe. For a while. Yet still he could not call out to the sexton or his gang of shovel men. And lest you, reader, think the boy a beast, know that he sought only to stymie Brù, to stop him from giving chase or sending his light-creatures after us when, five or six days hence, we, Calixto and I, would sail from Havana. As he, Cal, rightly supposed we would.

As for me, I'd specified burial in a mass grave topped with loose dirt; and as long as I had a coffin, its lid must be left *unsealed* so that I could rise of my own accord when ready. This Calixto saw to—by cash, as said, but also by haunting that boneyard as few ghosts ever had, coming each of those five days at dawn to both watch over my sleep and slip a crust of bread and some water to an ungagged Brù; which meals were administered with a knife held to the older man's throat, lest he cry out. Gagged again, Brù retook to his coffin for twenty-four hours more. It was a ritual repeated five times, and by it

Calixto kept Brù alive till I could rise and further decide his fate; for hadn't he presumed to decide mine?

As for me, I was left where I lay. As planned. In my closed coffin, with no need for a crack: When descending down to the depths of the disquieted dead, when *living* amidst their din—composed of secrets, oaths, promises, pain, and prayer, all of which I absorbed as inchoate speech, thereby relieving the dead of their disquiet and growing ever stronger myself— . . . when buried, I say, I did not need to breathe. This I'd learned. All I'd needed beside that rest, that strange sleep, was Sebastiana's Book. Of course, I could not read it as I lay. But when I woke, when I rose, I'd want it, yes, and I'd open it fast to find out that . . .

Hélas, I did indeed rise five days hence to find the dead quieted, and myself stronger. Not recovered, but recovering. And—blessedly—able to speak, able to call out to Cal where he sat atop a tomb staring at the darkening, starlit sky. Able, too, to discern, *to begin to discern*, what it was the alchemist had achieved upon me by the Great Work; and yes, oh so ready to search out light and peace by which to read, in Sebastiana's Book, what had happened to her, and how it was my path had come to cross that of Queverdo Brù.

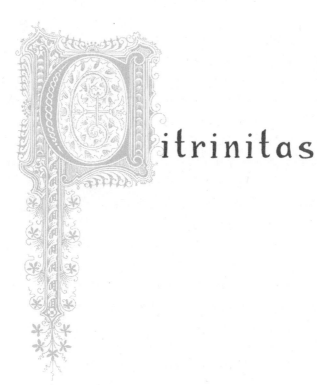

itrinitas

 *Chapter Nineteen*

For there is nothing which cannot be discovered
and nothing so secret that it cannot be known.
—Matthew 10:26

Oh, H., oh, my heart, what have I done?
If perchance you find this Book . . .
. . . Run, my heart!

Run? Not exactly.

We sailed from Havana as soon as we could, yes; but
we didn't run, it being rather late for the escape Sebastiana
had urged. And now that we had survived, there was no
one to run from . . . Brù? He was, well . . . contained.

And where was I to run to, go to? I had to read a bit
more in Sebastiana's Book before I could plot our
course. I had to use some deduction, too, as my sister
had written cryptically—she hadn't had enough time to
encipher those last pages—of her, or rather *their* destination, hoping to convey it to me whilst keeping it from
Brù, should he find her last *Book of Shadows* before I did.

Of course, I did learn the whereabouts of Sebastiana—and that Shadow-company she kept—albeit well more than a half year after I'd set out in search of her and her promised secrets; but let that revelation attend us whilst I say how it was we took our leave of Cuba and seek, too, to excuse what it was we did to Queverdo Brù.

As said, Calixto had returned to Havana more man than boy. What happened aboard the *Halcyon* I cannot here record: Cal never told me, and neither did I divine it, as to do so would have been . . . rude. I assume he'd had occasion to defend himself, and had done so to his satisfaction. He'd grown, yes; but I do not refer only to that growth one can record in units of measure such as those carved upon the cudgel, or shillelagh, of that Cuban dealer in coffins. No, I speak of growth of another kind as well: *inner growth;* which, I suppose, I furthered, as Calixto was fast in asking his questions of me once I'd risen. I answered each in turn, and truthfully. Indeed, I have not told Calixto another lie, not from that day to this.

His first question—and he was so confused it seemed he could have cried as I walked to where he sat upon that headstone—was *Had I died?* I had not. Neither as a result of the alchemist's efforts nor Calixto's in laying me down, coffined, amidst the disquieted dead. I descended to a death-like state, that is true, and so, *bien sûr,* I understood the boy's confusion. He saw me, after all, rise after five days in the dirt, days during which I'd needed neither sustenance nor air. Save for that last fact—that I'd no need to breathe—the death-state is akin to a bear's wintering-over in its den. Think of it (said I to Calixto, sometime later) as a sort of *spiritual hibernation,* from which I always rose revivified, renewed, stronger, and—to extend my ursine metaphor—hungry as a cub blinking its way out into the woods at winter's end. And if I hadn't hunger enough to swipe down a deer or set myself down in some mountain stream, there to glut myself on salmon, well, surely I could have sat for several courses at La Felicidad. And indeed, soon after my resurrection, I found myself standing in the shadows near said restaurant watching as Calixto secured from my old friend Joachim a pot of shrimp-thick stew, some bread, a small wheel of hard cheese, and a bottle of Rioja; all of which we carried back to Brù's.

Brù, of course, was not there. Brù we'd left behind us, in his crypt, bound but uncoffined. And though I do not seek to tag Calixto with the alchemist's fate—which, again, I cannot here record but may safely suppose along with you, reader—it is true that Calixto convinced me to leave the man behind, buried on the far side of the bay; which fast argument he prefaced with the second of his questions: *What did he do to you?*

Bref, yes, we left Brù behind, rode away from the cemetery—quiet now: I'd calmed it, drained off its disquiet—and went, by horse and barge, to Brù's house. I left the lot in my coffin, loaded now onto that same dray: We thought this the better plan, as the sexton was sharp-eyed, and one does not typically ride from a cemetery with company after one has come all alone. What's more: I was rather . . . bedraggled, despite having risen rather easily. . . . And I struggle here to convey the weight of that moment when one wakes to understand, or rather *to remember* that one has been interred; and, further, *to realize* that, if fate has somehow intervened—the denial or even the death of one's accomplice, perhaps, or the sick-making coincidence of someone having set atop the grave a marker or stone too heavy to displace— . . . *alors,* I will desist, will leave you alone, sister, with your own fears of being buried alive with naught to do but await the Blood. I cannot consider such a fate further without wondering what may have become of Queverdo Brù, and the guilt that would, or might still ensue—coming to mind, if not heart—can be of no use now.

. . . *What did he do to you?* Indeed, what *had* Brù done to me? Settling into my coffin a second time, I asked Calixto to hold his many questions until we'd returned to Havana proper, to Brù's, until I'd washed and eaten and looked into Sebastiana's Book, which yet I clutched; *then*, I swore it, he'd have his answers. Brazen of me to put the boy off, considering; but I needed . . . *to live* before I could speak any sense, indeed before I could speak at all; for though my voice had returned, yes, still it stuck in my throat, like a rat scrabbling up a rusted pipe. And only when we'd returned to Brù's—and how wild the birds were now, wheeling through the courtyard, confusedly, and seeming somehow dimmer than ever before— . . . only when I lit a lamp in my room and looked into a mirror attached to the washbasin, only then did I see . . . *Enfin*, only then did I hear again Calixto's question. He'd not asked what *alchemy* Brù had done unto me; for Cal knew nothing, yet, of the Great Work I'd suffered. Simply, the boy had wondered, had wanted to know, how it was I'd changed so.

And I stared into that glass wondering, wanting to know the same thing. Was it the alchemist who'd done . . . *this*, or had the dead done it, as they'd changed me the last time I'd lain with them?

No answers. All I knew, all I *saw*, was that *I was not as I'd been before.*

My blond hair—the sole physical trait I'd ever taken pride in—had grown long of late. I wore it plaited (as Herculine) or ponytailed, tied off with a strip of dried dolphin skin (as Henry); but now, *mon Dieu*, it was a stream of silver I saw tumbling from my scalp! It was as if it had been *plated*—not plaited, as in braided, but sans the *i*, as in new-minted and so silvery gray as to seem almost blue. Was this some trick of the light? Perhaps so, for didn't I appear impossibly pale as well?

Mais hélas, non. This was no trick attributable to any lamp. To what, then, could I attribute said changes? Alchemy or the death-alliance? I could not be certain. . . . Simply: If earlier I'd woken from the death-state stronger, with my Eye fixed in its witch-shape, well, this time I'd woken pale as fish belly and with a crone's crown of hair. And this I was not happy about. At all.

In time, I'd reconcile myself to the changes—my new mane I came to consider rather pretty, in fact, and my paleness I could mitigate by steady exposure to the sun; but then, back at Brù's, I stood in a pose I'd often adopted: before a mirror, crying. Not so loudly that Calixto could hear me where he stood, exploring, atop the *assoltaire*. And oh, how I cursed the alchemist, cursed a blue streak aimed at Brù; and thusly did I try to relieve myself of what guilt I felt at leaving him where he lay, even though Calixto had told me, again, that the yard did a brisk business—this he'd overheard said by the sexton, that sot-with-a-spade—and few of those interred there were ever let to lie in peace for long: Eventually they were evicted, yes, their plots sold to those *more freshly dead*. And so, said Cal, Brù would be found. Sooner or later. Alive or . . . otherwise.

Cleansed and changed into my second-best dress, sewn of emerald silks—the *bolan* had not fared well buried—I climbed up to join Calixto atop Brù's roof. Eagerly? Not wholly; for I worried what the truth would do to him, to me. To us.

Night had fallen, and a salted wind blew in from off the bay. The moon, I recall, was shy on its left side; but by its meager light Calixto had explored. Now, lamp in hand, I joined him in the largest tent—the laboratory-cum-chapel—where he stood before the dark, carved-wood altar.

"What . . ." said he, haltingly, "what is this?"

He referred to more than the altar, of course. However would I answer? I'd been six months in search of an answer myself. I said, "Alchemy. That . . . man—his name was, *is* Queverdo Brù—he practiced, *practices* alchemy here." Still I could not speak of Brù in the past tense. To do so would have been to admit what we'd done: Left him, *alive,* to die.

" 'Practices'?" came Calixto's echoing query; to which I replied by turning my palms out and upward, and glancing down the length of my green silks. What I meant to convey was, *Yes, upon me.*

"You've changed," said Calixto, "it's true. But that isn't . . . bad, I don't think." The boy was uneasy, as who would not have been? The hour for answers had come.

I motioned toward the more comfortable tent, the one wherein I'd first been received by Brù. Soon we were seated on one of the white sofas, enough space between us for a bull to have charged through. This space soon was littered with the detritus of the meal we'd gotten from La Felicidad, or rather those bits of it I'd not devoured on the street. We were silent a long while, and it occurred to me that the boy was not . . . *mine,* was not won over to the Shadows and still might rise to run.

And so, yes: the time had come to tell my truths.

It will come as no surprise that I thought then of my own teacher, Sebastiana d'Azur, whose Book I'd carried up to the *assoltaire* along with the lamp. The Book, in fact, had not been out of my possession since Calixto had set it in my filthy hands five, nearly six days prior; and still, still I hadn't had time enough to read it in its entirety. I wanted nothing more, save for this: to tell my truths, to teach Calixto what he'd need to know if he were to stay, and *keep me.*

Thinking of my Soror Mystica—where, oh where was she? . . . and did I have that answer in hand, if only I could open her Book and read it through?— . . . thinking of Sebastiana, I heard again those words she'd uttered a decade earlier when she'd saved me. She'd spoken those words to me, *me,* strangeness itself; and still they'd been so very hard to hear, to understand, even as I knew that, with them, with those words, Sebastiana was ushering me into a world of wonders. How would Calixto hear that same sisterly refrain? He, who'd been only a witness to witchery and not a lost, lonesome witch, as I'd been? *Enfin,* I'd find out. Said I:

"There exists the inexplicable."

"Explain," said Calixto, *"por favor.* What cannot be explained?"

Parbleu! However to proceed? How does a witch usher her boy into the Shadows? . . . Still I hoped, *presumed* that Calixto would be my boy, my consort, if only I could keep him near, if only he didn't deny me and run.

Suddenly I remembered how Sebastiana had imposed order upon my own *initiation,* for want of a better word. Of all, *all* the questions I could have asked—and would have asked, had she let me—she allowed me but five, at first. Wondering if I could be as disciplined as she, I tried this, saying again to Calixto, "There exists the inexplicable. Ask me what you will, but only five questions for now. I will explain, as best I can, and you . . . you must trust, and learn."

Whereupon order went by the wayside: The boy began to blurt out his questions—they'd been ripening on the vine for a six-month—in an English much improved, owing to the *Halcyon's* British captain. I cannot recall, exactly, the first question that came, but too well I recall the answer it required of me:

"I am . . . a witch," said I; but those four weighty words were barely out of my mouth—in a voice not yet smooth, but decidedly mine—before I fell into a giggling fit. It was strange. And I couldn't stop. I'd felt something coming over me when first I'd begun to speak, but I'd supposed it would manifest itself as tears. But no: giggles; which grow less becoming as one ages, such that now I felt the fool.

Calixto was at first bewildered, bemused; but this, I saw, was fast progressing unto anger. Not good. Not good at all. Did he think I was teasing him? Of course he did; and indeed I might as well have announced that I was . . . *a unicorn,* or some other mythic creature. Knowing things had to worsen first, I forged ahead, drawing a deep breath but giggling still—they were as persistent as hiccups—and had out with it:

"I am a man. I am a woman. And yes, I am a witch."

This, improbably, settled us both. Somewhat. I sat back on the sofa. I stopped giggling. Gone were the creases from Calixto's forehead. His anger I'd assuaged. And I suppose the reason was this: Calixto had seen *proof* of those first two sentences, simple in construction if not content, and knew they'd have seemed as ridiculous as the third claim—of witch-ness—had he heard them first, before seeing the proof, the truth. Now I'd no intention of stripping to show said proofs again; but I could, and would, offer proof positive of the third claim I'd made.

In so doing I learned that again I'd strengthened where I'd lain, again I'd risen a stronger witch. So it was with ease that I made dance some of Brù's taxidermic tools, there, in that lesser tent separated from us by naught but night. Further:

"Brace yourself," said I; and I Eye-threw a beaker full of silvery goo against the smaller athanor, where it shattered, causing to come many hundreds of birds, all vying for the spilled elixir. It was then I understood that Brù had fed us all alike—from bowl, from trough . . . or by funnel—but the birds, having progressed further toward perfection than I, seemed to crave, *to require* whatever it was I'd spilled, such that now they attacked one another for access to it, silent all the while. This was unsettling. And at the same time, I'd a scared and confused Calixto to contend with.

Said I, meaning to distract him from the chaos, that quiet chaos of the birds, "I did it the same way with Diblis. I seized that beaker, there, the same as I did the marlinespike aboard the *Athée*, with my . . . my mind's eye, I suppose, with my will; and I drove it through his eye. Not that I'd meant to kill him, mind. I . . . I just did, that's all."

Calixto turned back to the birds, watched as they pecked at the last of the spilled elixir. As I watched the birds, backed by blackness, I saw they'd somehow . . . diminished, dimmed, yes, in the days Brù had been away. What would happen to them if they had no more of the elixir? And whatever said effect would be, would I suffer similarly?

It seemed I might be doing the birds a kindness if somehow I could herd them all into the athanor and burn them, burn all the light-beasts Brù had made.

The athanor . . . Seized by something within, I rose and hurried to it, leaping over ladder and steps as best my silks allowed. It was, as I supposed it would be, out. Rather, it had died down to a glow. Picking up that *tinajone*, that reservoir of rainwater, I tossed its contents onto the last coals burning deep in the belly of the furnace. At first the alchemist's eternal fire sighed, smoked, and died; but then there came a quiet burst of . . . color, yes, that blasted me back several steps. Strange; but I did not dwell on the effect; for the colors faded as fast as they'd come, and it was done: The lesser athanor was out. As for the larger, well . . . This, too, I put beyond use, swinging a maddened hammer till Calixto came up behind me. He put his arms around me. He calmed me. I'd begun to cry as I swung at that kiln, that fire-coffin Brù had built for me, and in which he'd intended to render me down to Stone. No creature—be it a *sur*-sexed witch or whatnot—would ever meet such a fate. I saw to it. . . . And to further ensure that no sister would ever step through Brù's jetty doors again, I set a warning hex upon his hearth before taking my final leave of it—a spell involving red pepper, hydrangea, and galangal. . . . Understand: Still I assumed the Duchess and Sebastiana had suffered there, in Havana, had somehow been *done to death* or had their Red Ends hurried by Brù once he'd used them to find and lure me, his Rebus. Oh, but I couldn't contemplate the sad ends of my sisters, not then.

Only as I stood shaking in Calixto's embrace, only then did I come to understand how close I'd been to a strange, very strange end. Stranger by far than the Coming of the Blood. And returned to the sofa, seated shoulder to shoulder with Calixto, I told him all I could—about Sebastiana d'Azur and the Duchess, and how they'd led me, innocently, to Brù; about how he, the alchemist, had seen me as his salvation, as the hermetic androgyne in whom he could culture the Stone, thusly achieving his own Perfection, or immortality; et cetera. I held back none of what I knew; yet I knew, too, that all I spoke seemed too strange to be true. To another sister, let alone Calixto.

"The inexplicable . . ." said Calixto after I'd gone on at length, such that my sore throat was sorer still, and my voice ground down to a whisper, sounding like some thick-skinned fruit being run along a rasp. "The inexplicable," said he. "I see." And improbably, *inexplicably,* it seemed he did. Or leastways he'd heard and seen enough not to run. That said, he stared at me, hard, before letting his eyes fall to the Book that sat upon my lap and which doubtless seemed, *ah,* finally, an *explicable* thing: a book, merely. How strange could it be?

Quite strange, in fact.

In the stillness that ensued, and all through the hours leading up till dawn, we read from Sebastiana's *Book of Shadows,* both of us, passing it back and forth and reciting till we tired—reading aloud, my voice returned: It was a muscle that wanted flexing—and other times sitting shoulder to shoulder and reading in silence whilst one of us held high the lamp. Calixto questioned me as to the contents. I explained as best I could. And what we did not read that night atop the *assoltaire,* we would soon read at sea; for that night I learned where it was Sebastiana had gone when she'd escaped Brù, as indeed and blessedly she had. Strange, her destination? Not so very. What was strange was where she'd come to Cuba *from,* and why.

 # Chapter Twenty

. . . and the azure gloom
Of an Italian night, where the deep skies assume
Hues which have words, and speak to ye of Heaven . . .
—BYRON, Childe Harold's Pilgrimage

ROMA, READ THE HEADING ON THE BOOK'S FIRST PAGE; and this was followed by a date—*mars, 1836*—some eighteen months prior to the night Calixto and I sat reading upon the roof.

As you well know (wrote Sebastiana, addressing me), *I have not, of late years, committed pen to paper, neither answering all your letters—for the which you'll forgive me, won't you, heart?— nor keeping a Book of Shadows, though I hope and trust you pursue the latter, writing for the benefit of our sisters-to-come. Likewise I have not wished to travel, or you'd have found me by your side, as long ago promised. I am old. I know it in my bones and in my Blood. And I have grown accustomed to the comforts of home, such as they are.*

Why then do I find myself seated in this coach, and wrapped in furs against this wintry chill, and bent over this Book, cut pens and empty pages attending me? Why do I commence here, having just arrived in Rome after a bone-bruising trip of some weeks' duration, a tale the end of which is yet unknown to me? Why have I woken, just now, to raise the black shade, situate myself as above-described and write? To you. — Because, heart, we are here, and come for one reason only.

But wait, H. I cannot yet divulge what it is has called me so far south, has summoned me, as now Asmodei returns, walking straight-backed—angry, that is—and cutting a diagonal across this People's Plaza, this Piazza del Popolo, having just dealt with the penny-men of the papal custom house. His stride, his mien is such that I see the red-trousered soldiers turning toward him, like boats buffeted by his wake, yet they dare not stop him, dare not subject him to more of their silly controls. — Amusing, really, their reaction, and interesting that people still react to Asmodei as they have all down the years of our acquaintance—and can it be, truly, that those years now number nearly fifty? Still he scares people, even soldiers standing here in our own emperor's stead. — But I have watched time work upon him, H., have seen the changes age has wrought, and today's Asmodei would not treat you as once he did, a decade past. I know it. — I watch him. Still he stands tall, broad-shouldered and blond, with an Olympian's grace and, at present, his still-handsome features masked, marred by a grimace, the cause of which I am about to ascertain. Certainly it is owing to some perquisite insisted upon by the Pope's poppets. — He comes. And so, à tout à l'heure. — Much more to come, my heart. Much.

To Calixto I explained that Sebastiana referenced Asmodei, a man—I forwent the charade Asmodei had once played upon me: of his having been *demon-born*— . . . a man she'd met during the red days of the French Revolution. Neither did I say that Sebastiana held herself responsible, in part, for said Revolution, as some of her clumsier Craftwork had sped its coming, nor that she'd let her guilt over same send her into seclusion. But I did tell Cal how Asmodei had disdained me, nay, *detested* me since first we'd seen each in the shadows at C——, the night of my rescue; and how that disdain, that detestation—all

born of his fear that somehow he'd lose his witch to me—had deep-
ened, till finally he'd struck. I made no mention of the particulars—
the poison, that is—but did own that I'd had to leave my sister's
Ravndal. I'd a mission to see to, it's true; but also I, or rather we—
Sebastiana and I—feared for my safety. . . . Asmodei, said I, was a man
I never needed to see again, *merci bien.*

As supposed (resumed S., some while later), *this temper-flare of A.'s we may
lay at the slippered feet of the Pope, whose minions (says A.) have extorted us, have
made us pay in order to pass into these precincts. —— "Why are we here anyway?"
asks Asmodei. And it is true: I have always avoided Rome, since that long-gone day
when crowds drove me from the city owing to some ceremony of one of the Piuses.
The Sixth, I think it was, who then was Chief-Priest of this place. And rich as they
are, you'd think one of the popes might purchase a greater store of names from which
to draw, and leave the bothersome numbers be. I jest, yes, but the humorlessness of the
Catholics has long caused me to chuckle, and I cannot help but tug at the strings of
such sanctimony. —— I always skirted this papist place, it's true, much preferring
Naples even though Vesuvius sat offshore as rumbly-grumbly as Asmodei now is,
seated across the coach, knowing not that I write to you, but busy talking blue about
all the "detestable" soldiers—the more detestable, says A., as they are our own, placed
here by our Louis-Philippe to shore up papal rule, I suppose. So, too, does he hiss at
the many tourists who crowd this plaza and slow our coach, dismissing them with
compounded epithets, calling them "ring-kissers," "miracle-mongers," and worse. —— Il
m'amuse, vraiment, though I do not look forward to telling him the true reason
for this trip.*

*Our coachman asks down, Where are we to go? And so I must set these pages aside,
though already you return to me as a result of a score of simple paragraphs. —— Know,
H., that despite a silence that must have seemed, at times, willful and cruel—and perhaps it was—I have missed you, as a mother must her child. —— Zut! I am told now
by A.—who thinks I record my impressions of the plaza, as a meandering tourist
might—to desist and direct the driver. I must decide which of the three streets spoking*

off this plaza we are to take. As I haven't peace and privacy enough to listen for what it was first called me here, and determine our route thusly, I suppose I will simply guess and listen for the voice later.

It was not a true voice, no. More of a presence, I suppose. — Tout vite, I will tell you, and let these men wait: I was walking on the strand last month, February, when first I heard it, sensed it as once I sensed your nearness, your presence, and your peril. — Yes, H.—and I suppose I ought to have written this already—I have been summoned here by a witch as innocent as once you were.

It is certain: A new witch rises here in Rome. Less certain, my heart, my Herculine, is what she has to do with me, with you. Something, it seems.

Zut encore! These men devil me so! Je m'excuse, but again I must stable this quill, till next I can take it up. I trust it shan't be long.

And so, promising more, she signed off: *S.*

From the Piazza del Popolo they rolled further into the city, Sebastiana, on a whim, having given the order to take the Corso, the road that separates two churches consecrated to Mary: Santa Maria dei Mircoli and Santa Maria di Montesanto; thusly occasioning comment from Asmodei relative to how, in Rome, one cannot swing a cat without smacking it against some holy precinct.

Further progress found them settled at a pensione sitting just south of the Palatine Hill, near the Colosseum. Their room Asmodei had chosen, as its windows opened toward the southeast, sparing him that view of St. Peter's gilded dome, which seemed to cap every other aspect of the city. From a terrace bared of fruit by a lingering winter, the two could see as far as the Via Appia; which roadway Asmodei would gladly have continued on, riding right out of Rome. But no, insisted Sebastiana, she'd business in the city. Whereupon Asmodei, as prone to anger in his dealings with others as he was to acquiescence when dealing with his witch, his all-but-wife, acquiesced, yes, and resigned himself to accompanying her on a trite, all-too-typical tour of the city's artworks, thinking that is what Sebastiana had meant by "business."

Similarly, he'd not questioned Sebastiana weeks prior, when she'd returned from a stroll upon the strand to announce that her days of leisure, of lassitude, had lapsed—those days had accrued to years, in fact—and that a visit to Rome might be just the thing to inspire her, to cause her, once again, to take up her brushes. This had pleased her paramour, and he'd agreed to pack for a trip of unknown duration. Off they'd gone, shuttering Ravndal and heading south with both Roméo and his Derrich accompanying them, the latter pair happy to take their leave of both the coach and their compeers somewhere upon the Mediterranean coast, where they'd overwinter with Sebastiana's feline familiar, Maluenda, all three pleasuring in the fact that the whiteness underfoot was sand, not snow. Of course, Roméo knew the truth occasioning the trip. . . . And a blessed thing it was, reading Roméo's hello as conveyed in Sebastiana's artful script.

Reality or ruse, I cannot say, but page upon page of Sebastiana's Book told—in words and sketches both—of their taking just such an artist's tour of the city. And though Sebastiana had advocated, in an earlier Book, seeing art *tout seule,* lest another's impressions impinge upon one's own, Asmodei accompanied her everywhere whilst they were in Rome; such that I realized his jealousy had not lessened despite fifty years' worth of proof that she was his, and he hers. No one—man, woman, witch, or otherwise, come forth from either Light or Shadow—could set them asunder. *They were one,* inseparable as any sculpted pair they'd see in the city's many museums.

Calixto and I read aloud from that catalog of their listed preferences—Sebastiana's for Raphael, in particular, and Asmodei's for any large-format paintings treating of pestilence or plague, slaughter or sin. She, of course, preferred portraits; though all, or nearly all that she saw—and she spared only the Rembrandts—suffered her critical eye as sickness might be said to suffer a surgeon's. And even Asmodei, being neither *an adept nor an admirer*, came to marvel at what had been sculpted from the marble cut from the mines at Carrara. Thereafter, he sought out sylphs, sirens, and the like, and adored them in his way—until, of course, he was heard to hiss at the cicerone leading them and others through the Palazzo dei Conservatori when he, the cicerone, requested, kindly, that Asmodei not handle the art. Or rather, not *fondle it*; for he, Asmodei, had taken to testing, by hand, the curves of hips and the heft of breasts.

He is incorrigible, wrote S.; but by the row of exclamation points following this opinion I knew the man amused her still; and I, seated beside Calixto, could only hope that fifty years forward we'd know a like affinity.

> *He follows me everywhere, everywhere, asking only when we'll eat. This, of course, complicates my mission.*
>
> *I have no doubt that a sister is here, and needful. Last night, she flitted through my dreams, seeming, most improbably, a two-headed creature of some kind. Or perhaps she sat astride such a one. I woke not knowing. But so certain am I now of her presence here, it seems I must have been dubious before. She is here, yes, and wants discovery. — But however will I seek this new sister with A. trailing me so? I despair of finding her—let alone having time alone with her—under present conditions. It may come to pass that I will have to tell A. the real reason we've ridden this far southward; but—I know I needn't remind you of this, heart—mellower though he is, still he is disinclined to share me with others, sisters particularly.*

※

Disinclined, indeed. He'd nearly killed me.

Meanwhile, here we are in a wintry-gray Rome longing for spring. The fruit trees bear only ice and the fountains are frozen. Sad, seeing the city deprived of the trickle and spill of all the fountains. Romans commit the memory of their immortals to that most unstable of elements, water. And everywhere, when the weather is clement, one finds, one hears the up-gush and fall of water commemorating consuls, emperors, popes, and such. Not now, though. Winter is a cruel season for commemoration, I suppose.

And so we plod about the streets with my medieval Mirabilia Urbis Romae *as guide. It is a huge, cumbrous text, folio size, and is, surely, quite valuable. I like it, as it renders Rome in sixteenth-century terms, casting one back to a city that has since sunk thirty meters down, owing both to Time and the Tiber, which latter river does sometimes rise up to refute its banks. Too, it amuses us both, the* Mirabilia *does, as when it warns of such things as "the dragon said to lie beneath the Temple of Vesta."*

Oh, but lest I give myself over to art and amusement—it pleases me, H., to see that still I could—and forget why it is I've come, I have Roma Aeterna *to remind me that yes,* tempus fugit, *and I had best be about my truer "business." — But what can I do now but wait, listen, and hope our sister discloses herself? It's been four nights since the above-mentioned dream. And by day I watch for her, looking, as lecherously as Asmodei does, at every passing contadina in her scarlet head rags and silvery bangles. — Meanwhile, yes, we meander, at museum pace. This frustrates my companion, whom I can no longer trust to self-tame in more staid surrounds. And so we must keep to outside places, such as the many forums, which seem but quarries. But it is bitter cold, and I want art, not rocks. — We have compromised on the Colosseum. We go this day at dusk.*

And so they'd been five days in the city, going gallery to gallery, before Asmodei gave over all efforts at "self-taming," and they took to the Colosseum. By midnight of the night in question, they'd be glad they had. More precisely: Yes, they both gladdened—if *gladden* be the word—albeit for different reasons. Asmodei pleasured in the Colosseum's lore, the stories of gladiatorial gore. Sebastiana, for her part, found herself open to the ancient arena's ghosts, past and present; and, thusly attuned, she heard again the new witch's call. Less glad she was, of course, to hear in it such distress.

———————————————— ❋ ————————————————

 # Chapter Twenty-one

... the graves stood tenantless and the sheeted dead
Did squeak and gibber in the Roman streets.
—SHAKESPEARE, *Hamlet*

Have you never been here, H.? I think not. I think you have stayed on the Atlantic's far side since first you crossed it, non? *If you have not been to Rome, pardon my presumption as I tell you, Do Not Come.*

You've written me of your death-alliance and I understand, as sisters before you have suffered a like affliction. Suffered and benefited both. —— Oh, but Rome? Heart, hear this: The dead are everywhere here, and I wonder if a witch such as you wouldn't suffer too greatly, so greatly that the resultant gain in strength would not justify the cost. Here every stone seems to sermonize, as do the dead themselves. Disquieted, don't you call them, those who are dead but not yet departed, who linger to demand redress of a sort? —— And nowhere are the Roman dead more in evidence than here, at the Colosseum.

The spirit of this place is extreme, so extreme that even the mortals hereabout seem to sense it, yet know not why they are driven to extremes themselves—it is a dangerous place (so say today's Ro-

mans), its shadowed, stony corridors clotted with persons in extremis, *stealing, loving, selling themselves, and such like. — Of course, I am close enough where I sit in this coach, fur-covered and comfortable, to sense the Colosseum's many merits, morbid as they are, but, ach! my man insists we explore further. And so, I must stop writing, wrap myself, and venture forth, toward the Arch of Constantine, which sits none too distant, and upon the walls of which I see warring friezes seeming deep-cut and quite detailed, owing, no doubt, to the moon's playing upon them. — It's quite the sisterly moon tonight, indeed, and yet it strengthens me not at all.*

I am tired, yes, and weaker than I was when last we met, H., weaker even than when Asmodei and I arrived here in Rome. Is it listening for the sister-call, watching for this witch that enervates me so? I wonder.

— Yes. It is as feared. Asmodei will not leave me here alone with my pens and blank pages, with you, my heart, my H. It is dangerous, says he. I have the coachman for protection, say I, but Asmodei counters that it is the coachman he fears. And so I must close now.

As we proceed upon the saint-named street I shall tell Asmodei all that I have read in my Mirabilia, *the unnamed writer of which I imagine lingering, here, now, at the Colosseum, these three hundred years on. — Concession? Compromise? Regardless, it is how Asmo and I love, and have loved for half a century. — And so,* à bientôt. *More later, my love.*

I can only guess what it was Sebastiana had learned from her ages-old *Mirabilia*. Doubtless it was accurate enough, as Rome has been touristic for twenty-plus centuries; but I warmed at wondering who but Sebastiana d'Azur would bring to Rome a guidebook warning of dragons rather than one commanding *Turn right here, left there*, et cetera, the result being naught but wariness and a checked list of *Things Seen*. . . . But as Calixto had need of more regarding the Colosseum, as did I, and as may you, sister, let me here digress, and beg pardon for the next, fact-packed paragraph; which, in its way, will speak of *my promised surprises*—plural, yes; for there were two.

Anno Domini, 80. The Colosseum is completed under the reign of Domitian; which achievement is marked with one hundred days of games during which five thousand animals are slaughtered. Gladiators and slaves—cheered by a hundred thousand bloodlusting Romans— shared the same fate within its rounded walls. Of course, by the time Sebastiana entered the arena alongside Asmodei, the games—if not their ghosts—were long gone; and the place has since devolved to little more than a quarry from which blocks of travertine are extracted for use elsewhere in the ever re-architected city of Rome. Indeed, nowadays it seems the Colosseum sits as a mere moss-grown monument to the Christian martyrs said to have been sacrificed there. In their memory, a black, oft-kissed, consecrated cross stands center-all. Elsewhere, everywhere, there grows, untended, the worldliest of crops: It is a veritable *jardin botanique,* the Colosseum, owing to those seeds shat, in their death throes, by the animals and slaves brought from all the world over to die in Rome, *for* Rome, for the appeasement of its gods and the amusement of its people. . . . Sebastiana was right: It was a sight I'd not have wished to see—and one I would have avoided— whilst alive: The disquiet would have been too great.

. . . *Alors,* it was a wintry night when they went, yes: cold and perforce quiet, only the odd goat agraze upon that odder greenery, and only the heartiest, most hardened of tourists daring to brave the Romans then present. *I fancied,* wrote S., *that every other pocket showed a knife-glint of silver, blued by the moon.* She may have been right; which is not to say she was fearful, weakened though she was—and when Calixto asked me what was wrong with S., I could not say, though already I knew she'd begun to sense the Coming of the Blood— . . . no, she'd not have been fearful; for she'd Asmodei at her side, and what's more: She had herself, and she has always been fast with the Craft. *Enfin,* woe betides anyone seeking to better *that* sister, thought I, and I said as much to Calixto.

Sebastiana wrote of passing, unimpeded, the French sentinel; of

---

※

seeing those who picnicked by lamp- and moonlight; of joining the night-party within the Colosseum, part pagan and part papistical; and of listening to those who sang, lustily, despite being shushed by two pilgrims seeking to walk the Stations of the Cross, as set out last century by Benedict XIV when he'd sought to shift the balance of the Colosseum from quarry back to church. With glee, Sebastiana told of the drunken tenors' victory; but in a rare nod to sanctity, she'd had Asmodei carry her to the black cross, which she kissed. *Each buss*, she boasted, *earns one seven years' remission from the pains of Purgatory (which I suppose are plenty!). Eight, nine, ten kisses it was, for a total of seventy years of remission—just more than my life's span!—and what better way for a woman of advanced and fast-advancing age to benefit from travel, now that she has accumulated the bulk of her sins and her remaining temptations are few?*

I was heartened to see she'd enjoyed herself; and she had, till she heard again the sister-call.

I write now by the light of a rising sun. I have slept fitfully, and could not settle anything onto my stomach once we'd returned to the pensione. Asmodei sleeps on like a rock in a stream, ignorant of all that washes over him, over us. By which I mean, of course, he does not know what is to come, nor could he appreciate the gravitas of all that passed last night as we left the Colosseum.

She called to me again, H. So clearly I could tell from whence the call came. There! said I as we walked slowly back to our coach. Greatly agitated, I grabbed the arm of a passing rustic. What lies out there? I asked of the man, who seemed a veritable satyr, drunk as he was, and clad in goatskin breeches worn hair outward.

I had let fall my furs to point southeasterly from where we stood, the Palatine rising at our right and the oval course of the Circus Maximus sitting not far ahead. There! I said again, shivering, spinning the satyr round to see where it was I meant to point. He'd little French, this creature, but he was happy enough to gaze off into the middle distance, into the dark, and when finally he understood what it was I sought, he said, or rather asked, Le Terme di Caracalla?

❊

"No, not the baths," *I answered in a child's Italian,* "beyond that."

". . . Via Appia?" *he asked.*

"Ah," *said I,* "si," *and I asked further what lay along that ancient road, out beyond the city itself. The satyr shrugged. He'd had enough of me, and would have ambled off if Asmodei had not interposed. Having regained his attention, I asked again, wordlessly, with but the wag of an extended finger,* What lies beyond? Out there? *Again the satyr stared, squinting, as if he might truly see what it was I sought. Finally, comically, he wheeled back toward me, and, raising a filthy, shushing finger to his wine-dark lips, said,* ". . . La via delle catacombe." — *So that now I know where she is, where she waits, where she calls out from—some catacomb beyond the city walls. But why? Is she, too, death-allied. And what adds such distress to her unconscious cry?*

To sleep now, again. In sleep I shall open to our sister's call, hear her, hopefully, as once I heard you, H., when you suffered so. If not, if no call comes, we set out southeasterly at dusk—when the robbers rise, and the catacombs are crowded—to seek out the death-den in which this troubled witch sits, supposing, surely, as all new witches will, that she is alone in a world too wide.

Leaving Havana, we had but a short sail to where we hoped to find Sebastiana and those with whom she had sailed, many months prior, from Naples.

This was coincidence. The company had hied southward to Naples from Rome, finding there a Spanish ship soon to set out for Havana. *Havana . . .* wrote Sebastiana, much later in her Book.

When I learned we'd an option to sail from Naples to Havana, I thought back to two letters I'd recently received—quite surprising, this—at Ravndal. They'd come from a monk—though of course he was no more a monk than I, that beast, that Brù—resident in the Cuban capital. He'd heard of me and, more significantly, you, from your Duchess, who, desponding of all she'd lost of late, spoke secrets she ought to have kept. Doubtless she thought Brù was of the Shadows, and disclosure would be safe.

❋

*Or perhaps he tricked her, as he did me. As he has you, perhaps, though please please
please may it not be so! — Oh, H., how I wish I'd known then, in Rome, what soon
I was to learn in Havana. Had I, we'd never have set sail, but would have summoned
you home instead. If only I'd known. If only . . .*

But stay. I speed the narrative, and quote my sister out of context.
Far better to rejoin her in Rome, the Colosseum behind her and the
catacombs before.

Weakened as Sebastiana was—*deafening,* she wrote, *is the sound of a
sister's distress*—and with what strength she could summon focused on
salvation, Sebastiana followed her consort to the catacombs that day.
It had fallen to an increasingly suspicious Asmodei to ask where, precisely, they lay, how best to get there, et cetera.

And in asking this of their *hotelière,* Asmodei received a most surprising response: His questions all were answered—indeed, maps were
proffered and drawn upon—but said converse concluded with the un-
smiling signora arching one black brow and saying she'd no rooms that
night. With apologies she asked Asmodei and Sebastiana to pack, depart, and not return. This they did, reading their rousting from the
pensione rightly: The catacombs were known as thieves' dens, and
none who had business there would find themselves welcomed
elsewhere.

Sebastiana was sympathetic, wondering how the unfound sister had
fallen so. Asmodei, I imagine, was just as glad to trade the poshness
of the pensione for the rough-and-tumble of whatever might come;
and therefore, typically, he asked few questions of his witch. However,
I thought it telling that Sebastiana took care to write—without ad-
monishing comment—that Asmodei had loaded both his boots with
knives, and set a squash-size blackjack inside his belt. As for her, she'd
spells at the ready, and would sow warnings in the minds of any who
approached them impurely, or even impolitely.

The Via Appia runs still from Rome, as it has for some twelve hundred years. Armies beyond number, predators and protectors both, have smoothed its stones with their sandals. Pilgrims, too. And into its flanking fields there have been laid centuries' worth of the deceased, *ad catacumbus,* in galleries of many stories dug down into the soft, reddish rock. Some catacombs have caved over time, and are lost. Others, surely, are yet to be discovered. Still others sheltered those infamous Italian *banditti* as well as the less active, discarded citizenry of Rome. . . . What sort of sister would Sebastiana find in such a place? I was curious, yes; but my curiosity ceded to a cold chill as Calixto read aloud *a single detail* Sebastiana had culled from her dream, and pursuant to which she would seek the lost sister in *a certain catacomb:* namely, that of San Sebastiano.

We'd each a torch wound in pitchy rags that guttered and spat and sucked at the air as we descended. So began Sebastiana's report, written the night of her find.

> *Down we went, into the dankness, the cold and the dark of the centuries-old crypt, behind a guide we hired for six scudi but whose eye yet glinted of gold, which is to say robbery. Greed glittered in the man's eye like the ores threading through the walls closing all around us. Of course—no fool I—my furs, jewels, and other such adornments I'd left in our coach, locked against our own driver as well as any others who'd come. And the coach sat close by the Aurelian wall, a whistle away from where we entered the catacombs as have how many pilgrims preceding us? — Of course, we were no pilgrims, as it was not our own salvation we sought.*

Reference here was to the pilgrims who'd long come to the tomb of Saint Sebastian—yes, *my* Saint Sebastian—but also to other tombs said to be in that same space, tombs so old as to predate Sebastian's decease. Sebastiana saw varieties of *Petrus et Paulus, Requiescat in Pace,* scratched into the red-brown rock of the catacombs; for the bones of the Apostles Peter and Paul, thrown from Rome during a period of Christian persecution, are said to have been brought there. Later, with Sebastian martyred and interred in the days of Diocletian, even more pilgrims came in pious procession, till finally a church was built to cap the acres of columbaria holding the memories, if not the actual re-mains, of the three saints.

But then, a decade or so ago, the catacombs sat untended and under the control of such types *as would stab a Frenchwoman foolish enough to descend in furs,* furs that would have been coveted not only for the wealth they conveyed but also the warmth.

In fact (wrote S.), *we'd dirtied down, as seemed wise, lest the living inhabitants of the catacombs think to profit from our presence by violence. Our guide I'd succeeded in dissuading, peppering his wine-swelled mind with warnings, till finally he led us on, docile as a donkey and inured to all the death. Of course, I could not tell him who or what it was we sought. Neither did Asmodei know; but as my demon fancied himself "at home" some meters belowground, he let off bothering me about my strange "business."*

"This way," and "Now that," said I, leading our party by the sense I had of the sis-ter's nearness, a sense as real as those cold currents of air that came whistling past us, and of a provenance just as mysterious.

Down, further down. At times we had to stoop, whilst at other times our guide held high his torch to show a black line burned onto the rock above us. Passageways ran off to either side of our route, recessing into darkness. Fearful, it was, wondering what lay within that darkness. Of course, my fears were not of the dead, but rather of those who were alive, there, somewhere, in the dark.

It seemed a certainty that we'd climb down to Hades, and indeed Asmodei hissed in seeming imitation of his torch, asking was it Persephone we sought. It was then I saw that he understood why it was we'd come. Precluding any questions, I pushed him ahead of me, whispering that he ought to keep close to our guide lest we lose him to the dark, or the depths, or desertion. — Yes, I came last, and though the dark behind me was extreme, I thought it best to be the rear guard, as it were, lest the others see me so, slowing to look onto every coffin-length shelf, bending to take in the lower berths and going onto tiptoe to see the topmost. I found only the dead decaying unto dust. Found only bones and bodies. None of which were hers. What I knew, my one surety, was that I sought a living witch. I quite doubted a dead one could call as strongly as this witch had the night prior, as we'd left the Colosseum.

In time, growing colder yet ever more certain she was near, I moved to the fore of our threesome, Asmodei and our guide coming behind me in order. In time, too, as I'd suspected he would, our guide fell behind us, further and further still, till finally he was one with the dark, departed. I cared not at all, as now I knew the witch was near, quite. — But would she be able to guide us back to the light?

I worried that this was too much witchery for Calixto's consideration, but when I asked how he was faring—and at this point in our
second go-through of Sebastiana's narrative we were already at sea, in
a boat not much bigger than a skiff, a boat the sailing of which so
busied the boy that I'd long been reading aloud—he shrugged, and
parroted a bettor's phrase he'd picked up aboard the *Halcyon:* "In for a
dime, in for a dollar," said he. And so I resumed; as now:

When found, wrote S. of the new witch, *she was positively feral.*

They'd gone on without their guide, stepping over mounded
bones and trash that told of the catacombs' living inhabitants. Rats
rummaged at eye level. The cold was extreme, but so, too, was the
sister-call. So *extreme,* said S., she'd thought her head would split. . . .
Mind, it was not a call, per se, not a vocalization issued with intent.
Rather, she—this witch—finding herself in trouble of the insur-
mountable sort, *put out her peril;* yet did so no more consciously than
I had years ago, when I'd summoned Sebastiana similarly. Think of
it, sister, if you've yet to hear it, as a flower of Fear loosing its
scent.

———————————— ❋ ————————————

Asmodei saw by my increasing upset what I was about, and thusly had his own suspicions confirmed. This I sensed, and so did not turn back to see it writ upon his stone-set features. He'd not have approved such a mission as this. As you know too well, H., Asmodei wants no witches but me. — Jealousy. — But this witch, I knew, was distressed nearly to the point of death, and I'd not let that come to pass. No indeed. Asmodei be damned. — And hadn't I heeded this call come from another country? Hadn't I forsworn the comforts of Ravndal, such as they are, to ride to Rome in wintertime? Why? Soon I'd meet the reason. Or reasons. Read on, heart, and so, too, will you.

At a too literal dead end, I stopped. I lowered the torch—the smoke from which was stifling to sight—and I listened, as now the call had evolved into sound itself, which is to say I heard crying along with rat-scratch on stone, and the drip of water, and that whistling that sounded like the slow off-seeping of souls. And then, shush, *a cat. No. Not a cat. A child's cry. Coming from on high.*

When I raised the torch to the topmost shelf, I caused her to recoil, fast, and issue another feline hiss. She withdrew, yes, but not before I saw her turned Eye, strong as any I'd ever seen.

I called up to her. Once, twice, thrice I called before she came forth to show again that Eye—its toad-footed pupil surrounded by bright blue iris—set in a face caked with dirt. Her cheeks were sunken, bespeaking starvation. Dirt had matted her dark hair. But no aspect of her filth, of her fate-to-date, could dull her beauty, beauty of a particular type, beauty that seemed somehow familiar.

Now we'd found the witch, Asmodei stood behind me sighing, sighing so heavily as to cause his torch's light to dance upon the black walls around us, rendering them red. I stood wondering who to task myself with first, Asmodei or this witch-child, who'd endured a rough decade of life if she'd endured a day. — It was then she withdrew. And only when it seemed I'd have to make Asmodei climb the three tiers of tombs and take the child in hand, only then did she show her face again, and . . .

Was it the darkness, the swirl of smoke and shadow? Or could this child truly have those two heads I'd seen in my dream? Hideous thought, this. Hideous sight, too. But

❋

of course I was wrong. — It was a second child I saw, a boy, brighter, blond, come up from back in their shared crypt, so slowly and so close upon his sister it seemed they shared a neck. But, no. What they did share was that same beauty, borne on the same blood. Here were twins, a boy and girl, who—brace for it, H.— looked like the two parts of you.

 *Chapter Twenty-two*

Over the course of the Ages, I have been the boy and the girl,
the tree, the winged bird, and the mute being of the depths.

—EMPEDOCLES

WHEN FIRST I'D HEARD THOSE WORDS— *. . . A BOY AND
girl . . . like the two parts of you*—I felt faint. Whatever had
Sebastiana meant? Where was *the sense* in what she said? I
had Calixto read the page again and again, and again.

Could it be? No. Impossible . . . Or was it?

I thought, or rather *wanted to think,* and therefore did,
that Sebastiana had only meant to say that the new
witch, being young and in distress, had reminded her of
me, of the me she'd saved at C——. Ditto the boy, of
course, he being her twin.

Still, when first I'd heard her words spoken by Calixto atop the *assoltaire,* a chill had come over me—as
though someone had settled onto my shoulders an icy
cloak—and I felt faint; *had wanted to faint,* in fact. The second time I heard those words, reading them myself—we
were already at sea, as said, our small boat bobbing on

the blue like a cork; for the weather had not yet turned red, as soon it would—I did not feel faint, but still I could not reconcile *the sense* of the words with my . . . suspicions. And so I skimmed S.'s words and let go my suspicions, dropping them into the sea like stones.

. . . Ignorance may well be bliss; but when one is so *willfully ignorant,* as I was whilst reading on, sailing on, well then, something is awry, amiss. I'd need . . . *others* to tell me, to show me what that something was.

Though I'd wanted to stay seated upon the *assoltaire* till I'd turned the last page of Sebastiana's Book, whereupon I'd begin to turn them all a second time, I knew I could not. . . . What about Brù? What if he were discovered whilst still we sat in his house, and he brought to bear upon us forces natural or otherwise? And what of the light-birds growing ever dimmer, and whose flight had slowed so? Would I stay to watch them and their fellows dim unto death, or worse still, *survive?* No. I would not. . . . Best to leave.

Already I'd read enough of Sebastiana's Book to find out, to deduce, where it was she attended me. That is, if all had gone as planned since she'd signed off—*Run!*—and hidden her Book in Brù's library.

We agreed, Calixto and I, that I would wait in my let room on the Calle Lamparilla whilst he set about securing us a boat. This had been the boy's idea, and I need not detail here my relief at hearing him employ that collective pronoun, *us.* I will say only that said relief was extreme, and came concomitant with that warming of the throat that betoken tears; but these I stifled. . . . Yes, said Cal, we'd need a boat of our own. We'd a sail of no more than two days' duration, said he, "and that's if we're wind bound." But if the winds and sea (and Fate) cooperated, we'd be with Sebastiana a half day after setting out. Further, if we sailed in a boat of our own, we'd have no worries relative to passports or questioning port-folk.

Calixto knew who to see. He was off like a shot, down the Calle Lamparilla. Then: "Money," called he a moment later, returned to stare up from the street, and pat his empty pockets, "I'll need money." Somewhere he had the half-wages handed him upon the *Halcyon*'s return, but he doubted those monies would suffice; so—trusting, learning . . . —I dropped down from my second story sill that pigskin purse containing all the money I had with me in Cuba. Calixto caught it, and ran. And it would be less than truthful of me to say that, as I watched him round a corner and disappear, I did so without worry, without wondering if I'd ever see him again. Such thoughts crossed my mind, yes; rather as a rake does dirt. But somehow it would have seemed . . . *unlearned, distrustful* if I'd held back even a single coin; and so I had not. Down I'd dropped it, all. What could I do now but wait out the night, trusting in Calixto whilst learning more of Sebastiana's story?

She referred to the witchlings as *the children*. This discomfited me. And so I was glad when finally she told their names: Léopoldine and Luc.

At first they'd refused to descend from their death-den; which, said S., judging by what she could see of its contents, they'd occupied for some while. In a fore-corner, set upon what appeared to be a pelvic bone, a black candle burned. Beside it were mounded smaller animal bones—the detritus of eaten things—as well as pits and rinds and suchlike, the sum of which totaled to starvation. An orange sat moldering, already half-rotten and resembling a moon slipped into partial eclipse. There were two tied-off bundles of cloth, a Bible, and, *even more disturbingly* (said S., quoting A.), a rat; which latter creature the boy, Luc, held to his chest as if it were his heart. He fed it from a crust he ought to have eaten himself.

Finally, after Sebastiana had shown her own Eye, Léopoldine

agreed, tacitly, to descend; but her brother would have to be helped. This she said in Italian, *with a Tuscan rusticity of accent,* said S., *that told, too eloquently, of the rougher company she'd kept of late.* For how long, one could only wonder. The boy, at first, spoke not at all; leastways, not above the whispers he set directly into the pink and pointed ears of his pet; but when finally he spoke, telling his sister and their saviors that he'd not part with the rodent, he did so in French; and thusly did the four-some discover they'd a language in common.

This, of course, facilitated things. Soon the party—with promises made, and the rat retained—quit the catacombs, Luc in the lead; and all four, nay, five of them retook the coach and rocked back to Rome proper.

Rooms were let near the Circus Maximus, two only; for the twins would not separate, not even to wash, and once a meal was had, they napped. Or rather: *They fell into sleep,* wrote S., *descending as if dropped from a height.* But not before they'd begged from Sebastiana her hatbox, used to house her sable toque, and begged to be let to bore holes in its satiny top: A rat's house, it would be.

> *At first* (said S.), *before I'd agreed to let them punch holes in the box's top with the awl-like thing Asmodei proffered—having had it on his person previously, for reasons of security, or so I supposed—the boy, Luc, thought we meant to smother the rat, and had his sister accuse us accordingly. Asmodei laughed, as indeed he had thought of smothering the rat. And when the argument with which I refuted the children's accusation—Whyever would I use a hatbox handed me by the Countess Skavronsky to settle the hash of a rat when a heeled shoe would work just as well?—found not its mark, I consented to the ruination of that hatbox that had made its way from Russia to Rome, only to meet this most improbable and ignominious end. — His fears al-layed, young Luc fell asleep curled before his sister, his hand fallen onto the hatbox, where it lay on the carpet, his fingertip atop one of the aforementioned airholes lest his pet wake to worry that he'd been forsaken, boxed, and forgotten.*

As I sat reading on the Calle Lamparilla that night—or mightn't it have been morning already?—I heard a whistling-up from down in the street: Calixto had returned. I sighed, sighed like a damsel spared her distress.

The first thing Calixto wanted to know was what it was I'd read, or rather learned in his absence. He nodded at Sebastiana's Book, and I wondered if he took it all for novelizing of some sort, the work of some perverted peer of Miss Austen's. I promised to catch him up at sea, to tell him all I'd read and now knew—though, in fact, what I'd read and knew were yet quite distinct—but first, said I, what about a boat? Had he hired or bought a boat?

"I have," said he, proudly; whereupon he tossed back to me the purse I'd dropped down to him earlier.

"But," said I, "this feels heavier than before." And it did, much.

"I didn't even need all my pay," said he. "What's left over I put in the purse; but it'd be best, I think, if you held to it. I'm too easily . . . tempted. Tempted is the word, *sí?*"

"Tempted is the word, *oui.*"

I took back the purse; and in so doing I began to thank the boy for all he'd done—and *not done:* the disdain, the denial, the disappearing I'd half expected—and heard issue from my mouth words I'd had cause to utter but once before, to Sebastiana: salvation, loyalty, and the like. At this the boy blushed; and when he asked me to desist, I did; for I'd begun to blush as well. More: Calixto suggested I might want to wait on words of thanks, as he'd yet to deliver me to my Sebastiana. Said he, as a dog's-body, as a ship's boy and, most recently, as a sailor aboard the *Halcyon,* he'd requited himself passingly well—this I was heartened to hear, as the Calixto of six months prior had not held so high an opinion of himself—but now we'd a bumboat we'd have to run alone, just we two, and surely the sea would test us. "Test *you,*" I said; explaining that though I'd been to sea, my sailing skills were best summarized as "knowing how to stay out of the way."

"That's good." Calixto laughed. "Most lady folk . . ." and here he skidded, like a lark landing on ice, and sought balance, as so: ". . . most landlubbers, I mean, haven't even *that* skill, and shipboard, in a squall, say, are about as handy as a foot."

I swore I'd do my best. He said I might have to, and then some; for heavy clouds had come on after sunset, betokening rain and a general worsening of the weather.

I asked if he—". . . being a sailor"—thought we ought to put off the hour of our departure, which we'd determined would be dawn. He deferred to me; but in so doing, he offered up an old sea adage, leading me to surmise that still he wanted to sail at dawn, and therefore thought we'd survive the essay. And so it was we rested and read a few hours more, turning the key on my let room at first light and setting off in search of our newly acquired . . . Stay: I almost wrote *ship*, when our boat was no more a *ship* than I was *lady folk*.

A bumboat, it was. Calixto could have bought a fleet of such bobbers, surely, with his Barcelona pay; but that sharp-edged thought I left unsaid, knowing it was born more of my fear than any impecunious impulse on the part of my companion. Still, upon seeing the boat, I stammered: "Are we . . . ? Will we . . . ?"

"We are," said he, "and we will."

I worried that perhaps the boy had acquired *too much confidence* in sailing to Barcelona and back.

Lest I shame my sailor, I boarded. Oh, but lest you, reader, imagine I refer to a seacraft *of grander scale*, I say again that ours was but a bumboat, a runabout; and to board her one hiked high one's pants or petticoats, waded out to where she sat, her keel clear of the sand, and clambered aboard via a verb that exists in no language I know. It was a sort of grab-hold-haul-and-roll, and in attempting it, I recalled a

sight I'd once seen: A former shipmate of mine, drunk and rather cor-
pulent, warring with his bunk such that I'd wondered, the whole time
I'd watched him with my insomniac's eye, if he was struggling *into* or
out of his berth; for each confrontation—man versus berth—had
ended in a draw, till finally the carpenter went topside to sleep in a
more amenable hammock. Now here I was, no more graceful than he,
trying to launch myself from the sea and into the boat, my skirts
aswirl and my bare feet sinking so deeply down I was certain I'd soon
feel a Chinaman's tickling touch. A sudden splash scared me, quite,
and as I turned to bat away whatever sea-creature had come so close,
too close, I felt the sea itself sinking—as if some Providential plug
had been pulled—and . . . and before I understood what he'd done,
Calixto had dropped beneath the water's surface; whereupon he set his
shoulder to my bottom, and, standing, shoved me aboard, such that
suddenly bumboat seemed too apt, too embarrassing a term.

"My skirts . . ." said I, mortified. "I ought to have worn slacks,
or . . ."

Smiling, Calixto launched himself as I could not—*bref:* easily—
and took his seat upon a bench at the bow. His back was to the open
sea, mine to the beach. At our feet were provisions aplenty. From these
I looked up to see my companion smiling still; and though he tucked
his chin to his shoulder, trying to hide his smile, it told in his blue
eyes as well.

Said I, "I am able to row, you know." Was I? I supposed so. Rather,
to row seemed simple enough.

"Thank you," said he, "but I would rather you read."

And I did: I read aloud as Calixto rowed; and so it was I did not
see Cuba recede.

※

Chapter Twenty-three

A terrible childbed hast thou had, my dear,
No light, no fire: th' unfriendly elements
Forgot thee utterly . . .
—SHAKESPEARE, **Pericles**

SEBASTIANA AND COMPANY HAD COME TO CUBA IN GREATER
style than Calixto and I left that island nation, *bien sûr;*
but my sister had more money than Midas (and a rather
more magical touch, too).

They'd arrived some months before me, and had already left by the time I came to Cuba in pursuit of Sebastiana and her secrets, finding only Queverdo Brù.

They, the foursome, with rodent in tow— . . . *et quelle
drôle de famille!* wrote S.—had stayed another week in
Rome, *spoiling the urchins,* according to Asmodei, before
heading southward to ship out of Naples. This exten-
sion of their stay was owing to Sebastiana's desire to find
the children's mother; who, swore Leo, had died some
seasons past, *"when the roads had all been purple."* So: spring-
time or summer, that would have been; but whenever
Sebastiana had pressed the witch, she'd had little more

to report of her mother—whether out of reticence or ignorance, Sebastiana had been unable to say.

> *I asked, more than once, if her mother had been able to do with her eyes what we*
> *could, showing the Toad. She said no. — Was she not a witch, then? Or was she, but*
> *knew it not? — You see, heart, still I'd not surmised what you're fast surmising,*
> *surely.*
>
> *I asked Léopoldine how her mother had died. If the Blood had come to her, it was a*
> *cruel question. This I knew, and I'd never have asked it of Luc. But the witch-child*
> *took the question in stride, answering in pantomime—as she'd not the requisite*
> *French—and acting out a persistent, plaguey cough. Ah, thought I, then it was the*
> *Coming of the Blood. But when I asked, pointedly, and with apology, if there'd been*
> *an excess of Red, the witchling shook her head, calm as you please, and said, "Blood,*
> *do you mean? No, there'd been no blood." Apparently, the mother had coughed herself*
> *into her coffin, et c'était tout. — But if the children's mother hadn't been a witch,*
> *wherever had Leo's witch-ness come from? I'd never read of anything like it: a witch*
> *"of woman born." Mortal woman, I mean to say, and not witch-woman. I confess, I*
> *fell so far as to wonder if the twins' birth hadn't been, quoi? Inversely immaculate,*
> *might I say? Had they sprung up from the soil as sports of nature?*

Others, less tolerant than my Sebastiana, would have recoursed to
the word *freaks.*

> *What of the father, then? Where was he? But this question brought nothing but the*
> *shrug of four bony shoulders, as neither twin knew of a second parent.*
>
> *Had they been to France? Léopoldine thought not. Luc answered by asking, in French,*
> *"What's France?"*
>
> *How was it, then, that they knew the language of that place? Said Leo, they'd spo-*
> *ken two languages, always—one with their mother, another with everyone else. Who*
> *else? Was there family? — It seemed unlikely that we'd find any family, as we'd found*
> *the siblings starving, three stories below the Church of San Sebastiano, all but buried*

themselves. Still, it seemed I ought to ask before spiriting the twins from the city, tak-
ing them back to France, or elsewhere. And of course, if they did have family hereabouts,
and we found them, this family, if they'd known of the siblings' plight, their troglodytic
life, well, yes, they'd be made to answer for that in full, and fast. And better off they'd
be answering to me rather than Asmodei, who kept clear of Leo but had begun to be-
tray an affinity for Luc.

Questions about the children's paternity went unanswered; neither
was any family found. That is till the day, four days after being drawn
up from the depths, that the witch Léopoldine suggested *a trip.* Luc
was very much disinclined to take said trip, and cried against it, consoling himself with that rat that (said A.) *had grown as big as Madame Du
Barry's right buttock.* And doubtless it was true; for Sebastiana told of
those four days being devoted to naught but sleep and sustenance.
She'd let the twins—and the rat, which Luc hadn't even thought to
name—indulge themselves, such that at first they'd sickened and *spat it
all back,* said S., and I too easily imagined a mess made up of all those
things children will choose to eat; but in time she righted their diets,
and *a bit of ruddiness returned to their cheeks, and their flesh let go its stranglehold
of their bones.* The girl, especially, strengthened; and it was opined she'd
a constitution twice as strong as her brother's. He—*le pauvre, si perdu,
avec son rat bien aimé,* the little lost boy with his beloved rat—seemed
born of more runtish stock than his sister, and indeed had come up
from the catacombs limping. This was an injury his sister attributed
to an anonymous coachman of Rome, who'd whipped the boy down
when first he'd leapt upon the running boards to beg; and said
injury—caused by *the crush, the crunch* of the coach wheel on his foot—
had occasioned not only his limp but that *surnom* Asmodei soon be-
stowed upon him: Byron, or Lord B.; the point being that the boy had
nothing at all in common with the late, rakish poet save lameness.

Sebastiana—who, of course, referred to the boy only as Luc, *mon vieux*, or a nickname more beneficent than Byron—saw the boy fall pale at the mere mention of the aforementioned trip; and, though he had only just begin to speak to the two-legged and more senior members of their band, she knew then that they had to go. Had to follow Leo whither she might lead them. Perhaps then they'd find answers; whereupon they'd be able to plan.

> *And so* (said Sebastiana), *that fifth morning of our acquaintance, we four and a rat rode out of Rome, to a cemetery so near those same catacombs that it seemed the buried, unboxed dead, reduced to bone, must surely show themselves stalagmitic belowground. — One had no need of Sight to know that Leo meant to show us a grave. That same grave, surely, that frightened Luc so much that he stayed behind—seated atop the driver's box, beside Asmodei and our hired man—as the girl and I progressed, in silence, from coach to that sepulchral storehouse of the past.*
>
> *I knew whose grave it was we sought, but still I read the standing stones in vain. Of course, I ought to have asked at some point during the five days previous if the twins' mother had had a name. This I'd not thought to ask, stupidly; and when finally I did ask, in the cemetery, I felt cold, cruel, and Leo's silence seemed a just response.*

But lest Sebastiana judge herself too harshly, she added that she doubted either of the twins would have spoken the name if she'd thought to ask it earlier; for even now, Léopoldine, *the bolder of the two by far*, deigned not to speak her mother's name, choosing instead to lead Sebastiana to the stone on which it was inscribed.

Indian Key—and such was our destination, quitting Cuba—was, by then, a wreckers' outpost of some repute (most of it ill), sitting midway up that string of keys which culminated, southerly, in Key West, the latter city dangling like a diamond at the end of a beaded string. Why Sebastiana had not gone to Key West in escaping Brù, I did not know. This would have been the commoner route, as Key West lay but ninety miles north of Havana, whilst Indian Key sat a half day further north; but Sebastiana had not often opted for the commoner route in her progress through life; and what did it matter to me: I'd have gone to the moon in pursuit of her now.

. . . And so, yes, we'd set off from Cuba, refusing that most basic of sailorly truths: We had too much sea before us, and too little boat beneath.

Calixto worked our vessel as expertly as the seas allowed, rowing and sailing it, alternately; for, yes, we'd one sail—the size of a fat man's nightshirt—which, though it showed itself holey when first we unfurled it, seemed our salvation. Happily, the rains held off, and the Straits were smooth enough *once we gained them; it was the waves that came before the Straits* that bedeviled our boat. . . . Sailing inside that reef that shadows the coast of the keys, one is spared such waves; for they break upon the reef itself, and come to kiss the keys like a suitor on bended knee. The larger Gulf, however, or that part of it sitting *outside the reef*, shares not that barrier's breaking benefits. There the waves rise, and rise, and rise some more; and what such waves might have done to our bumboat, well . . . *Hélas:* Here we were at sea in a teacup of wormy wood, *sans* barometer, in the season of sudden hurricanes. Rolling, rolling, surging and slipping, dropping from crest to trough, there I sat, green at the gills. Now and again I shut my eyes—clenched them tightly as fists, truth be told—and imagined myself aboard a blue steed, riding, riding toward my sister, toward Sebastiana. All the while I held fast to her Book, of course, and would have sunk to the Gulf floor with it in my clutches if our bumboat had gone over, as several times it seemed it would.

Enfin, of that trip I'll say no more than this: *It ended;* but before its end I'd taught Calixto the French verb *vomir*, and was so earnest a tutor I even demonstrated its meaning, thrice, by tossing my own ballast overboard. Blessedly, embarrassment was done: *The boy knew me now;* and if he'd not denied me already, it seemed unlikely he'd do so over a little sea-spill.

The main problem pursuant to the state of the sea was this: It kept me from reading as I wished to; for the ink from Sebastiana's pen seemed to liquefy upon the page, and my blue sunshades might as well have been fishbowls for all they settled the words on which I trained them. So it was I was left to wonder, to worry, and slowly to dread *the truth* of what already I'd read; and, *je vous jure,* the more I read, the more said truths surged within me, settling my stomach not at all.

I knew the name, H., and so, too, will you.

Leo—and, heart, the girl is tall, standing to my bosom already, at ten, nearly eleven years of age—*Leo, I say, led me through the cemetery, walking atop the graves, not skirting them as the faithful might and the superstitious surely would. Some of the graves were freshly filled, whilst others seemed ancient. On we walked amidst the tomb-shapes, such that I felt myself a pawn in an overlarge game of chess. The child's Eye was in evidence all the while, such that I supposed its having turned was all that kept her tears at bay.* — *You see, H., I wanted to believe, as every woman will, that all children once loved, and later miss and mourn, their dead mothers.*

Overnight, it seemed, Roman winter had ceded to spring. Riding out along the Appian Way, the hills showed a green that only heightened my memory of their having been gray when last we'd come, and the flat brick and fieldstone of our surrounds—tombs, distant towers, the city walls and such—glistened, as if the sun meant to tattle, to tell of gold having been hidden there, mixed into their mortar. The air was still clear and chill, but the sun was much warmer than previously it had been, and on a mission of less import, I might well have stopped, set myself upon a stony mount and shown the sun my shoulders, bared them to the warmth I'd sought all winter long. — *The cold, H., seems now to go bone-deep. So it is with the old, I suppose.*

Suddenly the child stopped. Had she stood gazing downward, as one does in a grave-yard, perhaps I'd have realized we'd arrived. Instead, Leo looked skyward. A sister more sentimental than I might say "heavenward," excepting that soon it was evident the child's thoughts hied not toward Heaven but rather Hell.

Casting her turned Eye back to earth, Leo focused upon the plot at our feet, stubbled like an indigent's chin, rough with weeds and winter-browned grass. And then she brought back her new-bought boot, cocked it, and shot a rock at the headstone. It hit hollowly, and seemed to mimic the only other sound around us, that of a sexton's shovel chipping at the still-icy earth. Shocked, I watched as the witch stepped onto the grave itself, such that now she'd have been standing on the deceased's chest if six feet of earth and some planks of pine had not separated them. Worse still, I watched as she, leaning lower, spat. Spat!

I'd not time enough to express my shock, as quickly I looked to where the witch-child's spittle shone upon the stone and saw there the name of your nemesis, she who'd betrayed you in every way a decade past: Peronette Gaudillon.

Of course, the name had affected me when first I'd read it at Brù's, but not so *bodily* as now; for, reading it a second time, I retched. And oh, how I wished I could commit all my memories to the sea similarly. Spill them all, spew them, watch them spread—slickly, as scum—till the sea diluted and disappeared them.

"H.?" said Calixto, ". . . Are you well?" Before hearing me spill my upset a second time, he'd sat staring ahead, one hand upon the helm; for we'd entered the smoother waters of the Straits now and a slight wind found our sail. He'd assured me the worst was over: We had only to steer along the lines of a wrecker we'd sighted, headed landward, as surely she'd put in at Indian Key. "H.?" he called again; for he'd begun to refer to me as Sebastiana always had. "Are you all right?"

I was not. . . . Unbelievably, perhaps, I'd been reading this part of Sebastiana's Book *again*, and wondering, *again*, who the new witch's mother might be, casting back through all the Books I'd read—at Ravndal, and at Cyprian House, especially—and asking myself, *again*, Who, who . . . ? Had the children's mother been mortal, as Sebastiana

had supposed? I, too, had never read of a witch "of woman born."
Had she been a sister unknown to the sorority? . . . *Enfin*, there the
pieces lay, spread before me, not yet *of a piece*; but oh, how fast that
puzzle assembled itself as now, *again*, I read that name in Sebastiana's
script:

Peronette Gaudillon . . . I'd not thought of the girl for some while;
but, still, the name of one's first love sears itself onto one's soul like a
brand, does it not? The more so, surely, when first love ends in fury,
in flight, as it had for us both.

"H.," asked Cal, "who is this, this Perry—"

"Peronette Gaudillon," said I, the bile welling. Indeed, the vomit
that clung to my tongue tasted of her name. "She is . . . *was* a girl I
once knew."

"Knew . . ." echoed Calixto. He was a sailor, after all, and heard the
word *knew* as the euphemism I'd not meant it to be; but which,
nonetheless, it was. *Knew*, yes. I'd known the girl in both the sailorly
and biblical sense; but that was a story the particulars of which I cared
not to recount. . . . Yet I had to, *non?* I'd sworn there'd be no more lies,
no more dissemblance; and if soon we were to meet my . . . *Alors*, the
impossible word stuck in my craw—*How could this be?*—and ceded its
place only when I spewed onto the sea that third and final wave of
stomach-rot, of soul-rot; whereupon I rinsed my mouth with rum,
breathed deeply, and swallowed a quarter bottle more of the stuff.
Thusly fortified, I told the tale as fast as I could. Calixto sat rapt but
rowing all the while, such that soon we achieved Indian Key; where I
found, yes, *family*.

> *Pardon me, heart* (wrote S. whilst still aboard that brigantine out of
> Naples), *if I err in this sketch of the particulars relevant to this Peronette-creature
> and the peril she put you in, some years past.*
>   *She was, was she not, the niece of the fair but ineffectual, the feeble mother superior*

of that wretched convent school from whence we rescued you? What a cesspit of impiety that was! — Of course, I could confirm this myself, and spare you some paragraphs of pain, if only I had at hand my copy of your first Book of Shadows to which you committed this story, ever heedful of our rede: Write, that our lives might benefit the sisters-to-come. And you've done that well, heart, far better than I. But I haven't the ciphered copy of the Book you sent from Florida. I read it, assuredly so, but it never occurred to me to carry it Rome-ward, as I'd no idea the new witch I sensed was born of relations, let me say, recounted therein.

And there were relations, were there not? —Why do I even ask, when the proof sleeps in the next cabin?

As I recollect the tale, the troubled child, Peronette, arrived, in ribbons and bows, befurbelowed, and was consigned to your care, she being sharp-of-sense but dismissive of study. You were to help her learn. Proximity led to passion, as sometimes it does when girls grow up together, till you found yourself smitten, all but entranced. Though no witch was she, this P., well she might have been, bewitched as you were. — Blame not yourself, heart. The inner lives of girls are poems, progressing unto dramas as they age. So it goes. — And though I know not the full story of the night in question—did it not storm, and did not the minx slip into your bed in search of company, comfort, and acts more corporeal? — I know quite well the story of your need. How ignorant, how innocent you were, my H. And such traits no doubt were set in relief by love and its first-time expression. — I ask, What but Chaos could have ensued?

But, heart, hadn't there been blood? I believe there had been, yes. First blood. And too, pardon me, H., but surely there'd been a measure of surprise on P.'s part when in you'd slipped your man-part, and spent yourself. Did you not presume consummation? Evidently not, as you knew nothing of your nature then, neither as man-woman nor witch. — Parbleu! The lies and truths we tell ourselves, simply to sustain our sanity! — My heart breaks anew to think of you as you were, H., so confused, so alone, so wholly unknowing of all and everything.

And so you, my heart, no one could condemn. Doubtless you surrendered to instinct that night, and did as desire bade you do. — As once I told you, sister: One cannot condemn a creature for doing what it is in its nature to do.

———————————— ✳ ————————————

Thereafter, though, things fell apart fast, did they not? Recrimination, there'd been. Denial. Accusations of deviltry and satanic influence. — Ha! If only they'd known, those nuns and girls, how we waited in the Shadows, we creatures come aborning from their worst dreams. Incubus, succubus, sister-witch and a man claiming descent from demons. — I have long allowed Asmodei that charade he played upon you, H. Forgive me. But you've loved, and lost, and need not be taught the definition of indulgence.

Dreadful they'd been, those girls and nuns. Especially that wimpled bitch, Sister Claire de Sazilly. Sister to whom, I wonder, if not Satan himself? Evil enwrapped that one like a second skin and, à vrai dire, I've yet to suffer a moment's remorse for what befell her. Who, if not the wicked, should suffer? Non reliquet Dominus virgam peccatorum super sortem justorum *reads the psalm, non? "The Lord will not let the rod of the wicked rest upon the lot of the righteous." (Titter not, sister: I once had a Bible.)*

As for the girl, Peronette? Perhaps, for her, I might have found a measure of pity. She'd shown an inclination toward evil, too, it's true, and yes, she'd used and abused you, but once she'd run from the convent school, well, let me say that not all the world welcomes the unwed and pregnant, ma soeur. *No matter their means. She might have escaped the convent school in a coach crowded with riches, but what then? Where to, once she knew the truth of what you'd set inside her? I imagine life, for her, devolved fast once it was known she'd fallen. And indeed I might have pitied such a one as P., were it not for all I've learned in Rome, truths that I see written on the faces of these twins, Leo and Luc:*

Truth the first: They too were abused by Peronette Gaudillon.

And, truth the second: They are you, these two.

— More to come, heart. Now I must sleep, as the roll of this ship unsettles me. I'll need what strength I can summon if I'm to survive this crossing to Cuba, to the monk Queverdo Brù. And oh, H., how I hope you are in receipt of my command to come and meet us there, in Havana! I've such riches to confer unto you now, living riches. — Surprise, indeed!

But more of their story is wanted than I'll ever draw from the twins themselves. So, on the morrow, I'll slip into the ship's surgeon's lair, avail myself of his medicaments, and see if I can't back-cast a spell of Sight. In so doing, I shall be able to gather scraps of story, at least, and thereafter sew for you a truer tale. — Yes, tomorrow, heart, I'll See what truths I can See, and thusly spare your having to Sight those truths yourself. I fear they will be difficult to witness. And in so doing, I will spare, too, poor Léopoldine having to summon her past. Luc, even if he had sister-talents of a sort—and he does not, I'm sure of it—well, still he is inclined to cry at odd times, and I would not see such tears, neither recollected nor newly shed. — It is sad to see them here, H., as they sleep, suffering the dreams they must suffer, and knowing how they'd have benefited from your presence in their lives. If all goes well, they will, still.

And she closed with a toad-sketch.

 Chapter Twenty-four

I am all the daughters of my father's house,
And all the brothers too.
—SHAKESPEARE, Twelfth Night

I'D KNOWN FROM CERTAIN PRECAUTIONS THE CYPRIANS
had bade me take that impregnation was a possibility
when . . . *relating* with me; for yes, ejaculate results from
that double-spill of mine, that twofold, capital-*E* Ec-
stasy that was the envy of all the witches. Still, I was not
sure of my potency. Neither did I know, for sure, if I
could become pregnant; though the mother role seemed
far less likely to eventuate for me as, in the common
parlance, I had never received *my monthly bill*. (More envy
amongst the Cyprians.)

And even this scant knowledge of my body had come
much, much later in my life. Whilst at the convent
school, I'd known nothing. *At all.* Knew only that I, my
self, was a secret I'd best keep; and so I had kept it. Until
that stormy summer's night when the world as I knew
it was torn asunder, split into two parts: the Light,

wherein I was unwanted; and the Shadows, wherein I was welcome. . . . All of which is to say that it had never dawned on me, then or later, that I'd sired . . . Shadowlings—*two*, no less!—on the night I surrendered to instinct and did what I did with Peronette Gaudillon.

Sebastiana, it seemed, had been unable to procure, from amongst the ship's *materia medica*, those ingredients requisite to even the simplest of Sighting spells; and of course, she had no pharmacopoeia of her own: She'd left her own supplies at home, and found she'd neither the time nor inclination to acquire more as they rode from Rome, south to Naples. What's more: Sebastiana wrote so sympathetically of the children, calling them *les trésors*, that I wondered if perhaps she'd *chosen* not to peer into their unpleasant past. Regardless, she came to refer to the twins as treasures, equating the party's ride from Rome with that of Napoléon I's soldiers, who, on a summer's day nearly forty years prior (*1799, says Asmodei*), had ridden from the Eternal City with treasures of their own.

> *As Chateaubriand observed* (wrote S.), *Attila had required but X number of pounds of pepper and spices to surrender his hold on Rome, but Napoléon sought lucre enough to fill the Louvre. Amongst this lot were such treasures as that dear little Spinario. Have you seen this statue, H.? I suppose not, as now it sits returned to Rome, rightfully, and you've not been here. It depicts a boy seated and bent, trying to extricate a splinter from his left foot, and if you were to see it, heart, you'd see in it your little Luc, himself troubled by the same* pied gauche. — *The which, I might add, has responded well to potions and poultices applied by yours truly. I don't know that he'll ever be "un-Byron'd," as A. says, but certainly his gait is much improved since the day he came up from the caves.* — *Yes, the* Spinario *sits returned to Rome, alongside much else of the spoils of those imperial wars, as one of the umpteen Piuses somehow got back those prizes he'd no doubt pilfered himself. And so, too, will you see your treasures returned to you, heart.* On arrive, mon amie. Attends-nous.

But it was they who'd have to wait for me; as, owing to the duplicity of Queverdo Brù, they'd have to quit Cuba in advance of my arrival. We missed one another by mere days. And they'd been on Indian Key for more than a half year by the time Calixto and I sailed to that place in pursuit of them.

Havana, for Sebastiana, had been a debacle from the day she arrived.

Here (she wrote), *one wears the heat like a hundred-pound hat or a wig of the ancien régime! The dust, the dirt, the incessant dirge-like play of the soldiers on parade, it is detestable. — Who is this monk? Where is he? And where, my heart, are you? — I confess I am tetchy. The long days at sea have sapped me terribly, and truly, I don't know how I'd have fared if I hadn't had nos trésors looking after me.*

Heart, they are healing. Luc talks at times, and walks now with his weight—such as it is—shared by both his shoes, or nearly so. Boots, not shoes, I should say, as we made time in Rome to outfit the children, Luc choosing a suit cut from parson-dark dimity, and Léopoldine opting for three dresses so dainty, so delicate, so high style as to belie, utterly, those rags we found her in. — She, too, is a delight, albeit aptly named. Yes, heart, she has the temper of a lioness, which, of course, A. likes to test. Rather, liked. Past tense. As recently he teased the child beyond her tolerance for it, and rose the next morning to find a whip's worth of his prized hair still asleep upon his pillow. I, of course, have brokered a truce, which has so far held, and there have been no difficulties since, A. busying himself with Luc above deck whilst Léopoldine and I . . .

Suffice to say, H., that she is as quick a teach as you, and wakes each day at dawn, as do I, and comes to me with her Eye already turned and wondering what the day's lesson will be. She wants this witchery. Like no other witch I've known or read of. Such that I, with yet a week to go before we reach the Cuban port, am tired! I look forward to conferring this acolyte unto you, H. She'll be the strongest amongst us, of that I'm sure. She is slowed neither by age, as I am, nor shame, nor self-doubt, as once you were. — How I hope to meet you healed, my heart. — Must nap now. I close by saying, again, that Léopoldine wants this witchery, and I warn the world: World, beware!

In time, they reached Havana; and the two—Sebastiana and Brù—met, in accord with those particulars put forth by S. in a letter she wrote and posted from Rome once she'd decided to sail and settle "my secrets" with me. Said letter arrived four days in advance of its sender; and Brù met the party portside.

Asmodei, of course, had resisted Sebastiana's decision. He threatened to ride back to France, to not accompany the party; but in the end he conceded, as Sebastiana had known he would. *He depends on me,* she'd written. *He'll not go without.* A far greater surprise it was to read in S.'s Book how Asmodei seemed to enjoy the children's company—the boy, his Byron, more so than Léopoldine, the latter having earned a wide berth for herself, as described above. Too, it seemed Asmodei hankered to see the ocean's far shores. And, said S., quoting her consort with diplomacy, *He wonders what's become of you.* No doubt he did. But so, too, might frontiersmen watch a forest burn, wondering what would become of the wood? . . . Asmodei? His company was but the price I'd pay to see Sebastiana again. And to meet my . . . *what?* Spawn? So . . . biological. Progeny? So . . . biblical. *Hélas,* I would have referred to them as children, but that seemed a right I'd yet to earn.

Would that I could include in this record the correspondence of Sebastiana and Queverdo Brù; but I cannot. His two letters to her—in which he wrote, so pointedly, of me—are lost; though Roméo, returned to Ravndal, sought them high and low. Sebastiana could not recall where she'd put them. . . . Memory, yes, served her less and less well. As for her eventual response, posted from Rome the same day she commanded me, *Come to Cuba,* well, that letter Brù surely secreted away somewhere.

Sebastiana, who later confided in her Book—suspicious from the first, perhaps—that Queverdo Brù was not the man, the monk, she'd expected to meet, had been doubly disappointed to discover that I'd not yet arrived in Havana; and when she mentioned sailing to St. Augustine in search of me, well, *At this Brù lit up, verily, such that I knew he'd not known where you were resident, and straightaway I regretted the disclosure.* Brù recovered to lie that I'd written him of illness, nothing serious at all, and that I'd be delayed; but yes, oh yes, I was coming. . . . Understand: My absence was no less of a bane to Brù than it was to Sebastiana: He needed her to lure me to Havana, and he could only hope she'd do so before she herself decided to depart. And if she *did* decide to depart, well, he'd have to . . . make her wait. Somehow. He'd not come so close to Perfection to see it—and his Rebus—slip away now, at the whim of a witch.

How he held to Sebastiana and Asmodei both is hard to say; but—and each of us has our weaknesses, *non?*—it seems fair and accurate to say he held to S. with luxury and to Asmodei with decadence, two commodities easily come by in Cuba. A tired, wan, and wasting Sebastiana—she had begun, shipboard, to write again of the Coming of the Blood—Brù installed in a fine, *very* fine hotel with views of the bay. Asmodei he'd accompanied to cockfights in the Extra-muros and, within the city walls, those other pastimes common to every port. Too, Brù hired a tutor for *the treasures;* and thusly did their formal education, in English, begin, whilst Sebastiana slept, and Asmodei, unwilling to attribute her malaise to anything more than the effects of sea travel, amused himself portside. All the while they waited on me; and none more intently than Brù.

Cagily, the alchemist kept his guests from his home, saying he'd a maiden aunt in his care and joking, to Asmodei at least, that a bequest from said aunt was both imminent and contingent upon the quiet she sought, nay, *demanded* as her days dwindled down. Neither did Brù arouse suspicion owing to his dress; for Sebastiana wrote in her Book—the Cuban entries in which were few—of Brù's being rather nattily attired whenever he visited her at the hotel, *not monkish in the least.* She made no mention of the burnous, nor of those scars upon his neck that yet were livid when I arrived in Havana; and that were caused by . . . *Alors,* I outpace myself, and must first preface things, thusly:

Léopoldine, some weeks into their stay, took it upon herself to trail Brù from the hotel at which they were resident. He'd come to see Sebastiana, as he had twice daily since their arrival and installation at—he insisted—his expense. Indeed, so often did he come that Sebastiana grew immodest and met the monk abed, dressed in the flimsiest of her blue robes. And rings, many rings. Léopoldine would tell me much later that Sebastiana had never met Brù without setting some stones upon her fingers: clue the first, said Leo, that Sebastiana had come to suspect Brù of being something other than what he wished to seem.

Bidding Luc stay behind and tend to a tired S., Léopoldine quit their room, their top-floor suite, to follow Brù after an afternoon's visit. Both she and her brother could summon a Shadow-quality well suited to surveillance and the elusion of authority, a talent not inborn—as Luc, indeed, has no such talents, witchery being a woman's gift . . . in every case save mine, I suppose—but rather bred during those months alone in Rome, after the death of Peronette, when they'd had to steal food and slip about unseen in order to survive.

It was dusk, with darkness coming on; and against that darkening, against the slow-dropping drape of night, Léopoldine saw the light-birds rise above that house through the tarry doors of which Brù had slipped, looking first this way and that. Had he seen her? Sensed her? She thought not. At first she'd taken the birds for ash, swirling up from a fire unseen. But no: They moved, they flew more mindfully than ashes might, dipping and darting, sometimes slipping into unison and seeming a tablecloth sewn of light—so said Léopoldine—being snapped clean of its clinging crumbs and whatnot.

It must have been the bee hummingbirds Leo saw that night, surely; and lucky she was that they'd not swarmed her, as they had me, stingingly.

Léopoldine left Brù's street that night—and how I shivered when later I heard her tell the tale, reminded as I was of my own suffering and so very grateful for her own escape—and returned to the hotel, where she told only Luc of her double discovery: Brù's house and birds. And Luc, of course, believed her, as he believed everything his sister told him; because, 1) She never lied (to him); 2) Anything could be true; and 3) It was just easier that way. Luc added suspicions of his own to that litany of his sister's. Rather, not so much suspicions as this tale of . . . strangeness:

Their tutor—whom together they derided to a degree that tells the man was well paid by Brù; for otherwise he'd have run from *les trésors*, who could be troublesome, and who doubtless he wished were treasures of *the buried sort*— . . . their tutor, René, had, the day prior, offered Luc a Spanish coin in exchange for an answer, in confidence, to the question *How does your sister pee?*

"How do I what?" cried Leo upon hearing this.

"How do you pee," said her abashed brother. "You know, when you have to make water and—"

"*Tu es bête!* I know what it means, *to pee*. But why would the Nose want to know that?" Evidently, said tutor was cursed with a prominent proboscis.

"I don't know," said Luc, drawing the earned coin from his pocket with a smile.

"What did you say?"

"I said I'd only ever seen you poop." And they laughed as Luc tossed the coin out the window, down onto the street. . . . I doubt the twins ever returned to René's tutorials, going instead to that place where they were wont *to play* whilst in Havana: the cathedral. Yes, the twins had discovered the statue of Saint Sebastian, and though they'd later say they went there *for peace,* I supposed their purposes were plainer; for Luc was a long while letting go of his pickpocket-ish ways, from which both he and his sister profited.

Of course, hearing the tutor's strange question, I knew what it was Brù, his employer, was trying to discover: Had I sired an androgyne? Had Brù a lesser Rebus already in his midst? If so, he could speed his plan without attending me. I suppose he thought he'd have his answer if only he knew how Léopoldine peed, seated or standing, or, ideally, I suppose, switching betwixt the two, as I was wont to do whilst alive. . . . Brù. The fool!

Of course, I had not sired a child bearing my stranger traits. Léopoldine was but a girl, and Luc but a boy. . . . But it'd be a while more before Queverdo Brù learned this.

. . . Finally, one day, Sebastiana decided she was strong enough to sail. In truth, she wrote, she feared the Blood was near, and would not suffer it without seeing me again, now that I was as close as St. Augustine. Sensing that the treasures had a secret between them, she sought it; and Luc told all, as his creamy complexion has never allowed for lies. Léopoldine expounded—Brù's house, the birds . . . —and was congratulated. Said S., she had suspicions, too, but she had been too weak to seek out their truths, by divination or deed.

Now, knowing what the twins knew, S. supposed it might be time to *pop in* on Brù. A social call, she'd say, ascribing her knowledge of his home to coincidence or sister-instinct. She, nay they—for she'd bring Leo along—would thank Brù for his hospitality. They'd bid him adieu, *with all regrets.* And so, off the two witches went whilst *the boys* busied themselves with the baggage; for all four—sadly, the fifth member of their party, Luc's fattened rat friend, had expired at sea, and went to his eternal rest in the Countess Skavronsky's hatbox, crowded with three types of cheese procured from the ship's pantry—

. . . all four, I say, were to set sail for St. Augustine on the morrow. There they'd surprise me. As indeed they would have. . . . Had they ever arrived. . . . Had I still been resident in that city, and not sailing up the seaboard, toward Savannah and the Havana-bound *Athée*.

To render here an account of this *social call*, as paid by the witches upon an unsuspecting Brù, I must needs resort to what I know of the persons involved and, further, fictionalize the particulars. Sebastiana, you see, after this visit, wrote only to warn me: *Run!* And neither witch ever recounted said call in detail. Understandably. I, too, was happy to leave the alchemist where he lay—literally—and so never pestered my sisters for all the particulars.

That said, I must somehow plug this present hole in my narrative lest the ship of story sink, and in so doing I ask your indulgence. To do other than tell the story in full—albeit with recourse to some *fictioneering*—would be to lose the trail, as it were, that will eventuate in *my present state*. And by *state*, I refer not to that of a witch-soul occupying a putrefying child—though I must, *must* speed this pen or seek a second host, as soon *ma hôtesse* will harden beyond use, will begin to stink and leak such that I'll not be able to sustain this charade, as so far I have: I am a puppeteer, if you will, pulling the strings of Twitch and Pulse and emitting moans, such that the ship's surgeon is caught where I want him: He cannot yet pass my hostess to the captain for committal to the sea, but neither can he speak to my would-be mourners of recovery. In fact, *contagion* is the operative word; and *my* operative, the helpmate with whom I sail—and who has yet to enter this narrative—has only to spread word of contagion to keep our shipmates from this cabin. Otherwise, we'd know no peace at all, my hardening hostess and I.

No, by *my present state* I mean god, goddess, ghost; which sounds . . .

---

grandiose, granted. Indeed, "Be dead and be done with it," my helpmate is wont to say. She wishes I'd desist, and simply take another host
when we reach our destination. "What's the hurry, after all?" is the
question that comes with a smile; but she, being mortal, cannot comprehend the urgency of what I wish to do. Which, precisely, is this:

Tell the tale of *my* end to *its* end. . . . And to do so, I must here
resume my embellishment, my embroidery—hence, your indulgence,
sister, if you please—of that part of the tale I did not witness myself; namely: My Soror Mystica's departure from Cuba with *the treasures* in tow.

 *Chapter Twenty-five*

I have long dreamt of such a kind of man,
So surfeit-swelled, so old, and so profane;
But being awake, I do despise my dream.
—SHAKESPEARE, *Henry IV, Part II*

THE WITCHES SURPRISED QUEVERDO BRÙ ATOP THE
assoltaire, and found him dressed not in a suit of black
linen and silk but rather in the sweat-stinking burnous.
Léopoldine led Sebastiana through the streets of the old
city, walking more slowly than the situation seemed to
warrant: Though still young, Leo had never been innocent; and now she suspected, knew, and wanted Brù,
whom she sensed was a traitor to both her discoverer
and to the Shadows, wherein she already felt at home.
But caution was called for: Sebastiana, unsteady on the
cobbled and unpaved streets, and shadowed beneath a
parasol of yellow silk, could only walk so fast; and too
sudden an approach to Brù might stir the birds and alert
him of their coming. Above all, surprise was the element
they'd need to maintain if they were to strip Brù of his
dissembling ways.

Léopoldine, it was, too, who pushed wide the black and tar-tacky doors. Through these they stepped, into the midday shade of the porte cochère. There, Leo took from her pocket a bun, or some bread, or some friable thing, which she'd carried to distract the birds—with crumbs—should they come. Of course, neither Leo nor Sebastiana had expected to see peafowl, large, luminous peacocks and peahens, rushing to them in the shade of that entryway large enough to ac-commodate a carriage and four. It seems the fowl came at the witches less intently than they'd come at me. Doubtless they, too, had been surprised that quiet afternoon, the only noise being that which fell from the *assoltaire* and told that Brù must be, improbably, upon his roof, working at some mechanical thing; for the noises the witches heard were those of grinding, stirring and such. And this quiet held, despite the coming of the peafowl; which pecked at the crumbs cast by Léopoldine as if out of habit or from memory: They'd long ago come to disdain all but the elixir.

A quick survey of the courtyard and surrounds showed the witches the way up, up to the *assoltaire*, where the tops of tents could be seen. Their ascent was steady and slow, and, if the truth be told, stealthy; till finally, heedful of both the bats overhead and the light-birds twinkling in the creeper, like constellated stars, the witches stood atop the *as-soltaire*, in sight of Brù, who yet believed himself alone amidst his tents.

Sebastiana, of course, had seen her share of Shadow-lairs, of ate-liers and laboratories such as Brù's; but Léopoldine must surely have been awestruck. Indeed, S. later said she knew Brù as an alchemist the minute she saw the athanor. As for Léopoldine, well, her mind grew crowded with questions, questions she'd have cast crumb-like before Brù if only she'd been let to. ("She is her mother-father's daughter," Asmodei was sometimes wont to say.)

Queverdo Brù—and once there was a time when I thought it'd be amusing to back-conjure the scene, so as to see his face as he turned, stunned, at Sebastiana's summoning cough; but I dared not do it: One does not divine the past for sporting purposes; nor the future, for that matter— . . . *alors*, Brù, with what excuses I cannot imagine, must have wheeled from his work; but soon he recovered and bade his visitors sit on that same white divan onto which I'd later fall, stupefied, drug-struck. But already the surprise of their approach had shown the witches that Brù was, yes . . . *other* than he wished to seem.

In prior meetings with Brù—first at certain sites he'd shown the party, and later, when Sebastiana had weakened further, at their hotel—he'd not spoken of the truths he sought; nor did he tell Sebastiana why he so coveted my company. But there atop the *assoltaire*, with the athanor and all the lesser tools of his trade in array, she saw his purpose: He was indeed, albeit improbably, a puffer, as once alchemists had been called, owing to those blowing bellows with which they tended their never-dying fires. She'd known, or supposed, that some alchemists practiced still, seeking to render gold from dross in accord with age-old recipes; and she supposed further that such men were charlatans, as the greater part of their forebears had been. This Sebastiana said to Brù within minutes of her arrival. Further (and how Léopoldine brightened when later she told me of S.'s gathering her strength to dress Brù down), she chided Brù for the lies in his letters; though, said she, she'd never suspected him of *mere* monkery. Neither could she have known, then, that it was not simply gold-essay that concerned him; but when Brù began to blather of Perfection, et cetera, Sebastiana's suspicions, already confirmed, ceded to fear. A charlatan, a quack, yes; but whenever men—be they monks or magicians, or equal parts of both, as was Brù—begin to talk of immortality, and justify all Means leading to that End, they are not to be trifled with.

"Leo, heart," I can hear Sebastiana say, words accompanied by a wink of her turned Eye, "would you excuse Señor Brù and myself, please?"

Léopoldine would have resisted, surely, had it not been for the wink or the tip of the chin or whatever it was that conveyed Sebastiana's true intent; which was to free Leo to have a look around the place; for hadn't they bypassed three stories of rooms? None of which housed, Sebastiana supposed, a dying aunt.

If Brù balked at this, well, the witches had already put their plan into play, surely, with Léopoldine descending and saying, in her still-halting English, that she wished to pet the oddly white peafowl, nothing more. Meanwhile, S., regal upon that snowy divan, asked the first of many questions to come; which, it is easily imagined, may have been this:

"What do you want with the witch Herculine?"

Brù, not wholly disarmed, lied. Of course he did. But his lies, whatever they were, would have allayed my sister's new, *alchemical* suspicions not at all.

I know she went on to question Brù about his birds, and about Ouroboros, the snake, which hung, heavily, upon a forked branch of cypress standing upright in the corner of the tent in which they sat. More lies from Brù; such that Sebastiana stopped listening; for she learned more from the man's eyes, which did not meet her own— which she left turned, purposely so—but rather looked past her, to where Léopoldine had disappeared down the stairs. His discomfort was evident. Quite. He worried what the younger witch would find. And well he ought to have; for already Léopoldine had explored the library, finding the alchemical texts yet not knowing them for what they were. Still, so unvaried a collection told of too pure a purpose. And this—so perspicacious was she, even at ten or eleven—worried my witch. And if already she wondered if trouble were a-brew, she wondered and worried the more when she progressed from the library to try the unlocked door of the room next to it, the Stone Room. . . . Brù, never suspecting that the witches would come to bother his abode, had not locked the door of the room in which I'd suffer so.

———————————— ✣ ————————————

Léopoldine would report that she'd explored the Stone Room, and its strangeness, as long as her turned Eye allowed; for the accompanying headache was extreme. . . . To clarify: Leo had not willed the Eye herself, but rather the room had seemed somehow to elicit it. This further told of trouble. Still, she'd have explored more, eager to please Sebastiana with a fuller report—Were those wings upon the wall, flapping still? And how could the redness be at once so stony-looking yet soft to the touch?—but . . . something was wrong. She knew it. Sensed it. Scented it upon the air, as a dog does fear.

Léopoldine's fears riled her witch's blood as well as the walls of the Stone Room; for, in time with her increasing dread, the white-flesh began to writhe, to wriggle, to flap in mockery of its respective *living functions;* and the pieces of imperfected Stone—which she too took for rubies, as a ruby had been the last stone Peronette Gaudillon had had to sell to survive when cast aside by her last protector, and the proceeds from its sale had secured that garret in which the three had lived, and in which Peronette had slow-died of consumption, alternately coughing up both a blackish, treacly substance and bitter accusations aimed at her children, whom she'd long seen as the *antithesis of treasure*— . . . the pieces of stone, I say, had begun to swell and shape-shift upon their nails, as if jellied. This I'd witness myself, some six months on; and let me add that the sight of the Stone Room in that state was something that bound us, somehow, Leo and me, each to the other.

Léopoldine left the Stone Room and tried to set aside her fears, and wondered where else she might look; but it was then, returned to the terrace and standing in the shade of the creeper—it, too, seemed somehow animate, illuminate . . . —she heard that most discomfiting of sounds: silence. No voices drifted down from the *assoltaire* or the tents atop it.

As Leo ran the angles of that terrace, she roused the light-birds from their roost. The bats fell, too. Surely the courtyard was then chiaroscuro'd, seeming naught but shadow or light. And when the witch achieved the spiraling staircase, she slipped upon its first step, falling to settle onto a knee now gashed and bleeding, badly, her Blood being *up*, as it were. The pain receded a moment later; for she looked up to see the stairwell darkened and somehow . . . constricted, the change in its aspect attributable to the presence of Queverdo Brù, who stood several steps above her where she knelt.

He asked—too solicitously—if she was well. She responded with silence as she stared up at Brù, silhouetted by the light cast by the remaining bats. Finally, she stood, fearful not of Brù, but rather the too-tiny bats, whose larger, black brethren she'd come to loathe whilst living in the caves of Rome.

Standing at the bottom of the stairwell, Leo determined to somehow push past Brù and the bats. She charged, only to find herself in the man's arms, wherein she suffered his scent, his perfume, such that, to this very day, she drowns the memory of it in a scent all her own, a perfume so potent it quite overwhelms the violet odor occasioned by my *coming down*, as we call it. Oh, but worse than the hold the alchemist had upon her, and worse than his scent, much worse, was *the play of his hands*; for these Brù worked, obscenely, meaning to discern, finally, if she, my daughter, was doubly-sexed as well. Poor Leo. She was shocked into stillness. She'd seen such *congress*, let me call it, when things in Rome had progressed from bad to worse, and she and Luc had stood nearby, silent in the recess of doorways, watching whilst strange men offering coins were let to cover their mother in shadows; but she'd never known such acts herself, *bodily*. A few men had tried, yes, in months past, soliciting her in Italian—a language Leo all but scraped from her tongue the moment Sebastiana descended, saw her, showed her Eye, and said "bonjour"—but those men, well, she'd been able to send them away, let me say; and away they'd gone, yes, some bloodied and others cursing her—*Stregha!*—for that particular pain she'd willed onto their private parts.

Enfin, it is easily supposed that, had Léopoldine had her wits about her that afternoon, and had she met Brù upon a playing field rather more level than a spiral staircase slick with batshit, she'd have bested the man such that he'd have begged, *begged* for such an end as that interment that would be his fate, some months hence. *Hélas*, this was not the case. . . . Only when Leo heard the alchemist rip the blouse she wore, which had been gifted her by Sebastiana, well, that rip, that shredding of sheer and wondrous silk, more so than the man's hands upon her, strangely, is what allowed Léopoldine to rouse herself and strike; the result being this:

Brù, tumbled to the lowest step, found four scratches set into the right side of his neck by the recently lacquered nails of Léopoldine. Now she stood in ascent, atop the stairs; from whence she turned and climbed—blouse torn, skirt askew—till she stood atop the *assoltaire*, watching, wondering as . . . *Could it be?* Or was this a trick of her turned Eye? For it seemed, indeed she'd have *sworn* that the sofa upon which Sebastiana sat, with her back to the stairwell, and seemingly oblivious to all that had transpired there, was *alive*; for all along its humped back a whiteness writhed, as if a . . .

"Snake!" hissed Léopoldine; and she leapt and ran to the tent in question, bounding up before Sebastiana to find her sitting stock-still and silent, and somehow . . . golden. As if dusted with the ore. Again she named the predator.

"Yes, heart," said S., "I know it is a snake; and much as I'd like to move, I find I cannot." Only then did it seem she saw Léopoldine before her, in disarray, one budding breast bared. Said S., later, it was then she understood, finally, fully, why it was Brù sought me: He'd use me, alchemically, for my *sur*-sex, my duality. "Where is he?" she asked of Leo, tentatively. "Did he do . . . ?"

Léopoldine put her off, pointing behind S. to the on-slithering, pulsing python and looking this way and that, desperate to determine what bound Sebastiana to the sofa; for she was certain to be strangled if . . .

"Come closer," commanded S., coolly. And when Léopoldine approached, warily—bats were bad, but a python twice as long as she was tall was positively, *quoi?* . . . *Perilous,* yes—Sebastiana slowly raised her arms. "No, no!" said she when Leo tried, quite logically, to tug her from the sofa. "We mustn't move too quickly. The snake is too near, and wants this leaf Brù blew onto me."

"Leaf?" echoed Léopoldine. . . . Indeed, gold leaf clung to Sebastiana's face and neck, her hands, and brightened, too, the blue, light-weight robes she'd worn for this *call,* as it were, in concession to the Havanan heat. It was the gold that drew the snake. And for its snack of gold it would strike.

"Take these," said S. now, referring not to her proffered hands but rather the rings upon them. "Take the rings of gold—there, there, and there," and with a twitch of her fingers she indicated which rings she meant, "and . . . and feed it."

"The snake?" asked Leo. "Feed your rings to the snake?" Already the python was near enough Sebastiana to flick its split tongue onto her shoulder, to take its gold-treat flake by flake.

"Yes, dear," said S. through a clench of teeth, ". . . not the rings, *the gold* of them." Still the child stood there, uncomprehending. "Heart," said S., "see that saucer, there? . . . The black one, yes. Take my three rings and drop them into . . . into the milk or whatever that is, and bring the bowl here. *Vîte!*" Whereupon the younger witch, though still not knowing the *why* of it all, obeyed; such that Ourobouros soon ate, *ate,* from its black bowl set onto Sebastiana's upturned palm, three rings of gold, each worn by S. that day for a purpose of its own:

Onto her thumb she'd slipped a band inset with peridot (for "purity"), whilst onto her first and third fingers she'd put rings showing jade (for "the promotion of psychic strength") and lapis lazuli (to draw "the higher self"). Too, she'd sported two double bands of purest malachite, for—said she, later, with a laugh—"the warding off of evil. . . . Oh well."

My sister, you see, had rightly supposed that the strangeness, the luminescence of the animals under Brù's care, was owing to something alchemical; and as all things alchemical devolve to gold in some way, it seemed she and Leo might succeed in distracting, with that element, the python, whose purpose—as put forth by Brù, when already the snake had snuck up behind Sebastiana and it was too late to move— was plain: The python was to contain—literally, if need be—the older witch whilst Brù descended in search of the younger.

Blessedly, Sebastiana had supposed aright: Ourobouros turned its intentions, and its tongue, from my sister's shoulder and neck toward her hand, and down the length of her arm it came. It was all, *all* Sebastiana could do to support the snake's density, its watery weight, its slickness and chill. Léopoldine watched Sebastiana struggle, but what could she do? Sebastiana warned her to stillness: Too sudden a move and the python might strike, and there'd be no extricating her then. . . . Finally, slowly, Sebastiana lowered her arm onto the sofa, and there she sat the bowl down, balancing it carefully; for if it spilled, well . . . And then she moved out from under the python—quite snaky herself, as Leo tells it—and stood to take a shaking Léopoldine in her arms.

Together the witches backed from the python to the tent's far edge, watching as Ourobouros took the rings onto its tongue, one by one. "It's a strange man we've met this day, heart," whispered Sebastiana. "Where is he now?"

Unfortunately, the answer to that question came from Brù himself, bloodied at the neck but risen to stand at the head of the stairs: "Congratulations," said he with a hiss as he bowed to both witches.

Leo would later laugh, admitting that she'd hoped at that very moment to learn from S. that witches do indeed fly; for, with Brù blocking the stairs, there was no other way off his rooftop.

A conundrum, then; one that could only be solved by confrontation.

Sebastiana he'd meant to strangle, and Léopoldine he'd sought
to . . . unsex; and so it is surprising, yes, that Queverdo Brù survived
to greet me in that same tent some days later, his neck scarred by a
daughter I'd yet to learn of. And indeed, the witches could have done
away with Brù in myriad ways, witchly or otherwise; but Brù, too, afforded some measure of offense. He knew now that Sebastiana had already commanded me to come to Cuba, and he knew, too, where to
search me out if I never showed. As a lure, S. had outlived her usefulness. As for Léopoldine, well . . . he'd learned she was no Rebus. How
then did the standoff end? I will let Sebastiana tell it; for, some while
later, she took up her Book once more, to close the story of her
Cuban sojourn; like so:

> Oh, heart, regrettably, perhaps unforgivably, I chose to believe the last of the al
> chemist's lies—much to Léopoldine's dismay, might I add, she being stronger than I and
> flush with witch-sense I ought to have heeded—and I acceded to Brù's suggestion that
> we leave in peace, we witches promising a spell-free departure in exchange for Brù's
> telling what he knew of you.
>
> Yes, H., Brù implied he had news of you, which he'd hoarded. I saw no other choice,
> as the day's dread events—je déteste les serpents!—had drained me, had so
> weakened me I could not draw from Brù, by witchery, what he knew, but had to rely
> on his speech, his lies. —— H., pardon my blunder. —— But let me say, too, that I be
> lieved the Blood might come to me there, where I stood, upon a Cuban rooftop, and I'd
> not risk such an undignified demise. And though I'd the want to put the man down,
> truly I did, as one puts down a dog, I hadn't the will, nor the simple strength, and
> I dared not turn Léopoldine loose upon him, as I'd begun to tutor her in the subtleties
> of the Craft, the whiteness of the Work, and feared she'd stray down a darker path if

the first of her works was the murder of Queverdo Brù. — And so, yes, when the al-
chemist said he'd a second letter from you, of more recent date, one in which you'd put
off my command, saying your health, at present, precluded all travel, well, I believed him.
Pitifully so, never even asking him to show said letter, though he did give an address in
St. Augustine, the same that I now know to have been false. — Le bâtard! — My
strength recovered now, how I'd like to retake to that rooftop and change the day's end!

As it was, the witches left Queverdo Brù's *in peace*. Or as peaceably
as possible. Said S., recounting the tale of their departure, *The child's*
Eye did not settle for an hour or more, and she had to walk home head bowed, with
me leading her by hand, lest it be seen.

Léopoldine seemed less bothered by Brù's accosting her than by the
mysteries she'd uncovered, and which she thought would remain mysteries forevermore; i.e., the Stone Room, a description of which she struggled to convey to Sebastiana. The more Leo spoke, the more thankful
Sebastiana was for their peaceable escape. Oh, but now their problems
were manifold: How to rendezvous with me in St. Augustine before Brù
could? And what if the alchemist had lied (as indeed he had)? What if I
were en route to Havana in search of my sister and her secrets? What if
I arrived and found only Brù? What would I do then? Of course, she
tried to find me by listening, in the witch-sense of the word; but I was
not in distress then—chronic melancholia notwithstanding—and even if
I had been issuing a silent *au secours*, it is doubtful Sebastiana could have
heard it; for the travel, the turmoil of late, had weakened her so. Moreover: A witch's powers decrease as the Blood comes closer.

More immediately, Sebastiana worried that Asmodei might learn
of the day's events and their effect upon her. If so, how would she
keep him from killing the alchemist? And should she? Wrote S.,

I kept the day's secrets, or rather altered them in the telling. In this, Léopoldine swore
her collusion, her cooperation. And I did so not to mark any merit of my own, or to

dissemble, but rather because my Asmodei has always wanted to kill for me, and I have never let him. Neither I nor the world stands to benefit from such Red tribute as that. And certainly I could live guilt-free to the end of my days knowing I'd let an aged alchemist live to the end of his, pursuing his secrets, tending his athanor high above the streets of Havana. — Or so I thought then. Today, my decision would differ. And Brù would die.

The party's departure from Cuba was not delayed, but rather split. That is, the day after they'd surprised Brù at home, they sailed in pairs, as per this newly made plan:

Asmodei and Luc would sail to intercept me in St. Augustine; or, if need be, at sea, if already I'd sailed for Havana. In so doing, they'd keep me from Brù; for Sebastiana had slipped and spoken of St. Augustine as my home. Thereafter, we three would sail south to meet Sebastiana and Léopoldine upon Indian Key; which place had been decided upon by Sebastiana. She'd heard much of the island from Asmodei, who'd learned of it whilst drinking in the portside sinks he favored, and frequented, whilst in Havana. It seemed a suitable rendezvous: a set-apart place peopled by sea types disinclined to question newcomers, lest they be questioned in turn. And its population— tens of transients, perhaps a hundred—offered, in the aggregate, protection from the pirates and Indians who preyed upon the area's lone sailors and settlers; yet Indian Key was not so populous as Key West, where Brù—if he chose to pursue the four, and began his search in *the logical place:* the keys' prime city—might hide amidst the shadows cast by that island's several hundred settlers.

And so, two ships sailed, the one carrying Asmodei and his Lord B. to St. Augustine, the other set to make the shorter crossing to Indian Key. There the witches would inveigle themselves, and await our reunion. . . . It was a plan, yes, one further refined and put into fast effect at dawn of the day of sail; as so:

Witch-work was wanted. . . . Two spells would suffice, thought S.

Said spells Sebastiana was too weak to work herself. She'd not slept the night prior, passing a white night in order to write those words in her Book that ended with her imperative to me, *Run!* Additionally, she'd written two words in our familiar cipher of old: *Indian Key*. And so it was she turned to the children.

Having first secured an oath from Léopoldine to the effect that she would never, ever, cast a spell upon Luc without his knowledge, Sebastiana led the young witch in her work. As for Luc, well, he was happy to hear he'd a part to play in the plan.

. . . Understand: Neither child knew they were setting off in pursuit of a parent—Sebastiana, thinking *that* news was mine for the telling, had sworn Asmodei to secrecy as well—but they were happy to leave Havana, and quite cooperative, doing *exactly* as Sebastiana bade them do. If all went well, thought they, they'd meet another witch and please their sister-savior in the process.

Enfin, the question to be answered was this: How—if Asmodei and Luc failed to find me in St. Augustine or at sea, and I ended up in Havana— . . . how could Sebastiana communicate to me both her warning and her whereabouts? As known, she wrote it in her *Book of Shadows*. But however was it that said Book found its way into Brù's library, where I, in turn, found *it*? Like so:

Léopoldine cast a Shadow-spell upon her brother, under cover of which he slipped through Brù's black doors and into the library unseen. There he lay the *Book of Shadows* down, as directed by S., first cutting the heart from the Delphinus and attaching to said volume that dissembling spine-like ribbon reading *Labille-Guiard*. . . . As for the spell itself? Simple enough; but it rendered the already sly child all but invisible.

Requisite to the spell's success was a suitable effigy of Luc. As clay could not be found fast enough, wax was used: Five candles were

※

melted down to malleability and molded in the hands of Sebastiana and her most willing pupil, Léopoldine. They fashioned the wax to represent Luc, replete with strands of his hair and—here apologies were made—a left foot twisted inward, just so, lest the spell prove *in-efficace*. (People's inclination to turn from the lame further contributed to the spell's efficacy, of course.)

Blackness was wanted as well, as a quality of the poppet; for this would ensure Luc would not be espied in the streets. Onyx and hematite were pried from Sebastiana's remaining rings—these being the blackest stones literally *at hand*—and pressed into the effigy's chest. Luc swore he felt the pressure of this upon his own chest, and compared it to climbing from the Tiber after too long a swim. Asmodei, for his part, returned to the hotel short hours before he and Luc were set to sail, his errand a success: He'd procured black feathers, black velvet (satin would have sufficed), and a black box, all three of which were purposed in accord with common witch-sense: The feathers were pressed onto the effigy's back ("Ouch!" said Luc, with a wink at his startled sister) so as to ensure *fluidity*, fleetness of foot, and all but literal flight, whilst the black velvet was wrapped round the finished effigy, for *quiet*, and, finally, the whole of the poppet was placed into the box, for *concealment*. The spell thusly cast—"That's it?" asked an incredulous but rather self-satisfied Léopoldine—Luc set off from their hotel. There was nothing the others could do now but wait whilst the boy worked; and this they did, hailing the returned hero within the hour.

The Book in place, the party progressed toward the port by way of the cathedral, where Sebastiana sprinkled a handful of hexed sapodilla seed at the feet of her namesake's statue, knowing I'd find that, too, if ever I made it to Havana. Her hope was that I'd feel the hex's effect and suppose my sister had been there. And though I heard and heeded the statue's call, I did not extrapolate as my sister had wished: I did not understand she'd ensorcelled the statue; nor did I see that, in so doing, she meant to hint of having found the twins in those Roman catacombs bearing the martyred saint's name. . . . *Alors*, so it sometimes goes with Craftwork—it is neither as easy as faith, nor as sure as science.

Then, finally, the party sailed in teams of two, knowing not that I had already set out upon the St. John's; from the mouth of which river I'd sail on to Savannah, there to meet Calixto, Diblis, and all manner of darkness aboard the *Athée*. . . . *Alors*, so it sometimes goes. . . . And when they failed to find me, and all four reunited upon Indian Key, a return to Havana was deemed too risky: It was doubtful a weakened Sebastiana would survive the sail, let alone another encounter with Queverdo Brù.

I did survive Havana, of course; and so, led by my sister's Book, and helped by loyal, much loved Calixto, I was able to search out Sebastiana and company where they'd encamped upon that key, hoping I'd someday show. Hope, yes; it was hope—Sebastiana would say— that staved off the Coming of the Blood, *her* Blood . . . hope and her newfound treasures.

Thusly did it all came to pass; till finally Calixto and I sailed within sight of Indian Key. There, upon a jutting pier, I saw by late daylight two figures, one seated and one standing. The robes of the former were as blue as blue can be, bluer than sea or sky, azure blue; and so I knew it was she: Sebastiana d'Azur. Standing tall at her side, waiting with her, shading her from the sun with a parasol, was . . . my daughter, my witch, my Léopoldine. And coming down the pier, dragging a man whose broadness of shoulder, whose blondness bespoke Asmodei, there came a boy, himself blond, moving as fast as his left leg allowed.

Calixto paddled us nearer the pier, smiling all the while. When he raised a hand to wave, one, two, three, four, *enfin* eight hands rose fast to return his wave. (*Bien:* six hands at least: I cannot aver that Asmodei waved.) And watching as Léopoldine helped Sebastiana stand, I, too, stood, unsteadily, in the bumboat, and waved, waved both arms as if I meant to fly. My heart, it burst like a star, save stars only burst when they die and *I'd survived,* blessed be. And if I thought anything, *anything at all* as I stepped onto that pier and into the arms of kin, it was to wonder, wordlessly, how a place I'd never been before could feel so much, *so very much* like home.

 *Chapter Twenty-six*

Post equitem sedet atra cura.
Behind the rider sits dark care.
—HORACE, **Atra Cura**

"*Mes enfants*," SAID SEBASTIANA, BRIMFUL OF TEARS AND putting forth Léopoldine and Luc, "may I introduce your . . . your Herculine. *Dites bonjour.* . . . Rather, say hello."

And they did; he bowing, she keeping her distance whilst deigning to nod. . . . You see, Léopoldine had suspicions she'd yet to share with her brother. It was, *après tout*, a mere question of mathematics: If she, Leo, were a witch—as she most decidedly was—yet her mother, Peronette Gaudillon, had been mortal—as *she* most decidedly had been—and further, if I, a witch of "certain attributes," as S. had described me to her charges, had met Peronette ten-plus years prior, and now Léopoldine and her brother were ten-plus years of age, *alors* . . . The child, as I say, was sharp as a tack, nay *a stake*, and sensed from the first what said attributes were. . . .

Moreover: Asmodei had not honored his vow of silence on the subject; and even Sebastiana, as the months had passed and she'd despaired of ever seeing me again, had begun to speak of me in terms parental, if not paternal.

"Hello," said Léopoldine, finally, in her accented English; for Sebastiana had deemed that French be spoken only in the Shadows, only at home; where, in the half year past, Léopoldine had learned all, *nearly* all Sebastiana could teach a young witch. Luc had been under the aegis of Asmodei, which scared me when first it became apparent; but each adult balanced the other somehow. Sebastiana had seen to this. . . . And in extending a large and slender hand, quite like mine but showing still the softness, the rounded angles of her age, Léopoldine showed me her Eye, the pupil pushing out into an iris of blue, quite bright—which trait she shared with her brother. *Enfin*, here she stood showing me the Eye, which, between sisters, is sometimes a challenge, sometimes a salute.

What to do? What to say?

Turning from Leo, I bent to take a handshake and kiss from Luc, the latter seeming a tear set onto my cheek, light yet somehow dense. His nails showed half-moons of blackest dirt, and dirt, too, showed in the lines of his sweat-slickened palm; such that the whole of his proffered hand was . . . perfect. Absolutely perfect.

The two parts of me. Indeed. It was eerie and wondrous at once.

I looked again at Léopoldine, taller, brunette to her brother's blond—and only in Léopoldine's feline grace and Luc's wiliness, blunted by the shyness he'd inherited from me, surely, did I see the slightest hint of Peronette Gaudillon—and with a crooked finger I pulled my shaded spectacles to the tip of my nose, peering down over them to show the girl my own Eye. Further, I whispered that it was fixed, and that *that* was a story I'd tell her in time, if she were inclined to hear it.

"*Vous êtes . . . ,*" she began in French before looking back to Sebastiana and righting herself, "You are very strong then, *non?*"

"I suppose I am, yes," said I, hopeful she'd not hear my words as boastful. In truth, standing there on the weather-beaten, widely spaced planking of the pier, tearful and tense, and so excited I wondered how I'd draw sufficient breath, I did not feel strong, *not at all.* And when I turned from *her treasures* back to Sebastiana herself, well, I knew then I'd depleted what strength I'd held in reserve.

I'd waited long years to see, to kiss and hug again the woman, the witch who'd discovered and saved me; now here she was. . . . True, Sebastiana was unwell, and perspiring, such that I could only wonder how long she and Leo had waited upon that pier, S.'s parasol insufficient shelter from the sun; for she, Sebastiana, had recently divined the day but not the hour of our arrival, urged, verily *urged* to do so by her pupil. (Younger witches do not fear divination as older ones do.) . . . I saw the decade's effects upon Sebastiana's face. I shan't call it damage; for it was not that: Still she was beautiful, but her black hair now streamed silver at the part, and lines had deepened beside her eyes— eyes whose blue told in her adopted Shadow-name, *d'Azur*—and her mouth. Her body, too, had changed, barreling a bit in the middle: She'd lost her waist but had not run to fat, not at all. At present, she was perspiring, yes, having not acclimated to the weather of the American South; and, in fact, she never would: From that day to her death, I never once sat in conversation with Sebastiana without fanning her, directly, with a fan from her collection, or indirectly, by tying to a finger or toe one of several strings Asmodei had rigged to fans upon the ceilings and walls of our every room, themselves ever a-churn at the end of longer strings, pulleys and belts. . . . So it was that, despite my wanting to hold on to Sebastiana forever—and she, me—we drew apart, concluded the mutual introducing (during which Asmodei, wordlessly but with evident discomfort, remarked my turned Eye) and proceeded up the pier and onto Indian Key proper, toward shade and—as offered by Leo, with S.'s prompting her toward politesse— lemonade. Léopoldine and Sebastiana led; followed by Calixto, who walked warily, in silence, beside Asmodei; and Luc, who, sliding his hand into mine, looked up to say, with a wide smile both toothy and true, that a ball was to be held that day at dusk in honor of a physician and his family, newly arrived upon the island.

"A physician?"

"Yes," said Luc; and lest he embarrass me—for he thought I did not know the word in English—he leaned nearer to whisper its French equivalent, *"un médecin."*

"Ah," said I, "I see: *un médecin."*

"Oui, c'est ça." At which words Sebastiana turned, though it seemed she stood too far ahead to have heard the boy, and showed her Eye to him, *at him.* "I mean, yes," amended he, "a physician. . . . And a ball! Though Sebastiana says it is not a ball, not really, but more of a party."

"A party," said I, no better an interlocutor than a parrot; for I was nervous. . . . Was there blame for me here? If not from *my children* then from myself? Sadly, there'd be no blame; for Leo and Luc both so blamed and despised their dead mother for all she'd done—a list of which would add naught but sadness to this record—and the effects of which linger still, in Léopoldine's temper, in Luc's sad dismissal of himself (*Je suis nul,* he is wont to say when sunken low: "I am nothing"), that it seemed they'd no blame left for me. *Me;* whom the twins seemed to judge on terms all their own, Leo needing to satisfy herself that I was *of the Shadows,* and strong, and Luc needing only to know that *I'd stay.* . . . Oh, but yes, Peronette had inflicted upon the two a decade's worth of damage, which could never be wholly undone, not by love, spellwork, or aught else. And as for the hurt I'd come to feel over *all they'd suffered* at her hands, and in my absence, well, let this suffice: I saw my heart as a house, and said hurt I stowed in a room I determined never to enter.

Alors, onto the island we went, Luc dragging me up the pier as earlier he'd dragged Asmodei down it. "We have lots of parties here," said he; and he leapt at the prospect, *party,* as every boy ought to, but he came down crookedly upon that still-lame left foot—booted, whilst the other was bare—twisting his ankle and stumbling such that again Sebastiana turned, as did Asmodei. With assurances from Luc, though, our progress resumed; and this time it was I who reached down my hand in search of his.

Improbably—or so one would have thought—there was indeed a party on Indian Key the night of our arrival. This was fortuitous, said S.—stopping to spell *fortuitous* for Leo and Luc—as it would allow us to celebrate yet spare us having to suffer the attention to be accorded the honorees, one Dr. Trevor and his wife, come with two daughters and a young son in tow. . . . In the Shadows one *suffers* attention, it's true.

"*Ce n'est pas un vrai bal,*" said a smiling Sebastiana, later, when we'd a moment alone, "but, as they call it a ball, well, I do not disabuse them of the notion." She, of course, had been to balls in all the capitals and finer châteaux of Europe, and knew whereof she spoke; but the colonists of Indian Key had been kind to her since the day she and Léopoldine had arrived. As she told of those early days upon the key, and of how fearful she'd been thinking she'd never see me again, her Eye turned. And something in her regard led me to . . . *to lie;* but these were the whitest of lies, and I excused myself even as I spoke them. I apologized to Sebastiana for the lateness of my arrival, saying I'd had to wait in Havana for Calixto to come back; and I'd not had to expound upon this: so said her sly smile. Further, I said that yes, I had

met Queverdo Brù; but, sensing his motives were both odd and ill, I'd
kept from him, despite his insistence, till finally I'd had to put him off
permanently. Thusly did I lead my sister to believe that I'd not suffered at the alchemist's hands, that I'd partaken of his library, yes, but
had *put him off* with words alone (and not, *mon Dieu,* entombment!).
Did she believe me? Had she divined the truth of my time in Cuba? I
cannot say; but upon the pier, when first she saw me, she commented
upon my pallor, and twirled strands of my silver hair betwixt her fingers. In so doing, was she encouraging confession? Again, I cannot say;
but if so, well, I chose celebration over confession that day. And thereafter, discretion came to seem the wiser course; thusly were the hor-
rors of Havana put behind me.

Sebastiana and Asmodei were settled and content upon Indian Key.
They were welcome amongst the island's salts, lost types, and miscre-
ants, she *grâce à* her money, he *à cause de* his might. . . . Money and might
mattered there, upon Housman's key.

Housman, Jacob Housman, was lord of all the island; and the fact
that he had allowed first Sebastiana and Leo, and, later, the rest of Sebastiana's party, to settle on *his* island—everyone referred to it
thusly—was owing to several factors rather more specific than money
and might.

Sebastiana flirted with Housman, to be blunt; but she did so delicately, and in so witchly a way as to secure his dog-like devotion whilst
sparing herself the enmity of his missus. Too, there may have been
spells put into play. I cannot say; for on the topic my sister was coy.
Moreover: Housman feared Asmodei; which fact—and one had only
to spend a moment in the presence of both men to see Housman's fear
as factual—told more about Asmodei than it did Housman; who'd
sailed down from Staten Island some few years prior and proceeded

to develop the eleven-acre island into a port prosperous enough to rival St. Augustine, some several hundred miles to the north, and Key West as well, a day's sail southward. Housman, I mean to say, was a man of few fears; but Asmodei was one.

Five grand, I once heard it said: That was the price paid by Housman in '31, when he couldn't have been much older than I was when first I arrived on his island (thirty or so). He'd sailed southward with cash and sufficient reason to live on the lam. And if the law, or Law, was another of Housman's fears, he must surely have felt safe upon his key; for there the laws were his, and he was the Law.

Housman had talked the island out of the hands of a man named Gibson, who'd known not what he had. A waystation it was then, nothing more, with a tumbledown hotel of two stories wherein the wreckers would sometimes stay, amusing themselves with Gibson's bowling pins and billiard balls, as well as with those things more commonly partaken of by seamen come ashore: whores, to be blunt; and booze. But Housman saw more in store for the island, which militarists might have deemed *strategic* in its location: thirty-five miles from Carysfort Reef—where wreck upon wreck foundered, their wares to be shared by whatever crew claimed them first—and quite near the sinkholes of Lower Matecumbe Key, from which freshwater was readily drawn. Too, Indian Key had long been reputed to be mosquito-free; and though it was Housman himself who spread this rumor, there was, owing to the island's placement and its patterns of wind, some truth to his claim. . . . *Bref*, it was, or would be, a most livable place.

And indeed the island developed, Housman staking out its streets, its houses and groves, and seeing, too, to the importation of workable soil and rather less workable seedlings. Slaves, too, to do said work, of course. To support his wreckers, who in turn supported him and his island empire, Housman built warehouses, wharves, and several cis-

terns, one of which was carved from marble during our tenancy on the
island at a cost of four thousand dollars. He drew to the island all
manner of men whose skills were requisite to the realization of his
dreams: blacksmiths, boat wrights, carpenters, caulkers, cooks, et
cetera; and upon Indian Key they all lived in harmony; for Housman
insisted on harmony, ensuring it with his henchmen and the occasional harangue, delivered within earshot of all and sundry.

Such was Indian Key when Calixto and I arrived, that winter of '38:
a most prosperous place; . . . and where there is prosperity there are,
perforce, parties.

Léopoldine had baked a cake as "the family's" contribution to the ball;
but this confection had come from the oven so crooked and over-
cooked as to seem not only alive—its pudding-like interior supporting
a pulse of sorts—but inedible as well. So imposing was this pastry that
Luc asked if he might be let to "kill it with a coconut," which instrument he'd found on the sands outside the kitchen door and brandished
now with great show. The query amused only Asmodei. Sebastiana—
was she stifling a laugh herself?—said no, and would Luc please set the
coconut down outside; whereupon she commiserated with Léopoldine,
herself being of scant use in a kitchen. But what to do? They'd said
they'd bring a cake to *le bal.* . . . Could it be rescued, this cake?

Calixto and I sat watching, sipping our lemonade, whilst the two
witches iced the cake; but they'd have needed tar and caulking to reshape it sufficiently; and, what's more, the cake had yet to cool, so that
the icing they'd concocted slid from its sides like sap from a tapped
tree. When next Luc suggested a suitable end for the cake—that he be
let to pass a chain through it and use it to anchor his canoe—
Sebastiana and Leo acceded with shrugs and wry smiles, whereupon
the men turned mirthful; and I would have joined in but for the chill

I suffered at hearing again Asmodei's laughter, the same sound with which he'd once scorned me so.

The promise of a cake was fulfilled with punch instead; a punch so potent the original promise of a cake was fast forgotten, and the party, thusly fueled, proceeded apace.

. . . Oh, how we danced that first evening, on that tiny key set into the sea. Only my memories are more sublime than the night itself.

The "ballroom" consisted of planking set atop the smoothed sands of a piazza topped by a pergola of sorts, through the beams of which a flowering vine was woven. Not long after our arrival, there I'd stood, helping to hang lanterns from these same beams: We'd set white candles in glass, and in turn set the glass within shades of pink paper, so as not to confuse—and draw to us—any ships that might have spotted red or white lanterns from sea. (It was difficult to dance in that pink light, dimmed further by my blue spectacles; but I benefited from the effort, being able to attribute my clumsiness to poor eyesight and so excuse my omnipresent spectacles.) Plank tables overlain with lace were piled with delicacies—no finer fare could have been had in Havana or Key West—and set with tableware that told of the island's chief trade: The flat-, stem-, and hollowware was all fine yet mismatched, much of it bearing the monogram of whoever had lost, or *thought* they'd lost their wares to the sea. . . . Indeed, there was no telling what one might find on the island, owing to the way things arrived there rather than sinking onto the seafloor. So it was that Housman had in his house a pianoforte lost by a marquis, who'd sought to ship it home to France from New Orleans; and we, in our house, had a harp none of us could play but which served, said Luc, as a suitable shredder of hard cheeses. It was to that pianoforte, in fact, as well as the multipurpose harp, that we danced that night; for the elder of the Trevors' daughters tapped at the former whilst her little sister plucked at the latter.

Yes, we danced; in nearly every permutation our party allowed: Sebastiana walked her way through a waltz with Calixto, whilst Asmodei and Housman, both, seethed upon the sands; Asmodei and Léopoldine extended the terms of their truce for the duration of a ring dance; and Luc and I clomped through a quadrille neither of us knew, nor stood a chance of learning; and so it went, the sole exception, the sole permutation not coming into play being that of Asmodei and myself. *That* I was not ready for. Instead I danced with the wreckers and turtlers and other types who asked me.

I even danced that first night with Housman when Sebastiana, somehow, with a single gesture, demurred, declined his suit and cast me into his arms in her stead, all at once; for yes, he was our host, and no one settled on Indian Key without his clearance. I earned mine that night, as my sister had hoped I would. So, too, did Calixto earn his clearance when, within a week of our arrival, he crewed to a wreck alongside Housman, showing his seamanship and returning to gift me with some of the salvage: a leather-bound set of Sir Walter Scott's works as well as a weighty volume wherein were gathered the collected plays of my beloved bard. . . . And by attending *le bal* in the same dress of emerald silk I'd sailed in, I determined, unwittingly, who it was I'd be for some years to come: Herculine, and not Henry.

. . . So it was that we arrived on Indian Key. So it was that Paradise ensued. . . . It ensued, yes; but it did not, *could not* endure. Soon our Sebastiana would be dead. And not long after, we'd *all* draw deeply of death; and a most baneful draft it would be.

 *Chapter Twenty-seven*

With meditating that she must die once,
I have the patience to endure it now.
—SHAKESPEARE, *Julius Caesar*

W̲E ALL SIX LIVED IN A TWO-AND-A-HALF-STORY HOUSE
of yellow-painted clapboard that extended out over the
shoreline on the island's quieter side; such that the
waves, as they came to lap at the house's piles, seemed to
do so silently by day but were a lullaby at night. I hear
it still, that sea-song. And those waves, that slow and
steady tidal clock, mark the measure of those recollected
days, days that now seem dream-like, less than indus-
trial, *enfin*, well nigh indolent. Indeed, it seems we did
naught but study and love. Till the onset of death, that
is; whereupon our world turned on its black axis.

Our house was the island's second largest, after
Housman's. It had been built of late by our host for Dr.
Trevor and family; for the doctor—not a physician, in
fact, but a doctor of the scientific sort: *a horticulturist*—
had written some months earlier to inform Housman

that Congress had recently passed an act granting him, Trevor, *a town-ship*, if you will: a six-mile square, somewhere upland of our key, nearer the peninsula's tip, which he'd be free to plant in accord with his purposes. And in exchange for housing, et cetera, Housman partnered with Trevor in this concern—the Tropical Plant Company, I believe they called it, a title so unoriginal as to presage the company's fate. The horticulturist, you see, was never happier than when he sat in converse with his well-cataloged seeds and shoots; but he was so *boring* a man (may he rest in peace) that it's a wonder those same seeds and shoots didn't wither before ever coming in sight of soil or sun. As for Housman, he'd ambition; and dreamed of revenue streams flowing, *flooding* from those fields planted with agave (or sisal; for rope), cochineal cacti (for dye), mulberry trees (feed for silkworms), and all-purpose sea cotton; but, eventually, Dr. Trevor's *deliberateness* got the better of Housman's ambitions, his dreams. . . . Still, it was those early hopes of Housman's that accounted for the luxury of the house intended for the Trevors, but which Sebastiana bought for a song—and with, perhaps, a spell—shortly after she and Leo arrived on Indian Key; for Trevor had the bad fortune to arrive some months after my sister and some few weeks prior to Calixto and me. We, of course, moved into the same house; but the late-arriving Trevors had to wait out the construction of the island's third mansion whilst living in the wreckers' hotel; wherein, said Mrs. Trevor—a woman strung more tightly than our harp—every day they risked their daughters' ruin. So it was that the aforementioned ball had been held in the hopes of pacifying Mrs. Trevor *post* her receipt of the change-in-plans.

Our house, as said, had a half story at its top: the perfect atelier; and to this no one save us three witches were admitted. So excluded were our fellows that one day, as we proceeded upstairs—S., followed by Leo, followed by me—we found nailed to the door of our den the severed head of a paddle, upon which the men of our household had burned the words, *The Witchery. No Admittance.* And therein we studied and worked what Craft we could; beginning with a survey of the keys' fauna, which Dr. Trevor abetted—not always knowingly, it's true: What specimens we could not beg or buy we sometimes stole—though his concerns were of Commerce, ours of Craft.

Sebastiana and I soon found our interest in witchery renewed owing to the fact that we were no longer sisters-in-solitude—no fun at all, that; rather like setting a table for one with crystal and silver—and, of course, we'd Léopoldine urging us on. If I thought I'd been a querist of the first order when first I'd come to the Shadows, well, Léopoldine put me to shame. Sebastiana had been right: She *wanted* the Craft, and badly so. She read all we could provide her with; such that soon I'd written to Eugénie in New Orleans, asking that she ship to us whatever *Books of Shadows* she could spare. Too, that sister with whom I'd shared so much in Gotham—and who then was warring with Marie Laveau for control of the shadowed core of New Orleans—sent supplies we could not procure on our key, though, in fact, this was a short list; for we'd a steady stream of ships from which to draw, and with which to send orders to Key West, Cuba, St. Augustine, and elsewhere.

Yes, as a student of the Craft, my daughter—never can I call her that, even now, without a hitch—excelled. So, too, did she shine in the first-floor parlor; wherein, on Monday, Wednesday, and Friday mornings, I taught her more traditional things alongside the Trevor girls, Sarah and Jane, aged thirteen and nine, whose inelastic minds slowed our studies somewhat; but still progress was made in English, penmanship, and other such topics, including the more general sciences and geography, although Dr. Trevor—rightly, if snidely—deemed those subjects beyond the ken of his daughters. But Leo wanted study of the half-story, witchery sort more; and there we'd find her at all hours of the day and night, secreted away with the Books and such (. . . "like someone else I once knew," Sebastiana liked to say).

Lest we slight the men in our lives, tutorials were held in the same parlor on Tuesday and Thursdays, attendance being mandatory for Luc and Timothy Trevor, aged ten; though Calixto would come when on-island, and Asmodei, too. The latter made it known he was there only to preclude any mischievousness on the part of the boys—for such there'd been, in spades, when at first I'd tried to educate all five children *ensemble;* and I'd believed him, and suffered his evident disinterest, until the day, surprising all present, he asked a question. *Of me.* And pertaining to English, the particularities of which plagued him. Thusly did we begin to set our differences aside. And thusly, in that parlor, did I begin to . . . *befriend* the man who'd once tried to poison me. ("You'd not have died," said he, dismissively, when finally I confronted him. "If I'd wanted *that,* I'd have milked the venom of a heartier toad." . . . So went apologies in Asmodei's world.)

It was via learning, too, that Léopoldine and I grew closer; but it must be admitted that she turned to me not as a parent, but rather as a tutor, a witch whose knowledge (such as it was) she came to covet. For months at a time, we shared a bedroom—we'd four upon the second floor: one for S. and Asmodei, one for Calixto, one for myself, and one for the twins; but they, Leo and Luc, were let to pitch cots wherever it pleased them, whether beside one of our beds, or out upon the sleeping porch or pier, if the winds were right and the mosquitoes put off—and when Léopoldine and I shared a room we'd talk ourselves to sleep, more often than not, she asking all, *all* about the life I'd led but declining, with silence, never tears, the questions I asked in turn, touching upon her life. When on occasion she answered these questions, she did so in terms of her twin; and only by extrapolation did I learn what life had been like *for her,* as she'd been ever and always at Luc's side. What I learned sometimes saddened me; and when finally, heatedly, Leo asked me to stop apologizing for things I'd not done, I did so. Still, regretfully, I must own to something that stands between us, something that I know would not be there if only I'd known of the twins' birth, if only I'd been there when . . . *Hélas*, here, too, I'll stop my apology, and say only that I long wished for some aspect of the Craft that could undo the calendar; for I wanted nothing more than to shear ten years from it and return to a time *I might have been there* to raise my children up.

As no Craftwork can affect the calendar so, I was fated to be not wholly a parent, not merely a friend, but *something else*, something for which a word is wanted. Oh, but understand: Love came to us all, and we tended it as best we could. There were tears, of course; such as when Luc, stung under his arm by a bee, came running up the house's long pier crying, passing me where I sat—upon the porch, a volume of Paracelsus open upon my knee—and crying out for Asmodei; who proceeded to pack the boy's armpit with soothing mud, as I might easily have done. On another occasion—one occasioning tears: mine—Léopoldine, who'd been sleeping in my room, began to bleed—in the monthly, not sisterly sense, *blessed be*—and, saying not a word to me, decamped to Sebastiana's side. . . . *Enfin*, in living I have learned that self-pity is a currency best hoarded and never spent.

. . . Our house—atelier above, with bedrooms below this, and two parlors upon the first floor—was flanked by a wide porch. Both parlors gave onto this porch, but it was the larger we converted into a classroom, Asmodei overseeing the shipwright's assistant who came to line that room, as well as the witchery, with shelves. The secondary parlor we set up as one would expect, with sea-stolen goods Housman had gifted to Sebastiana. We'd a dining room, too, of course; and therein, at Sebastiana's insistence, the family dined at least four nights out of seven. One's absence from dinner required a sound excuse;

though Sebastiana never pressed me on my appetite, much diminished since I'd suffered those . . . *feedings* from Queverdo Brù.

Of course, none of us would abide being served by slaves; of which, sadly, we'd a surfeit upon the island, Trevor himself having come with four. Instead, we hired the two half daughters of a twice-widowed turtler, each of whom, improbably, was named Catherine, and came to be known as Kit (who cleaned and served), and Kat (who cooked). We'd no choice, really: We'd all have wasted away, or worse, if we witches had taken to the kitchen. Still, so guilty were we over our dependence on the turtler's daughters, we paid them twice their asked-for wages, asking only that they, 1) Leave the upper half story be; and, 2) Never tell their father what we truly paid them, as already he deemed himself entitled to half their supposed wages.

Capping the house was a cupola, accessible only through the witchery; and there Léopoldine or myself might be found in the hours after dawn, seated at a small desk and chair Calixto carpentered specifically for that space, reading by sunlight that would heat the room to extremes by ten, *ante meridiem.*

We'd a cellar of sorts, too, sitting as if in opposition to the cupola. One accessed this via a trapdoor in the pantry, a shed-size room set between the lesser parlor and dining room. Down through the trapdoor one went, into water; for said door was cut into the floor of that half of our house which sat stilted, if you will, out over the water. Seawater filtered through our cellar, passing through the slatted, lattice-work walls which progressed down the length of our pier, toward deeper water. This cellar had been built as a kraal: a pen in which to keep turtles or other sea-specimens until such time as they might . . . die for our delectation. But, as Kit and Kat brought us our turtle steaks fresh from their father's hooks, Asmodei refashioned the kraal till it suited the boys as a tidal pool or watery playpen.

After our arrival, as the months fast accrued onto years, first one, then two, the island continued to grow; till, midway through our second and final summer there, Indian Key sat crowded with forty-odd structures of assorted purpose, from the pleasure palaces of the wreckers—which were off-limits to all of our party, said S., save Asmodei and Calixto, of course, the former a regular in those precincts, the latter going there only in search of work; for Calixto had begun to crew more regularly with Housman's men, setting off into the Straits for days, sometimes weeks at a time; during which time, it must be said, I missed him progressively less, or rather *tried to*, telling myself I'd reached that age at which the heartsick ought *to try* to stop loving those who cannot love them in kind, as was our sad case— . . . *alors*, in addition to those pleasure palaces we had now a post office, for which Housman had lobbied hard, and which connected us to a larger world whenever such connections were wanted. Thusly did I write to Eugénie, as said; receiving in return Books, supplies, et cetera, yes, but also, without fail, an invitation to come to New Orleans with *Sebastiana and all her brood;* which trip we might have taken, had Sebastiana been well and the rest of us less happy than we were. . . . Oh yes, we were happy. For a while. Then there came the Blood.

Poor Léopoldine.

She woke one morning in her cot and watched, watched (said she) the redness drip from the sodden sheets covering the bed beside her. Only as she woke the more, only as she watched the more, did she realize what the redness was; whereupon she rose screaming and woke Asmodei where he lay. His roar in turn brought the islanders to our door. I had first to put our neighbors off, then console Leo and Luc, explain to Calixto what had happened, and somehow control Asmodei, who rocked in the reddened bed, holding a lifeless Sebastiana to his chest as a crying child does a doll.

À vrai dire, there was no controlling him. Leo and Luc watched his heart spill till it seemed each twin sought to climb into the other's skin, so tight was their sad embrace. Calixto succeeded in silencing Asmodei by the insertion into his mouth of a bone-length piece of driftwood, which Luc would later find beneath the bed, a molar set into it like a stone. There was nothing more we four could do but leave the lovers be. We'd all said what had wanted, had *needed* saying; for Sebastiana, knowing her hour was near, bade us speak our hearts in turn. Asmodei, ever in denial, had declined; such that now he said his good-byes the only way he could: *the articulation of tears;* whilst the rest of us waited out on the sleeping porch in silence, each with his or her chosen memories.

Blessedly, the Blood had not snuck up on Sebastiana—as it had her own Soror Mystica, the Venetian Isabella Téotocchi, who'd fallen to it on the Rialto, in plain sight of passersby—and so we'd been able to prepare ourselves the week prior, as it became apparent that Sebastiana would not rise from her bed again. Yet we were not prepared. One never is; for Death knows things the living do not. But still . . .

Léopoldine had promised Sebastiana she'd write her own Books for the sisters-to-come, and she listened with Eye-turning intensity as S. spoke to her of sagacity, of sisterly will and responsibility. From Luc, from Calixto, and even from Asmodei, Sebastiana had elicited oaths of loyalty sworn to us witches, and to one another. She spoke of family, and saw that forgiveness was sought and granted. (I speak here of Asmodei and myself, yes.) And during *un entretien* that lasted till sleep overtook her, Sebastiana counseled Calixto and me on our love; for such was the thing between us, yes: *love,* albeit not of the active, consummative kind. . . . How I'd cried that night, sad, so terribly sad, yet freed, too, in hearing Calixto speak words he'd long withheld: He did not disdain me *for what I was,* but rather had found, to his own great regret, that his love for me would not evolve, no matter how he wished it to, no matter how he willed it to. *He did not desire me.* And with tears of his own he apologized, not for that lack of desire, but rather for the long, long while he'd left our love undefined.

. . . Me? What can I say? I'd passed that last week at Sebastiana's bedside. So, too, had Leo. And both of us, of course, bore the added difficulty of knowing, or rather *believing*, that the Blood would come for us similarly; which knowledge affected me more than Léopoldine, for whom death was yet an abstraction. For me, of course, it was rather more than that. *I knew death.* And I sat bedside hoping Sebastiana's would be quiet, that she'd shed life and go, not linger as so many do. Should she linger, yes, I might never need to lose her; but I did not want that *stasis* for her, that ghostly role.

Leo and I laid fresh linen beneath Sebastiana, all of it dyed to her preferred shade of blue, and when she'd sufficient strength we spoke of spellwork and travel and such, she listing all she wished for us. We, in turn, did all we could for her: Not only had we dyed the linens, but I'd ordered blue candles down from a Boston chandlery, and I'd had a seamstress on-island sew shades of blue silk, and it was blue this and blue that till finally Sebastiana asked, in a whisper, that I desist, as she'd prefer to depart with blue *still* her favorite color.

She grew delicate in her last days, and bruised easily as the Blood began its end-work; but she knew no pain, only a terrible, terrible lassitude that stole words from her before she could summon strength enough to speak them. Still, she, too, was glad to have sensed the Coming of the Blood, and said so; said, too, that she'd lived her last years as she'd wanted, and had not merely attended her Red Ending. We ought to be sure, said she, to do the same.

The waiting was the worst part. All during it, Asmodei drank the days away, and fought whomever he could fight. (Cruelty he knew. Sadness he wanted no part of.) Calixto was called down to the hotel on two occasions to retrieve him; and as Asmodei slept off one such debauch—always at S.'s side, and always crying; such that his sober tears, stifled though they were, replaced the sea as our lullaby—Calixto risked a two-day commission to Key West, from whence he returned with roses; for I'd told him of the *roseraie* Sebastiana had once kept at Ravndal. Indeed, rose petals came from that faraway place, set into a long letter of farewell sent by Roméo and read, to S., by me. Luc, for his part, continued to run about and play with Timothy Trevor, coming bedside every few hours to report to Sebastiana their progress in taming a certain crane. Already they'd tamed a cormorant, said he, proudly. And each time he left Sebastiana's room, he did a jig of sorts; this to please S., and make her smile, but also to thank her, again and again and again, for the gait she'd given back to him by craft-work and care; for he walked normally now, or nearly so, though Asmodei still was wont to refer to him as his Lord B.

All such visits ended at the first signs of the Blood. This was my decree. Leo, too, I excused: She knew of the Blood, yes, but would not benefit by seeing it come.

. . . And it did come. Not as a flood. Not at first. Rather it came creeping; as on the day Sebastiana and I sat in converse, she feeling stronger till there came from her ears and nose a scarlet trail, slipping to slicken her neck and upper lip. Her gums, too, began to bleed; such that her teeth turned red and she had to spit the sputum away. Such red incursions as these increased that final week. So, too, did the bruises, which betrayed the busyness of the Blood beneath her skin. These I could smoothe away at first, working my hands over those spots, colored jade-unto-gray, and gray-unto-black, where the Blood pooled. The longer it coursed, the longer she'd live. Stopped, it'd be as a dam set to burst. Distressingly, her nails came from her still-ringed fingers, fell as leaves do from autumnal trees; but this she did not feel, and as I slipped her arms under the blue sheets, neither did she have to suffer the sight of it. . . . Oh, but perhaps she knew; for it was not long after this that she bequeathed to me—and by me she meant *the family*—her rings and all else that had been hers, including, specifically, the care of Asmodei. Over this we shared our last laugh. *Care*, queried I . . . *Asmodei?* "Yes," said she, emphatically. I'd never seen her Eye stronger. So it was I promised her that I would care for her consort as best I could, as best he'd allow me to; and no, he'd never know I'd sworn to do so.

Thereafter she declined fast. The Blood came in increments at first; but then . . . *enfin*, there were symptoms I shan't expound upon here. Indeed, I'll say no more than this: Sebastiana d'Azur died as she'd lived: *avec dignité*. Nothing, not even the Blood, could strip the witch of that.

We were all of us an hour or more upon the sleeping porch, all save Asmodei; who finally fled the house and took a rowboat out to sea, disappearing for a day. I worried that already I'd failed Sebastiana, regarding his care. But when he returned, disheveled and reeking of drink, he came rolling a barrel of rum up our pier, onto our porch, and into our parlor. I knew it was rum, recognizing the name of the Cuban distillery stenciled on the side of the cask. *Bon*, thought I, bracing for our first postmortem battle; for I'd not have him drink his life away before the eyes of Leo and Luc, and perhaps he'd choose to dull his heartache with drink, but as for the rest of us, well . . . And so went a speech I never gave; for:

Soon a second casket of sorts—a coffin carved of tamarind—sat in our parlor, delivered courtesy of a bereaved Jacob Housman. Indeed, it was his own casket, which had long lain in wait; for a man of no few enemies lives, I suppose, in time to that tick-tocking clock that culminates in a coffin. But he'd offered his to Asmodei not an hour past, when he, Asmodei, had sought out Housman at his warehouse to deliver news of Sebastiana's death; which we'd kept secret for several reasons, not the least of which was the fact that the corpse continued to bleed. Further, Asmodei announced that there'd be a service at sunset, Housman officiating (as our common cleric had long since damned us all and departed).

"That's all well and good," said I, "but—"

And what I'd intended to say was that one could not simply plant a witch in the ground, coffined or otherwise, as if she were some seedling of Dr. Trevor's; for there were concerns: What if some latent power of hers precluded this, and the witch's body—or worse, her residual soul—rebelled, bounding up and bursting though the coffin's tamarind top? How would Asmodei like to explain *that* to those who'd gather to say good-bye to someone they'd thought was dead? (In truth, I didn't suspect Sebastiana would react to interment thusly; for *she'd gone*, I knew it.) And what if Housman sent for some off-island, collared type who'd come spouting some papist palaver? What if he'd haul Sebastiana off to be buried somewhere in consecrated soil? We'd have to follow. What then might become of me, amidst the disquieted dead? . . . All of which questions Asmodei answered before I could ask them, saying:

"Hush . . . I have a second body in the boat, beneath the pier."

"A second *what*?" And though I thought to send Leo and Luc from the room, I saw there was no point. They'd be party to whatever would come to pass.

"Stop your aching," said A., "I didn't kill anyone. . . . I found it."

" 'Found it'? *Eh bien*, but it's nonetheless dead, *non?*"

Calixto stood at the window of the parlor now, and reported that the island was abuzz. Word of the death had spread. The women were gathered into gaggles. One of them already wore an armband of black crepe. Slaves had been sent to rake the sands of the piazza and drop that plank flooring upon which we'd danced the night of our arrival. . . . Whatever had Asmodei gotten us into?

"I get it," announced Léopoldine. And she did, explaining thusly:

We'd bring the second body—dead of a gangrenous sea-injury to his leg, or rather, the resulting amputation; and "found" courtesy of a barber in Key West who'd only recently hung out a surgeon's shingle and wanted no one to know he'd had to box-up his first patient— . . . we'd bring it up, up through the trapdoor and set it in the hardwood coffin, bury it in Sebastiana's stead with whatever obsequies were wanted by a heartsick Housman and his islanders, all of whom had liked "the French lady."

"But," said I, "what of Sebastiana?" And I pointed upstairs, as if anyone present had forgotten where she lay.

"Rum," was Asmodei's one-word answer. *Rum?*

Now it was Calixto's turn to explain; and taking my hand, he did so. "Rum, yes," said he. "Alcohol is a . . . preservative."

"You want to . . . *to preserve her?*" Horrified, I asked this of Asmodei; for I thought he meant to . . . to pickle the witch, to put her up like last season's jam.

"No," said he with heat, "what I want is to send her off as I, *as we* wish to."

And so we did, crying—as best we could—through the conferral of a one-legged stranger into a shallow plot dug on Indian Key, and only later, much later that same night, setting our beloved Sebastiana into a barreled rum-bath. Of course, lest we spill and waste the stuff, as displaced by our sister's body, well, there was drinking to be done. And why not? In this we all participated, even Sebastiana's treasures, whom I granted one goblet each. Owing to so inebriate a wake and the success of so insane a plan, well, we fell to laughing, all five of us, and nearly smothered ourselves in our attempts to stifle, lest our house seem not one of mourning but mayhem. Then, at night's end, the rum slowing in its course, we drew all our shades against the coming sun, lay where we chose, and cried ourselves to sleep.

Some days later, at dusk, our funeral party reassembled to slip down through the pantry floor and out to sea under cover of our pier; for, after considerable discussion and some debate, we'd struck upon what seemed, at the time, a suitable, respectful send-off for our beloved Sebastiana.

 # Chapter Twenty-eight

Thou know'st 'tis common; all that live must die,

Passing through nature to eternity.

—SHAKESPEARE, *Hamlet*

*I*T WAS NINE DAYS LATER, TO BE SPECIFIC, THAT WE SLIPPED away from Indian Key, at dusk, in two boats the oars of which we'd wrapped in canvas, so as to quiet them in their locks. Asmodei and Luc sat in the first boat—the man at the oars, the boy holding steady the cask containing Sebastiana's body; whilst in the second Calixto rowed Léopoldine and myself.

We'd waited *three days* for the last of the Blood to seep from our sister, from her every orifice; and a red mess there had been, too, with only Leo and I to tend to the sheets that grew sodden and had finally to be buried, to wash the slow-cooling flesh, to air the room at sun- and moonrise and rid it of its ferric tang. Meanwhile, it was left to Calixto and Luc to put off the islanders; who, for the most part, left us to mourn at home, alone; though they did indulge that most mortal of mournful impulses: They cooked, and baked, and deposited at our door food enough to feed a legion. And as the two Catherines had had to be put off—with pay, *bien sûr*—during these proceedings, it was Luc who took charge of this windfall, eating himself sick and setting the rest to rot upon our groaning sideboard.

When finally the Blood was done, and the redness had run, had spewed and seeped and sluiced from Sebastiana's body, we waited *three days more*; for, if the ancients are to be believed, it is during this time that the soul either snaps its etheric, silver cord—the Ensilvering, this is sometimes called; and I'd seen it in the past, both at natural speed and hurried by violence—or, conversely, it shows itself yet tethered to its corporeal host, to *the material*. . . . And then we waited *one day more*, to be sure of Sebastiana's soul having dissevered itself from the body before us—I did not see my sister Ensilver, as doubtless she'd been ready to rise and had done so at speed—and further, because the ancients cite the seventh day after death as that when *the typical soul*, if freed, begins its ascent. . . . So, a week it was; whereupon we waited *two days more*; for I thought it best to attend a coming full moon, by the strength and light of which we'd benefit, surely.

The key we sailed to bore no name we knew; but it had a beachhead, and sand into which we could stake our lanterns. It was unsettled, of course, small and mostly marsh, and otherwise nondescript; indeed, I cannot now summon further description of it, save to say it sat too near Indian Key. *That*, of course, was the grave mistake we made (which pun I shan't excuse) in solving our problem; which was:

What to do with Sebastiana's body? *The actual one*, not that which had been pomp'd and circumstanc'd to the Great Beyond by Housman.

We'd finally settled Sebastiana onto a stool set in the cask; for, in the course of preparing the body—washing it, sewing it into its blue winding sheet, et cetera—Leo and I noticed . . . *enfin*, let this suffice:

Death had begun to express an interest in our sister's remains. Upon which topic I'll offer no more, as I am reminded here how the Reaper stakes a similar claim upon my ever-hardening hostess, here, now, shipboard; and so I hasten:

Onto that ill-chosen key we carried all we'd brought from home, all of it requisite to the simple rite we'd decided upon; central to which would be a pyre. With fast-fire we'd speed our sister on her way. And if anyone came to the key, curious, drawn by the fire, well, by then we'd be gone, leaving naught behind but ash and a charred circle of sand. And to ensure the speed of Sebastiana's ascent as well as our own escape, we had jugs and jars of fuel, fast-burning oils, varnishes, et cetera. With these we'd soak the mangroves and other wood we'd gathered, Calixto first fashioning the larger, sturdier logs into a bier on which to set the cask whilst Luc broke the rest down to tinder. Asmodei, meanwhile, stood at the water's edge, staring out to sea with his right hand at rest upon a barrel, wherein sat his beloved.

Enfin, we'd build a pyre, read a fast rite—all, or *nearly all* of what needed saying had already been said as Sebastiana lay *in articulo mortis*—and in so doing we'd speed our sister to the Summerland. Such was our plan.

It was as comforting a notion of the Afterlife as I'd ever heard, the Summerland; and it was the one I chose for Léopoldine and Luc. And for myself.

The ancients held that the souls of the newly dead dwelled in the ether surrounding the moon; and made their way thence by trailing the long, long line of lunar luminescence laid onto the sea. Ascending thusly, the dead retrace the routes of their birth; for birth, it was held, happened when a soul had passed through the four realms—from the *material* to the *lunar,* thence to the *solar,* where souls not yet finished with their work in the material realm burn, as light, before proceeding to the *stellar*, there either to stay or to await rebirth and a return to the material. And so, in being born, or reborn, souls ricochet (". . . as when you shoot jacks," said I to Luc, who struggled with the concept) down through the planetary spheres, taking from each planet a portion of its nature and incorporating that as *personality*. Hence, the study of astrology. Indeed, the seed of Léopoldine's abiding interest in the zodiac was sown the day I first spoke to her of the Summerland.

As said, I supposed Sebsatiana had left the material realm easefully, and at speed, having no further work here on earth. Those who linger—*the disquieted*—are typically those who have lived a life defined by hate rather than compassion, by intolerance, jealousies, et cetera. *That* was not my Sebastiana, surely. Moreover, if it is true that the soul chooses its own route toward rest, toward the Summerland, be it fast or slow, final or not—a belief very much borne out by my own dealings with the disquieted dead, by the way—I knew Sebastiana would not *choose to return* but rather would fast accede to the Summerland and there stay, a Star.

First, though, we'd send her body up behind her, *via fire;* for fire would be the surety of her end and her ascent. . . . What I'd not counted on—foolishly—was how brightly, how hotly, how very *strangely* her body would burn, fueled by those flammables and rum, yes, but also by sister-blood. The cask, you see, burst like a bomb, and the whole of the pyre burned as a beacon upon that beach; and so it was that, having set out to honor life, in the end we summoned death as well.

For more than two years, we'd lived beneath the Emperor Housman, suffering his imperiousness with a nod and a smile, less grateful for his protection than we ought to have been; for upon Indian Key *we were safe*. And when on occasion his temper had flared and affected us adversely—owing, usually, to something Asmodei had done or said—a smile from Sebastiana smoothed things over. Yes, in a word, we'd all been *safe* upon Housman's key, safer than we knew.

In the years prior to our arrival upon Indian Key, war had marked the Florida territory. I, in sailing to Havana, had been all too pleased to quit the war-torn peninsula; and once I'd returned to it, I was distracted by *la famille*. Which is excusable, I suppose. What is *not* excusable was my denial of the dupe I'd been, my denial of the role I'd played in the conflict in question: the Seminole Wars. And only much later would I tell my kin all, *all* that had happened in years past. . . . I won't say I lied; but I had found it quite easy, *enfin* too easy to remain silent upon chosen topics.

The hostilities—begun long ago, when first the red- and whitemen met upon the Florida shore—were heightened when the United States won the peninsula from Spain in 1821; whereupon that maniacal militarist, Andrew Jackson, proceeded to push its native inhabitants into the unsettled West. *Removal,* was the euphemism, though *murder* might have been the better word. And this was nearly achieved by the end of 1835; but then the remaining Seminole, led by Osceola, rose, rebelled. And in December of that same year, I found myself at the center of a conflict—a *massacre*, it was—that left one hundred soldiers slain, chilled the blood of the settlers scattered about the peninsula, and led to the further escalation of those long-simmering hostilities.

Of those events and my role therein, I'll say no more; neither did I detail my shame for the education or edification of Léopoldine and Luc. Rather, I sent Calixto to St. Augustine with keys and careful directions, and from my long-shuttered home on St. George Street he gathered some monies—the which I added to Sebastiana's store—and that second *Book of Shadows* to which I'd committed my story. This I let the twins read. And the interested witch is referred similarly: Seek said

Book amongst the sisterhood, if you wish; for it has been widely copied, and continues to be bandied about the Shadows.

After said massacre, I all but buried my head in the Florida sands, retreating, a sister-in-solitude; till finally I acted upon Sebastiana's command and sailed to Cuba. There, in Havana, the peninsular war had seemed remote; and so, too, did it seem upon Indian Key, where we were happy together, and wanted no news of war.

News, mind, which would have told such stories as these:

How, one week after the massacre of Dade's one hundred men, a Seminole war party had slaughtered the family of William Cooley, southward and across the territory, at New River; from whence some two hundred scared settlers then fled to Key West coincident with their requesting from the navy a fleet of warships; which ships came, and were often espied from the cupola of our house by, yes, yours truly, who persisted in thinking their purpose a remote one, one that had nothing to do with *me and mine.*

How, in July of '36, Seminoles stole from their strongholds in the Never-Glade to attack the lighthouse at Cape Florida, killing its keeper and his assistant.

How, in October of that same year—whilst I was yet resident in St. Augustine—a band of seventy natives sailed over Florida Bay and destroyed the lighthouse at Carysfort Reef and, too, set upon a schooner riding at anchor off Tavernier Key.

How, in June of '37, the captain and crew of the Carysfort Reef lightship were killed as they came ashore at Key Largo to gather wood and water.

Et cetera, and so on.

. . . There were periods of recess during those years, yes, when the Seminole who refused *to remove* returned to the swamps, ceding the land to the settlers, and ceding the seas to those who protected them: That naval squadron consisting of schooners, gun barges, and some sixty-odd vessels of shallow draft, and therefore better suited to the Straits: flat-bottomed boats, canoes, and suchlike. In the midst of one such recess, a more formal truce was agreed to; but this—in May of '39—had been broken when a band of Seminoles sacked an army sutler's store, a trading post, on the banks of the Caloosahatchee, leaving eighteen dead soldiers whose bodies said, in *terms certain*, that the truce was broken, the war renewed.

Tensions were high in '40, '41. Rumors were rampant, too; in fact, even we had heard it whispered that a band of Spanish Indians—so called because they'd long been abetted by Spaniards in Cuba who begrudged the loss of the peninsula, and funded the Indians' fight against the *yanquis*—were encamped at Cape Sable, under the leadership of Chakaika; from which place it was but a short sail to the settlements at Key West, Key Vaca, and, yes, Indian Key.

But which of these were they more likely to attack, if attack they did?

Key West, sitting so far southerly, and well protected owing to the wealth and influence of its citizenry? Doubtful.

Key Vaca, sparse with settlers barely able to sustain themselves on the scrubland? Perhaps; if the Indians could content themselves with an easy, retributive spill of blood, but no booty.

What about Indian Key then, *our* key? Where—to judge by the concussive, multicolored display that was Sebastiana's send-off—the navy or, more probably, Housman himself had secreted a store of munitions that might well turn the war in the Indians' favor, if only they could . . . Oh, but to benefit from said armory they'd first have to find it. And search they would, starting with that lesser key to which we'd so clumsily called their attention, and progressing to the key upon which we lived; and upon which, owing to us, blood was soon to be shed.

In deciding to light Sebastiana's pyre at night, we knew we ran the risk of detection; and we'd taken what precautions we could.

Léopoldine and Calixto had been days sewing the mourning cloaks we'd wear: night-dark, nearly formless, the fabric of which—bolts of black and navy serge, ordered down from an upholsterer in Charleston sometime prior, when S. had been abed for a full week without rising—was sewn so as to fall, fully, from our outstretched arms. We'd all five don our drapery, join hands, and with our backs to the beach, and our capes spread, bat-like, we'd conceal the fiery rite from those at sea, ever watchful for fires and signal lights. Inland, we'd mangrove growth and a slight dune for concealment; and in the lee of the latter we'd build the pyre. There'd be smoke, yes; but we hoped the smoke would rise to seem one with the slow-floating clouds, which were as tufted, torn cotton, and came as if to clothe but never conceal the full moon.

Again, such was our plan. In reality, we found ourselves standing not before a funereal fire but rather *fireworks;* for the cask and its beloved contents rose in the reds of the Blood, and the blues of, *quoi,* sister-soul? We'd no recourse but to back from the fire, from the flames, to stand where the water lapped at our legs; and even there the heat was so intense we cowered beneath our capes, which soon were so dry, so hot, it seemed they might combust. We dipped down into the surf. We wet our capes and saw the fabric steam. Tears on our cheeks dried before they could fall. . . . Of course, we had no hope of hiding the fire.

What to do? Whom would we draw? . . . At the time, I thought only of Housman's men; and so tried to conceive of a suitable . . . *untruth,* should they come to ask what we were doing upon an unsettled key an hour's row from home, at midnight, beneath a full moon, black-clad and cowering before a burning . . . something? I cannot now recall the particulars of said untruth; for the fire affected me *terribly:*

Upon my tongue I tasted Brù's elixir for the first time in a long, long while, and I grew faint, confused, and was at once *drawn to* and *repulsed by* the fire. Indeed, Léopoldine would later say she'd stopped me when it seemed I'd walk from the water toward the raging flame. . . . *Hélas,* the details of our dissembling are of no import now, and neither were they then; for Luc spoke words of greater weight, words that I heard with a chill, words that roused me from my *fire-trance:* "What about the Indians?" he asked. And as he and the other three mourners turned to stare at me, I saw I'd been alone in neither wondering nor worrying about them. . . . Indeed: *What about the Indians?*

We all agreed: The wisest course of action was to quit the key as quickly as possible. But would we leave Sebastiana's body behind us, half burned? Her soul, I assured the twins, had already acceded to the Summerland. I wanted to believe this as well; and I recall stealing a seaward glance out to where the moon shone silvery blue upon the water.

Finally, the flames began to fall; and the fire burned as *normal* fire will. Relief, then: Perhaps we'd not been espied. Still, best to bid our sister good-bye, rake her bones from the ash, and go. Oh, but there were no bones, so brightly, so hotly had the fire burned. Calixto raked the fire, raked the ash with the tool we'd brought for that purpose; but . . . nothing. Somehow this saddened me beyond measure; for I understood, finally, that my sister was gone. And I'd so wanted a bone, something of Sebastiana to hold to. A memento mori. Leo, alone, understood this; for she, too, had hoped for a bone or a seashell's worth of ash. Sentimentally so, yes; but it is also true that there's great potency in such—bone or ash, achieved when sisters are rendered down similarly—and doubtless Léopoldine hoped one day to put her relic to purpose, to powder the bone or drop the ash into a potion. But there was nothing. No bones at all. And what ash Cal raked from the fire was white, all but indistinguishable from the sand. . . . But if there was nothing to take from the rite, neither was there much left to hide. So, as some of us cried, as others incanted, we shoveled sand onto the pyre, smothered the last of the fire, and raked the site smooth.

Then we rowed home in silence, tethered our two boats to the end of our pier, and snuck into our house, Leo and I upon the pier— trusting in our concealing capes, yet waiting, too, for a cloud to oc- clude the moon—whilst Asmodei, Calixto, and Luc crept in the watery way, wading in beneath the pier, through the kraal, and up through the pantry's trap.

I slept fitfully that night of the rite; but not so the next: I was deeply, dreamlessly asleep when woken at dawn by a single rifle shot.

A hard rain had fallen that early August night, the kind of rain that brings the frogs forth to croak and climb every slickened surface, that floods smaller boats, that quiets the birds whilst riling with wind the trees in which they roost; and all through the long rain one hundred Spanish Indians had lain in wait upon Lower Matecumbe Key. At first light, they came in their long, cutout canoes to Indian Key to search out that store of munitions Sebastiana's send-off had betokened.

. . . As for Housman and his lot, they'd heard tell of the nearby fire—a crew anchored out on the reef had seen it, and so, too, had a cutter on patrol—but whether or not anyone had sailed to investigate, I cannot say. The day after the rite, Asmodei had resumed his drink- ing down at the hotel; but now he listened as well for any suspicions amongst the wreckers. Cal had made the rounds similarly, concluding that the islanders were wary, were on alert, even though it was widely deemed "un-Indian" for a war party (if such it was) to have betrayed themselves so. Others, less sanguinary, attributed the flames to a light- ning strike. . . . Blessed be, no one looked askance at our house.

By consensus, Housman's militia had been convened. These thirty-odd men—all the able-bodied whitemen on-island, and six slaves; and a force including Calixto but not Asmodei, who'd refused conscription by pouring a rum drink into the cap of Housman's "lieutenant" —were *called up*, as it were; and even this term was strange to the men, the lot of whom were better suited to a broken-bottle brawl than organized battle. So it was that, as the Indians came ashore that day at dawn, what arms and ammunition had been amassed for our defense—*not* the armory the Indians had hoped for, surely—sat locked in glass-fronted cabinets in the Housman's parlor. And it was there, to the Housmans' house sitting across the piazza from ours, that the islanders, militia or otherwise, were running, all of us having been woken by that same rifle shot. This I witnessed from my window. Worse: I saw that the Indians were winning the aforesaid footrace.

As the story would later be told—and told, and told again, elaborated upon till it bore the sheen of history—an insomniac carpenter of our acquaintance (the same who'd built our shelves) had gone out onto his second-story porch to greet the morn; and by the sun's rising light saw seventeen canoes pulled up onto the strand. The fact that said carpenter—whose name I know but will not here record, so as not to shame a blameless man—*counted* the canoes speaks too eloquently of the mien of our militiamen; but no matter. And it is neither he nor they, neither the carpenter nor the militiamen, who bear the blame for having brought on the attack. No indeed . . . *Enfin*, when the carpenter came across the war party en route to Housman's house, his ensuing cries—for he was cruelly met—woke a neighbor; and *he* it was—many would later claim this distinction—who fired the warning shot that woke us all to a day the likes of which every settler in Florida feared.

We five met upon our second-story landing in various states of dress and wakefulness. Asmodei, naked to the waist and wild-at-eye, already held a firearm. He and Calixto shared a look, the subject of

which was Luc; and before the boy could speak, Asmodei commanded
that he stay with his Eye-turned sister and heed my every word. And
so our party was sundered: Out into the fray went Asmodei and Calixto, leaving me with the twins and that firearm, the business end of
which I kept upturned (as if *it*, not I, would decide when it would fire).

"Hide!" was the last word I heard as the men bounded downstairs
and out our door. Luc took off after them, Leo and I crying after,
"Come back, come back!" But he descended only to block the door
behind his heroes, mustering all his might to tip a fauteuil and jam its
uphostered back beneath the porcelain knob. . . . *Hide!* But where? . . .
The witchery? This was my first thought; for there we'd always felt
safest of all, and from the cupola we could look down into the piazza.
But what if the house were breeched—and we'd not fend off the in-
truders for long, not with a fauteuil and a single firearm that I was
afraid of, and which had an unknown number of bullets in its belly—
. . . *alors*, it was not a matter of if, but rather when. The house *would
be breeched*, it being the island's second biggest and second best. One had
only to come up onto the porch to kick in a parlor window. Even easier: The school-parlor door that gave out onto that same porch had
only a hook and eye holding it fast. I went so far as to worry that a
water-minded warrior might come up through the kraal, through the
pantry floor . . . and it was then I knew what to do.

I led the twins downstairs and into the pantry. Luckily, Luc—
who'd matured into an adventurer of sorts, in his dreams if not yet his
deeds—had, some months prior, petitioned to be let to nail a rug
atop the trapdoor, the better to conceal it from whoever or whatever
pursued him in said dreams, the contents of which he was more likely
now to share with Timothy Trevor than Leo, the latter caring for
naught but the Craft. And if that little green *tapis*, cut to exceed the
trapdoor's dimension by two inches, and tacked atop it, had seemed a
folly then, well, in time we'd see that it had saved our lives.

———————————————— ✳ ————————————————

It was low tide when the Indians struck; and so there the three of us lay upon the shadowed sand, the warm water lapping at our legs. We were belly-flat, lest we be seen through the kraal's latticed sides. Thusly positioned, we could see but a portion of the piazza and the houses on its far side: Housman's, from whence screams came, and the Trevors'. Upon the porch of the latter I, nay, we three saw Timothy Trevor standing, shocked, staring at we knew not what. (Indeed, it was the slaughter of his sister Sarah; she who'd so liked to trail through a French text whilst I read, her finger as light upon the page as the smile upon her lips.) . . . Timothy, *le pauvre*. How I pitied the child where he stood, a stain spreading to cover the crotch of his red night breeches. I so pitied him, in fact, that I did not shush Luc when he called to the boy, though Timothy stood too far away to hear and our safety, our very survival depended on our silence, our staying secreted in the surf beneath the house. In my turn, I called to the boy. Silently, of course: sister-style. So, too, did Leo. I cannot say which of us he heard, but soon Timothy Trevor bounded off the porch and sped, *sped* out into the piazza, headed for our home and the secret place beneath it, wherein he and Luc had often played. He'd find a way in. Or so we hoped whilst waiting, waiting for the trap to open so we could steal the boy down to safety.

But Timothy Trevor never came; and when finally we heard footsteps upon our steps, upon our porch, and upon our parlor floor—in came a window, *crash*—they were booted, not bare, and far heavier than those of a boy weighing some seventy-odd pounds. Yet his was the name we heard in a voice rendered hoarse by fear, and calling out in a half whisper, half shout:

"Timmy! Timmy!" It was Dr. Trevor. Doubtless he'd seen his son set off across the piazza, headed toward our house. I stood now, my toaded Eyes unhidden and my white nightshirt wet and clinging to my . . . *to me*, showing secrets none but those in the Shadows knew, but still I grabbed the ladder mid-rung: I would climb up, push open the trap, and call to Dr. Trevor, tell him Timothy had not come, and . . . But as I made to push upon the trap, more footsteps were heard upon the porch. Muffled footsteps, with bare heels landing hard above us; and this was enough to tell us the Indians had come, four, five perhaps. The twins pulled me back down onto the sand. And there we all three lay, listening as Dr. Trevor, in halting, timorous Spanish, pled for his life.

We heard the fauteuil all but thrown from the door. It toppled the harp, which fell—quite dissonantly, quite . . . Chaotically—onto the pianoforte. We heard, too, the crash of crockery let to fall onto the pantry floor, just overhead.

From the first floor up, Dr. Trevor was made to lead the Indians on a search of our house, though he'd never been beyond the parlor himself. What must he have made of the witchery? I wonder. He saw it, this I know: all the labeled jars of this and that, flora and fauna, the Books we'd had from Eugénie, our white- and black-handled knives, those mortars and pestles requisite to the making of powders, of potions, et cetera. I know the doctor saw these, yes; for, having led the Indians through the witchery and up to the cupola, there he was killed and scalped. And not in that order: So said his screams, which left us shuddering on the ever-colder sands.

As the Indians descended from that first survey of our upper floors, carrying what loot they could, there I lay, listening, cold in the marl, the mud, all the tiny shells feeling like tacks, with a child crying into either side of my neck, knowing, *knowing* we'd die if the trapdoor were opened. I saw, *tried to see* naught but darkness, tried to stave off the light. Opening my eyes, I watched as an unshelled hermit crab scuttled across the sands; and I wished, wished that we might shed our home as easily as he, shed it and slip into the sea, into safety, and *away*.

Still the heels hammered above. . . . Never had I felt so fearful, so helpless; *but what could I do?* Foolishly, I'd set the pistol upon the sands, where now the waves had claimed it. Wet, it wasn't likely to fire, was it? I thought not. What other means of defense did we have? Witch-work? A spell of strong effect would take time, even if Leo and I colluded; and even if we *made* the time, there, upon the sands, what spell might we effect with our hands and souls atremble? I thought of a *cache-cache* spell—so named by the Burgundian sister who'd first cast it—by which we might better our chances of hiding, if not escaping; but I did not know it by heart, and the Book in which it was written sat in the witchery, which now seemed as far away as the moon. The moon . . . Sebastiana . . . With these fresh-minted memories there came tears. Stalled of late by fear, now they began to flow. And I don't know what I would have done had it not been for my late sister's treasures, *my* treasures, my twins; for whom I had to be strong.

We lay in hiding long enough to see the tide rise further up those piles crusted by crustacea. Above us silence alternated with footsteps. We did not know whose they were—Indian or Islander—and we could not call out lest the islanders were being led by the hostiles, who'd brought them as bait; for the sounds of a search could be heard over-head—closets being opened and tossed, beds being overturned—as we, or rather the inhabitants of a house as large as ours, were sought. We listened carefully—for Asmodei, for Calixto—and spoke no word but one: *warehouse;* for it was there, down near the island's primary pier, that war was being waged. We heard the war whoops, heard the occasional cry of a woman, heard what shots could be gotten off. Other than that one word, silence had somehow been decreed. That way we'd not have to voice our worst fear: *That Asmodei, Calixto, or both, would die defending the island.*

This fear I had soon to address; for I could not continue simply *to wish* that Sebastiana watched over us all. Something had to be done. What if the men had already fallen? What, then, were we waiting for? Our neighbors? The navy? And if either of those did come, was I to crawl from our cave nearly naked, showing my fixed Eye and aught else? Hardly. Indeed, I might be better off if the Indians found me. . . . *Enfin,* I rose, shivering, kissed the twins, and told them to stay where they were—to which they agreed, falling into each other's arms such that I saw, *verily saw them as Sebastiana had,* down in the catacombs, near starving and stilled by fear, though now Leo knew what she was and Luc, well, he had his wiles—and I said, nay, *swore* I'd return.

I listened at the trap: nothing. And so I pushed upon it, slowly, slowly, but dared not look behind me to where the light fell upon the trembling twins. From its far side, I shut the trap, smoothed the green rug over its outline, and even took care to replace those shards of pottery and pieces of silverware I'd displaced.

I'd hurry, yes indeed; for my objectives were few: Somehow I had to let Asmodei and Calixto know where we were; I wanted, too, to see what damage had been done to our home, the witchery in particular; and finally, I would shove aside Sebastiana's bed, pry up the floorboard beneath it, and retrieve that strongbox that held the larger part of our wealth: specie, assorted deeds, jewelry, et cetera. If events progressed from bad, *very* bad to worse, and we had to escape, we'd need what wealth we had.

Daring to peer from the same window through which I'd looked at dawn—for I'd gone to my room to retrieve a robe of some sort and my spectacles, sorry but nonetheless necessary—I saw . . . *nothing at all.* Stillness. The islanders were either engaged in the defense of the island or had hidden. Or been killed. Indeed, there lay sweet Sarah Trevor, limbs splayed, turned to those odd angles that tell of a sudden, disquieting death. Another body lay beside Sarah's: either her sister's or mother's: a reddish caul—the result of her having been partially scalped?—concealed the face, and so I cannot name her. But both women died, that I know. And blessed it seemed, somehow, that Dr. Trevor lay slain a story above; for how might a father survive the sight I saw, and that further truth we'd learn: Timothy Trevor, poor Timothy Trevor, waylaid midway through the piazza, had hidden away in a small cistern set above the smithy, and when later that building was burned, he'd been too fearful to come from it; and so had boiled.

. . . I'd gone up to the witchery first. . . . Ruination; such that, not knowing what I could save, I let it all lie, hoping we'd be able to set it aright in time; for never, *never* did I think we'd lose our island to the Indians, for once and forever. Moreover: I saw that the Indians had explored the witchery with . . . *intent;* which is to say they'd unscrewed jars they might otherwise have smashed, untied burlap bags they might otherwise have cut, et cetera; all of which told of their imminent return. They might not find the armory they'd sought, but here was something else altogether. . . . And lest they come to discover me mourning the loss of our atelier, I left it, climbing first to the cupola; wherein I found Dr. Trevor's body badly used, indeed in a state I shan't endeavor to describe, save to say its aura was already showing silver. Unsteady as I was, I stilled myself and managed somehow to step over the body, push open a blood-splattered windowpane, and affix to the sill a length of blue, *azure* blue cloth: a sleeve torn from off a dress of Sebastiana's. In setting out that pennant, I hoped to convey thoughts of our sister to those who'd know it for what it was; and who then— how I hoped it!—would understand my plan, *the only plan open to us;* for already lesser buildings at the island's edge were burning.

Coming down from the cupola—wherein I'd become light-headed, unable now to discern the silver of Dr. Trevor's soul from the indrifting smoke—I passed through the witchery and closed the door; for thusly had I found it. But then, impulsively, I pried from the door the graven paddle head with which the men had gifted us in happier times. Why? I might have said I'd sought it for protection; but, in truth, I may somehow have known that we'd never return to Indian Key. . . . And indeed, none of us would. The island would be lost.

Housman and his wife—coming downstairs to find militiamen and Indians warring in their parlor—had stolen out their back door in their nightclothes, and made their way off the end of their L-shaped peer, their two dogs in pursuit. These latter Housman had had to drown, lest their barking betray them all. And eventually the couple waded and swam to Tea Table Key; whereon Jacob Housman sat shoreside, watching as his island burned, watching, too, as the Indians sent shot at the slow-coming navy, shot fired from those same six-pounders he'd long ago bolted to the wharf behind his warehouse for his empire's defense.

. . . Thusly accoutred, carrying naught but a paddle head and a strongbox, I clambered back down into the kraal; and never had I been so happy to see Asmodei, who stood therein, the water risen to his waist and to the twins' shoulders. I asked, wordlessly, *What of the island?*

"Lost," said he.

"And . . ." I began; but Léopoldine spared me, whispering:

"Calixto!" And pointing to the end of the pier, where he clung to a pile behind which, half-hidden, the larger of our two boats bobbed.

. . . *Sebastiana,* I'd meant to convey with the pennant. Had the men seen it and perceived my plan? I did not know, not then. In fact, Asmodei had; and so he'd returned home, relinquishing the hotel to the hostiles who'd already taken the warehouse; but Calixto had not, and yet he'd struck upon the same plan: We'd sneak away as we had two nights prior, all five of us, *alive;* albeit soon to be adrift.

Part Four

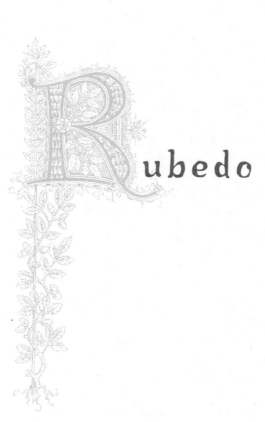

Rubedo

Chapter Twenty-nine

... how came I thus, how here?
—MILTON, Paradise Lost

*I*F WAR IS MERELY A SCORE—AS SO OFTEN IT SEEMS—A matter of *we* VERSUS *they,* *then* let me say that *we* lost seven souls in the attack on Indian Key whilst *they,* the Spanish Indians, would lose ten; when, within a few months, ninety-odd soldiers under the command of Colonel William Harney—himself a survivor of the Indian attack upon the Caloosahatchee outpost—stole into the Never-Glade, to the Indian encampment.

This avenging corps was led by a slave of our late acquaintance, name of John, though Housman had called him Neptune; for the bondman feared the sea and would only work the wharf, where he was the first man to meet every returning crew. Neptune, along with a slave woman of the Trevor household and her two children, had been taken from Indian Key by the Indians. Perhaps they'd gone willingly: Many slaves did so, finding more fairness amidst the redmen than the white. Perhaps not. Regardless, Neptune either left or escaped alone, and eventually made his way back to Housman in Key West; whereupon the latter brokered him, as guide, to Colonel Harney. . . . *Enfin*, the corps in their canoes found the Indians; and in the battle, or ambush, which ensued, the Indians lost five warriors—Chakaika amongst them—to bullet and blade, and five more to the noose when the soldiers' canoes were deemed too unsteady for the taking of captives.

After the raid—through the end of '41, and into '42—naval forces in the keys were doubled; and soon the fleet's six hundred or so men had rousted all but the most resolute of the Indians from the southern swamps. The rest of their tribesmen had been murdered or removed. Thusly did the Seminole Wars come to an end, first by deed and later by decree; and those with a far greater claim on the land than the whitemen lost it.

. . . So, too, did we several hundred settlers upon Indian Key suffer and disperse, a goodly number of us going north, whilst others—both the hardier folk, such as Housman, and the lost folk like us—sailed south to Key West, there to start anew.

History holds that the defense of Indian Key was a failure. In truth, it was a farce.

Some of the escapees—amongst whom we numbered, yes, though I do not refer to our party; for we, by paddle and sail, and consensus, went into the Straits and thence to Key West, declining the offer of a captain whose schooner we met at sea and who offered to put us ashore at Cape Florida, where we might await a steamer that would take us to St. Augustine— . . . escapees *other than us*, I mean to say, had hied to a navy schooner anchored off Tea Table Key; and there they apprised a midshipman of what already was being referred to as *the massacre*.

This lesser officer, whose duty it was to nurse the naval ill, determined to launch a counterattack with the aid of his dozen charges, six of whom were sick, and six of whom were *sick unto death*. A barge was manned, and to its thwarts were tied two four-pounder carriage guns; but when finally this barge was poled within striking distance of the hostile-held warehouse and fired—which shots we had heard with hope—the guns recoiled and rolled into the sea. At this turn of events the midshipman wondered if it wasn't the wiser course to return to his schooner, and protect *it* from the savages; who surely would come. But the Indians did not come. Instead, they stayed to sack the key, sailing off later that day in low-riding canoes laden with loot. . . . And oft have I wondered what the Indians took from the witchery. Or did they burn the house and *all it held,* as they had the hotel, the warehouses, and even the wharves? I do not know, and so cannot say; for the Wheel of the Year began to spin, and quickly so, upon our unexpected departure from Indian Key, and I never bothered to back-conjure such details as these.

But yes, up it all went, in smoke; and down went Housman, unto ruin. Within the month he'd quit his key for good; and shortly thereafter, with the Northern Law and his creditors descending, he was forced to sell, at auction, all he'd been able to salvage. About this he was not happy, not at all; and lest you wonder how I know this, let me say *he told us so*. Indeed, with Sebastiana gone, Housman felt free to loose upon us a stream of invective so blue, so bitter, so laced with accusation as to . . . *Enfin,* I'd not have minded as much if he'd not calumniated us *in public,* and upon a day when we were all so hopeful and happy; for, of we five, only Calixto had ever been to an auction before.

And the more Housman railed against Cal, against us, *the higher we bid* for pieces of his seized estate; till finally we were the owners of a quite sizable schooner—one hundred and twenty tons, she was, seventy-seven feet of Jamaican dogwood and mastic trim, measured stem to stern—as well as three slaves and assorted housewares.

The housewares—crystal, silver, furnishings, and such—we needed.

The slaves we freed, of course. Two—a couple—sailed north with letters of manumission, whilst the third—a stout woman of middle age whose bill of sale said she'd been "seasoned" in the Bahamas, and whose name was Euphemia—chose to stay with us; and happily so. She, our sweet Euphemia, was well paid to do all we could not: She oversaw those who cleaned both our newly bought house on Front Street as well as the cabin—wherein she lived—and kitchen behind it, from whence she came to us twice daily, at noontime and supper, bearing dishes delighted in by all but me (being of ever-diminishing appetite) and Asmodei (who angered our cook, disdaining as he did her liberal use of spice).

As for the schooner, well . . . It was pricey, yes; *mais hélas,* a plan had had to be made.

. . . In the strongbox I'd retrieved from beneath Sebastiana's bed I found a sapphire the size of a thrush's egg, and rubies so numerous we might well have spared some for Luc to skip as stones. Too, there were jewels not in their raw state but arranged: *jewelry,* in a word. I was surprised to see Sebastiana had carried these with her from Ravndal, first to Rome and thence Cuba, but not so Asmodei. He said our sister had carried her jewels with her wherever she went, not as a miser might, but rather as a woman would, a woman to whom memory mattered; for amongst the lot were rings that had been gifted to her straight from the fingers of kings, as well as the daintier digits of her onetime patroness, Marie Antoinette. And the rubies alone, as sold by Calixto in New Orleans, whence he ventured with letters of introduction from me to the witch Eugénie—letters that (as ever) solicited news of the Duchess, but told, too, of all that had happened of late, and wherein I excused my absence, which was owing, said I, to the twins ("Can you *conceive* of it?" I asked of Eugénie, adding with a wink-in-ink, "Apparently, I could!")— . . . the rubies alone, I say, financed the schooner (bought at six percent off for cash, *merci bien*).

Once we'd agreed upon our plan, it came to seem Sebastiana's legacy: With her money—a *monstrous* sum as compared to mine—and with her memories, she staked us to a new start.

So: We'd really no choice but to buy all that would establish us as wreckers. *Wreckers*, of all things! (I was, yes, the last to assent to said plan.) And if Housman cursed us, so be it. Of course, we— Léopoldine and I—could have met his curses with those of the sisterly sort, but we did not. Leastways, *I* did not. As for Leo, well . . . Though she denied it then and denies it still, she, embarrassed as she was at the auction by Housman—and angry, too, such that her Eye turned and she had to bury her face in my bosom (cold comfort, that) lest it be seen—may well have cursed our former keeper; for, within a half year, humbled to dust, and whilst working a wreck on equal terms with men who'd once been his hirelings, Housman was crushed between two rolling boats and buried at sea, *sans cérémonie*.

Understand: We'd not sailed from the burning key blithely. No indeed. There'd been trembling, there'd been tears; and, too, we feared we'd be seen and pursued by the Indians. And indeed we were espied, and shot at—blessed be, we'd already rowed beyond the range of their rifles. Luc worried, then, that we'd be fired upon by the commandeered cannons at wharf's end; but evidently we in our launch were deemed unworthy, *a waste of shot*. Neither did the Indians set out after us in their canoes; and for this I was doubly grateful, as, in trying to assuage Léopoldine's fears that the canoes would come, I had said they would not.

"And *how* do you know that?" she asked, holding tightly to a cry-

ing Luc. There was both sarcasm and defiance in her tone, and cu-
riosity, too: She wondered *how I knew.* Had I seen, or rather Seen, future events as I spoke of them?

When I confessed that I had not, well, then Leo turned *truly* defiant, asking what good were our gifts—hers and mine—if we refused
to use them? Here she referred, of course, to divination, or sisterly
Sight, of which both S. and I had warned her (despite, or rather *due to*
Leo's talents for same, which far outstripped ours, even then). "Is it
not so," she asked at sea, when we'd been silent some time, having already set our southerly course, "is it not true to say we might have
drawn down visions of . . . of *that*?" And lest anyone—myself or the
three males, intent upon our every word—mistake her meaning, she
pointed with the whole of her arm, flinging it back toward our former home on the now smoldering key.

"I suppose so," said I, weakly.

"Then why, *why* did we not do it?"

For this I'd no answer (*fear* seeming an insufficient response). And
when I turned to Calixto and Asmodei, they turned away in silence,
the former seeming sympathetic, the latter not. They, too, wondered
why we hadn't divined an attack in which we might well have lost our
lives; especially seeing as how there'd been rumors and suspicions, the
lot of which had resulted from Work we'd done unwisely: Sebastiana's
sloppy conferral unto the Summerland.

As we sailed on that day in silence, northbound vessels sailing past
us to the site of the attack—we waved to say that yes, *we'd escaped*, and
yes, *we were well*—I sat astern wondering why the future, or rather the
Sighting of it, frightened me so. And it was true: We might well have
been four, or three, or two in our boat, rather than five. . . . Could anything worse than that ever eventuate from a bit of Sight?

If more was said of divination that day, I cannot recall the converse; but in the days and weeks to come, I returned to Léopoldine's

question, driven both by my wonderment and her sullenness, which endured to the point of distraction and ended only when finally I summoned the family to say, *to swear* that thenceforth I'd watch for such dangers, do my best to See them before they came to pass. At this I heard huzzahs, none louder than Léopoldine's; for of course she assumed that she'd be let to divine as well.

She was not. Not at first . . . Whereupon her sullenness resumed, and she showed me her Eye with insistence.

"She is thirteen, *at most*," I protested to the men when they came to me as one to petition on her behalf, and ostensibly so; in point of fact they'd already begun to conceive of a marriage most fruitful: Commerce betrothed to Craft.

"She is strong, H.," said Calixto; by which he meant many things: Léopoldine *was* strong, and less inclined to fright than I; she'd a talent that would have out, one way or another; and, finally, as witch, as woman, she'd not let herself be coddled much longer.

To some or all of which Asmodei assented by saying, too pointedly, "Let her work. She is a stronger witch than you. . . . Sebastiana always said so."

"Do not presume to sway me," said I, heatedly, "by setting words in the mouth of my dead sister!" And I stormed from our house— not literally, no: It was the lot of . . . *a different witch* to be allied to the weather—and I walked up and down Caroline Street. (And if I'd already acceded to the family's request and divined our future, surely I'd have Seen that Caroline was the same street on which we'd build our present home, the whole of which we refer to as the Witchery.) After this pacing of the street, I returned home, once again convened the four, and amended my announcement of some days prior, promising that not only would Léopoldine and I use the Sight *together* to ensure the family's safety, but we'd work it toward our betterment as well. *En bref,* our profit.

Whereupon there followed more huzzahs and hugs; which I took greedily, supposing (rightly) that they'd stall when I went on to say, as then I did:

"However, I have one condition."

"Speak!" hissed Asmodei; for already the sun had set, and he was deep in his cups: Unable to sleep since the loss of his love, he'd redoubled his drinking such that now he sloshed away his nights—first with simple rum, and later that absinthe he decocted himself—and slept away his days.

"However . . ." I resumed, "I've a condition to which you all must agree."

"*Speak!*"

If Asmodei was angered, the others were rapt; but suspense had not been my intent. "If we are to explore . . . *profit*," said I, wondering would the word be *curse* or *charm*, "it must be to fund something more than ourselves, something . . . larger."

Silence; born of both surprise and relief. "That's all?" asked Calixto. ". . . Agreed!"

And the twins, as one: "Agreed!"

Asmodei deigned to nod his assent; whereupon our talk progressed to *how*. And it was then Calixto told of a rumor he'd heard concerning Housman's ruin; which rumor eventuated in the aforesaid auction at which we—*most* improbably—first announced ourselves as wreckers.

Chapter Thirty

We must take the current when it serves,
Or lose our ventures.
—SHAKESPEARE, *Julius Caesar*

KEY WEST THE TOWN SITS NESTLED IN THE NORTHWEST-ern corner of the key known by the same name, and which the compass sites as laying just north of latitude 24°, 30' and just west of longitude 80°, 40' . South of Key West no American can say they are *at home*.

In ages past the Spaniards called it *Cayo Hueso*, or Bone Key—too aptly named a home, perhaps, in my case. This was owing—legend says—to a skirmish long ago fought on the island's shores, the resultant dead of which (conquistadores all) were left to rot till their sun-bleached skeletons jangled in the easy surf like the bells on a baby's booties. Doubtless it was the Calusa, or perhaps the Tequesta, who met and slew that party sometime in the 1500s; whereupon Spain ceded the keys—known then as *Los Martires*—to the natives for some one hundred years, trading with them, yes, from the safety of Havana, but not daring to settle.

Gradually, with gifts, with trinkets, with rum and lies, the Spanish won the natives to their side; till, by the turn of the seventeenth century, the South Florida natives were sailing the Straits to trade in Havana, their dugouts weighted with fish, ambergris, tree bark, fruits, pelts, and suchlike. Thusly did the natives acquire a veneer of Spanish culture whilst simultaneously sealing their fate; for the trust arising from this trade would prove their downfall.

. . . Now, begging pardon, I'll sew the rest of the requisite history from scraps; as so:

At the end of the French and Indian War, in 1763, Spain and England swapped land: Florida for Havana, which city the British had captured. When the Spaniards—whom the keys natives had let settle, eventually—left the peninsula for Cuba, they took many of the natives with them, some free, others as slaves. When, twenty years on, at the end of the Revolutionary War, Florida was *retroceded* to Spain, that nation's second, short-lived tenancy began; but this had little effect upon life *as it was lived* in the keys by those hardy, not to say *foolhardy* folk who'd since settled there.

Oh, but then another twenty years pass—1803, if I am to be precise, as we dead so seldom are—and the United States acquires the Louisiana Territory. The resultant increase in shipping between that place and sundry other ports shows, plainly, that Key West is to the Gulf what Gibraltar is to the Mediterranean: *important*. Yet, as a result of Spanish laxity, the waters thereabouts are lawless; and soon they grow crowded with wreckers, pirates and privateers—this last group being, in sum, *sailors who pirate with their government's permission*—some of whom perished, and some of whom profited from that reef which gives the Gulf its teeth.

The plate ships of the Spanish were forever running aground, depositing their gold in *God's watery vault* as they carried it betwixt Havana, home, and other states of the Spanish Main. So, too, did lesser ships founder in the Gulf. Soon, salvage was seen as sport—risky, yes, but worth the rewards. It was not long before those sea types freed at the end of the War of 1812 drifted south on the Gulf Stream, some in search of pure, piratical profit, others trolling amongst the finny tribes of the sea. And indeed it was these last, fishermen—Northerners, to a one—who'd be the first to settle at Cayo Hueso; which name they, in their way, corrupted to Key West.

By the early 1820s—that is, twenty years prior to our arrival—the waters off Key West were rife with wreckers and turtlers, still based in New Providence, Bahamas, as well as fishing smacks come from Cuba and (in the winter) the American North. To such types the seas were profitable, paradisiacal; . . . but still a problem persisted: *pirates;* whose sadistic ways were legendary:

Once, in 1823, the captain of a schooner, captured at the northern entrance to the Straits, had both his arms dissevered at the elbow for refusing to tell the boarding pirates where his money was hidden; though, when finally the captain told where said coin was cached, the pirates put out his eyes, tied him down on a bed of oakum—having already stuffed some of that tarred and turpentine'd hemp in his mouth—and set him alight. Their blood-thirst unslaked, the pirates proceeded to hang a lesser seaman from the yardarm and crucify the boatswain by spiking his feet to the deck and his torso to the tiller; whereupon, for pure piratical pleasure, they blew the ship's dog to smithereens by the application of a swivel gun.

Yes, pirates were a . . . *problem,* one which lessened the appeal of settlement in the keys. But they were soon to be run off; for, in 1822—one year after Spain ended its second tenancy in the Florida Territory, ceding it to the United States—the navy of the latter country sought to establish itself at Key West, where the harbor was determined to be both wide and deep, and there they based the Mosquito Fleet (as it came to be called), whose purpose was to put down piracy. This the fleet achieved, and fast; such that it has long seemed to me that the pirates' defeat must have been a most ignominious one, accomplished as it was by vessels bearing such names as *Fox, Weasel, Terrier,* and *Ferret.* Rather like salting the wound, that; . . . but never mind.

When it seemed the piratical fires were about to be doused, men began doing with titles and deeds what it is men are wont to do; and ownership of the island passed through a succession of Johns, men whose sameness of name betokens a sameness of intent: *profit.* And so, the island that had been granted by the then governor of Florida, Don Juan de Estredo, to Juan Salas, in 1815, for *favors rendered unto the Kingdom of Spain,* now passed into the hands of one John Simonton; who, in 1821, bought it for the rounded sum of two thousand dollars. Simonton, in turn, profited by portioning off his parcel to the Johns Whitehead, Fleming, Warner, Mountain, and Strong; all of whom profited in turn by . . . *enfin,* tales of *mere* profit are so common they grow tiresome in the telling, *non?* . . . All save ours, of course; to which tale I now return via these few words regarding wrecking.

Wrecking is a trade as old as the reef, surely. Natives are known to have rowed out to wrecks as early as 1622, when a hurricane set a Spanish flotilla upon the reef's spars; but the facility with which the Indians stripped the ships of their gold tells that they had been diving for quite some time. Indeed, the Spanish seamen marveled at how deeply the Indians dove, and how long they held their breath, unto drowning, unto death; . . . but what *won't* men do in their desire for gold?

. . . By the year of our arrival in Key West, wrecking was the mainstay of the economy. One would have been hard-pressed to find, amongst the island's thousand-odd inhabitants—*odd,* indeed—

someone *not* engaged in the trade, though the principals were few. These men owned the large wreckers—and there were perhaps twenty, twenty-five such ships then, supported by lesser vessels beyond number—as well as the requisite wharves and warehouses, and those shops provisioning the industry, i.e.: boat wrights' facilities, chandleries, sailmakers, et cetera. They were all Housmans, these principals, or cut from the same cloth as he; but the *real* Housman they hated for his . . . lawlessness; for they were all proud to say they'd *evolved* from piracy; and though they hadn't, not really, it is true that wrecking, by then, was far from lawless.

Courts of admiralty had been established, of necessity; for the reef claimed, on average, a vessel per week. Probably more: If the ship's captain or the wreck-master (for a fee) managed to refloat a ship, the incident went unreported to the Wreckers' Court, as we called it; for there, *process imperiled profit.* The courthouse itself was infested with underwriters and other such, black-suited types—they'd have circled like carrion fowl, had they been able to fly. But, of course, court could not be avoided if a wreck were contested. In such cases, the concerned parties—captains, wreck-masters, owners, crewmen, supercargoes, insurers, et cetera—went before the presiding judge, who awarded salvage based on those rules of wrecking which had been put in place to distinguish the enterprise from piracy, *expressly so;* namely:

1. The first vessel to arrive at a wreck was declared its *salvor,* and the captain of said vessel became *the wreck-master,* assuming:
2. The captain of the wrecked vessel agreed that:
   a. His ship had indeed wrecked; for often a half day's delay in these dealings would allow the tides to extricate the vessel; and:
   b. He accepted the terms—percentages and such—proposed by the wreck-master.

If conditions *a* and *b* (as set forth above), were met, then:

3. All salvors arriving subsequently had to apply to the wreck-master (and not the captain of the foundered ship, who had, under Rule 2, relinquished all authority) for a role in the salvage effort; and, if said roles were granted, and terms agreed to, then and only then did . . .

4. Salvage begin.

     And, if the salvage itself—by which I refer not to the act but *the wares thusly recovered*—went awry, and was contested, the court was resorted to, claims and testimonies were made and taken, till finally the judge rendered his award according to:

     Rule 5: The precept of "no cure, no pay." In other words, had the wreckers *actually* salvaged the wreck—the cargo being of primary concern, the ship itself secondary—or had this been effected by the captain, or Providence (which loftiness referred to the aforementioned tides), or had all of the above played their part? If so, well, this was sticky business indeed.

     If the judge ruled in favor of the wreckers—as often he did, being either *in the pocket* or *on the payroll* of one of the abovementioned principals—percentages of salvage (Rule 6) were awarded according to:

     a. Its worth; i.e., *the cargo's cash value at market*; and:

     b. The risk the wreckers had run: *Had the ship in question been taking on water? If so, at what rate? Had the seas been rough or smooth? Was fire at issue? Had men been lost in the essay?* Et cetera.

All of which points were spoken to by the suitors, who could number four, five, six, or more, in proceedings that might drag on for days, thusly keeping captains and crews aground and *costing all concerned*. Oh, but if the wreck were worthy, and the judge found in favor of the wreckers . . . *enfin,* fortunes might be made; as had happened some few years prior to our arrival:

One Captain Geiger, in his ninety-four-ton *Caroline,* had mastered the salvage of *America,* incontestably a total loss when it ran onto Loggerhead Reef in the Dry Tortugas, and for his efforts was awarded $47,971, a sum I well recall; for Calixto, when first he presented his vision of the family's future to us all, not long after our escape from Indian Key, repeated the figure time and again. Indeed, it was Geiger's windfall that persuaded me to accede to the plan and cast my lot in with the others; whereupon we proceeded, *unanimously,* to the Housman auction.

When finally we found ourselves in possession of all a wrecker needed, and *most all* of what a wrecker could want—anchors and chains of various design and grade, long hawsers, fenders, axes, awls, and saws, as well as dewatering devices, winches, grappling hooks, et cetera, the lot of which was unfamiliar to us all, save Calixto—there remained but one question; and from it our success depended:

Seeing as how all successful salvage stemmed from speed, how were we *to ensure* that we'd be the first to arrive at a wreck?

The answer, though simple—we, Léopoldine and I, would divine the wrecks before they occurred—seemed *all but impracticable,* at first; for it required mastery of that most slippery of the sister-sciences: Sight.

 *Chapter Thirty-one*

Would God I could awaken!
For I dream I know not how;
And my soul is sorely shaken . . .
—Edgar Allan Poe, "Bridal Ballad"

*E*ager as we were, and nervous—seeing as how we'd spent a great deal of the legacy resettling ourselves—Calixto wasted no time in taking our enterprise to sea. Indeed, we bought the schooner on a Wednesday, saw her overhauled that Thursday, and by Sunday her papers and register had been changed, such that henceforth she would be known as the *Soror Mystica*. We christened her thusly, with a *bash* of bottled rum across her bow and smiles sent skyward.

Calixto, with Luc and Asmodei assisting, combed the port for the requisite crewmen. Having solicited ten, nine were signed: The tenth man came wharfside so drunk that Asmodei dunked his head—and nearly drowned him, as I heard it told—in a briny barrel of pickles before kicking him home, as one would a cur;

this despite, or perhaps *owing to*, Asmodei's own penchant for drink and other narcotizing substances.

Enfin, it was a Sunday when we all sailed for the first time about the *Soror Mystica*. The sky was cloudless, the seas smooth; and we were all as happy as we'd been for a long, long while.

The wreckers' routine soon passed from tedium to torment; and though none of us voiced our doubts, surely each of us questioned the wisdom of what we'd done; for whilst the men failed at sea, we, Leo and I, failed within our Front Street home.

Not for want of trying, of course. On Front Street, we slow-built a witchery as best we could; but each day we worked therein, we felt the loss of all we'd had to leave behind on Indian Key. Still, we made do:

At Léopoldine's urging, we charted the stars from the witchery's second-story windows. In truth, I was no help at all; for I found I'd neither aptitude nor affinity for things zodiacal (. . . too *mathematical* for me). Meanwhile, my contribution to the Work was the *colorizing of our efforts*, but in this I failed; for, though I'd procured candles of every color, I'd forgotten that only Calixto could know his astral colors (blue and black), as only he knew his date of birth (September 26). . . . Of course, I knew the date of the twins' conception—remembered the day and the date quite well indeed: the twentieth of June—and though it was therefore likely that they were Aries (white and pink), they might also have been Pisces (white and green). So, in the end, we burned all the colors we cared to burn (*lampadomancy*); for we were wont to work at night, and needed the light, though we made sure to burn a preponderance of green (*for finance*), light blue (*for health*), and purple (*for ambition*, though it seemed we'd a great deal of that in the family already).

Whilst Léopoldine persisted in her analysis of the stars, the planets, et cetera, my Craftwork was rather less lofty, rather more *terrestrial:* I worked with herbs, spices, flowers (*floromancy*), and such; for still I shied from the Sight, and, truth be told, sought to make a nice home instead. Leo, of course, shied from no aspect of the Sight, and this frightened me; but it was not long before she met with some success, announcing that—owing to the sun's placement in this house, Mercury's in another, and the moon's in a third . . . or something like that—a wreck was likely. Well, a wreck was *always* likely; but still we sent word (ciphered, of course, as Luc had proven himself quite adept at ciphering, devising a new one for our use from Scott's *Ivanhoe*) out to the *Soror Mystica* by way of a father and son and their nimble little smack.

Surprisingly, encouragingly, a wreck was indeed spotted the next weekend: The brig *Marion Ashby* reefed and began to bilge, and so hoisted her colors upside down at half-mast. Problem was, it wasn't the *Soror Mystica* that espied this signal of distress. Indeed, we were the sixth wrecker to arrive on site, and Calixto's suit for a role in the salvage—the *Marion Ashby* had a bellyful of common furniture and cabinet ware come from Boston, a share of which would have benefited our still bare-boned household—his suit was denied. Rather too jauntily, in Asmodei's opinion; whereupon the wreck-master heard himself cursed from the deck of the *Mystica* and had to duck—so Luc reported—when a rubber fender came hurtling over the bulwark toward his head.

. . . Asmodei. His grief was worsening, eating at him as teredo worms do ships' wood; and in time it would sink him just as surely.

As word spread of there being a madman aboard the *Soror Mystica*, Asmodei began to stay ashore. It was an arrangement that suited him well, and sadly so; for the slow life of routine, as lived aboard a wrecker lying at anchor, waiting, and waiting some more, maddened him; so, too, did his hired shipmates, Asmodei being accustomed to no company but Sebastiana's. Further, and worse—such that already I began to feel I'd failed my sister, who'd consigned her consort to my care—there was no role for Asmodei to play in the witchery—discounting those of *skeptic* or *cynic*; and so he fell to frequenting a Greene Street establishment, a lean-to of timber and tin, known as *The Throne of the Goat*. There he steeped himself in rum, rather as he'd once done Sebastiana; but if alcohol preserves the dead, it tends toward the opposite effect upon the living. Soon drink was Asmodei's daily work; and this he pursued with diligence, drinking till the onset of dreams, and sobering at no one's insistence, not even that of his Lord B., who begged.

. . . But I shall set this particular sadness aside, and return to the problem then at hand: How to arrive *first* at a wreck?

Léopoldine abandoned the stars a while, as I did my herbs; for together we decided to task ourselves with stronger Work. . . . She is rather *persuasive*, our Leo.

In the meantime, and no thanks to us, the *Soror Mystica* happened upon her first wreck:

The *Tennessee*, sailing from Bordeaux to New Orleans, ran onto the reef well north of what had once been Housman's key and began to ship water, badly so. Calixto and crew heard the report of ordnance, a single cannon being fired, reloaded, and fired again, as fast as its mechanism allowed: *Vessel in Distress*.

Arriving well ahead of any other wrecker, and having their suit accepted by a captain as distressed as his vessel, our crew set about a salvage operation that was more dangerous than they knew. The *Tennessee* had fallen over onto her beam-ends, and the sea was washing over her in a mass of foam, rolling her heavily, side to side, with two masts al-

ready having gone by the board. Some of her many passengers—
passengers, yes: not a wrecker's most wanted cargo—were already in the
water, clinging to what was afloat and crying to the crewmen of *"des
requins!"* —indeed, there were sharks—in a language Luc alone knew.
He it was who comforted the passengers plucked from the sea, and he
it was who received the lion's share of honor when the *Soror Mystica* returned to port, all parties accounted for *and alive.*

Though the nonliving salvage from the *Tennessee* was of little
worth—Calixto had ordered that the ruined ship be stripped of her
metal parts, her copper sheathing, her iron chain plates, et cetera—the
Soror Mystica was hailed for its heroism, and never again was she (or any
of our later vessels, for that matter) shunned when arriving at a wreck.
Still, though, we were some months away from arriving *regularly* at
wrecks, let alone *first.*

Whilst the men sailed the Straits with lessening patience, Leo and I
resorted to types of divination untried for centuries, surely; and I
wrote to Eugénie in New Orleans soliciting more. She, in turn,
spread the word amongst our scattered sorority—and blessed be
that sister of mine, who, in late years, suffered the Coming of the
Blood whilst Working in her home on the rue Dauphine—and soon
Books of Shadows began to arrive by the semimonthly mails. It was my
habit to read through these first, of course; and I claimed seniority
over Leo in doing so, though she was wise to me and would often
say that I ought not to feel obliged to protect her so. Oh, but I did,
and with reason: On those occasions when our Work had brought
dreams, she'd Seen them strongly, much more so than I, and even
minor revelations seemed somehow to deplete her, to cause her head
to ache, to send her to bed for days at a time. . . . . Was she, I wondered, allied to Sight as I was to the dead? Regardless, Leo's hunger

for Sight was undiminished. "I'll sleep it all off if I must," said she, oh so casually.

And I was right to watch her, to protect her, yes, despite her desire for independence. Or rather, *because of it*. And indeed, when first I lapsed, leaving her alone one afternoon whilst Euphemia and I, with proceeds from the salvage of the *Tennessee*, set out shopping for house-wares and such—*needful* things only, mind; for I'd not forgotten our vow to fund something larger than ourselves if ever we were to suc-ceed on a scale we'd not yet approached, *à moindre dire*: in fact, funds were low and in recent months we'd had to learn *economy*—I returned at dusk to a sight the likes of which . . .

Stay: Let me preface the following by saying, *by allowing* that Léopoldine was what, fourteen, fifteen perhaps? *Curious*, in other words, both as a woman and as a witch; though which species of cu-riosity was worse I'd have been at pains to say.

Alors, this is what happened that day:

Via Eugénie, we'd received a copy of a Book once kept by a sister of African birth who'd lived and died in the islands; and though I'd yet to read it all the way through, still I'd seen that it touched on rites quasi-religious—*bref*: voodoo—and so I had hidden it; . . . but not well enough.

Later, having slept for two days straight, waking neither for food nor drink, nor to relieve herself, Léopoldine would say that she'd only hoped to send Calixto *something certain*, news of a wreck strongly Sighted; but why she'd turned to a spell, a rite so strange, so savage, well, *that* she could not say. But I knew and told her: It was the lure, the temptation of Sight that both Sebastiana and I had warned her of. When finally she woke and I learned *the all* of what she'd done, I made her write it down in her Book; and from said Book I had her recite the tale a second time, so as to be able to tell from the turn of her Eye if she stinted the truth at all. She did not, of course—

no liar, our Leo; and so it is I am able to relay the too truthful particulars, as so:

In the yard of that first of our two island houses, on Front Street, Euphemia kept—penned, caged, and roaming at will—animals that, whole or in part, and in ways which I did not care to consider, found their way onto our table as well as onto the *Soror Mystica;* for Euphemia and Simon, the ship's cook, working together, came *to admire* each other, so much so that in time he came to share her cabin and a wedding of sorts was celebrated in that same yard. . . . I speak of hens, of course, and the requisite roosters; but also Euphemia kept lesser fowl renowned for their flesh: squab, geese, and ducks. When these latter quacked, they suffered the hurled insults—not to mention shoes, conch shells, candlesticks, and anything else suitably weighty and at hand—of Asmodei, who hated, *hated* to be woken from whatever dreams he'd so *diligently* achieved with drink, with opiates, with ether, or with some admixture of the three. . . . Too, we had goats. One goat *fewer,* though, after the day in question.

Perhaps the fault was mine; for I'd told Léopoldine how a late Seeress of my acquaintance had found the future in the heated bones of hens, denuded in vats of devouring beetles. Nothing new, this: *scapulomancy,* sisters call it, commonly. But as the stripping of the bones—preferred are the scapulae, the shoulder bones, of larger beasts; or the knucklebones, the marrow from which, when heated, speaks with a sizzle some sisters are able *to translate*—takes time and, moreover, we'd no barrels of beetles at hand, *merci bien,* Léopoldine took it upon herself to speed a similar spell, found in that Book I'd intended to hide from her. . . . And I suppose it might have been worse: She might have happened upon my Tacitus, and therein read of our ancient sisters "consulting the gods in the palpitating entrails *of men.*"

As Euphemia and I were to be absent but a few hours, and Leo was to be alone—a state much attended, I suppose, seeing as how I rarely ventured out by day, a habit attested to by my ever-increasing pallor; for, if once the sun had tinted my skin to a tenable shade, now it burned it, painfully, such that I was white as fish belly, and with my silvered hair must have seemed . . . ghostly, I suppose—*enfin*, finding herself alone, Leo chose her goat at great speed. She led the ill-fated creature into the house—doubtless watching its behavior for signs (*hieroscopy:* the observed behavior of those about to be sacrificed)—and up to a second-story bedroom adjoining our witchery. Said room was spare now that Calixto and Luc had taken to sleeping aboard the *Soror Mystica*, whether she was at sea or in her slip.

. . . *Cephalomancy*, it's called: divination done by the reading of the cracks in an ass's skull occasioned by boiling. Léopoldine rightly supposed that a goat's skull would suffice. But why, *why oh why* she decided to slay the goat *inside* she never could say. *It was a lapse in sister-sense,* wrote she in her Book, a sentence rather more . . . *neat* than the scene I returned to that day at dusk. And though Leo long denied it, I believe she'd hoped to read the spray of the goat's blood upon our whitewashed walls (*haematomancy; dririmancy,* if the blood is let to drip, and the drippings are read) before progressing onto its entrails (*haruspicy,* as favored by the ancients of her detested Rome); specifically, the liver (*hepatoscopy*).

The liver, yes; for just as Léopoldine had attributed her astrological luck—whereby she'd seen as "propitious" the week in which the *Marion Ashby* would wreck—to the Babylonian zodiac, now she would scry as the Babylonian *baru*, or priests, once had: They held that *all a body's life*, both as it *had been* and *would be* lived, could be read in the four lobes of the liver, cut, of course, into fifty cubes. . . . Of course, it seemed to me then, and seems to me still, that the fate of one whose liver is extracted and cut into fifty cubes is rather easily foretold, *non?* But never mind.

With her white-handled athame, she slit the goat's throat, holding both her nerve and her nose as the animal bleated and bled. I imagine, too, that Leo had occasion—albeit unsought—to dabble in *scatomancy* that day; for surely the goat shat itself at the *slice* if not the sight of her knife. *Alors,* so far, so good (reported Léopoldine): The goat was dead, and its blood read (albeit to no avail). There remained but the dissevering of the head; for though we'd a cauldron big enough to boil the goat whole, Leo hadn't the time to heat sufficient rainwater within it—well water: *hydromancy;* spring water: *pegomancy;* rainwater, as preferred, issuing as it does from on high: *hydatoscopy*—to a suitable temperature, which is to say *a boil;* for she sought not to stew the goat but rather to render it down to its readable bones.

The head off—hard work, that; but Leo'd been prescient enough to carry a saw up to the scene of her would-be Sighting—into the cauldron she dropped the head, *plop;* whereupon she swung the crane so as to situate the cauldron over open flame, flame onto which she'd thrown rosemary for the heightening of Sight as well as the dulling of . . . Stink. Then, in defiance of that adage that advises otherwise, there she stood, watching, waiting for the water to boil, all the while asking simple questions *inwardly* whilst incanting, *outwardly,* "*Exurge, Domine, adjuva nos, et redime nos propter nomen sanctum tuum,*" which spell she—rather enterprisingly, I thought—derived from an old Psalter she'd found. . . . *Enfin:* lots of bubbles: an answer in the affirmative. No bubbles: a negation.

Just what questions she asked of the cauldron—in fact, she never even read the cracks in the poor nanny's skull—well, this was easy to surmise; for when I found her, fallen, and dangerously near the fire, still she held sea charts in her hands. *Will there be a wreck Monday on Alligator Reef? Tuesday on Loggerhead? Wednesday on the Quicksands?* Et cetera. A most tiring attempt at Sight, it seemed to me. And in addition to costing us a goat, she might well have hurt herself, might well have burned our whole house down—a house that reeked now of bled and boiled goat, *merci bien,* such that I was a whole day upon my knees with buckets and brushes—still I found I could summon little anger when finally Leo woke; for hadn't I made mistakes myself? Indeed I had. Far worse ones, in fact.

"I only meant to help," said she tearfully, and with her Eye turned. Moreover: Léopoldine apologized, in her way. Not for the Craft she'd practiced, mind, but rather for having snuck it. In time, we'd laugh at this "lapse" of hers—and there'd be more of both: laughter and lapses, as Leo explored her particular talents—but then, when first she woke, I knew she'd Seen something. It was writ on her face; and absurd though it sounds, I will say that *somehow she'd aged.* When finally we were alone, I asked her what she'd Seen, and her answer was threefold:

First, she asked, verily *begged* that I not tell Calixto what she'd done, a request that struck me as strange at the time; but to this I acceded. I was less than truthful, I suppose, in failing to inform Leo that Luc already knew—I'd told the boy, as I'd drawn the line at disposing of the slaughtered goat myself; . . . bad enough I'd had to dissemble before Euphemia, *suggesting* that perhaps the nanny had wandered off—and that Luc, in turn, had told Calixto. . . . Cal, of course, cared only that Leo was well; though, too, he very much welcomed the relay of what next Léopoldine told me:

Calixto was to watch for a ship whose initials were *F.C.,* as it was soon to wreck. This Leo Saw as she recited the alphabet over the cauldron: It bubbled over at the aforesaid letters. . . . Sure enough, the *Flying Cloud* went down within the month, somewhere west of the Marquesas; and though the *Soror Mystica* was not the first wrecker to arrive, still she shared in the salvage of kegs containing $25,500 worth of specie: An award large enough to allow us to lay the foundations for the Witchery on Caroline Street *and* commence the channeling of funds toward our chosen cause: abolition.

The last words of Léopoldine's tripartite apology were much the hardest to hear, literally and figuratively; for she whispered to me that one of us was to die within the year.

"You see!" said I, leaping up from her bedside, ready to rail. *"That* is why we must be wary of the Sight! . . . What are we to do now, now that we know . . . ?—" and already I was crying, trembling at the loss I'd just learned of, when a still-weak Léopoldine beckoned me back to where I'd been sitting and whispered one word more.

"What? . . . Leo," and I shook her by the shoulders, "what did you say? Who . . . ?" But already she'd relapsed into that sleep, that post-Sight trance of hers. By the troubled set of her features, by the hunch of her shoulders, by those tears that had fallen to chap her cheeks, I saw she'd learned a lesson; but so, too, had I.

. . . *Asmodei.* I heard the name long after she'd whispered it—it was as if it echoed through the room in which she lay—such that there was no denying what Leo had Seen and spoken:

Asmodei was to die within the year; . . . meaning, '44.

Chapter Thirty-two

For ye may all prophecy one by one, that all may learn, and all may be comforted.

—1 Corinthians 14:31

THOUGH ONLY A FEW YEARS HAVE PASSED SINCE THAT most immemorial year of 1844, it seems an eternity. Indeed, it may be an eternity *has* passed; for I have been dead several of those years. . . . My petite hostess here, however, is rather new to the Afterlife. She was quick to Ensilver and go, her soul being light and her earth's work done; but this body of hers goes about the lesser business of death *at length*, troubling my tale-telling efforts.

She has been dead for some hours, yes, but no one knows it, the ship's surgeon being rather simple and easily spooked. When warned of his approach by my companion (who raps thrice upon the wall of the adjoining cabin: the agreed-upon sign), I clamber back onto the bunk, just there, and cause to issue from this corpse noise enough to put the surgeon off. I twitch, too;

rather, *I cause* this child-case to twitch, and cause her eyes to roll and her lids to flutter. I can even summon the drum of a pulse, if need be; which mimicry sets the surgeon to doubting his third, steely, stethoscopic ear. For fuller, albeit indelicate effect, I let seep gases that hasten his departure. And depart he does, putting off the mourners-to-be with, "It shan't be . . . *it cannot be* but a few hours more." . . . Duplicitous of me, yes; but where would I be without this Missy, my amanuensis? And if I seem blasé as regards her body, it is because *I know what the body is.*

In many ways, she has proven a most amenable host. She is not stiffening as quickly as an older corpse might, though already I feel the rigor mortis descending—neck and shoulders stiffening—and this arm grows heavy, pulling this pen across the page as an ox does its plow. Nor does she tire, as a mortal might if asked to transcribe a tale of ten hours' duration. *Enfin,* she ought to serve me through to my story's end, as I need but a while longer to achieve *the present,* to tell how it is I, or rather we—my companion and I—have come to be here. And I will hasten, as the only thing worse than recollecting the events of '44 would be having to stall this story in order to seek another teller; yet I proceed *without ease;* for the memories of that year have long sat as if in a still, till now they have all but fermented, and are as strong as those too literal spirits that were the ruin of Asmodei.

Léopoldine and I wondered what use to make of *the truth* of Asmodei's imminent death. Surely, it would have come as no surprise to him; for *he sought it:* Leo Saw indications that Asmodei would die by his own hand. So: What point was there in telling him he'd soon succeed? None. Neither would he be dissuaded. This I knew. And so we began instead to wonder, and worry, what effect *the news* would have on Calixto—wise enough to be wary of the Sight, and inclined to put paid to all our efforts despite the profits they bore—and above all, Luc, who would try to save Asmodei, somehow.

As Leo said she would not desist in her efforts at Sighting—despite the lesson she'd learned, and no matter what Calixto might say—and as I'd no wish to find myself set betwixt she and Calixto on this question—for they often fought like . . . like what they were, I suppose: two people fearful of falling in love—we decided not to tell Calixto. Rather, Leo *convinced and cajoled* me not to tell. We did, however, tell Luc, eventually. And as for his attempting to save Asmodei, well . . .

He tried, yes, as I'd supposed he would; but there was naught could be done.

With our share of the salvage from the *Flying Cloud*, we four—Calixto, myself, and the twins—bought a large lot on Caroline Street, near Duval, and set about building the Witchery; but Asmodei, with his portion, bought *The Throne of the Goat*, and made of it his own little den of iniquity, within which he was, well, *iniquitous*, quite. He closed the groggery to all but those very few people he could suffer: seamen too old or inebriate to bore him with their sea tales; younger men whose criminal ardor amused him; and a few fallen, most *willful* whores whose services were on offer in a room behind the bar. At the Throne (as it was known), no one dared suggest that Asmodei had had enough to drink, ever—they'd have been banished or beaten, or both. And so he'd drink rum till he grew unsteady on his favored stool—the eponymous Throne, I suppose, he being the Goat upon it—and afterward stumble into the back room to sleep beneath his whores, as a trapper might his furs. Whether he sought solace in their . . . *charms,* such as they were, I cannot say; but I doubt it: All he wanted was to drink and sleep himself toward dreams of Sebastiana.

When Asmodei became inured to drink—too inefficient an inducer of dreams, too slow a soporific—he progressed unto opiates, the first of which he pilfered from the pharmacopoeia Leo had compiled, even though *narcomancy* held no allure for her at the time. Asmodei would lie in that back room of the Throne like some perversion of a Near Eastern pasha: pipe at his side—like an octopus it was, with arms enough for *all* to partake—and those whores at work around him. And when, predictably, opium lost *its* appeal, he progressed unto ether. Where he got this from, I have no idea; but by the time Léopoldine had divined his death, he'd gone from sitting at the bar before a saucer of the stuff—a saucer kept full by that barman whom both twins threatened at various times, but who had the protection of his patron—with a ragged, stained square of tanbark sail worn over his head like a hood, and weighted at the neck with a noose, lest any of that reeking solvent escape.

In the months to come, as he roasted himself on a spit of grief, Asmodei fell to drinking the ether. . . . He'd rinse his mouth with water, spit it out—spray it through his clenched teeth, in fact, or let it dribble down his ever-stubbled chin; whereupon he'd throw back just enough of the ether to cool his tongue and throat before drinking a whole glass of the stuff as if it were water. (This I saw him do, once, when I went to the Throne to dissuade him from his death-seeking habits, to try to talk him home. . . . All to no avail.) And then, as he reddened, as his laughter rang through the rotted bar, he'd swallow water enough to weight the ether, to keep it from evaporating in his esophagus before it could settle in his stomach and find its effect. This he'd repeat, all down the length of day and unto dreams.

In the last weeks of his life, Asmodei spoke hardly at all, and only to Luc (who now knew what his sister had Seen). Was this willfulness? Or had the ether scorched his throat? Regardless, Asmodei was beyond words, or nearly so; and what words he uttered came from him in a voice not his own: reed-thin, ruined. And when Luc was not at sea with Calixto, he kept watch over the older man as best he could—

and as best Asmodei allowed him to. Indeed, one of the reasons—*and only one,* as soon I'd discover to my chagrin—that Luc had taken to sleeping aboard the *Soror Mystica* even when she was in port was that her slip sat at the foot of Greene Street, quite near *The Throne of the Goat;* into which place he'd wander, as if for his amusement alone, taking a stool beside that man for whom, frankly, he'd an affinity I was neither able to share nor understand.

Finally, one night in late summer, Luc sought out Asmodei at the Throne, eager to share news he thought might amuse the man: Owing to a Sighting done, somehow, by Leo, Calixto had, two days prior, been declared wreck-master of the brig *La Maria;* and from the hold of that vessel—from the captain's quarters, in fact—Luc himself had salvaged a chest of French erotica. But Asmodei was not there. Neither was he at either of our homes: not the first, on Front Street; nor the one on Caroline, which was still but a one-story shell.

The hour now was small: one, two, perhaps three in the morning. The air was especially still, swamp-heavy, redolent of shore-rot and night-blooming cereus, the scent from which cacti so cloys at the nose as to make one *gag,* and *gladden* to learn that each of its few flowers is abloom but once a year. A full moon lit the empty streets, and by its light Luc sought out Asmodei. He found him on the shore, staring out over the Straits. Though he was moderately sober, still Asmodei mumbled at the moon, both where it hung overhead and where it shone upon the water as the ladder to the Summerland.

Whether the two spoke that night, I cannot say; but Luc would seem less than surprised when, some months later, in October, as an unforeseen gale blew in fast and the rest of us sought shelter, Asmodei sailed out to sea in a stolen sloop, never to return.

I imagine he, Asmodei, said his good-byes to both Sebastiana and his Lord B. that night. As for the rest of us, well, it was left for us to bid the man good-bye as best we knew how. . . . Luc, having hired a team of carpenters to dismantle, board by board, *The Throne of the Goat,* made a bonfire of it, and around this we stood one November night, staring into the flames; and when that fire had burned to naught, I, for my part, looked up to the night sky, to the moon, and swore to Sebastiana that I'd done all I could.

I will not say I loved, nor even much liked Asmodei; but still I felt his loss. In going, it seemed he took something of Sebastiana with him. And after his disappearance, his death, I grew lonely, to a degree I'd not known in years, not since quitting Cuba with Calixto and finding the family. This was owing to Asmodei's death, yes, in part, but also to . . .

Alors, would that I could give a good spin to Time on its axis and speed this story toward my death—it is *that,* after all, that I purposed to tell when I took this body over long hours ago—but I must first pen a few paragraphs more about the aforesaid loneliness and its *truer cause:* the ignominy of late '44.

By December of that year, having survived the October gale in which we lost not only Asmodei but also that house in which we'd lived since our arrival in Key West—it took on water up to its wainscoting, causing the floor to buckle and the wood of the walls to rot like meat set out beneath the sun—we were ready to move into the Caroline Street house, the Witchery; problem was, it was not ready for us.

It had been framed but only partially built before the storm; and so—blessedly—the winds blew through it. Now we began to build in earnest, and from the top down. That is, once the skeleton of it stood, we outfitted its tower and atelier first.

Léopoldine and I much enjoyed the planning of the top of the house, and the procuring of what we'd place therein; and so busy were we with this that we left the fuller construction of the lower two floors to Calixto and Luc; which charge they passed on to an able crew, well paid to complete the project at speed. These workmen were told two things:

One, that more than *the basics* were called for; by which we meant— and here let me say I'd feel shame still, were it possible, for acceding to the others' architectural wants, which so bespoke our being *nouveau riche*—a first floor featuring a double parlor opening off a foyer (marble-floored, *merci bien*) with a dining room opposite and kitchen-pantry combination sitting behind; also, there had to be an office, a billiards room (Calixto, Luc), and a library (me, admittedly). The second floor ought to comprise four bedroom suites.

Two: Said crewmen were told to spare no expense yet were warned (by Luc, by Leo) that every expense *would be watched;* and so glaziers came over from New Orleans, and masons came down from the North, as did boatloads of furniture ordered from Walter Corey's workshops in Portland, Maine; for I'd hoped—in vain— that by ordering from so far away we might stem a rising tide of jealousy evident amongst the islanders. Calixto even hired a mural-ist to adorn those walls Léopoldine opted not to cover in *papier peint;* and so it was we'd eventually dine in a room tricky with trompe l'oeil and telling, variously, the myths of the twins Artemis and Apollo (whose faces bore more than a passing resemblance to those of Leo and Luc), Poseidon (Cal), and Diana (for which I agreed to sit, reluctantly, having declined the twins' twinkle-eyed suggestion that I pose for either Hermes or Aphrodite, or both). It was all . . . *de trop,* truly.

. . . But latterly we'd struck upon a means of Sighting wrecks that seemed, indeed *was* foolproof; and we had only to refine it in the new witchery whilst on the floors below us men worked from dawn to dusk upon a mansion suited to our means; or rather, all we *supposed* we'd soon earn.

In those weeks between the hurricane rendering our former home inhabitable and the whole of the Witchery being completed, I took up residence in the tower. The others lived . . . elsewhere (more anon).

The tower was a squared, gabled affair through the *portes-fenêtres* of which one could access a sea widow's walk, though this latter feature came to be called, in our case, *The Ledge of Lucre*; for, in time, it would afford views of our warehouses, our ships, et cetera, all those trappings that betokened our success as wreckers. I set up a cot in the tower; and a humble, comfy little aerie it was, one I much preferred to that second-floor suite soon to be outfitted with a half-tester bed, bureaus of Brazilian rosewood, and rugs from some Glaswegian weaver, which last items Leo pushed upon me, opining that they were "oh, so plush *and seamless besides!*" Increasing the tower's appeal, I descended from it by spiral staircase to an atelier, a witchery that would have been the envy of any sister who saw it.

Again, having let myself be urged toward luxury by Léopoldine and Luc—who knew what it meant to go hungry; and whom, I reminded myself, *guiltily*, I'd sired only to learn a decade later that they'd been left to live alone in the catacombs of Rome—*enfin*, yes, guilty as I was, I acceded to certain . . . *indulgences*, let me say:

Luc, given to whimsy, had surprised me by buying from a photographer in New Orleans—" . . . and cheaply, too!" he enthused—a collection of glass plates, the after-product of portraits produced in his studio. These featured the faces of the dead; for yellow fever had raged there in that city of late, and the new art (or is it a science?) of Monsieur Daguerre took hold as photographs became the memento mori of choice amongst the many left to mourn. Said plates came from New Orleans with the abovementioned glazier, who no doubt proffered an opened palm upon being told his mission: Blindfolded, he was to be led through the witchery to the tower, where he was to replace random panes of glass with the photographic plates; so that in looking out over the island, to sea or sky, one found oneself gazing into, indeed *through* the faces of the nameless dead. Need I say this was a *most* eerie effect? Need I say, too, that it amused me no end, finding those faces as the sun or moon hit them just so? . . . I thought the idea inspired, and told Luc so.

Léopoldine, for her part, discovered she'd a penchant for silks and such; and it was as a result of this penchant—or rather the many, *many* purchases resulting from same—that I came upon a way for us to honor that oath we'd all sworn when first we'd decided to apply the Craft for financial gain. . . . Years earlier, whilst resident in Manhattan, I'd heard much talk about the brothers Tappan, Lewis and Arthur; who, with monies earned in the silk trade, had founded the American Antislavery Society (as well as the Magdalene Society for the relief of "penitent prostitutes," the establishment of which saw them derided by many working women of the Third and Fifth Wards, but not the Cyprians, nor I, now that I'd seen a lower breed of whore at work in the Throne). I wrote now to the Tappans—anonymously, of course—and solicited ways by which we might further the abolitionist cause (as well as that of said Magdalenes). Thusly did we begin funneling funds northward; as still we do, to this day. . . . And in time we had much, *much* money to funnel; such that great pains had to be taken to preserve our anonymity.

. . . *Enfin*, we had in the witchery proper all a sister could want; and though that room—the whole of the third floor, a pine-planked expanse broken only by four square supports—would come to contain all, *all and everything* requisite to the Craft, initially we tailored it to that means of Sight, as practiced by Leo alone, that soon had the *Soror Mystica* arriving first at every wreck of worth.

Axiomancy, it was; and in the witchery we worked it thusly:

Center-all, upon the floor, we'd had built, in brick, a broad and shallow pit. A six-foot circle this was, filled with cinders rendered more . . . *potent* by the addition of human remains (procured, more easily than the living would like to know, by Calixto and Luc—in league with Eugénie—on their trips to New Orleans). Onto the piney floor surrounding this pit—in a design seeming half bull's-eye, half globe—Luc copied a chart of the keys till the whole of the floor was covered, and in order to Sight we had to shove aside our worktables and other furnishings. This we did every second month—less frequently than the twins would have liked; but upon this I insisted, lest we Sight and salvage so many wrecks as to give rise to suspicion. Already there was envy; add to that suspicion and . . . Suffice to say: I'd not risk ruin; for tales found their way back to us, tales telling of the good that came of our funneled funds.

The floor itself, then, was a chart, showing not only the reef but all the keys and lesser features of the wreckers' water-world. The waters themselves were painted in shades of blue corresponding to soundings taken therein; though, I must add, our floor chart was only as accurate as its sources—old Spanish and British charts, imperfect in some particulars, erroneous in others; and though on one or two occasions this caused our Sightings to err, it was those same charts that caused the ships to wreck: *a wash*, in other words. A shame it is, though, that more than a quarter century after Florida fell into American hands, its waters remain so poorly charted. *Hélas*, as Leo is wont to say: "Others' pity, our profit." . . . *Enfin*, the whole of the floor was both accurate (enough) and artful, Luc showing himself as skilled

with paints as he was with pens, the latter attested to by the many
ledgers he kept, and in which he accounted for *every penny* we earned
and spent.

It was Luc, too, who was responsible for burning those fires that
heated the ash to the requisite temperature: It had to be warm, not
hot, at the hour of the Sighting. And at the appointed hour—as determined by Léopoldine, who now charted the stars with such delicacy she was able to determine not only the day, but the hour most
propitious to Sight—we'd all four gather in the witchery to watch her
balance an ax on end in the pit, mounding the ashes at its base tightly
enough to support it but loosely enough to allow it to pivot, as does
the arm of a compass. And pivot the ax head would, though not before Leo *persuaded* it with great patience—the ax itself is wont to tip—
and no small amount of spellwork. If a worthy wreck were
imminent—and we ensured a wreck's worth by burying gold coins in
the ash, so as *to witness* the Work—then slowly, slowly, almost imper-
ceptibly, the ax head would turn toward its location. The wreck being
thus *rudely sited,* we'd progress from the macro- to the microcosm: We'd
unfurl actual charts of the specified area on a tabletop, refining the
wreck's location by either *acultomancy:*

Placing twenty-one needles in a glass dish set atop the chart, slowly
we'd pour water (rainwater; *never* gathered in tin) over these to see if a
majority turned toward the same spot; or, failing this, *sideromancy:*

Whereby we'd read, similarly, the movement of straws placed upon
a red-hot pallet of iron (nota bene: the convex side of a shovel works
well).

Thusly did we arrive at the near-exact coordinates of wrecks-to-
come; and when Leo—with further recourse to her star charts—
discerned the likely date of said wreck, Calixto had only to see to it
that the *Soror Mystica* was nearer the site than any other ship.

Et voilà, so it was that we became rich. Very.

———————————— ✳ ————————————

———————

Hélas, before we were able to refine such Sight, and whilst still the Witchery itself was being built and I alone resided in its tower—like that storybook crone it would soon seem I'd become—the twins took up residence aboard the *Soror Mystica*.

And one night, determining to venture out, as I so rarely did—I drew stares, and well-meaning inquiries regarding my health; for, as the logical result of loss of appetite, I'd grown quite thin, which state was only heightened by my pallor and hair that had grown so silver I had to hide its night sheen beneath a broad-brimmed hat—I found myself headed down Caroline Street, toward the schooner in her slip.

It was midnight, surely; but into a panier I'd placed the makings of a snack: wine, some chocolates, fruits, and whatnot. I'd surprise *my three*, as I thought of them still.

Chapter Thirty-three

> . . . O, most wicked speed, to post
> With such dexterity to incestuous sheets!
> It is not nor it cannot come to good:
> But break, my heart, for I must hold my tongue.
> —SHAKESPEARE, *Hamlet*

I'D COME ABOARD THE *Mystica* QUIETLY, *so quietly* I'D LATER wonder if I hadn't half expected to find what I found, see what I saw; . . . or leastways some variation thereof.

And let this suffice on the topic of what I found, saw, variations thereof, et cetera: *It was a sight I never thought I'd see.*

. . . As for Sight of the other sort, yes, the irony is not lost upon me: I suppose I might have Sighted . . . this . . . them . . . *my three;* but it is a truism of the Sight that a sister most often Sees only what she looks for. And, as said, I'd never even have *thought* to See . . . this:

There they lay, asleep, the twins on either side of Calixto. It was dark in the captain's cabin, but not dark enough: By the greasy, glaring, golden light of an oil lamp, hanging high on its hook, I saw that they dozed in . . . in *a most intimate pose.*

Luc's long, lightly haired legs extended beneath a throw of sapphire hue, tangled at his knees as if placed there for effect by Titian or Tiepolo; and when I saw the scar atop his left foot—his nickname of Lord B. had long outlived his limp, but had disappeared with Asmodei—I had this thought, plain as if I heard the words spoken aloud: *He is grown.*

Of course, if asked, I'd have said I knew this, certainly: He was sixteen, perhaps seventeen, quite independent, really, with money and a mind all his own. Indeed, he was quite like Calixto had been when first I'd met *him:* similar in both age and aspect, though somewhat bolder. *He is grown.* And though I cannot say that I ever really parented the boy (even less so his sister)—truth be told, it was Sebastiana and even Asmodei who'd done more of that—still it stunned me to see, *so evidently,* that the boy had become a man. *He is grown.* And in the seven-some years since we'd met, what *had* my relationship been to the twins? Not parental, no, not quite. Sibling-like? Hardly; for that they *had* each other, as it were. Custodial, then? No, much more than that. *Alors,* no one word is sufficient; for I was what I was: a witch who'd sired twins and found them only after ten hard years had passed. And now here was the boy, *grown.* About to be *gone.* . . . *Enfin,* that's what the healed scar told me as I stood there at the cabin door, staring, stupidly, as yet unseen: It spoke to me somehow of the end of family, and that thought echoed as loneliness. Mine. Such that tears welled, very much against my will.

Shakily, I reached for a seat, a chair at the table still littered from their feast; and in so doing, I sent a bottle of wine onto its side. Empty, it rolled as bottles will on belayed boats: slowly, yet somehow more loudly than on land. Finally, it fell. The bottle broke. . . . And *my three* awoke.

They started. They sat up fast. Calixto clasped to his crotch more than his share of the sapphire throw, such that *now* Luc woke, saw me, and muttered a most emphatic *"Merde."* Whilst Cal and Luc tugged at opposing ends of the throw, seeking cover, Léopoldine sat there unsheathed—beautiful, shoulders back and breasts forward. And though it may seem I describe *a defiant stance*, it was not that at all; but neither was she shamed in any way. Simply put, *Léopoldine refused shame.* She always had. This I'd long admired in the witch; . . . though maybe not so much then, truth to tell.

Silence ensued. Silence endured. And all the while I cried.

Their assumption—a mistake, hastily made—was that I cried owing to what I'd witnessed. Not so. Rather, not wholly.

True: Though I'd long ago locked away my love (unrequited) for Calixto, it did not . . . *please me* to see him so. No. To say otherwise would be to lie. Yet my displeasure—the situation warrants a better word, but none comes— . . . my displeasure, I say, was short-lived, and ceded not to anger but understanding; for much came clear, then and there:

Léopoldine's determined Sighting of wrecks for Cal to chase; her coyness whenever our captain came ashore; the excess of *parfum* and maquillage she applied on those same occasions; and, of course, *the fact*—how had I not seen it as such?—that when the two were not flirting they fought, those two actions comprising the two sides of that most common of coins: *Love,* incipient. . . . It was then I wondered if I'd seen this all aborning? Had I chosen to turn from their attraction, dismiss it as *less than mutual,* a girlish crush? I had, and understandably so.

But what of Calixto's part in all this?

We'd all supposed Calixto preferred the *company and comforts* of men. This we'd never discussed amongst ourselves, of course; though Asmodei had on occasion called to our attention—and Calixto's, too—

the composition of the *Soror Mystica*'s crew. Whereupon Calixto would laugh, and wonder aloud what captain would not choose as handsome a crew as he could corral? And this Calixto did; the more so once Leo's Sightings obviated, somewhat, his need for the ablest of sailors. He had the pick of the portside litter, too, as it were. Everyone wanted to crew for us: We were successful, yes, and fair, but we paid a wage as well, whereas other crews were paid only their share of a salvage, and *no salvage, no share*. Indeed, when recruiting, Calixto would send the prettiest of petitioners to the front of the line, and on a line of another sort Luc would bid them sign.

So: That Calixto would ally himself to Luc surprised me less than that he'd do so with Léopoldine.

As for Léopoldine and Luc, what's to say? Taboos interest me even less than laws—all laws, that is, save *ours*, sister; which is this: *If it harm none, do what you will.*

. . . *Enfin*, theirs is a trinity that endures to this day; and so long as love lay as its base, *my three* will hear naught but blessings from me.

Granted: I was rather less resolute on the night in question. Indeed, I could not stop crying. My breathing was shallow, stertorous: I sputtered like a coal-choked engine; for the shock ceded in turn to surprise, followed by confusion, clarity (to a degree), and finally fear: fear of that loneliness I knew too well, and wanted no more of.

Of course, this I could not articulate, not then. Thusly was I subjected to apologies from *my three*, who came to me on their knees, and cried at my side for fear they'd hurt me. And though I was hurt, it's true, previously I'd have been devastated by such a . . . *development* as this.

Understand: The scene onto which I'd stumbled stunned me to tears, yes, and even tried my temper somewhat; but—blessed be—I neither did nor said anything I had later to regret or rescind. Simply, I quit the *Soror Mystica* once I could and, wine bottle in hand, walked the streets *through the dead vast and middle of the night;* which last bit comes from *Hamlet,* such that I am reminded that I retired to the tower at dawn, carrying thence naught but the Bard and letting it be known (by note) that I was not to be disturbed. For two full days I read; or rather, *re*read my preferred plays and poems, setting Shakespeare aside only to wonder, thusly:

What else *could* have become of *my three,* the twins being Shadow-born and Calixto an initiate? Wasn't it I who caused them to recourse to one another? It was, surely; though I in no way blamed myself for the nature of their bond, which seemed to me rather . . . *bold,* and somewhat worrisome. Less so, it's true, when they came to me in the tower on the third day, and we all four spoke again. They told me of a plan of six months' standing: Léopoldine and Calixto were to marry; out of love, yes, but also to quiet certain rumors that had arisen amongst the wreckers. This Luc approved—indeed, it had been his idea; for it would change the present arrangement but publicly. "So be it," said I, with a shrug and a smile I had somewhat to force, it's true.

Finally, the three, *my three,* exchanged a look; whereupon the men—being blond—flushed, and Leo's Eye turned, such that I feared I'd yet to hear the worst or weirdest of what they had to say. So it was with relief I heard them ask—it was Leo who spoke—if they were all still welcome to live in the Witchery. To this I readily assented, of course.

A toast was made.

And then I sent them all away; for still I was sadder than they knew. Sadder than *I* knew, in fact.

There was yet much work to be done if the Witchery were to be *perfectly* habitable upon the trio's return from Port-au-Prince, to which they'd sailed on a honeymoon of sorts. I found distraction in this work, which lasted many weeks longer than my discomfit did.

The wedding itself had been as small as we could keep it. No easy feat, this; for our wealth was ever more evident, and certain expectations had had to be met, lest our partners sour and business be compromised. Worst of all was learning, in the course of said ceremony and the requisite reception—held aboard the *Soror Mystica*, where all dined on the food of Euphemia and her Simon—that our townsmen had long since taken Asmodei for my (widowed) father (who had lost his wife/my mother in the Indian Key massacre), the twins for my children, and Calixto for a cousin of theirs. And it seemed stories abounded as to how my husband had met his end. The twins, of course, upped the ante on the day in question, and circulated slyly contradictory tales of how my late husband, their unfortunate and heroic father—whom they dubbed "the Colonel," that being the American appellation for all *men of merit*—had lost his life: fighting either the Greeks, the Turks, or the red tribes of Canada, depending. Thusly did I assume the status of widow—which suited me well, I suppose.

. . . *Enfin*, off *my three* sailed, finally; and I took charge of finishing the Witchery. Suddenly I was more *of the world* than ever I'd been before.

Upon their return, Léopoldine worked in the witchery, whilst her husbands, or brothers, or what you will, lay at anchor in the Straits, awaiting word of an imminent wreck. Meanwhile, with the larger Witchery nearly done, I attended to all manner of details, summoning architects and artisans of sundry skills. My plan was to achieve what it is we have, presently: an architectural hodgepodge that stirs no one's interest. That draws no one to our door. That elicits only derision from those *pretending* to taste.

. . . *Enfin*, the whole of the Witchery—from its whitewashed first floor up to its gray-painted second story and the black tower beyond—

⁂

resembles nothing so much as a chthonic wedding cake, the icing of which has begun to melt from too close proximity to the fires of Hell. . . . Just as I'd wished.

You see, I'd thought to build *an off-putting house,* as we of the Shadows want no strangers at our door, *merci bien*—and though Key West had grown, grotesquely so, since our arrival, and there were by then some *several thousand strangers* in residence upon the isle, this had its benefits, too, the primary one being that, amongst so many strangers, fewer could rightfully impose upon us as *neighbors*— . . . but, of course, the interior of the house was exquisite. That is, all of it save those few areas said strangers were most likely to see: the foyer, and the room to which it led, as directly as a chute to a shambles: the office.

The foyer I floored in marble the color of a streambed run dry. Its walls were unadorned, and left unlit. It was, in a word, *unwelcoming.* From a circular rod of brass affixed to the plaster ceiling there depended heavy-grade drapes of black damask, hung so as to stifle both the eye and step of anyone expressing an interest in the home's interior. Once inside the foyer, one's options were few: suffocate, or step to the right, into the office.

In the office, we had sometimes to suffer strangers, yes. We were too rich to keep *all the world* at bay, and owing to the exigencies of our business, well . . . Still, and by design (mine), the office was a place to which only the most macabre of men ever sought to return.

I saw to strangers' discomfort by ordering half-backed, armless, and cushionless chairs from the above-mentioned Mr. Corey, of Portland. Two of these—the legs of which I sawed down myself, so as to further unsteady our visitors—I placed before a desk of black walnut so vast one might have shouted across the Straits to equal effect. And if a stranger sought to tarry, well, down would come the skull.

Typically, Yorick—as the skull was called—was twinned to a brass cleat, and he and another object of suitable weight kept upright a row of books pertaining to maritime law; but when we'd reason to expect that someone would linger overlong, we'd take the skull down from its shelf and set it at the fore of the desk. Once, when a rival salvor began to bother Calixto, daring to turn his talk toward blackmail, he, Cal, sought advice of the skull, addressing it as *Grandfather*; whereupon the wrecker fled. Other curiosities—such as our dear Marian—furthered our cause of *unfriendliness* as well.

A most impressive specimen Marian was, too, or rather *is*; for she has endured since the day she came to us in a glass-fronted coffin of camphor wood, not so much salvaged as bought by Calixto off a salvor who'd "found" her in Macao.

Upon her red velvet, she lies to a length of nearly four feet. Hair that once was red, surely, spills from her shrunken head down over her shoulders, shoulders from which there depend two arms that cross over her chest, hands clasped, heart-high, as if in prayer; or perhaps to hide her withered paps. Prayerful, too, is her face—hence her name, and hence the Marian-blue veil beneath which we shield our Sea Virgin from the sunlight—though its features are less distinct than those of her body, the skin of which seems smoked, or salted, or otherwise preserved, whilst her scales yet shimmer.

They start small, the scales do, at about the height of her hips; from there they progress downward, diamantine, growing in size as they near the tip of her upturned tail. . . . No, no, no: our Marian is not a *real* mermaid. Leastways I don't think she is; but I cannot say for certain, as her sale was contingent upon Calixto's not lifting her from her casket, and neither have we done so since. To do so, perhaps, would be to discover the handiwork of some Eastern surgeon, who, with stitches and other taxidermic trickery, aligned two disparate species. But why ever would we disturb her? To learn her secrets, and thereby satisfy ourselves? . . . *Jamais!* To do so would be . . . dumb. And disrespectful.

And we *greatly* respect our Marian. So much so that we sometimes trundle her out from the office corner she inhabits, turn her toward the aforesaid chairs, and raise her veil so as to introduce her to our strangers. . . . And there, by the grace of *our* goddess, they go—those men who linger, those strangers we cannot otherwise shake.

So it was I put Marian to purpose on the unfortunate day I looked down from the tower, through the sun-shimmering portraits of our plaguers, to see the *Soror Mystica* arrive in port. Typically, this was occasion for celebration; but as I watched this day, I saw Calixto bound off her bow, with Luc following fast. Strange. *Most* strange: Calixto, as captain, was never first to quit the *Soror Mystica*.

I took up our spyglass, fixed it to my eye, and saw three black-clothed types standing in attendance upon the dock. These *crows* Cal and Luc approached; and none too pleased was I to see all five set off up Caroline Street, toward home, toward the Witchery, with something of a crowd coming behind.

I called down to Léopoldine, at work in the witchery. "No, none," said she when I asked if she had Seen any reason for such a parade as this. "I sent them to Sombrero Shoal," and here she took the spyglass from her Eye, turned to me, and added, ". . . business as usual, by my Sight."

"We'd best go down," said I, and we did.

When the party—composed of Calixto, Luc, and the black-clad men; and *not* that mob, most of whose members settled, rather impertinently, thought I, upon the wide steps of our stoop— . . . when the party came into the foyer, and into the office, it was to find we three, Léopoldine, myself, and Marian, turned toward the door.

"Gentlemen," said I, whereupon half bows were made and hats doffed, "please, won't you take a seat?" Two of them did; and whilst they sought an equilibrium they'd never achieve, the third man took two steps back from Marian, and looked to me. He'd have spoken, surely, but his mouth was fixed: a rictus. I smiled in response, nothing more; but then, shoving the skull aside, I settled my skirted hip onto the corner of the desk, arched an eyebrow high above the brim of my blue spectacles, and tacitly commanded Calixto to:

Speak.

 # Chapter Thirty-four

I fear I am becoming a god.
—VESPASIAN

Not only had we refined the means by which we Sighted wrecks, but we'd also been able to assess—by means of prevision practiced by Léopoldine, and concerning, largely, her star charts—*the status* of a wreck; by which I mean its . . . worrisomeness. Was it to be safely salvaged? Would it be worth the pains taken? And thusly we'd steered clear (literally) of dangerous or *controversial cargo*. Until the day in question.

"*Slaves*, did you say?" I asked this as I sat upon the corner of the desk, fingering the eye sockets of Yorick's skull so as to further discomfit all three strangers and distract the one who stood, and seemed to sway; for, though at first I'd thought Marian had had her effect on the man, I saw now that he was attempting to see *behind* my blue lenses, to my turned eyes. Had I let slip my spectacles earlier, so low onto my nose as to show my Eye? So sloppy of me . . . Regardless. Let the man see what he might with those tiny black eyes of his, eyes set in the flesh of his face as cloves are set in ham. We'd more pressing concerns at the moment; for one of the seated strangers, he with a parson's pursed lips, parted said lips to say:

"Yes, madame: *slaves.*"

"I see," said I, though I did not: It'd be some while before the whole of the tale were told, and I'd know what had transpired at sea. . . . Share in my then predicament, my puzzlement, a moment more, sister; for requisite to the telling of *that* tale is this bit of background:

The year before—and so I return, once more, to '44—there'd been a scandal at sea, the percussive effects of which were resounding still, through the Gulf ports as well as all the seaboard states. I refer to the fate of one Jonathan Walker, *Slave Stealer;* whose plight has been penned by the poet Mr. Greenleaf Whittier. Indeed, "The Man with the Branded Hand" had appeared, that very week, in the pages of our own *Gazette.* Begging pardon of the poet, I forthwith, and humbly, present the same story as prose:

On a July morn of that fateful year—and therefore coincident with Asmodei's long demise, though still some months prior to his death—a rival of ours, R.R., a wrecking captain whom I will not deign to name—though, should a reader familiar with either *this tale* or *those times* hazard that said initials stand for Richard Roberts, she would be right— . . . *enfin,* a certain wrecking captain sailed from Key West aboard his *Eliza Catherine,* a sloop of some eighty-odd tons. It was to be business as usual; and so it was, until, up-reef, his lookout espied a much smaller sloop. Thinking there was something strange in the sloop's tack, R.R. ordered her overtaken. It seemed the sloop's captain might be in need of assistance. . . . Or so said R.R. at trial, though in truth that old sea hound gave chase only after sniffing the scent of a Reward on the wind.

Roberts was right: In the sloop were seven black men and one white: Jonathan Walker.

Walker had taken seven slaves aboard his sloop in Pensacola—*to smuggle* seems the Southern verb of equivalence—and set out for the Bahamas, for freedom. This he did for no remuneration, for no reason other than *right*.

Oh, but R.R., whom already we hated nearly to the point of having hexed him—indeed, had I left it to Léopoldine, he'd be *sowing his seed* without effect; for, one night, when she'd heard Calixto complain of the rival captain, she'd set out for his house on Eaton Street, and there I'd found her, just in time, standing beneath a half moon and tying knots in a five-inch length of string— . . . *alors*, he, R.R., hauled the slaves and Walker to Key West, where they sat in the jail near Whitehead's Point before being transported back to Pensacola. There the slaves were treated in a manner meriting no words, whilst Walker was tried, convicted—in a trice, and upon Robert's testimony—and sentenced to be fined, pilloried, and branded upon the hand: *SS*.

Shamefully, Jonathan Walker sat in jail a full year more after the enacting of said sentence. And the shame is mine as well as all the world's; for though I was distracted, it is true—what with Asmodei fading, our home flooding, *my three* . . . frolicking—still I ought to have paid greater heed to Walker's plight; and paid, too, sooner than I did, those fines and court costs for nonpayment of which he was being held.

. . . Those men, Walker and Roberts both, may have decided my fate that day they met at sea; for whilst Walker further opened my eyes and purse to the abolitionists then at work in the North, Roberts, in his turn, tasked me toward his own ruin; and so it is that we, *la famille*, thereafter took *particular* pleasure in Sighting and salvaging wrecks which otherwise would have been his, the awards from which we have applied to the aid of bondsmen such as the seven he plucked from the sea when they were halfway to the Bahamas, and halfway free.

. . . So it was that when I said, "Slaves . . . ?" it was as though I'd lit a fuse, one that snaked around us upon the office floor. Such was the tenor of the times—worse now, and worsening still—in which Calixto, Luc, and the crew of the *Soror Mystica* salvaged the *Cimbrus*— out of New Orleans, and bound for Baltimore—near Sombrero Shoal, finding in its hold the following:

One thousand bales of cotton, most of which were waterlogged beyond worth, but some three hundred of which, after being weighed and marked at the Key West customs house, would go to a Boston trader for two dollars per bale;

Barreled corn that fast began to ferment, such that soon the fumes seeping from between the staves blinded the salvors, and Calixto ordered the *Cimbrus* fired down to her waterline so as to add both light and breathable air to the salvors' efforts;

And two slaves.

It was Luc who heard, found, and freed the slaves, diving into a hold that was half flood, half flame, whilst the *Cimbrus's* captain and supercargo, both men Louisiana-born, stood upon the deck of the *Mystica* bemoaning the loss of their cotton and corn, having either forgotten or forsaken the slaves in their charge.

Calixto sent word of the wreck and its cargo back to the admiralty court via one of the schooner's quarter boats; and so it was that— unbeknownst to Leo and me—already the wreckers were abuzz when the *Soror Mystica* returned to her slip; for Calixto had refused to lay claim to the slaves as cargo.

Thusly did the three *crows* in question—seated before me were a clerk of the court and the captain of the *Cimbrus,* whilst standing, nay, *swaying* was the supercargo, who'd have spoken on behalf of the ship's owner if he'd been able to speak at all— . . . thusly did those three men come to the Witchery, and into our office, to impress upon us the importance of our treating the slaves as cargo—*not* passengers; which claim had been Luc's idea as he sought to spare us proceedings too base (and too public) to partake of. Further, the men insisted we *dispose* of the slaves as later we would the bales of cotton, as we would *any other commodity*. Of course, I—who had to be consulted, as titular Head of House—backed Calixto on his anticlaim; whereupon the matter most unfortunately proceeded to court.

. . . When, on occasion, I felt guilty over the witchly way we built our wealth, I had only to remind myself of the way other wreckers did the same. *Bribery*, in sum.

And so it was that certain proponents of slavery influenced the outcome of the ensuing trial; for the judge found *in our favor*, this despite our waiving all claims to salvage, and ordered the slaves' owner— who'd broken none of the Laws of Man; for, though the importation of slaves into these rapidly *dis*uniting States has been outlawed since 1807, still the interstate trade is legal—to pay us one-third of the assessed value of the two bondsmen; which assessment was conducted, showily, shamefully, in open court at a trial the true topic of which was neither justice, nor property rights, nor shares of salvage, but rather *slavery*; and, further, the status of slaves as cargo and nothing more, not then, not ever.

Thusly were we forcibly awarded six hundred dollars' worth of Boston-bound cotton and five hundred dollars' worth of slave: Geronimo and Peter, by name. Worse, we were refused when we offered money equal to twice the slaves' assessed worth in attempting to secure their freedom. . . . By trial's end, we'd had to accept the award from the slaves' owner, and Geronimo and Peter had to go back to Pensacola, back into bondage. So spake the Law.

. . . We returned to the Witchery defeated; but, having banked our unwanted award, we all determined to Sight and salvage, with increased intent, as many wrecks of worth as we could. Eight months and five wrecks later, we'd amassed monies totaling many times the amount of the award, a sum so large, in fact, there was but one way *to ensure* its safe deposit in the coffers of our chosen cause: We'd have to sail it northward ourselves.

I sent the trinity in the *Soror Mystica*.

I watched from the tower that early morning they set out at the first of the ebb, with a fair wind at their backs. Calixto waved as best he could whilst working the ship's wheel. Luc climbed the ratlines to the crosstrees, as if to afford himself a better view of the Witchery, of its tower, of me. Léopoldine, standing astern, had in hand a spyglass to match mine, and so she saw me where I stood, waving, worrying that she'd not taken the time to Sight the *Soror Mystica*'s safe return.

"Don't worry so," she'd chided me the night prior, when I went to her in the witchery and asked what she'd Seen of their trip. "Nothing," said she, when pressed. And when pressed further still, Léopoldine reminded me that she'd not gone to sea in some time, and had never been to Man-hattan, and . . . *Bref*, she sought an adventure the outcome of which was uncertain. "For once," said she, smiling, "you and Sebastiana were right—the Sight can sometimes be . . . burdensome."

"*Now* you realize this, when all I ask is that you Sight the *Mystica*'s safe return, and . . . and assure me you three will be aboard?"

"Of course we'll be aboard, silly," said she. "But if it'll put you at ease . . ."

"I'd do it myself," said I, "if I'd any true talent for Sight."

"But you do," said she, "you do!"

✻

"Me? *Mais non!* It's you who has that gift. . . . What do I see but the too busy dead? That plus a nickel will buy you five cents' worth of candy, *chérie.*"

In truth, I was torn: As much as I'd have liked to know they'd all be safe at sea, and all return to me, to the Witchery—*après tout,* we'd not been apart much since finding one another on Indian Key, seven, eight years prior, and they were all I had—Léopoldine had been longer and longer in recovering from her recent Sightings, and I'd not have asked her for another. She was worn, and needed to go away for a while. . . . She, in her turn, worried about me:

Taking my pale, *horribly* pale hands in hers, she sought from me a promise: "Promise," said she, "that you will eat. Simon sails with us, but Euphemia is staying to cook for you, to care—"

"Oh, now, I don't need anyone to care for me."

"Still, she will be in their cottage on Whitehead Street, and will bring you meals straight from her stove. Promise me you'll eat them. Will you?"

". . . Promise or eat?"

"Both!" Whereupon our converse fast devolved to turned Eyes, tears, and a hug.

I never did promise, and so it can't be said I lied; for I didn't eat, couldn't eat, and hadn't eaten in some time. Food on my tongue— even Euphemia's food—was tasteless, and lay there like weights on a scale. When I chewed, my teeth, upper and lower, met as if they were metal, and the contact chilled me. To swallow was worse; and therefore— pardon my precision—I hardly ever shat. Worst of all, and so strange a habit that I came to consider it a vice, and did it only in secret, was this: When hungry—though it was not hunger at all, of course, but something . . . else—I craved but one thing: coinage, in gold; and these I carried, slipping them from the pockets of my skirt onto my tongue and sucking at them as if they were lozenges. . . . That oddest of hungers sated, I was left to wonder, yet again, what Queverdo Brù had done to me.

The alchemist's work had been slow to find its effect—slow, but steady. At first I'd thought my symptoms—the diminishing of appetite till finally I had none at all, and subsequently grew thin, skeletally so; the pallor of skin that the sun had come to shun; and the change in hair color, from blond to . . . *bright*, as if I'd locks of silver—bespoke the Coming of the Blood; but by the end of '45, I'd come to believe that it wasn't the Blood at all. It was Brù.

And owing to his alchemical work, I'd weakened, too; though still I might have sailed northward with the trinity, had it not been for that damnable trial and its most deleterious effect on my person.

My presence had been court-ordered, and I'd suffered terribly when made to testify. To the wreckers, I was mastermind of the island's most successful crew—*crews*, in point of fact; for we'd recently bought and launched a second, smaller schooner, the *Hecate*, as well as a ten-ton sloop we christened *Persephone*, both of whose crews, of course, sailed without benefit of the Sight, as their success (or lack thereof) was intended to balance the bolder work of the *Soror Mystica*. To those standing in countersuit to us, I was an agitator of the worst, most *Northern* sort—*en bref*, an abolitionist—and foreign-born to boot. And to all concerned, I was a woman. (*If only they knew* . . . said I to myself, time and again, *if only they knew* . . .)

It was at trial that once again I saw myself in the world's mirror. For a long while I'd only been in the presence of *my three*, or others somehow in my employ (the latter quieted by cash). But now I had again to suffer strangers, at trial and even en route:

One day, as I walked to court carrying both that parasol that I could not go without and my walking stick of curved birch, needed to poke back those many dogs somehow drawn to me, I heard the whispers, saw the scorn, and even felt it when, that day, a piece of slate came hurtling toward me and tore the sleeve of my dress. He who'd hurled it was a child, or was then; he's since grown to young manhood, and is known about town as Cavity, owing to his constant complaint, which no practitioners, no pliers, no opiates, have been able to relieve him of, and which Léopoldine laid upon him that very day, throwing her hex as fast as he'd thrown the slate whilst there I stood, a fool, atremble, worrying about the propriety of going before the judge in a dress less than perfect and seeking to soothe myself with a bit of fast-returning Bible: *Jesus, passing through the midst of them, went his way.* . . . Not that I mean to make comparisons, mind; but the passage did come back to me then and by its light I walked on, straight-shouldered, to court.

Oh, but after the trial, I retired to the Witchery. Nay, more truthful to say *I retreated to it.*

And there I remained. I could be found in the tower, typically, reading whilst the others worked at our wealth. Such was my pose when one day Leo called up to say that a letter had arrived from New Orleans, from Eugénie. . . . Its contents, let me say, were far from salutary:

She, my dear Eugénie—whom, inexcusably, I'd not seen since the dissolution of Cyprian House, though there'd been plans made and she'd become both friend and treasured auntie to the twins, and Calixto, too— . . . my dear Eugénie had begun to Bleed; so badly that she'd not bothered to cipher those ten lines in which she bade me good-bye and, *and* told me that finally she'd had word of the Duchess. She, too, it seemed, had begun to sense her Red End and had written to Eugénie so as to bequeath to me, by way of my sister, those many *Books of Shadows* the Duchess had crated and carried from Gotham. This bequest Eugénie had arranged: Three boxes—carpentered for the purpose, each big enough "to stow a sow," wrote she—were set to ship. . . . Eugénie. *La pauvre.* In a postscript she cursed Marie Laveau, most bitterly, and blamed that *voodienne* for somehow bringing on her Blood.

It was those *Books of Shadows* to which I turned whilst the trinity was away. Indeed, here let me quote Edgar Poe—that ghoul-haunted poet who so bedeviled my days when first I arrived in Richmond—to say:

> *Eagerly I wished the morrow; —vainly I had sought to borrow*
> *From my books surcease of sorrow—*

. . . A bit singsongish, that, and not his best effort; but nevertheless . . .

Enfin, some of said Books I'd read before, of course; others not; and still others the Duchess had collected in California, where she lived in late years, and where, for all I know, she died.

I had the crates—the interiors of which displayed shelves hewn of Brazilian rosewood, and red leather strapping by which to secure the Books—carried as far as our parlor. From there I carried them to the tower, two, three, or four at a time. There I stacked them, in order of interest. Those written in languages I read neither with ease (such as Russian), nor pleasure (German), I let lie; those in French rose to the fore, and I pored over each of those first in the hope that upon the turned pages I'd see Sebastiana's name (I never did). The others I read at hazard, with naught but a simple geographical bias: those of Western origin I read before those of Eastern, Northern before Southern.

And one day, when the Witchery had been too quiet too long, I set aside the Book I'd been reading—and in which I'd been in the pyramidal lair of some Peruvian sister—to take up some Shakespeare, as if to cleanse my palate of the Craft. Some while later, larking, I heard myself mutter a spell, and letting the much-thumbed book fall open at will, I Sighted with a bit of *bibliomancy*. Eyes closed, I poked at a page of *Twelfth Night*; whereon I read:

Journeys end in lovers meeting,
Every wise man's son doth know.

. . . But, thinking nothing of this at the time—indeed, Time and
Léopoldine, both, had shown that I had little talent for Sight—I
sighed, set the Bard aside, poured myself some lightly bewitched wine,
and went back to Peru.

 *Chapter Thirty-five*

If after every tempest come such calms,
May the winds blow till they have waken'd death!
—SHAKESPEARE, **Othello**

*I*T MAY BE SUPPOSED BY A SISTER FAMILIAR WITH NEITHER
the Sight nor the sea that the *Soror Mystica* would sail on
and on, and on. And why not? The supposition would
seem a safe one. She'd been sturdily built and was a
beauty, with her breadth of beam, and the rightness of
her waterlines, and the neatness of her navy-painted
sides, and the smoothness of her well-greased masts,
and the spiderish symmetry of her rigging, and the gen-
erous spread of her tanbark sails, and, above all, the
safety of that shallow draft that allowed her to sidle up
so elegantly to vessels that had wrecked in shoal water.
A beauty, indeed; and the envy of the Straits. And well
she *might* have sailed on and on, and on—some
schooners do, for thirty, forty, fifty years or more—if
only we hadn't taxed her so. And well we *might* have Seen
her demise, if only Léopoldine had looked.

Of course we *did* tax her, and Leo *didn't* look; . . . but truly, no one is to blame for the *Mystica's* later fate:

Léopoldine chose not to Look: a witch's prerogative, as the Sight is no easier to navigate than the sea. As for Calixto and Luc, well, a ship as *right* as the *Soror Mystica* all but begs to be used, to be let to run like a filly o'er the field of the sea.

It was that shallowness of draft that *most* made her what she was— a wrecker, nay, *the* wrecker; and never had this been more evident than in the months prior to the trinity's departure for Man-hattan, when we'd Sighted and salvaged those five wrecks that settled our wealth and all but sank our ship.

It was the salvage of the *Sofia*, off the Great Conch Reef, that did the greatest damage. The *Sofia* was the last wreck we Sighted before going to Gotham; and though Calixto was wreck-master, of course, he'd accepted the suit of four other sloops. So it was that forty-one wreckers assisted our tired, *very* tried crew of eight; and for twenty-odd hours they all earned their shares ($125 per) by off-loading (with due care) kegs of gunpowder. Late in the salvage the winds shifted, and so, too, did the *Sofia*, causing one of the other sloops to split its chains and hit the *Mystica* starboard, hard enough to sheer off a rail and stave in her side, just so. The hole—happily—sat above the waterline; and so Calixto was able to sail her home, where she was nursed back to health by the boat wrights in our employ. Soon the *Soror Mystica* was declared sound, and once again seaworthy—ready for her northward sail.

So: . . . yes, if only Leo had somehow Sighted all that; . . . if only we'd desisted, or drawn back in our efforts to ruin Captain Roberts and secure from those five wrecks funds enough to free a legion of slaves; . . . if only—

Hélas, hindsight, foresight . . . Sometimes—even for witches who Sight—there is only the present, ceding fast to the past. In time there is no time, as the sages are wont to say. And one is left with naught but lessons learned and tales to tell; like so:

They made it to Man-hattan, the trinity did; and once there placed our contribution—converted to specie, stocks, and drafts drawn on scattered banks—into the hands of friends of friends of the Tappans (the better to blur the lines of our bequest). It was the return trip that turned troublesome, such that Leo would write in her *Book of Shadows: Oh, for the ash, the birch, the willow bark with which to fashion a broom, a broom to sweep me from these heaving decks and fly me homeward—or toward land, beloved land!* Seems Léopoldine wasn't much of a sailor. Of course, she jested, as regards the broom; for, as you well know, sister, our supposed powers of flight were foisted upon us in ages past by those who could not catch us, and needed *a reason why;* but as far as I know, no witch other than myself has ever ridden the Aether, as it were. . . . Patience, now. I promise: I approach the point in my tale that tells how *that* came to pass; but meanwhile, let us return to a green Léopoldine and read a bit more written aboard the *Soror Mystica,* which heaved on the sea, as did she:

Neptune has seen fit to take me. She tends toward the theatrical, does our Leo; but still the sea passage was a rough one, as attested to by her handwriting: a scrawl, and nearly vertical upon the page. *And so do it! say I. Rise, Neptune, with your Trident and stick me, stick me with its tines! Run me through!* . . . Et cetera.

Sea travel, you see—which Léopoldine defined as "a line of tedium, stretched taut between two points of panic," referring, of course, to departure and arrival—was not all she'd hoped it would be. No indeed. Worse: She hadn't the means to See, *at sea,* her future, nor her beloveds', nor the *Soror Mystica's,* whose *whining spars, whistling cordage, and whipping sails* kept her awake at night, whilst during the day the sea *so slickened the ship from stem to stern* that recreation of any sort was deemed too dangerous: Cal and Luc had forbade her the decks. As to the wording they used, I can only muse; for Léopoldine is not easily constrained. In truth, though, I wonder how much Leo wished to recreate, truly, as, in her own words:

> *This infernal heaving mocks my "inner workings," and any foodstuffs I attempt to swallow soon find they must cede Right-of-Way to those I spew. And all the while C. and L., whom I hate, and the crew, all of whom I hate, go about their business side-mouthing remarks relevant to the green tones of my skin. Simon, the dog, went so far as to say, not an hour past, when he came into the cabin to gift me with a knob of ginger (to gnaw, against the stomach upset), that still I had vomit in my hair, "owing," he supposed, to my "most recent inspection of the schooner's sides." The gall! I swear I'd cast them all down into Davy Jones's locker if only I had the key, and then somehow I'd steer this tub landward, toward the nearest port, where I'd sell her as tinder and take a coach homeward!*

It was rough sailing, and I cannot say how I'd have fared in similar seas; but, too, Léopoldine stewed over being Sightless. This she confesses. So, too, does she write of soothing herself:

> *Blessedly—as our H. would say—I packed a pipe and opiates enough to see me into port. Now I will strap myself into our bed, our berth, our bunk—damn this sea vocabulary!—and smoke myself into a stupor. If later I wake to find myself lying fathoms deep, upon the seafloor, then so be it. Surely I'll suffer less upon the sea's floor than I do on its surface!*

And all that, mind, was written *before* the weather went red, which development left the next pages of Leo's Book blank for some days.

Some while after they'd been piloted from New York's harbor—
... and of course Leo had loved the city, *save for the snow,* to which she

was unaccustomed, whilst neither Calixto nor Luc cared much for its bustle and double-pace—a gale came on, and soon the *Soror Mystica* was pitching and tumbling in the seaways like a spun top, causing Calixto to worry, for the first time, about her long years of wear.

I fear we witches played a not so subtle role in all this; for Calixto, as captain, had come to count upon our protection, and thusly he'd surrendered a bit of . . . humility, let me say, when *face-à-face* with the sea. Too, he was less vigilant than once he'd been. Which is to say: Calixto decided to sail for home despite the harbor pilot's reproval, and despite the words of those crew members, including our much-trusted Simon, who advised that they seek the shelter of Chesapeake Bay once the winds came on and all went squally. Calixto said no. They'd sail. Unwise, perhaps? Arrogant? Yes. But I remain grateful; for if Calixto had taken the *Soror Mystica* into Chesapeake Bay and not gone to sea, I might never have met Grania Byrne, without whom . . . Well, suffice to say that I don't know how I'd have lived—or died—without my Lady of Eire.

She came from Skibbereen in County Cork, but she'd sailed from Liverpool in a "lumber tub" bound for Quebec. Its captain had oh so graciously allowed her and her mother to stow themselves (for fourteen pounds, mind) in a hold that would otherwise have been empty on its return trip. And though winter was no one's chosen time to cross, the situation in Ireland was already dire, and due to worsen: So said Bridie Byrne, Grania's Ma, whose gift—" 'tis hardly that," says Grania—was Sight, such that what Bridie Saw of the coming Famine brought on her Blood. So Grania believes.

Bridie, swollen as a tick and already turning blue, drew a last promise from her daughter: She didn't want to be thrown overboard till Ireland lay far, far behind them. Seeing all she'd Seen, Bridie wanted never to return there, above all not as "bones borne on a tide." As for England—and the English, for whom she harbored "a murtherin' hate" —Grania had her mother's blessings if somehow she could "get hold of one of me old bones," and with it manage to beat John Bull about the head and neck. "And best to start with your man Trevelyan," said she, meaning the English lord who'd recently referred to Irish hunger as "the will of Heaven."

The lumber ship, in the hands of an inexperienced crew, had lost its bearings in the gale; and though Calixto, in ordering a change of tack, told his crew he'd heard shots of distress above the howling wind—unlikely; the more so when later it was observed that the ship had no sizable guns; but the *Mystica's* crew, though mortals all, had grown accustomed to *the inexplicable*—it was, in fact, Léopoldine who told Calixto of the nearby *Belleforêt*, caring less (frankly) that there was a ship in distress than that there was a witch upon it.

Leo had woken with a start from her "poppy sleep," and would have considered the presentiment of a stranded sister merely the debris of her dream— . . . *a dream of India*, wrote she, from which she woke *drippy*; for in said dream she'd mounted both an elephant and its handsome mahout—had she not heard tell of how Sebastiana had sensed, similarly, both my distress in Brittany and Leo's own, in the catacombs of Rome.

So it was that the *Soror Mystica* sailed not toward the bay but further out to sea, Simon and others being heard to say, sotto voce, that Calixto meant to sacrifice them all; but when the dismasted, bilging *Belleforêt* suddenly hove into view—by which time they were nearly upon her—all hands readied to do what they did best: wreck, and salvage; and, as ever, they prized people over property.

The *Belleforêt* had already suffered—at half passage, and but days after the burial at sea of Bridie Byrne—the effects of an electrical storm. I've heard tell of such storms; wherein the air falls sultry and takes on a sulfuric smell, and sometimes there is to be seen those globes of phosphorescence, called *ignis fatuus*, or St. Elmo's fire, which, ranging in size from apple to pumpkin, alight—all too literally—upon the masts and yards, and there linger long enough to render any sailor superstitious, or rather *more* superstitious; for the lights are said to herald the devil, and doom. As surely they did for the *Belleforêt:*

In that same storm, lightning had struck the mainmast, shot down toward the deck, and sped damage to the four quarters of the ship via her chains; such that in the gale she'd dismasted—claiming, in her throes, three seamen—and now bobbed about, helpless as a cat without claws.

The lightning had put beyond use one of her longboats; and another, when launched, shipped so much water that down it went, taking with it an unknown number of unfortunates. Others leapt into the sea when the *Belleforêt's* decks tilted well past level and it seemed she'd capsize. These poor souls had not heard, or perhaps had not been able to heed, the crew, who, to a one, had cried that they ought to hold on; for in the sea they'd freeze. Still others, fully half the crew and twenty-some passengers, or a third of those who'd shipped from Liverpool—though not the captain, who did as a captain ought and rode the *Belleforêt* down—came onto the *Soror Mystica* by means of her quarter boats, her ropes, speedily rigged gangways and slides, and means even more desperate.

In the course of the rescue—it was not a *salvage* operation, per se, if the lives saved be discounted—as well as after, when finally she set out for the safety of Chesapeake Bay, the *Soror Mystica* showed her advanced age. And though she shipped some water herself, she'd survive awhile longer, and sail home to Key West once the requisite repairs were made; which repairs, I should say, delayed the trinity's return by more than a month, so that by the time they finally sailed within view of my scope, that spring of '46, they'd already written—

—※—

not in cipher, mind, despite all my warnings about our supposedly inviolate post—to tell what happened, to say that they were well, and to announce that they'd be bringing home a witch ". . . whom we think you'll like."

If Grania had not shown the Eye, they might well have left her behind, aboard the sinking *Belleforêt;* for she had refused, *refused* to let go her hold on both her cauldron and her dog. There she'd stood, mid-storm, arguing with Calixto, who fast assented to the collie, but *not* the cauldron; which, said he, would fall into the longboat like a cannonball. It was then Léopoldine came topside—against "orders," ha!—and, deck to deck, the two witches traded the Eye. It was more sensed than seen, I suppose; but it was enough for Leo to announce to Cal, "It is she"; whereupon Grania was let to drop down into the longboat—with both cauldron and collie—to be rowed over a short span of the rudest seas conceivable. Saved, she clambered aboard the *Soror Mystica* and stepped into a sister's embrace.

Grania is—irony of ironies—weather-allied; and so she and Leo both, having been tempered at sea, so to speak, took care to work some Craft before allowing a patched *Soror Mystica* to retake to the sea, setting out from the Chesapeake, and headed home. Each sister read the sky in her own way: Leo by some hastily acquired charts; Grania by the clouds, or *neladoracht,* as it is called amongst the Celtic sisters. Both Saw a smooth sail home.

Some months prior, Bridie Byrne had Seen a rough sea crossing— Grania, like me, and unlike her mother and my Leo, has limited talent for Sight of that sort—but still she'd insisted; and she and her daughter had set sail. Grania worried that her mother's mind was unsound, then; for how could all she'd prophesied come to pass? *Impossible;* or so it had seemed.

In tears, Bridie had told of the Irish being run off their land and onto the streets, there to live in "scalps"—holes dug and topped with naught but turf and sticks. There they'd die like dogs. Nay: There they'd die *to be eaten by dogs*, themselves starved unto desperation. She'd Seen children rooting about in blighted fields, looking for *pratai romhair*, whatever potatoes the diggers had missed some season past, which now would be rotten, if found, and unfit for fodder, but which nonetheless they'd roast in ashes and eat.

The blight, you see, borne on the breeze, had blown into the moist and mild west; and Grania herself, in the month they took their leave, had seen whole fields die overnight. And that was well before the worst of it, as later lice would carry fevers just as the wind had brought the blight, and the Irish would die, and die, and die. Of fevers both black and yellow. Of "the bloody flux." Of diarrhea, dropsy, and other diseases born of starvation.

Bridie had spoken of the coffin ships to come, too; and come they would, come they do, carrying countless Irish into quarantine, into penny-work, and far worse. "And them's the lucky ones what didn't 'go to sea' midways acrost it," says Grania, "dying only to be slipped down to the depths with a few words and a 'here's your hat' from your saints Peter or Paul"; for so it had come to pass for Bridie Byrne when the Blood had come mid-crossing.

Yes: Poor Bridie Byrne had Seen the Famine, and the crowded ships, and so had insisted on as fast a sail as she could afford for herself, for Grania, and for their familiar—the calico collie, Cuchulain—and for that cauldron; which was no mere bucket of blackest cannon shot, melted and remade, but rather was Cerridwen's cauldron, bequeathed to Grania by her grandmother, as it had been bequeathed to *her* grandmother in turn, and so on, and by the use of which she could . . . —

Stay. I skip; and I oughtn't to tell you any more about Grania Byrne's powers before I introduce her, properly; as now I will:

She stepped off the *Soror Mystica*—the wear on which was evident, yes, from the bald spots on her hull up to a mainsail that showed as many patches as "a cracker's underpants"; or so said Simon, who received from his Euphemia, even before she hugged him, a pie so sweet-smelling he had to hold it high, up and away from their two hip-high boys and a passel of dogs, all of whom had run toward our wharf as word spread of the *Soror Mystica*'s being spotted, and . . . —

But why do I stall? To savor my first glimpse of the witch Grania Byrne? Perhaps so; for the memory is precious. . . . But, as strange a claim as it may be for an immortal to make, I haven't time to stall and savor: These fingers have steadily stiffened round this pen, till now they seem a claw, talons upon a tree branch; and, worse, this body's blood, which gravity causes to well, has made bluing cushions of these buttocks. And so I speed, and summarize thusly:

Tall, broad-shouldered Grania Byrne stepped onto the wharf at Key West as though she were Queen Maeve returned to Tara.

She wore a black dress that buttoned up the left side of her neck, snug to her square jaw, and her red hair was a nimbus, whipping round in that same breeze that had set the sails to soughing. This I could not hear, of course, but rather saw; just as I saw with my spyglass, from the Witchery's tower, that cauldron Grania carried as effortlessly as another woman would a purse. It was bigger than a cannonball, and black as her dress, whilst the collie, Cuchulain, standing at heel, was patched with reds that matched his mistress's hair.

So focused was my scope upon this newly arrived sister, I did not see Léopoldine—or was it Luc, or Calixto?—point to the tower, as surely they must have; for, next thing I knew, there Grania Byrne stood, shading her emerald eyes against the sun and searching. Once she espied me, *there,* she waved. *Waved.* Whereupon I let slip the spyglass and, heart hammering, sank back onto my reading sofa, smiling so . . . *wholly* that it seemed the panes of the portrait'd dead could not contain themselves, and smiled in their turn.

 *Chapter Thirty-six*

For, tempering each other, heat and moisture
engender life: the union of these two
produces everything. Though it is true
that fire is the enemy of water,
moist heat is the creator of all things:
Discordant concord is the path life needs.
—OVID, *Metamorphoses, Book I*

THAT WAS THE LAST TIME I SAW GRANIA BYRNE IN BLACK.
It was all white thereafter, linen and lace, owing to that
heat to which the rest of us had become accustomed;
though still she favored dresses with high collars, and
those being hard to find in a tropical clime, soon she
found a tailor to fashion for her a type of under-collar,
a wimple-like thing whose buttons ran up her neck to
the base of her jaw. "We witches, what with bein' of a
certain age," said she, in a rare concession to vanity, and
in unsought collusion with me, both of us being about
forty, "oughtn't to show our necks so."

Of course, there was nothing unsightly about her
neck: It was long and lean and perfectly pearlescent, just
like the rest of her. Indeed, when shortly after her arrival, the *Hecate* salvaged the ship *Clairefontaine* off Pickles Reef and we found ourselves in possession of a

double string of pearls, I thought straight off of Grania and tried to impress them upon her. *I wanted her to wear them.* It was odd, how badly I wanted this. To the point where I was cruel in commerce, as I'd never been before, and referenced the Laws of Salvage in response to the marquis whose possession the pearls had been, and who wrote on behalf of his marquise, saying she was "all tears" without her double strand. *No,* I replied. *No, no, no.* And when the trinity exempted me, happily, from converting the pearls to cash, as was our custom— whereupon we'd send the cash northward, and to Ireland, as now we'd begun to do—I presented the pearls to Grania as a sort of welcome to the Shadows, to the family, and to the Witchery itself. It was *all-hands-on-deck* to get her to accept my gift; and once we'd induced her to do so, still she'd wear the pearls only over her high collar, and never against that flesh, that *exquisite* flesh that so mocked their luster.

Going about town in her white dresses, and with her red hair piled atop her head, well, let me say that it was not long before she bore the nickname Torch. This came into currency amongst the wreckers, especially; though no one dared let her hear it—in fact, she knew of the nickname and found it . . . *droll,* let me say, if not original—as the *true* torch burned in Grania's eyes, and she'd stand down before no man.

Soon she was well known all along the wharves; and allied as she was to our house—though no one knew *how,* precisely: sister? cousin? aunt?—Grania was accorded more respect than most newcomers, and *far* more than was considered an Irishwoman's due, surely. And her share of respect only grew as she began to work with us upon our wharves, and in our warehouse.

And oh, *mon Dieu, ma déesse,* that warehouse!

Of late we'd salvaged more than we could stow, or readily sell: perishables we disposed of quickly, of course, but as for the rest . . . The letters we had to post, the auctions we had to arrange! So very tiresome, it all was; and I'd have withdrawn from the efforts, had it not been for what they funded. The wares did tend to accumulate, yes; and hard as we tried to convert it all to cash, still the warehouse was crowded with cases of this, kegs of that, and more household *stuff* than Léopoldine could rotate into use at the Witchery. Said wares, mind, were not of the *ordinary* variety, either, as *ordinary* people tend not to transship their wares from Catalonia to California, from Marseilles to the mouth of the Mississip'. No: here were mirrors squared to the size of the downy mattresses standing beside them; here were such oddments as vases, vessels, and urns, of porcelain, of plated gold, of faience . . . the lot of them chipped, it's true; here, in short, were wares enough to cram to the crenellations another castle for "that Dog-Queen Victoria," as Grania called her. And in fact it was that very insult that inspired the solution to *the sole problem* pursuant to Grania's arrival at the Witchery: What to do with Cuchulain, that russet mutt that had never, *ever,* strayed more than a mile from its mistress's side?

Understand: It was not that I disdained the dog more than any other. I just didn't want him in the Witchery. . . . He looked at me funny—as all dogs and other animals did, and long had. Too, the dog was too fast to show its temper and its . . . *excess of teeth.* Until, that is, Calixto suggested I let slip my spectacles and show the mutt my Eye; whereupon he went all nuzzly, whimpering, and whatnot, and all were pleased. Except me. You see, I'd long avoided all animals—as being Lady of the Beasts was *not* my chosen role, *merci bien*—and those few familiars I'd tried to keep had died or wandered off, or worse. And so it was that Cuchulain went to the warehouse, where he lived *in royal splendor*—in quarters carpentered to Grania's specifications—and where, courtesy of Simon, he ate better than most men.

Sport that she was, Grania one day decided to make the most of the situation: She whispered something in the dog's ear, slipped off its leash, and sent it tearing down the wharf toward one of Captain Roberts's crewmen, the same who, some weeks earlier, had not given

Grania the welcome she thought she warranted—it had something to do with his whistling, I believe—and Cuchulain tore from the man's right buttock a steak-length piece of flesh; whereupon word spread, as Grania had intended, and we found ourselves in possession of *a watch-dog*. Then, finally, we were *all* satisfied—excepting, of course, he of the halved buttock; . . . *mais, c'est la vie.*

Only later would I see that it was part of the trinity's unspoken plan to have Grania become . . . well, *the public part of me*. And it's true: There were things, related to the wrecking, that I was either unable or unwilling to do, more so since the trial; and these Grania did—and did well—when she was not furthering our work in the witchery proper. . . . Though, in truth, Grania's talents wanted not the witchery but the tower.

At first, Grania did not see the glassy dead surrounding her. When finally she did, she started, falling back from those windows through which she'd begun to read the weather, exclaiming, with one hand on her heart and the other her pearls, "Goddess go well! Who in Hades are they, that lot there, *there?*" And she pointed with a still-trembling finger.

I laughed. So, too, did she, eventually; though for more than a week she warned of scaring me similarly, abandoning her plans only as she learned more of what I'd meant when earlier I'd said I was death-allied. "I've been accosted by the disquieted dead in graveyards from Gotham to the Never-Glade," said I. "Just *try* to scare me, sister." . . . In fact, if Grania had sought to scare me, truly, she had only to trick me into a crowd of strangers; for, as said, *I'd retreated.*

"I see," said she, speaking to the question of our talents, such as they were: "The one of you Sees the future," by which she meant Leo, of course, "and the other," me, "sees those what ain't got one."

"Plus ou moins," said I. . . . More or less.

And it was about that same time, not long after she'd come, that we all sat at table and listened as Grania explained her own gift. "Me ma, that was Bridie by name, Bridie Byrne—gone, she is, and may the goddess rest her—she passed down to me a wee bit o' Sight, as you call it, though 'tis *da-dhealladh* to us; but when I need, truly need the knowin' of things to come, I look to the clouds." Over dessert—one of Euphemia's pies, baked and left warm in a locker at our back door, and served now on saucers of sundry origin, and eaten with silver showing more graven initials than the alphabet would seem to support—she explained further, first observing:

"This one don't eat much, eh?" Meaning me, of course; as she made clear by the jerking of her thumb toward me, whilst her words were sent toward the table's far end, toward Léopoldine, who simply shrugged.

"Well, then," resumed Grania, "what I mean to say is that since Hector was a pup, I—"

"Huh?" I forget who it was said this, but I'll let the query stand without attribution; for it might have been any one of us.

"Oh," said Grania. "What I mean to say is that since I was a wee one, knee-high to a grasshopper, I . . . —

"Ach, as me ma would say, a story's best when plainly told, eh? . . . To you lot, especially," she added with a smile, "as no one told me it was a different language ye spoke here in Americay.

"And so . . . Since I was young I've seen meanin' above. In mares' tails and mackerel skies, and suchlike; though the cumulus, they're best for readin'."

"Reading?" I asked. "What do you mean by 'reading'?" Already I was charmed; so much so that I made no complaint when Grania set a second slice of pie upon her plate and brought Cuchulain onto her lap to eat it—an act that had the trinity sending smirky looks back and forth, so as to say, *We were right*. And they were; for the day I let a dog join us at table was, indeed, the day I showed myself smitten with its mistress.

"Well," said Grania, "all reading depends on the reader, don't it? Take a sister from Chiney, squintin' down into her teacup. She'll not See what you'd See, but still and all, that don't mean her readin' is wrong, now do it?

"As for me, I might See up there, in the tumble and puff, a fist, say, and I'll know it's no day for fightin', and I'll try me level best to let go of any and all slights done me that day. Or a lamb—don't ye laugh at me, now— . . . a lamb will show, tellin' of a new and good idea about to come birthin' from this ol' bean o' mine." And she knocked upon her head, lest we lose her meaning again.

Grania spoke further about her species of Sight that night, though not in great detail; for it seemed she and Léopoldine had hashed this at length whilst aboard the *Soror Mystica,* the two of them agreeing that Grania's gift was both particular *and* particularly well suited to wrecking; whereupon she'd been told all about me—and I do mean *all*—and invited to come to the Witchery.

For she Sees the weather, Grania Byrne does, *before it comes to pass.*

She'll go up into the tower, sit staring out the windows an hour or so, maybe shut her eyes—the better to See—and then come down to announce, "It'll be a mighty t'under tomorrow, it will," or "Rain today, comin' on about half-two." No mean feat, this, upon our southernmost key, where, according to Grania, the sky turns like a kaleidoscope.

Useful? Indeed; for Grania can forecast as far out as weeks and even months, with accuracy. Her prognosticating contributed to our planning from the day she arrived; for now we sought to baby the *Soror Mystica* with naught but blue skies and smooth seas, and sent out the *Hecate* or the *Persephone* in anything worse.

And then came the day, late in September, when already we were in love and I thought I'd been, *quoi?* . . . redeemed? saved? . . . *Enfin,* then came the day Grania descended from the tower to the witchery, to say

—————————— ✳ ——————————

to me, in a whisper, lest Leo hear, "Sure, I've never seen the like of it, I tell ye."

"What? What is it?" I got her a chair: I worried she'd fall, she swayed so. She'd unbuttoned her collar, the better to breathe. And she'd taken off the pearls in doing so, I supposed; for now, nervously, she fretted them with her fingers, rosary-like.

"A hurricane," said she. "No more'n two weeks' time . . . It'll kill, too, it will."

So it was that for the first time we applied Grania's Sight not just to our salvaging, but to our survival.

Grania Byrne . . . We knew each other from the moment we met; and—blessed be—she thought of my being hermaphroditic as a mere characteristic, akin to her being Irish.

Of course, the trinity—and Leo, especially—thought they'd come upon the match for me, and had amused themselves in arranging it. I was wary, as what witch wouldn't be? I'd read in the books of too many meetings amongst sisters that fast devolved to spectacle, to conviviality of the *two-cats-in-a-sack* sort. And though I was alone, and thought I'd live out my days alone, and loveless, still I'd nearly, *nearly* convinced myself that that was all I was: *alone;* not lonely. After all, I had my three—though they'd followed the lead of another Trinity, and now were One—and I had the Witchery, the Work, the Books. . . . Wouldn't that all keep me busy till the Coming of the Blood, or till Brù's work found its final effect? It would, surely. Still, on my worst days, I wondered, and *not* necessarily with dread, when the end would come. It's not as though I *awaited* it, or would have *welcomed* it, mind, but still . . .

Then came Grania Byrne instead, and I . . . revivified, and loved as I'd not loved in a long, long while.

———————————✳———————————

Midway through our mortal courtship—three months after her arrival, then, which puts the date at July of '46; . . . for three months from *that* date I'd be dead—our bedroom doors were as busy as those of the others. She'd come to me first. And though I'd kept "me works from rusting," as Grania would say, through the occasional self-pleasuring, still I was unprepared for her interest in my . . . particulars. She was *voracious*, let me say. . . . Indeed, I'd laugh if I could master the muscles of this Miss Lucy's throat; for if Grania were to slip into this cabin now and read this, doubtless she'd slap the face of the child who writes it, or rather seems to. . . . And as ever sisters did, Grania envied me my double-spill, and effected it so often I thought at one point I'd faint. Weakened as I was from surfeit of sex—it *is* possible, yes—I agreed to take food and drink; which by then I *wholly* disdained.

"You're old Tiresias, y'are," said Grania one day as we lay spent. She was combing her fingers through my too silver, too luminous locks. "So tell me then: Who is it gets the greater pleasure, the man or the woman? Sure, *you're* like to know, eh?"

I demurred, saying that for me, *in me,* the two were inseparable. When Grania pressed her analogy further—truly, she wanted to know who drew greater pleasure from sex, man or woman—I reminded her that when an arguing Zeus and Hera came to Tiresias to ask the same question—as he was supposed to have lived some portion of his life as a woman, owing to some strangeness involving serpents—Tiresias, in siding with Zeus, and answering *man,* had so angered Hera that she'd struck him blind.

"Aye, but I'd never harm ye, I wouldn't," said Grania; whereupon, with a reversal of my role, we resumed our lovemaking.

. . . *Enfin,* it was six months of bliss, from start to mortal finish; and it'd be blissful still if only I were alive and possessor of that body that once shamed me so. But I am not, and the bodies by which Grania loves me, and I her, are *borrowed bodies,* bodies brought back to life, *quickened* by us both, she with Cerridwen's cauldron and I with my invasive soul.

The idea was hers, though it did not come to her, of course, till *after* the hurricane, when the dead were plentiful and it was discovered that I was gone:

. . . *god, goddess, ghost.*

Chapter Thirty-seven

Hoc est enim os de ossibus meis et caro de carne mea,

et erunt duo in carne una.

This is now bone of my bones, and flesh of my flesh. . . .

And they shall be one flesh.

—Genesis 2:23–24

ACTUALLY, THE IDEA MAY HAVE BEEN MINE; LEASTWAYS IN its *first* application, before Grania thought to apply it to the borrowed bodies.

Grania, you see, suffered her first island summer terribly. She'd wear dresses as thin as modesty allowed—collared, of course—with ventilating slits sewn into the designs, like split seams. I talked her out of her coarse *inexpressibles*—figuratively, yes, but literally as well—yet still she perspired unto embarrassment. We carried fans—sea grape leaves, sewn together with hemp—but the effort required to stir a breeze only made us perspire the more, and so the fans were set aside, or reserved for the swatting of flies. Yes, pearls of perspiration were ever upon Grania's upper lip, slipping, with a sting of salt, into her mouth as she spoke; and thusly, said she, compromising her when amongst the men, the wreckers.

An hour down at the warehouse and she'd return to the Witchery "sopping," and wondering aloud if our chosen island wasn't Hell in the guise of Heaven.

And so, wanting, *needing* to please Grania, I sent word to Lemuel Corbeil, the island's other Frenchman, who then sought his fortune in the export of salt from our up-island ponds as well as the import of ice—though, in late years, Lemuel switched to sponging, and finally has found his long-sought fortune—and asked that two blocks of ice be delivered to the Witchery along with two long, tin-lined tubs of mahogany, sawdust, et cetera—in short, all things requisite to the prolongation of both the ice's life and . . . well, life itself, I suppose.

The ice and tubs I had Calixto and Luc haul up to the *Roseate Suite*—thusly did we refer (rather grandly, yes) to that fourth and smallest suite upon the second floor, which the twins had papered in shades of red, and adorned with roses, real and painted, both, in honor of Sebastiana and her horticultural hobby—and soon we were referring to the suite by a new name: the *Cool Boudoir;* for the ice, three feet long by two wide, and several inches thick, I set into the tubs, fashioning a sort of chaise longue by then draping the whole in crepe, or spun cotton, or another fabric light enough to let the coolness seep through. A few pillows, *et voilà!* On this icy divan Grania would recline, nude, till the cool pleasure of it ceded to cold pain; whereupon she'd rise and dress, refreshed and once again ready for the out-of-doors and her wharfside work.

And so: When later we needed a place to stow the bodies we borrowed, both of us knew we'd already struck upon the perfect place and the perfect preservative; whereupon the Cool Boudoir became the *Mourning Suite*. The room *did* face east, and saw the morning sun; moreover, we could reference the room beyond the Shadows, as no strangers would presume we spelled *morning* with

that extra, most moribund *u.* . . . . To tease witless strangers was
Léopoldine's want, never mine. "To the Mourning Suite," she
would say, commanding Corbeil's deliverymen, who'd then tong the
ice and carry it thence, under the strictest scrutiny—lest one of
them lose himself amongst the Witchery's upper floors—and all
the time those men must have wondered how it was that ice, delivered so often and in such quantity, prolonged the lives of cut roses;
for still we crammed the Mourning Suite with as many roses as we
could procure—so as to mitigate the stink of our oh so mortal
friends, whose visits were of some days' duration—and thusly did
we explain our need of Monsieur Corbeil's services: *What we hoarded
was roses, not corpses.*

The aforementioned *friends* we brought by cart to the back door.
On one memorable occasion, a corpse came in through the front door
at noon, rolled into a carpet. *Le pauvre* had been a long time sailing
from St. Augustine aboard the *Hecate* and, well, *he very much wanted the ice*
by the time he arrived at Key West.

Luc had made the acquaintance of a sexton in a St. Augustine
churchyard when he'd gone there to settle some business and retrieve
the last of my stowed things; and he'd convinced the sexton that the
bodies he sought would be brought to a physician, a Man of Science,
who'd pry them apart for *pure purposes only* and then reconstitute the ca-
daver before according it a send-off worthy of the Pope himself. This
the sexton *chose to believe*, of course, so as to set in balance the scales of
his own salvation; for, truth to tell, had we asked him to, the sexton
would have stuffed and trussed the corpses like Christmas geese once
he saw Luc step off the *Hecate* with his remuneration: a case of island
rum.

Hélas, men with addictions are so easily manipulated. . . . Indeed,
Luc had a similar arrangement with a Jesuit in New Orleans whose
addiction wasn't drink, but faith—capital-*F* Faith, Faith of the Inqui-

sitional, auto-da-fé sort. All I ever heard of our Father Time (so Calixto dubbed him) made Asmodei seem cherubic by comparison. And
though Father Time professed only to hate the sin, not the sinner, taking from that priest the city's "depraved dead" came to seem a rescue
mission of sorts; and in fact we "rescued" corpses too ruined for our
use, so as to spare them interment at the hands of the Jesuit, who was
wont not to bury them—albeit aboveground, in that manner of New
Orleans that scared me from the city all my mortal life—but rather
pile them in pits of lime and pitch dug bankside, near the battlefields
of Chalmette, so that their bones would marry those of the British
soldiers whom Jackson so famously slew there. He seemed quite demonic, that man—the Jesuit, I mean, not Jackson; though, I could
argue the demonism of the latter, too, given more time and a suppler
hostess.

. . . *Bref*, it has never been hard to find bodies. And when they'd
outlived—or should I say out-died?—their usefulness, which state is
most evident to the mortal eye and nose, we'd secrete them out of the
house at night and onto the *Hecate*—easily done, as carts were trun-
dled between the warehouse and the Witchery at all hours—and
thence out to sea, where *each and every one of them* was accorded their cer-
emonial due. The rites we read were part pagan, part papist; and
though by then I'd have quit the corpse, and risen, often I lingered
long enough to see the efficacy of those rites:

What remained of the soul's silver would seep from our wrapped
and weighted friends as they sank, spiraling back toward the surface,
there to bubble and break and release its violet scent as it ascended
toward the Summerland.

Understand: I did not return to those bodies for the trinity's sake.
They'd loved me in life, and had known me so fully and long that their

love would've endured my death. They'd no need of a corpse to contain me. They'd their hearts for that.

I came back from Beyond for Grania's and my benefit; for there is but one thing the heart will not, *cannot* abide: the loss of love when it is new. And Grania and I had been together but six months when I burned, and in burning learned what Brù had done.

Of course, we couldn't let on that we knew about the coming storm because, well, *How was it that we knew?* Neither would it have been right to leave the island in advance of the squall, to secure the warehouse and the Witchery as best we could and sail off. Then, too, Grania was at first unclear as to which direction the storm would come from, and so we might have set sail straight into it.

So we stayed, and were subtle in our precautions so as to stave off suspicion. Indeed, I was forever urging subtlety on the trinity, to whom the Burning Days seemed but a dream. (To me they were rather more real than that.) It had been my idea to sail *and sometimes fail* at salvage—I called this *safe*, whilst to the others it was *a waste*. Too, I'd advocated for less . . . *sisterly* names for our fleet, thinking it unwise for Leo and me to be allied to ships named for Queens of the Underworld, of the Night, of the Shadows. I'd lost that and other battles; but now, with the storm approaching, again I urged subtlety, though I knew there was sound reason in what both Leo and Grania said to assuage my worrying self:

We of the Shadows are spared discovery by the beliefs of those in the Light. Strangers do not believe we exist, and so we don't. Still, I said, the strangers thereabouts were soon to find themselves in extremis, and it'd be best not to tempt them toward suspicion by boarding up the Witchery, et cetera, before the barometer had begun to fall, and whilst the winds were yet still and the sky untroubled.

My words were heeded, and *subtlety* was ensured. Still, by the time the weather reddened, we'd rearranged the warehouse, just so. We di-

vested ourselves of baled cotton that had been sitting about, broker-
ing it up to St. Mark's at well below market price. Many casks, car-
tons, kegs, and bottles of liquor we let go as well. Much of the
furniture might need to be sacrificed, as there was only so much room
in the half story of the warehouse's loft, and already we'd packed it
with those things that would not suffer well a rising tide: barrels of
salt we were due to ship northward for Corbeil, smoked foodstuffs, a
large and gilded mirror Leo sought to save, et cetera. . . . Just where
the sulfur was, I cannot say. Perhaps it was present as a component of
some rubber-maid thing? Or in that case of medicaments Asmodei
had left behind? Regardless, the sulfur was somehow present, surely, as
was the abovementioned salt and the mercury backing the mirrors.
Otherwise, I'd not have . . . —

Hélas, I ought to hurry, but I find now that it's hard, this closing in
on tale's-end.

We witches knew that efforts to secure the Witchery, albeit subtly,
would be worthless. Neither Grania nor Leo Sighted the extent of the
damage to be done, though both knew it would be bad. And at the
first signs of the storm, we, along with all the other islanders, began
to batten down as best we could:

I placed all the *Books of Shadows* into the crates in which they'd come.

We carried Marian to the Mourning Suite, and stocked that room
with fresh ice.

And so on . . . Calixto and Luc saw to the *Soror Mystica,* speeding to
completion repairs they'd begun post-Gotham but bringing aboard
lengths of chain and extra anchors as well.

Finally, there was naught to do but wait.

Too late to sail, Grania had Seen that the storm would come from the
southwest. Now it was nearer, Leo could divine its path by those same

means she used to site wrecks. And so we were able to chart the storm's progress upon the witchery floor:

It would hit Havana. "Hard," said Grania. Thereafter it would stir the Gulf and Straits to a froth, and sit overhead a long and drenching while. "I See three days with little blue above," said Grania; and by *chaomancy*—from the Greek *chaos*, but meaning "the atmosphere," as read by wind direction, squalls, dust devils, and such—which Leo had been learning at Grania's knee, she, Leo, saw the streets of the town running like rivers.

This Sighting upset Leo terribly, and after it she slept for several days; for, ever since her northward sail, she'd suffered nightmares of death by drowning. No: Rather it was *surviving drowning* that she feared, sinking to the seafloor alive, or floating as shark-meal, all the while attendant upon the sole thing—besides exsanguination by bullet or blade—that will kill a witch: the Coming of the Blood. . . . Such were her nightmares; and so it surprised us all somewhat when she announced she'd ride out the storm not in the Witchery with us, Grania and me, but aboard the *Soror Mystica* with Calixto and Luc.

And indeed, early that morning of October the eleventh, when first the winds picked up, the trinity took our schooner from her slip out into the harbor, there to let her suffer the storm at anchor. Others soon followed suit, owing not so much to imitation as that old saw holding that in storms ships are safer at sea, where there isn't the worry of being dashed against the wharves by the wind and waves. The open sea relieved us all of *that* particular worry, perhaps; and one less worry was welcome after two weeks of worries in which some of us had Seen but all of us had learned the fate that none of us carried to articulate: The life we'd known, and which had suited us so well, was about to end. Ironically, it would be taken from us by those same elements that had brought it: water and wind. Further irony: If either Grania or Leo Saw the effects of fire upon our common fate, neither spoke of it. . . . Would that they had. Perhaps I'd have been more wary.

Fire . . . Water . . . The marriage of the two . . . I'll approach these subjects with . . . subtlety, yes. You'll grant me that, surely, sister, as it's myself I eulogize here.

. . . Grania and I discussed fire the morning of the storm: We thought it unwise to leave the witchery as it was; for what if events-to-come brought strangers to it as it lay, whole or in ruins? What then? And so we resolved to pack the cinder pit with our pharmacopoeia, and all our most damning paraphernalia. Into the pit went jars of pickled this, pots of powdered that, et cetera. Need be, we'd douse and burn it all.

By midday the storm was upon us, and the wind sounded (so said my Grania) "like somethin' crossways between all the island cats being crucified and some ol' crone keenin' her husband home." Daring the tower, we looked out at the *Soror Mystica* in the harbor; but we dared not tarry at the shuddering sill, as it seemed the dead-panes might pop and shatter at any second. From the smaller windows of the third-story witchery we watched the sea encroach upon the streets, and saw the winds render cannon shot of coconuts. . . . Later, it'd be seen that a one-by-four piece of the wharf had been driven by the wind through one of our own coconut palms, such that the tree was now cruciform four feet up its slender trunk: a Calvary perfectly suited to that cruel end Grania had imagined for the islands' many cats.

"Waves," said Grania in wonderment. "Damned I am if those be not waves down there in the street!"

"Then damned you are, my dear; for those *are* waves, I fear"; whereupon, portentously, I recited two lines of Ovid's that came to me then:

> *And flowing water filled the final space;*
> *it held the solid world in its embrace.*

And unhappily, unfortunately, I am able to report that the water, the waves, had already risen as high as the fifth step of our stoop, leaving but three more before the porch would be covered and the first floor breached. *Embraced,* indeed. This I'd learn as a result of what next Grania exclaimed:

"Me poor pet!" said she. "Cuchulain!"

"What of him? He's in the loft, is he not? As high and dry as any man or beast could hope to be?" We'd all discussed the best place for Cuchulain to be in the coming storm, and had deemed that the warehouse; for, being his witch's familiar, he watched the weather as closely as she and barked at it rather vexingly. Truth be told, no one wanted him about, barking back the wind and water. No one but Grania, that is.

"Aye, but he's leashed to the loft's ladder down low, as it was the wind gettin' into the warehouse that worried me the more. Oh, but now 'tis the sea risin' so as to . . . Goddess be damned! Why didn't I bring him here?"

"We discussed this and—"

"I know full well what was discussed, me love, but now me pet is there and I'm here, with the sea risin' to separate us." Her Eye had turned. "I don't like it, 'tis all. And if *you'd* a familiar, you'd know. . . ."

"*Parbleu,* not that again," said I, regrettably; for those were the last words Grania Bynre would hear from my mortal mouth, in my mortal voice.

Exasperated, I turned from Grania toward the witchery's windows. It was true, and frightfully so: *Here came the sea.* And the winds had risen, too, such that houses had begun to be unroofed: Sheets of tin spun above the flooded streets. I could no longer see the *Soror Mystica;* for the rain came on sideways now, and sprayed the windows with the force of buckshot. Something heavy hit the house, down low. I remember thinking that the windows of the tower would not, *could not* last for long; but when I turned to say as much to Grania, she was gone.

"Grania?" No response. I climbed to the tower. She was not there. I called out again, "Grania!" but I could hardly hear myself over the howl of the storm. . . . Could it be . . . ? Could she have . . . ?

The term *a fool's errand* seems hardly to suffice for what next I did; but let me spare myself the self-scorn and repeat what already is known: *I was in love;* and therefore twice, thrice, four times the fool I'd otherwise have been. Only love could have sent me out into that storm in search of a dog that, though I wished it no ill, certainly, was the last, *the very last* of the Shadow-kin I'd ever mourn.

. . . But that's what I did; though at first—having sought Grania high and low within the Witchery—it was my witch I was after, ready to chide her for braving the elements on behalf of her Cuchulain. Familiar or no, she ought to have known better. And I was keen to tell her so, and *carry* her back to safety if need be.

Once I stepped off that fifth, flooded step of our stoop, and waded down into hip-high seawater, I could not even raise my face to peer down Caroline Street toward the warehouse, toward where, surely, Grania waded before me; for the wind and rain came on *painfully*. My spectacles blew from my face. In an instant I was soaked through. But still I waded toward the warehouse, leaning into the storm and doubtless seeming as set upon my course as a ship's figurehead.

I never caught up to Grania, *because she hadn't gone out*.

She'd slipped from my side not to sneak out to save her Cuchulain, but rather to retrieve, from somewhere deep in our common closet, a clay whistle that had been her grandmother's, and had long been used to call Cuchulain's sires home over the fields and fens, the tones of which she hoped would rise to the dog's ears above the storm. Thusly would she—somehow—tell the dog to slip its leash. If *told* to do so, Cuchulain could and would obey, as he'd done the time Grania had sent him teeth-bared after the buttocks of Captain Roberts's man. And then, freed of his leash, the dog could scurry up-ladder to the loft.

All this Grania effected when finally she found the whistle, slipped through the witchery—wondering where I'd gone—and climbed to the tower; where, crazily, she raised a rattling window and stepped through it, out onto the widow's walk. She whistled as best she could. And turning back toward the tower window, wind-whipped and worried . . . well, it was then she saw me—my hair, said she, shone like a halo—fifty or so paces down Caroline Street: too far to summon home by whistle, by words, by any means she knew, though she tried, and cried my name from the tower till she feared the wind would take her and toss her out to sea.

Grania's whistle worked on Cuchulain, yes; for I found the dog loft-high in the fast-flooding warehouse. From there he snarled down at me where I stood, soaked, rather more than disheveled and none too happy. I asked where his mistress was. Had she come? Was she yet at the Witchery? (Already I half supposed my mistake.) Verily, *I made demands of a dog*. As if he'd the power of speech. But all I heard were the boards of the wharf giving with groans, and sounding like breaking bones. I'd have to take the dog and quit the warehouse quickly, lest I lose access to land, land that already bore all the aspects of the sea. Or I could settle with Cuchulain and hope the warehouse held; but the flooded floor shimmered now in the scanty light—none can say what that scummed, slickened water held—and boards had begun to blow off its frame. In the short while I stood trying to summon down from the loft the snarling mutt, enough water came into the warehouse to float things—cracked barrels, broken crates, bottles slipped from their shelves . . . —and to move them far from where they'd been when first

I'd entered the warehouse. The whole of the structure would go, surely, and the sole question was, or rather *seemed*, which element would take it: water or wind.

"Come!" said I to Cuchulain. He would not. I tried to imitate the Irish I'd heard Grania speak to him. Still, nothing. I wondered if he could not hear me over the storm's din. I shouted louder. More snarling. Perhaps he could not see me well enough to know I was not an intruder, the which he'd had to ward off on occasion. So it was that I cast about for a lamp to light.

I found one beneath the loft: a large lamp whose glass belly was gravid with oil. Lit, it would have illumined half the warehouse. I took it down from its hook, drew a long-handled match from a tin hammered to the fast-faltering wall, and struck it upon a strip of sandpaper, once, twice, thrice. . . . The lamp lit; but still I was raising its wick when I stepped out from under the loft, looked up, and saw the collie coming down upon me.

Owing to the weight of the dog, or the rising water, or my own fears, I lost my balance and fell backward. Though my fall was broken by the trough of sawdust and wood shavings into which I fell, my head met its wooden frame hard, *very* hard. The last things I recall are Cuchulain, barking, weighty upon my chest, and seeing the lamp I flung as I fell. Weighted as it was, the lamp went end over end toward the wall, spinning like a tomahawk. Doubtless it burst as it hit; and what had been light was reduced to its more incendiary components: oil and flame.

As for what those flames found first—the salt, the sulfur, or the mercury of the *prima materia*—I cannot say; for I lay unconscious atop that too conductive sawdust and tinder. . . . Perhaps it was the salinity of the seawater. Perhaps it was the storm-seasoned rain. In any case, it seems to me that *water* in one of its forms must have been the *magisterium,* that agent that provoked or leastways allowed the alchemical change. . . . *Enfin*, soon the fire had found the three elements of the *prima materia* and water as well, and so *all the colors came,* and when next I knew consciousness—what else to call it?—I saw that finally, *finally* the work of Queverdo Brù was done:

I was his Rebus, that alchemical vessel in which, *in whom,* his Great Work was achieved. Done, yes.

And though I'll never again live, neither will I die a second time.

 *Chapter Thirty-eight*

Nonne Salomon dominatus daemonum est?

Had not Solomon dominion over demons?

—LEONTIUS OF CONSTANTINOPLE

*E*VERYONE SAW THE WINDOWS OF THE WAREHOUSE GO red—the trinity, *my three,* saw it from the cabin of the *Soror Mystica* whilst Grania set her spyglass to the eye of a dead woman and watched from a tower window. Both witches sickened when the high windows of the warehouse blew, and the inrush of wind fed the flames; for they knew, *physically,* my distress. Of course, only Grania knew what had happened. Or supposed it. . . . So it was she keened along with the wind.

. . . As for the fire itself, well, I wrote about that as best I could and did so first, in what Grania refers to as the "pro-lo-glue" of the current volume. I shan't correct her either; for her way with English—which, at times, seems hardly our common tongue—charms me. And she, having been born to an oral tradition, is yet wary of all things literary—indeed, she knew nothing of the

Books of Shadows till she learned of them from Leo. Now she keeps her own, of course; the which no one is let to see, not even me. Yes, she recommended that I write of the fire up front. "Put the worst of it first," said she, "as not every witch is wise, and not every witch can be counted on to dig down to the seed of the tale."

. . . The seed.

It was sown by Queverdo Brù well nigh a decade before my death, and lay more or less dormant a long while, wanting only the confluence of fire and water to . . . *Enfin*, I suppose if Brù had had his way, if he'd been able to see his plan through and slip me—whole or cleaved into pieces, and somehow wedded to water—into that athanor of his, I'd have ascended sooner. . . . *Et pourquoi?* To serve him like Azoth, the demon Paracelsus is said to have trapped in the crystal pommel of his sword? Or simply as proof positive of all his puffery, of Perfection?

No matter now. The alchemist did not have his way with me, and if I am his Success, well, he knows nothing of it. I lived ten years beyond my escape from his house, from Havana. Alive, I learned the *ars vivendi*. Dying, the *ars moriendi*. And now there stretches before me all eternity. So far the state suits me. It has been . . . sweet, *merci bien*. Neither will I bemoan any *bad luck*; for, after all, and as Proverbs 3:16 puts it:

> *Longitudo dierum in dextera ejus et in sinistra illius divitiae et gloria;* or: Length
> of days is in her right hand, and in her left hand riches and honor.

What witch would ask for more?

. . . Oh, but there is one thing that troubles me time and again: *What will the death of my beloveds bring?* I fear—if fear it be—a loneliness greater than any I knew whilst alive; for who will I watch over when they ascend in their turn? Will they all achieve the Summerland, *sans moi*? Will

I be let to follow? If not, well, I suppose I'll simply stay in death's dream state and no longer descend into borrowed bodies; as I did, for the first time, within a week of my death in the warehouse, brought back by the brass bells, the spells, et cetera, and all else Grania and the trinity tried in summoning me home.

Oui, oui, oui, and blessed be, they all survived the storm, Grania in the Witchery and the trinity at sea. . . . Less fortunate was the *Soror Mystica:* Weakened as she was, she finally went down and slumbers at "full fathom five."

. . . Grania, *la pauvre,* for a whole day she thought she'd lost us all. I was gone. She knew it. Still, needing to see the scene of it, once the waters receded and the streets—though chockablock with barrels, boats, and even bodies—were passable, the waters only knee-high, she went to where the warehouse had stood. She found naught but timber, both charred and soaked. And standing in the drizzle to which the storm had ceded, beneath skies cruelly blue, she looked down to find Cuchulain at her side. How he'd escaped the fire and flood, I cannot say; but if Grania sought further confirmation that I had *not* died, she had its opposite now from her familiar, who told her, by the tone and pitch and length of his howl (*ololygmancy,* this is, oft referenced by sisters more *familiar* with canine *familiars* than I) that I was indeed gone; whereupon, she sank into the sea of the street and . . . —

Stay: I've no wish to speak of a grieving Grania.

Instead let me say that she learned the same way—from Cuchulain, who quieted as she whispered their names into his triangulate ear—that the trinity was alive, albeit at sea, and unseen from shore. Summoning what strength was left to her, she hired a search party, put Simon at its fore, and sent them off in one of the island's few floatable boats.

They were found some three miles northwest of the harbor, in shoal water, sitting upon the scarred hull of the tipped *Soror Mystica.*

Strewn about were other boats that had gone fully bottom's-up, a three-masted square rigger that had rolled onto her side, several dismasted schooners, and a broken-up brig. (Admittedly, some consolation came when later we learned that the storm had tossed Captain Roberts's *Eliza Catherine* onto Key Vaca.)

The afternoon prior, as, I suppose, Grania and I hunkered down within the Witchery, and the winds came on, the *Soror Mystica* rode to two anchors—starboard and port—with nine hundred feet of chain out. They'd brought down the yards and secured them on deck, so as to lessen the windage aloft; but as the worst of the winds buffeted the old gal, she swung broadside to the direction of the wind, and in so doing put too great a strain on her anchors. By the time I reached the warehouse, the risen sea would have been washing over the *Mystica*'s decks; and by the time Luc thought he saw fire on our wharf, water was already rising in the hull, and the trinity—yes, Léopoldine as well—were busy bailing as best they could. Soon afterward they abandoned their efforts; for the starboard anchor chain parted and the *Soror Mystica* began dragging her port anchor. The compasses were wild, and the storm precluded mortal sight; so it was that we, *my three* and I, were all set adrift at the same hour, they across the harbor, and I across the sky.

Many wreckers went down that day, and nearly all the island's boats suffered some degree of damage. When once again the *Hecate* was afloat, she and the *Persephone* towed the *Soror Mystica* into deeper seas; and there we sank her. The moment her mast went under, two dolphins broke the surface, as if to say they'd see our good schooner down, and home.

The boats bore not the brunt of it, of course.

The storm toppled the lighthouse at nearby Sand Key, as well as our own; and in so doing claimed both light-keepers and their families—fourteen from the Key West light alone. And near where that light had stood, on the island's southwestern shores, a cemetery was churned up. Coffins and corpses, both, were blown into the branches of trees. The living, some of whose homes fell or flooded fast, thought they'd be safer *outside*, and so hied to the island's high point. There several of them died when the trees they clung to were torn away, roots and all, and sailed off like skiffs on a sea of wind. It was held that forty-odd of our fellow wreckers were lost as well, all up and down the keys. Even the town's horses and horned cattle went to their rest—one steer, in its throes, destroyed a Duval Street saloon; and, some days later, saws were requisite to the removal of its remains. Of the island's eight-hundred-some structures, few fared as well as the Witchery; where nothing was lost but the dead-panes, which shattered, finally. These Léopoldine salvaged, cutting her fingers and crying as she sought to reassemble the now-familiar faces and set them into frames.

Leo, you see, was not quite right after the storm and that second ordeal at sea; but, as the strong will once they've seen and survived their worst fears, she'd grow well again. In time. You see, Calixto and Luc simply refused to let her surrender her sanity. It was not easy, no; but in their efforts they were aided by . . . *enfin*, suffice to say *we all were aided* by my return.

Would I could say I simply rolled back a rock after three days away, but *my* resurrection was rather more . . . *necromantic* than that.

. . . As said, the Witchery stood strong through the storm, and all repairs were fast seen to. Of our *enterprise*, though, we'd naught left but the lesser schooner and the sloop—and, yes, *a bankful of savings*. Few went wrecking then, as there was salvage enough to be done in the streets. And whilst others went about the rebuilding of Key West, life within the Witchery was something it had never been before: *mournful.*

Calixto and Luc suffered the loss of the *Soror Mystica,* and had their hands full with a dazed and dissolute Leo, who hauled out from a closet Asmodei's hookah and by diverse means of Sight found the island's stashed opium. As for Grania, well . . . They all four mourned me, but Grania's loss was such that she returned to the witchery two days after she'd last seen me there, alive, and set about her summoning. She'd not let me go. "Love," she says, "is for holdin' to, no matter *the how* of it."

Having cleared the cinder pit of all we'd thought we might have to burn, Grania had Luc lay a fire. Beside this she set a crane, and upon its arm—swung out over the flames—she hung her cauldron. Cerridwen's cauldron. And out of the crates came all, *all* the *Books of Shadows.*

Upon the balustrade of what now was, in fact, a widow's walk, Grania strung strings of brass bells. Onto the lips of the larger bells she'd had Léopoldine scratch the names of the seven planetary spirits; for in the Books she'd read of the necromantic bell of Girardius and thought, *Why not?* She'd not the means to properly season the bells—which rite requires lengths of green taffeta (which patience could have provided her with, perhaps), but also "a settled cemetery," of which there was no hope, not then; and so she settled on brass ships' bells and the inscribed names of Aratron (for Saturn), Bethor (Jupiter), Phaleg (Mars), Och (the Sun), Hagith (Venus), Ophiel (Mercury), and Phuel (the Moon), as Léopoldine's sidereal talents were not to be wasted. Then, with all, or *nearly all,* in readiness, Grania called the trinity to the witchery, told them the details of her summoning plans, and, hearing it huzzah'd and heartily approved of, asked Calixto and Luc to acquire the last things requisite to the rite:

They'd have to harvest two bodies from amongst the hurricane's dead.

Lemuel Corbeil extorted a high price for what ice he had left— and, *grace à* Grania, Corbeil was spared Leo's wrath, or surely he'd have been made to rue such ill-got profit—and the *divans of the dead* were re-made in the witchery. Onto these were lain the two bodies, each having died in the days after the storm. One was known to me: She was old Mrs. Bernard, the upholsterer's wife, or widow, I suppose; for her heart had stopped after she'd learned they'd found her husband drowned in his shop, where he'd been pinned to the fast-flooding floor by four fallen bolts of silver damask.

The other corpse was that of a wrecker new to town—from Bedford, Mass., thought Luc—who'd come to Key West with a brother, neither of whom could have been a quarter century old. The brothers had crewed aboard the *Lafayette,* but, for reasons fated to be forever unknown, this particular boy had not sailed the day before the storm; and so it was he heard the news hard: The *Lafayette* had gone down with all hands; whereupon the distraught sailor suicided himself by ingesting full bottles of lampblack and rum: a most carbonaceous cocktail, surely, but one which left him looking much as he had whilst alive; which is to say: *handsome.* Tall, broad, black-haired, and tan . . . Sad? Incontestably so. But I haven't time to mourn *le pauvre.* Instead let me return to the tale as told me by Grania, and report that she was pleased with the procured corpses; for she'd charged Calixto and Luc with procuring two that were passably pristine and unlikely to be looked for. This they'd done. Now it was down to her.

At first, things did not progress according to plan. No surprise there, I suppose, seeing as how said plan had been hatched by a heartsick witch reliant upon the *Books of Shadows,* a goodly number of which were written in languages she did not know. With difficulty, and resorting both to dictionaries and Leo—when she was not deep in her dreamless poppy sleep—Grania read the ones in English.

In these there was much related to the drawing down of demons, yes; but this begged the question: *Was I a demon?* If so, ought she to summon me? If not, could I even hear and heed her call? . . . Of course, my Grania was not the first sister to be confused by such questions, as Egyptian, Grecian, and Roman theogonies, all, waver as to whether those spirits to whom the living appeal are angels or demons. The Books she had before her settled the question not at all; but still she determined, still she *dared* to try and draw me down. . . . And lest you wonder, sister, whether I am angel or demon, I add here that I am both. So, too, are you.

Soon it seemed Solomon was the key, as several sisters sang his praises. He, son of David, otherwise Suleiman-ibn-Daoud, was not only the wealthiest of all monarchs but the wisest as well, with secret knowledge that made him commander of all beings celestial, terrestrial, and infernal. So it was that Grania scoured our collection for word of Solomon, and came upon the Books of several sisters who'd excerpted his *Clavicule,* better known as *The Black Book.* This text has been integral to the conjuration of spirits since first it began to circulate (not coincidentally) in the first century of the Christian era. Just when it passed from the Byzantine into the Latin worlds, none can say for sure; but pass it did, into the hands of popes such as Honorius III, Leo III, John XXII, and Sylvester II, sorcerers all, till finally, in 1350, Innocent VI ordered all extant copies burned. Of course, no self-respecting sister or sorcerer parts with such a book upon orders of a pope; and indeed such edicts often have an effect *opposite* to that intended, as in this case: *The Black Book* was widely copied throughout the Middle Ages, later finding favor with such types as the androgyne-king Henri III, as well as his witch-mother, Catherine de Médicis, till eventually it was printed, late in the Renaissance, by Petrus Mozellanus. A printed edition, however, is held to be far less potent than one copied out in the practitioner's hand. Blessedly, the Duchess had bequeathed to me one such *Clavicule de Salomon*, copied by a Florentine sister named Simaetha; and it was within its covers of green grosgrain that Grania found what she sought:

The ritual itself.

Of course, as any gifted witch will, Grania made it her own.

Into Cerridwen's cauldron—and Cerridwen is naught but the Celtic Ceres, really, a goddess of both the Under- and Otherworlds, to whom Grania's foremothers had long sacrificed sow's blood, boiled in the cauldron, to spur a good crop and sometimes summon the spirits of the dead—*alors,* into the cauldron went not sow's blood but rainwater cut with a few, *very* few drops of both the widow's and the suicide's blood—no more than was easily wrung from their fingertips. This was brought to a boil. And as it bubbled, they all began their incanting— all save Calixto, of course, who sat silently by, not being *of the Blood*.

"We conjure thee, Herculine," they began, each of the three reading the rite as written out by Grania on blank pages torn from the back of my last *Book of Shadows*—"virgin parchment" is what's called for, and those pages seemed to Grania to be as close as she was likely to get— ". . . and in the name of all goddesses and gods who reign, and in the name of our redeemers, our spirits, and our most merciful consolers, and by the powers secreted in the High Empyrean, we conjure thee to appear instantly and without delay, in comely shape, and without noise or harm done to our persons."

Whatever did they think I'd do? Come as the hurricane had?

Regardless, they read the rite, thrice through, on three successive nights. And when I did not appear they began to add to it whatever high-sounding sonorities they could cull from the Books; such as:

"Muerte, Etam, Teteceme, Zaps . . ." said by a sister from Saragossa to cause figures to appear on the surface of any liquid; or:

"Hereto we conjure you by the Living God El, Ehome, Etrha, Ejel aser, Ejech Adonay Iah Tetragrammaton Saday Agios other Agla ischiros athanatos amen amen amen!" And, further, they resorted to such call-and-response as:

". . . galatim, galata, caio, caila"; to be answered with:

". . . Io Zati, Zata, Abbati, Abbata, Agla."

Too, they tried this thirteenth-century claptrap, by which the sorcerer Salatin was said to conjure demons:

"Bagabi laca bachabé, Lamac cahi achababé, Karrelyos . . ." and so on, all of it sounding nonsensical to them, too, even as some unspecified portion of it found effect.

. . . To die is to die, but to be dead is to dream. Leastways so it was and is with me. And what first woke me from death's dream state were the bells, the brass bells tinkling atop the Witchery. It was well after midnight, but not yet morning: the small hours so conducive to summoning. A waxing moon lit the ruined town. It was as though the bells had woken me where once I used to slumber and dream, in my, nay, *our* second-story suite. And when I woke *I was undead*—call said state what you will—and I saw, *saw* that I had descended. . . . I speak not of *literal* descent, mind. I did not drop into those bodies as stars fall from the firmament. Rather, I refer to that action that is the opposite of *ascension.*

No sight. No thought. Not at first. But I could hear, and I heard the incanted words, and I drew strength not so much from the words themselves as from the voices of those who spoke them. And *strength of will* is what's needed—the strong wills of the summoners as well as that of the one being summoned; for by force of will they draw me down, direct me, and by force of will I slip into the borrowed bodies.

———————————————— ✳ ————————————————

. . . It is but a simple, watery displacement: my silver, my soul, swapped for what remains of theirs, the corpses'. Sometimes there is resistance, or disquiet—easily overcome; sometimes there is too much residual silver and I must share the body awhile, the two of us ensouled together. This can be torturous, or Peace itself, depending on the soul-state of the departing dead. In the end, the body will be mine to borrow if we—I and the summoners—will it; whereupon *I give its gore new life*. And it is through the borrowing that I become god, goddess, ghost. . . . Again, call me what you will. It matters not a whit to me.

It was on the fifth night, midway through the second reading of the three-day rite, that I woke to Grania's voice alone. Previously, I'd been present; but I'd not been able to make my presence known. Now I would. *I willed it*. . . . They'd all read the rite through, and the summoning tired them. Even Léopoldine, who'd felt my presence but hadn't dared encourage Grania by saying so. Indeed, the trinity's efforts were now turned toward consolation. They told Grania she'd done her best, as had they all, but it was time to abandon both the rite and the bodies, as the former hadn't worked and the latter would fast progress unto putrefaction. The widow's particularly: flies had found their way into the witchery and laid their larvae on the body's points of in- and egress: the eyes, the mouth, et cetera. (The sailor, fortunately, still was firm and fresh, much like live-flesh.) Grania, in her grief, refused to desist, and determined to read the rite twice more, as prescribed, and on her own if need be. So it was that I heard her voice alone, woke—it's really no more mysterious than that: *the progression from dream to wakefulness*—and descended, determined to show myself. Somehow.

. . . Did I *choose* the sailor? Perhaps I did. I know that later we'd laugh, and I'd boast that I was a most obedient soul; for hadn't they commanded me to take a "comely shape"? And comely the sailor was, still, despite death's having worked some days upon him. Regardless, and whether by choice or not, on the fifth night of the rite I found myself within the sailor's body, the which he'd fast abandoned; for he'd sought death as now I sought its opposite. I heard Grania, yes, but still I couldn't summon strength enough to master the sailor's body, to see with its green eyes, to speak with its deep voice, let alone to locomote via its slackening muscles, all of which I can do now, of course, albeit with an ease relative to my host's state of decay; which, when it worsens, sends me back to Aeternitas, if you will, there to sleep and await another summons.

And so the fifth night passed. *Fortunately,* my beloved read the rite once more.

That sixth night all was as it had been before. The waking. The descent. The slipping into the sailor's corpse. And I heard Grania's reading of the rite, sad now, and irresolute: things it had not been before. Had she lost belief? She hadn't, no; but wondering thusly, I summoned will enough to open the sailor's eyes, just so, but only to see Grania's white-clad figure quitting the witchery.

A single lamp and several black candles burned on, and by their light I saw that the widow was gone. The sailor Grania had held to one day more. I knew: It was now or—*literally*—never.

Beginning with the bones and moving on to the muscles, I sought mastery of the sailor's body. Soon I stood, swaying. I, or rather he, or rather the body, was unclothed; for Grania had abluted and perfumed it, and had kept it ready for my coming. Soon I knew no confusion but the corporeal: I was a bit clumsy at first, yes. But through eyes not mine, I saw where I was. And with ears not mine I heard, *heard* Grania's tears. *There. Downstairs.*

I went toward the stifled sobs, drawn there, and upon the second-story landing I stood in the dark before our door, listening. And oh,

if that sailor's heart had borne blood and a beat, it would surely have broken, so sad was Grania's mourning song.

The bedroom door sang back upon its hinges as he, as it, nay, as *I* pushed upon it. A full moon had risen to blue all and everything, and so it was that Grania shone, verily shone as slowly she sat up in bed, opened her arms, and whispered me home.

 *Epilogue: Cauda Pavonis*

To him that overcometh will I give . . . a white stone.
—The Revelation of St. John the Divine

MY BELOVED HAS BUT ONE COMPLAINT AS REGARDS MY After-state and the borrowing of bodies: that the voice she hears is never mine. She prefers to read what I have written; for then, says she, *she hears me.* Thusly have I written this testament; for her, now, and in the future for you, sister-unseen.

The future . . .

Enfin, we remained in the Witchery for some while after the storm. I suppose it has been nearly a year now. Oh, but the island has changed, irrevocably so; and we have no need of Sight to see some of what the future holds:

We never again went wrecking, as something of our spirit sank along with the *Soror Mystica;* but, too, it would seem the industry is on the wane. With Florida now a state, and its coast growing ever more crowded, the surrounding waters are sure to be charted; and better charts—not to mention those railroads that now stitch across the northward plains, and the steamers supplanting sailing ships atop the seas—will cut the occurrence of wrecks. And so be it: "'tis progress, I suppose," to quote Grania Byrne.

Worse by far, and the thing that has decided our departure: Léopoldine has Seen that Florida as well as all the other, fast-*dis*uniting states will redden with war. She Saw this, and *strongly so*. And though she cannot say when, *war is in the offing*, and when it comes it will give rise to legions of the disquieted dead. I'll not be here for that, *merci bien*, even though the dead disquiet me less, now that I am amongst their number. Neither do any of the family wish to witness a war, nor suffer the aforesaid Reign of Death that will follow fast upon it. . . . And so, we sail.

Where to? *Alors*, I have not been party to all the particulars, but it seems we—Grania and I—are sailing to Boston, thence to steam aboard the *Chariclo* toward England and a place too aptly named: Gravesend, on the Thames, near to London. Thereafter, it will be decided: Grania's Ireland or my France? It matters not a whit to me, of course, and I will let the family decide. . . . No easy matter, that; for Léopoldine lobbies hard for London whilst Grania yet disdains the English; too, Calixto and Luc seek a coastal home on the continent, so as to reestablish themselves as seaman. . . . *On va voir;* but wherever we settle, it will be together. On that we are agreed.

The trinity sails behind us, and a Boston rendezvous has been arranged. They had first to seal the Witchery, and then settle the *Hecate* into the hands of a Carolina merchant before coming northward by coach. The *Persephone* we let to Lemuel Corbeil—cheaply, quite, though the lease is contingent upon our having full rights to reclaim said sloop should we decide to return to the island. In truth, I suspect our island days are done. Leo says she did not See us there, but neither can she be certain; for when she cast her Sight further into the future than ever she had before, and saw the coming Cousins' War, the dream was too extreme, too troubling, to discern its every detail. Indeed, having Sighted same, Leo slept four days straight and *still* woke troubled, atremble; whereupon we all five agreed: We'd sail from these dissevering states before the coming conflagration.

. . . *Bien,* here is Grania now.

Under cover of morning's dark—not to mention that fear of contagion that has given Miss Lucy and me peace, as I'd hoped and supposed it would—Grania has slipped into this cabin from the one adjoining to report that no other passenger has fallen to fever. This is good news: The disembarkation in Boston won't be slowed by quarantine. Yet it is likely that the captain, upon learning (albeit belatedly) of little Lucy's death, will persuade her mourners to confer her unto the sea, soon, *today*, whilst still the waters beneath us are suitably deep and distant from port. And so I must speed in speaking of our plans:

Grania is to meet the trinity some days hence—a date dependent on both the successful disposition of the *Hecate* and the vagaries of stage travel; whereupon, if the witches deem it wise, they all four will settle themselves in the *Chariclo*'s finest suites and set out seaward. Will I descend? Doubtful, as bodies are typically not let to linger aboard ships; but I will do my best to be near. And will *seem* as near as Léopoldine; for it's likely she will Sight and smoke herself into a stupor, *la pauvre*, the better to forbear the sea crossing. . . . Yes, I must now surrender this child's body to her family, and to its lot, its watery plot, and ascend; but Grania sails with all her *summoning stuff*, and I know I shan't be gone for long.

Enfin, the sun rises now and this porthole burns like Brù's athanor of old. Grania has cleared the candles by which I've written, ranged

---

❋

the room, and now she is settling the bunk upon which I must lay this body down; for my love reminds me that the surgeon is soon to come. And when he does come there can be no one *present* but Grania; who, days ago, offered to nurse the girl and "help her go."

My love. My Grania . . . Blessed be she who loves me despite this discorporeality, who loves the ghost or godhead I've become. And though neither of us would *choose* a love of this sort, let me say that still it is far better than its opposite: loss. . . . And lest I doubt Grania's abiding love, there it is, *there;* for she wears it.

To explain:

Naught of worth could be culled from the ruins of our warehouse—it all went up as *all the colors came,* as the alchemists' *cauda pavonis,* or peacock's tail, spread its colors amidst the transmogrifying fire; and there was only ash, and mud. Oh, but Calixto—loyal, loving Cal—dug in the muck in the days before my first descent, and he found it.

It: all that had become of me: an egg-size stone bright as light, perfected: the One Stone, the Philosopher's Stone. . . . This Calixto presented to Grania Byrne. This she has had set in an emerald casing, its clasp gold-filigreed. And this she wears ever and always— sometimes as a brooch pinned to her omnipresent collar; sometimes pendant from a gold chain long enough to let the Stone hang over her heart.

. . . Commotion. I hear crying: mourners. The surgeon comes.

I must and will ascend, to Aeternitas. Oh, but first I wait for . . . Yes: There it is: Grania's kiss, set upon this jaundiced and hardened hand. "Rise now, love," says she, "and listen for me heart's-call. It won't be long in comin', that ye know."

And so I must go, and do, conferring this, my last *Book of Shadows,* unto Grania Byrne, asking that she sign her name beneath mine as

Possessor of the Stone and keeper of all my secrets, truthfully told this sixth day of August, eighteen hundred and forty-seven.

Blessed be,

H.

And may the goddess go well,

Grania Mary Byrne

———————————————— ❋ ————————————————

ACKNOWLEDGMENTS

Thank you to my agent, Suzanne Gluck, and my editor, Sarah Durand, as well as their respective assistants, Erin Malone and Jeremy Cesarec. And heartfelt thanks to my family, without whom . . .